Desmond Bagley

Desmond Bagley was born in 1923 in Kendal, Westmorland, and brought up in Blackpool. He began his working life, aged 14, in the printing industry and then did a variety of jobs until going into an aircraft factory at the start of the Second World War.

When the war ended he decided to travel to southern Africa, going overland through Europe and the Sahara. He worked en route, reaching South Africa in 1951.

He became a freelance journalist in Johannesburg and wrote his first published novel, *The Golden Keel*, in 1962. In 1964 he returned to England and lived in Totnes, Devon, for twelve years. He and his wife then moved to Guernsey in the Channel Islands. Here he found the ideal place for combining his writing with his other interests, which included computers, mathematics, military history, and entertaining friends from all over the world.

Desmond Bagley died in April 1983. Two previously unpublished Bagley novels have since been published: the first, *Night of Error*, was published in 1984, the second, *Juggernaut*, in 1985. Both were on the bestseller lists for many weeks.

DESMOND BAGLEY

FLYAWAY

HarperCollins*Publishers*

HarperCollins*Publishers*
77–85 Fulham Palace Road,
Hammersmith, London W6 8JB

This paperback edition 1993
1 3 5 7 9 8 6 4 2

Previously published in paperback by Fontana 1979
Reprinted fourteen times

First published in Great Britain by
Collins 1978

Copyright © Brockhurst Publications 1978

ISBN 0 00 616611 3

Set in Baskerville

Printed in Great Britain by
HarperCollinsManufacturing Glasgow

To Lecia and Peter Foston
of the Wolery

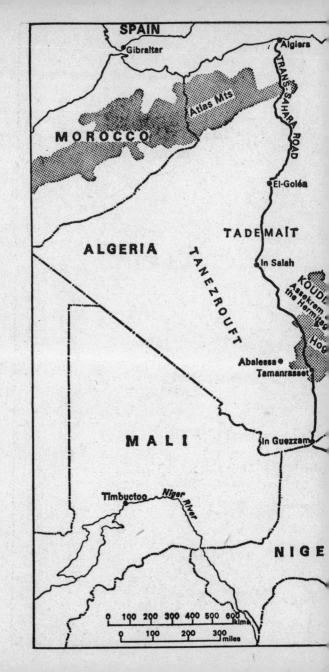

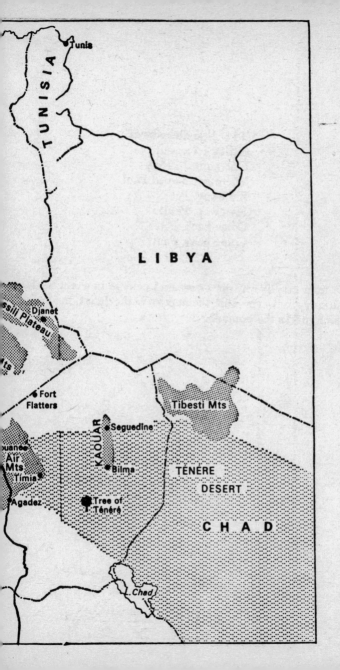

Two little dicky-birds,
Sitting on a wall;
One named Peter,
The other named Paul.
Fly away, Peter!
Fly away, Paul!
Come back, Peter!
Come back, Paul!

No man can live in the desert and emerge unchanged. He will carry, however faint, the imprint of the desert, the brand which marks the nomad.

Wilfred Thesiger

One

We live in the era of instancy. The clever
chemists have invented instant coffee; demonstrating
students cry in infantile voices, 'We want the world, and we
want it *now*!' and the Staffords have contrived the instant
flaming row, a violent quarrel without origin or cause.

Our marriage was breaking up and we both knew it. The
heat engendered by friction was rapidly becoming unsup-
portable. On this particular Monday morning a mild
enquiry into Gloria's doings over the weekend was wantonly
interpreted as meddlesome interference into her private
affairs. One thing led to another and I arrived at the office
rather frayed at the edges.

Joyce Godwin, my secretary, looked up as I walked in and
said brightly, 'Good morning, Mr Stafford.'

'Morning,' I said curtly, and slammed the door of my own
office behind me. Once inside I felt a bit ashamed. It's a bad
boss who expends his temper on the staff and Joyce didn't
deserve it. I snapped down the intercom switch. 'Will you
come in, Joyce?'

She entered armed with the secretarial weapons – stenographic pad and sharpened pencil. I said, 'Sorry about that;
I'm not feeling too well this morning.'

Her lips twitched in a faint smile. 'Hangover?'

'Something like that,' I agreed. The seven year hangover.
'What's on the boil this morning?'

'Mr Malleson wants to see you about the board meeting
this afternoon.'

I nodded. The AGM of Stafford Security Consultants Ltd
was a legal formality; three men sitting in a City penthouse
cutting up the profits between them. A financial joke.

'Anything else?'

'Mr Hoyland rang up. He wants to talk to you.'

'Hoyland? Who's he?'

'Chief Security Officer at Franklin Engineering in Luton.'

There was once a time when I knew every employee by his given name; now I couldn't even remember the surnames of the line staff. It was a bad situation and would have to be rectified when I had the time. 'Why me?'

'He wanted Mr Ellis, but he's in Manchester until Wednesday; and Mr Daniels is still away with 'flu.'

I grinned. 'So he picked me as third choice. Was it anything important?'

The expression on Joyce's face told me that she thought my hangover was getting the better of me. A Chief Security Officer was expected to handle his job and if he rang the boss it had better be about something bloody important. 'He said he'd ring back,' she said drily.

'Anything else?'

Wordlessly she pointed to my overflowing in-tray. I looked at it distastefully. 'You're a slave-driver. If Hoyland rings I'll be in Mr Malleson's office.'

'But Mr Fergus wants the Electronomics contract signed today,' she wailed.

'Mr Fergus is an old fuddy-duddy,' I said. 'I want to talk to Mr Malleson about it. It won't hurt Electronomics to wait another half-hour.' I picked up the Electronomics file and left, feeling Joyce's disapproving eye boring into my back.

Charlie Malleson was evidently feeling more like work than I – his in-tray was almost half empty. I perched my rump on the edge of his desk and dropped the file in front of him. 'I don't like this one.'

He looked up and sighed. 'What's wrong with it, Max?'

'They want guard dogs without handlers. That's against the rules.'

He raised his eyebrows. 'I didn't catch that.'

'Neither did Fergus and he should have. You know what I think about it. You can build defences around a factory like the Berlin Wall but some bright kid is going to get through at night just for the devil of it. Then he runs up against a dog on the loose and gets mauled – or killed.' Charlie opened the file. 'See Clause 28.'

He checked it. 'That wasn't in the contract I vetted. It must have been slipped in at the last moment.'

'Then it gets slipped out fast or Electronomics can take their business elsewhere. You wanted to see me about the board meeting?'

'His Lordship will be at home at four this afternoon.'

His Lordship was Lord Brinton who owned twenty-five per cent of Stafford Security Consultants Ltd. I got up and went to the window and stared at the tower of the Inter-City Building – Brinton's lair. From the penthouse he overlooked the City, emerging from time to time to gobble up a company here and arrange a profitable merger there. 'Four o'clock is all right; I'll tell Joyce. Is everything in order?'

'As smooth as silk.' Charlie eyed me appraisingly. 'You don't look too good. Got a touch of 'flu coming on?'

'A touch of something. I was told the name of a man this morning and I didn't know he worked for us. That's bad.'

He smiled. 'This business is getting bigger than both of us. The penalty of success.'

I nodded. 'I'm chained to my damned desk seven hours out of eight. Sometimes I wish we were back in the bad old days when we did our own legwork. Now I'm shuffling too many bloody papers around.'

'And a lot of those are crisp, crackling fivers.' Charlie waved at the view – the City of London in all its majesty. 'Don't knock success on this hallowed ground – it's immoral.' The telephone rang and he picked it up, then held it out to me.

It was Joyce. 'Mr Hoyland wants to speak to you.'

'Put him on.' I covered the mouthpiece and said to Charlie, 'You might like to listen to this one. It's about time you administrative types knew what goes on at the sharp end of the business.'

The telephone clicked and clattered. 'Mr Stafford?'

'Max Stafford here.'

'This is Hoyland from . . .'

'I know who you are, Mr Hoyland,' I said, feeling like a con man. 'What's your trouble?'

'I've come up against a funny one, sir,' he said. 'A man called Billson vanished a week ago and I've run into a blank wall.'

'How critical is Billson?'

'He's not on the technical side; he's in the accounts office. But . . .'

'Have you checked the books?'

'They balance to a penny,' said Hoyland. 'It's not that, sir; it's the attitude of the company. I'm getting no co-operation at all.'

'Expand on that.'

'Well, Billson is a bit of a dumb bunny and he's getting paid a lot more than he's worth. He's on £8000 a year and doing the work of an office boy. When I asked Isaacson why, I got a bloody dusty answer. He said the salary structure is no concern of security.'

Hoyland was annoyed, and rightly so. I was annoyed myself because when we took on a contract it was stipulated that *everything* was the concern of security. 'He said that, did he? Who is Isaacson?'

'Chief Accountant,' said Hoyland. 'Can you get on the blower and straighten him out? He's not taking much notice of me.'

'He'll get straightened out,' I said grimly. 'Let's get back to Billson – what do you mean when you say he's vanished?'

'He didn't turn up last week and he sent in no word. When we made enquiries we found he'd left his digs without explanation.' Hoyland paused. 'That's no crime, Mr Stafford.'

'Not unless he took something with him. You say he isn't critical?'

'Definitely not. He's been a fixture in the accounting department for fifteen years. No access to anything that matters.'

'Not that we know of.' I thought about it for a few moments. 'All right, Mr Hoyland; I'll have a word with Isaacson. In the meantime check back on Billson; you never know what you might find.'

'I'll do that, Mr Stafford.' Hoyland seemed relieved. Bucking top management was something he'd rather not do himself.

I put down the telephone and grinned at Charlie. 'See what I mean. How would you handle a thing like that?'

'Franklin Engineering,' he said reflectively. 'Defence contractors, aren't they?'

'They do a bit for the army. Suspension systems for tanks – nothing serious.'

'What are you going to do about it?'

'I'm going to blow hell out of this joker, Isaacson. No money-pusher is going to tell one of my security officers what concerns security and what doesn't.'

Charlie tilted back his chair and regarded me speculatively. 'Why don't you do it personally – face to face? You've been complaining about being tied to your desk, so why don't you pop over to Luton and do some legwork? You can easily get back in time for the board meeting. Get out of the office, Max; it might take that sour look off your face.'

'Is it as bad as that?' But the idea was attractive, all the same. 'All right, Charlie; to hell with the desk!' I rang Joyce. 'Get on to Hoyland at Franklin Engineering – tell him I'm on my way to Luton and to hold himself available.' I cut off her wail of protest. 'Yes, I know the state of the in-tray – it'll get done tomorrow.'

As I put down the telephone Charlie said, 'I don't suppose it is really important.'

'I shouldn't think so. The man's either gone on a toot or been knocked down by a car or something like that. No, Charlie; this is a day's holiday, expenses paid by the firm.'

Two

   I should have remembered Hoyland's name because I remembered his competent, square face when I saw it. He was a reliable type and an ex-copper like so many of our security officers. He was surprised to see me; it wasn't often that the top brass of Stafford Security appeared in the front line, more's the pity.

His surprise was mingled with nervousness as he tried to assess why I had come personally. 'Nothing to worry about,' I assured him. 'Only too glad to get away from the desk. Tell me about Billson.'

Hoyland rubbed his chin. 'I don't know much about him. You know I've only been here three months; I was transferred here when Laird retired.'

I didn't know – there was too damned much about my own firm I didn't know. It had grown too big and depersonalized. 'Yes,' I said.

'I took over Laird's files and checked his gradings. Billson came well into the green scale – as safe as houses. He was at the bottom of my priorities.'

'But you've rechecked since he disappeared?'

Hoyland nodded. 'Forty-four years old, worked here fifteen years. As much personality as a castrated rabbit. Lodges with a Mrs Harrison in the town. She's a widow.'

'Anything between him and Mrs Harrison?'

Hoyland grinned. 'She's seventy.'

That didn't mean much; Ninon de L'Enclos was a whore at eighty. 'What about girl-friends?'

'Not Billson – the girls didn't go for him from what I've heard.'

'All right – boy-friends?'

'Not that, either. I don't think he was the type.'

'He doesn't seem much of anything,' I said caustically.

'And that's a fact,' said Hoyland. 'He's so insignificant he hardly exists. You'd walk past him and not know he was there.'

'The original invisible man,' I commented. 'All the qualifications for a sleeper.'

'Isn't fifteen years too long?' queried Hoyland. 'Besides, he left everything in order.'

'As far as we know, that's all. Do the Special Branch boys know about this?'

'They've been poking around and come to the same conclusion as me.'

'Yes,' I said. 'Billson is probably in some hospital, having lost his means of identification. But there is a mystery; why was he overpaid and why is management being coy about it?'

Hoyland nodded. 'I talked to Stewart about it first – he's Billson's immediate boss – and he pushed me on to Isaacson. I got nowhere with him.'

'I'll see what I can do,' I said, and went to find Stewart, who proved to be a sandy Scotsman, one of the new breed of bookkeepers. No dusty ledgers for him; figures were something which danced electronically in the guts of a computer.

No, he had no idea where Billson might have gone. In fact, he knew nothing about Billson, full stop.

'Isn't that a little odd for a department head? Surely you know something about your subordinates?'

'He's a very strange man,' said Stewart. 'Reserved most of the time but capable of the most frantic outbursts occasionally. Sometimes he can be very difficult.'

'In what way?'

Stewart shrugged. 'He goes on about injustice; about people not being given the proper credit for achievement. He's very bitter about it.'

'Meaning himself?'

'No; it was always about others. being repressed or cheated.'

'Any political implications?'

'Not at all,' said Stewart positively. 'Politics mean nothing to him.'

'Did he do his work well?'

Stewart offered me a wary look and said over-carefully, 'He did the work we asked of him to our satisfaction.'

'Would you say he was an achiever himself?' I smiled. 'Was he in line for promotion, or anything like that?'

'Nothing like that.' Stewart seemed aware that he had spoken too quickly and emphatically. 'He's not a dynamic man.'

I said, 'When did you join the firm, Mr Stewart?'

'Four years ago. I was brought down from Glasgow when the office was computerized.'

'At that time did you make any attempt to have Billson fired or transferred to another department?'

Stewart jerked. 'I . . . er . . . I did something like that, yes. It was decided to keep him on.'

'By Mr Isaacson, I take it.'

'Yes. You'll have to ask him about that,' he said with an air of relief.

So I did. Isaacson was a more rarefied breed of accountant than Stewart. Stewart knew how to make figures jump through hoops; Isaacson selected the hoops they jumped through. He was an expert on company law, especially that affecting taxation.

'Billson!' he said, and smiled. 'There's a word in Yiddish which describes a man like Billson. He's a *nebbish*.'

'What's that?'

'A person of less than no account. Let me put it this way; if a man walks out of a room and it feels as though someone has just come in, then he's a *nebbish*.'

I leaned back in my chair and stared at Isaacson. 'So here we have a *nebbish* who draws £8000 for a job worth £2000, if that. How do you account for it?'

'I don't have to,' he said easily. 'You can take that up with our managing director, Mr Grayson.'

'And where will I find Mr Grayson?'

'I regret that will be difficult,' said Isaacson in a most unregretful manner. 'He's in Switzerland for the skiing.'

He looked so damned smug that I wanted to hit him, but I kept my temper and said deliberately, 'Mr Isaacson, my firm is solely responsible for security at Franklin Engineering. A man has disappeared and I find this lack of cooperation very strange. Don't you find it odd yourself?'

He spread his hands. 'I repeat, Mr Stafford, that any questions concerning Mr Billson can be answered only by my managing director.'

'Who is sliding down hills on a couple of planks.' I held Isaacson's eye. 'Stewart wanted to fire Billson but you vetoed it. Why?'

'I didn't. Mr Grayson did. He said Billson must stay.'

'Surely you asked his reasons.'

'Of course.' Isaacson shook his head. 'He gave none.' He paused. 'I know nothing of Billson, Mr Stafford, other than that he was . . . protected, shall we say.'

I thought about that. Why should Grayson be Billson's fairy godfather? 'Did you know that Billson was "protected" when Stewart wanted to fire him?'

'Oh yes.' Isaacson smiled a little sadly. 'I wanted to fire him myself ten years ago. When Stewart brought up the suggestion I thought I'd test it again with Mr Grayson.' He shrugged. 'But the situation was still the same.'

I said, 'Maybe I'd better take this up at a higher level; perhaps with your Chairman.'

'As you wish,' said Isaacson in a cold voice.

I decided to lower the temperature myself. 'Just one more thing, Mr Isaacson. When Mr Hoyland asks you for information you do not – repeat not – tell him that what he wants to know is no concern of security. You give him *all* the information you have, as you have given it to me. I hope I make myself clear?'

'Very clear.' Isaacson's lips had gone very thin.

'Very well; you will allow Mr Hoyland access to everything concerning Billson, especially his salary record. I'll have a word with him before I leave.' I stood up. 'Good morning, Mr Isaacson.'

I checked back with Hoyland and told him what I wanted, then went in search of the Widow Harrison and found her to be a comfortable motherly old soul, supplementing her old age pension by taking in a lodger. According to her, Billson was a very nice gentleman who was no trouble about the house and who caused her no heart-searching about fancy women. She had no idea why he had left and was perturbed about what she was going to do about Billson's room which still contained a lot of his possessions.

'After all, I have me living to make,' she said. 'The pension doesn't go far these days.'

I paid her a month in advance for the room and marked it up to the Franklin Engineering account. If Isaacson queried it he'd get a mouthful from me.

She had not noticed anything unusual about Billson before he walked out. 'No, he wasn't any different. Of course, there were times he could get very angry, but that was just his way. I let him go on and didn't take much notice.'

'He was supposed to go to work last Monday, but he didn't. When did you see him last, Mrs Harrison?'

'It was Monday night. I thought he'd been to work as usual. He didn't say he hadn't.'

'Was he in any way angry then?'

'A bit. He was talking about there being no justice, not even in the law. He said rich newspapers could afford expensive lawyers so that poor men like him didn't stand a chance.' She laughed. 'He was that upset he overturned the glue-pot. But it was just his way, Mr Stafford.'

'Oh! What was he doing with the glue-pot?'

'Pasting something into that scrapbook of his. The one that had all the stuff in it about his father. He thought a lot of his father although I don't think he could have remembered him. Stands to reason, doesn't it? He was only a little boy when his father was killed.'

'Did he ever show you the scrapbook?'

'Oh yes; it was one of the first things he did when he came here eight years ago. That was the year after my late husband died. It was full of pictures cut out of newspapers and magazines – all about his father. Lots of aeroplanes – the old-fashioned kind like they had in the First World War.'

'Biplanes?'

'Lots of wings,' she said vaguely. 'I don't know much about aeroplanes. They weren't like the jets we have now. He told me all about his father lots of times; about how he was some kind of hero. After a while I just stopped listening and let it pass over me head. He seemed to think his dad had been cheated or something.'

'Do you mind if I see his room? I'd like to have a look at that scrapbook.'

Her brow wrinkled. 'I don't mind you seeing the room but, come to think of it, I don't think the book's there. It stays on his dressing-table and I didn't see it when I cleaned up.'

'I'd still like to see the room.'

It was not much of a place for a man to live. Not uncomfortable but decidedly bleak. The furniture was Edwardian oversize or 1930s angular and the carpet was clean but threadbare. I sat on the bed and the springs protested. As I looked at the garish reproduction of Holman Hunt's 'The Light of the World' I wondered why an £8000-a-year man should live in a dump like this. 'The scrapbook,' I said.

'It's gone. He must have taken it with him.'

'Is anything else missing?'

'He took his razor and shaving brush,' said Mrs Harrison. 'And his toothbrush. A couple of clean shirts and some socks and other things. Not more than would fill a small suitcase. The police made a list.'

'Do the police know about the scrapbook?'

'It never entered me head.' She was suddenly nervous.

'Do you think I should tell them, sir?'

'Don't worry,' I said. 'I'll tell them.'

'I do hope you can find Mr Billson, sir,' she said, and hesitated. 'I wouldn't want to think he's come to any harm. He really should be married with someone to look after him. His sister came every month but that really wasn't enough.'

'He has a sister?'

'Not a real sister – a half-sister, I think. The name's different and she's not married. A funny foreign name it is – I never can remember it. She comes and keeps him company in the evening about twice a month.'

'Does she know he's gone?'

'I don't know how she can, unless the police told her. I don't know her address but she lives in London.'

'I'll ask them,' I said. 'Did Mr Billson have any girl-friends?'

'Oh no, sir.' She shook her head. 'The problem is, you see, who'd want to marry him? Not that there's anything wrong with him,' she added hastily. 'But he just didn't seem to appeal to the ladies, sir.'

As I walked to the police station I turned that one over. It seemed very much like an epitaph.

Sergeant Kaye was not too perturbed. 'For a man to take it into his head to walk away isn't an offence,' he said. 'If he was a child of six it would be different and we'd be pulling out all the stops, but Billson is a grown man.' He groped for an analogy. 'It's as if you were to say that you feel sorry for him because he's an orphan, if you take my meaning.'

'He may be a grown man,' I said. 'But from what I hear he may not be all there.'

'I don't know,' said Kaye. 'He held down a good job at Franklin Engineering for good pay. It takes more than a half-wit to do that. And he took good care of his money before he walked out and when he walked out.'

'Tell me more.'

'Well, he saved a lot. He kept his current account steady at

21

about the level of a month's salary and he had nearly £12,000 on deposit. He cleared the lot out last Tuesday morning as soon as the bank opened.'

'Well, I'm damned! But wait a minute, Sergeant; it needs seven days' notice to withdraw deposits.'

Kaye smiled. 'Not if you've been a good, undemanding customer for a dozen or more years and then suddenly put the arm on your bank manager.' He unsealed the founts of his wisdom. 'Men walk out on things for a lot of reasons. Some want to get away from a woman and some are running towards one. Some get plain tired of the way they're living and just cut out without any fuss. If we had to put on a full scale investigation every time it happened we'd have our hands full of nothing else, and the yobbos we're supposed to be hammering would be laughing fit to bust. It isn't as though he's committed an offence, is it?'

'I wouldn't know. What does the Special Branch say?'

'The cloak-and-dagger boys?' Kaye's voice was tinged with contempt. 'They reckon he's clean – and I reckon they're right.'

'I suppose you've checked the hospitals.'

'Those in the area. That's routine.'

'He has a sister – does she know?'

'A half-sister,' he said. 'She was here last week. She seemed a level-headed woman – she didn't create all that much fuss.'

'I'd be glad of her address.'

He scribbled on a note-pad and tore off the sheet. As I put it into my wallet I said, 'And you won't forget the scrapbook?'

'I'll put it in the file,' said Kaye patiently. I could see he didn't attach much significance to it.

I had a late lunch and then phoned Joyce at the office. 'I won't be coming in,' I said. 'Is there anything I ought to know?'

'Mrs Stafford asked me to tell you she won't be in this evening.' Joyce's voice was suspiciously cool and even.

I hoped I kept my irritation from showing. I was becoming pretty damned tired of going home to an empty house. 'All right; I have a job for you. All the Sunday newspapers for November 2nd. Extract anything that refers to a man called Billson. Try the national press first and, if Luton has a Sunday paper, that as well. If you draw a blank try all the dailies for the previous week. I want it on my desk tomorrow.'

'That's a punishment drill.'

'Get someone to help if you must. And tell Mr Malleson I'll meet him at four o'clock at the Inter-City Building for the board meeting.'

Three

     I don't know if I liked Brinton or not; he was a hard man to get to know. His social life was minimal and, considered objectively, he was just a money-making machine and a very effective one. He didn't seem to reason like other men; he would listen to arguments for and against a project, offered by the lawyers and accountants he hired by the regiment, and then he would make a decision. Often the decision would have nothing to do with what he had been told, or perhaps he could see patterns no one else saw. At any rate some of his exploits had been startlingly like a magician pulling a rabbit out of a hat. Hindsight would show that what he had done was logically sound, but only he had the foresight and that was what made him rich.

When Charlie Malleson and I put together the outfit that later became Stafford Security Consultants Ltd we ran into the usual trouble which afflicts the small firm trying to become a big firm – a hell of a lot of opportunities going begging for lack of finance. Lord Brinton came to the rescue with a sizeable injection of funds for which he took twenty-five per cent of our shares. In return we took over the security of the Brinton empire.

I was a little worried when the deal was going through because of Brinton's reputation as a hot-shot operator. I put it to him firmly that this was going to be a legitimate operation and that our business was solely security and not the other side of the coin, industrial espionage. He smiled slightly, said he respected my integrity, and that I was to run the firm as I pleased.

He kept to that, too, and never interfered, although his

bright young whiz-kids would sometimes suggest that we cut a few corners. They didn't come back after I referred them to Brinton.

Industrial espionage is a social disease something akin to VD. Nobody minds admitting to protecting against it, but no one will admit to doing it. I always suspected that Brinton was in it up to his neck as much as any other ruthless financial son-of-a-bitch, and I used the firm's facilities to do a bit of snooping. I was right; he employed a couple of other firms from time to time to do his ferreting. That was all right with me as long as he didn't ask me to do it, but sooner or later he was going to try it on one of our other clients and then he was going to be hammered, twenty-five per cent shareholder or not. So far it hadn't happened.

I arrived a little early for the meeting and found him in his office high above the City. It wasn't very much bigger than a ballroom and one entire wall was of glass so that he could look over his stamping ground. There wasn't a desk in sight; he employed other men to sit behind desks.

He heaved himself creakily out of an armchair. 'Good to see you, Max. Look what I've gotten here.'

He had a new toy, an open fire burning merrily in a fireplace big enough to roast an ox. 'Central heating is all very well,' he said. 'But there's nothing like a good blaze to warm old bones like mine. It's like something else alive in the room – it keeps me company and doesn't talk back.'

I looked at the fireplace full of soft coal. 'Aren't you violating the smokeless zone laws?'

He shook his head. 'There's an electrostatic precipitator built into the chimney. No smoke gets out.'

I had to smile. When Brinton did anything he did it in style. It was another example of the way he thought. You want a fire with no smoke? All right, install a multi-thousand pound gadget to get rid of it. And it wouldn't cost him too much; he owned the factory which made the things and I suppose it would find its way on to the company books under the heading of 'Research and Development –

Testing the Product'.

'Drink?' he asked.

'Yes,' I said. 'The working day seems to be over.'

He pressed a button next to the fireplace and a bar unfolded from nowhere. His seamed old face broke into an urchin grin. 'Don't you consider the board meeting to be work?'

'It's playtime.'

He poured a measured amount of Talisker into a glass, added an equal amount of Malvern water, and brought it over to me. 'Yes, I've never regretted the money I put into your firm.'

'Glad to hear it.' I sipped the whisky.

'Did you make a profit this year?'

I grinned. 'You'll have to ask Charlie. He juggles the figures and cooks the books.' I knew to a penny how much we'd made, but old Brinton seemed to like a bit of jocularity mixed into his business.

He looked over my shoulder. 'Here he is now. I'll know very soon if I have something to supplement my old age pension.'

Charlie accepted a drink and we got down to it with Charlie spouting terms like amortization, discounted cash flow, yield and all the jargon you read in the back pages of a newspaper. He doubled as company secretary and accountant, our policy being to keep down overheads, and he owned a slice of the firm which made him properly miserly and disinclined to build any administrative empires which did not add to profits.

It seemed we'd had a good year and I'd be able to feed the wolf at the door on caviare and champagne. We discussed future plans for expansion and the possibility of going into Europe under EEC rules. Finally we came to 'Any Other Business' and I began to think of going home.

Brinton had his hands on the table and seemed intent on studying the liver spots. He said, 'There is one cloud in the sky for you gentlemen. I'm having trouble with Andrew McGovern.'

Charlie raised his eyebrows. 'The Whensley Group?'

'That's it,' said Brinton. 'Sir Andrew McGovern – Chairman of the Whensley Group.'

The Whensley Group of companies was quite a big chunk of Brinton's holdings. At that moment I couldn't remember off-hand whether he held a controlling interest or not. I said, 'What's the trouble?'

'Andrew McGovern reckons his security system is costing too much. He says he can do it cheaper himself.'

I smiled sourly at Charlie. 'If he does it any cheaper it'll be no bloody good. You can't cut corners on that sort of thing, and it's a job for experts who know what they're doing. If he tries it himself he'll fall flat on his face.'

'I know all that,' said Brinton, still looking down at his hands. 'But I'm under some pressure.'

'It's five per cent of our business,' said Charlie. 'I wouldn't want to lose it.'

Brinton looked up. 'I don't think you will lose it – permanently.'

'You mean you're going to let McGovern have his way?' asked Charlie.

Brinton smiled but there was no humour in his face. 'I'm going to let him have the rope he wants – but sooner than he expects it. He can have the responsibility for his own security from the end of the month.'

'Hey!' I said. 'That's only ten days' time.'

'Precisely.' Brinton tapped his finger on the table. 'We'll see how good a job he does at short notice. And then, in a little while, I'll jerk in the rope and see if he's got his neck in the noose.'

I said, 'If his security is to remain as good as it is now he'll have to pay more. It's a specialized field and good men are thin on the ground. If he can find them he'll have to pay well. But he won't find them – I'm running into that kind of trouble already in the expansion programme, and I know what I'm looking for and he doesn't. So his security is going to suffer; there'll be holes in it big enough to march a battalion of industrial spies through.'

'Just so,' said Brinton. 'I know you test your security from time to time.'

'It's essential,' I said. 'We're always doing dry runs to test the defences.'

'I know.' Brinton grinned maliciously. 'In three months I'm going to have a security firm – not yours – run an operation against McGovern's defences and we'll see if his neck is stuck out far enough to be chopped at.'

Charlie said, 'You mean you're going to behead him as well as hanging him?' He wasn't smiling.

'We might throw in the drawing and quartering bit, too. I'm getting a mite tired of Andrew McGovern. You'll get your business back, and maybe a bit more.'

'I hope you're right,' said Charlie. 'The Whensley Group account is only five per cent of our gross but it's a damned sight more than that of our profits. Our overheads won't go down all that much, you know. It might put a crimp in our expansion plans.'

'You'll be all right,' said Brinton. 'I promise.' And with that we had to be satisfied. If a client doesn't want your business you can't ram it down his throat.

Charlie made his excuses and left, but Brinton detained me for a moment. He took me by the arm and led me to the fireplace where he stood warming his hands. 'How is Gloria?'

'Fine,' I said.

Maybe I had not bothered to put enough conviction into that because he snorted and gave me a sharp look. 'I'm a successful man,' he said. 'And the reason is that when a deal goes sour I pull out and take any losses. You don't mind that bit of advice from an old man?'

I smiled. 'The best thing about advice is that you don't have to follow it.'

So I left him and went down to the thronged street in his private lift and joined the hurrying crowds eager to get home after the day's work. I wasn't particularly eager because I didn't have a home; just a few walls and a roof. So I went to my club instead.

Four

I felt a shade better when I arrived at the office next morning. I had visited my fencing club after a long absence and two hours of heavy sabre work had relieved my frustrations and had also done something for the incipient thickening of the waist which comes from too much sitting behind a desk.

But the desk was still there so I sat behind it and looked for the information on Billson I had asked Joyce to look up. When I didn't find it I called her in. 'Didn't you find anything on Billson?'

She blinked at me defensively. 'It's in your in-tray.'

I found it buried at the bottom – an envelope marked 'Billson' – and grinned at her. 'Nice try, Joyce; but I'll work out my own priorities.'

When Brinton had injected funds into the firm it had grown with an almost explosive force and I had resolved to handle at least one case in the field every six months so as not to lose touch with the boys on the ground. Under the pressure of work that went the way of all good resolutions and I hadn't been in the field for fifteen months. Maybe the Billson case was an opportunity to see if my cutting edge was still sharp.

I said abruptly, 'I'll be handing some of my work load to Mr Ellis.'

'He'll not like that,' said Joyce.

'He'd have to take the lot if I was knocked down by a car and broke a leg,' I said. 'It'll do him good. Remind me to speak to him when he gets back from Manchester.'

Joyce went away and I opened the envelope and took out a four-page article, a potted history of the life and times of

Peter Billson, Aviation Pioneer – Sunday Supplement instant knowledge without pain. It was headed: *The Strange Case of Flyaway Peter*, and was illustrated with what were originally black-and-white photographs which had been tinted curious shades of blue and yellow to enliven the pages of what, after all, was supposed to be a colour magazine.

It boiled down to this. Billson, a Canadian, was born appropriately in 1903, the year the first aeroplane took to the sky. Too young to see service in the First World War, he was nourished on tales of the air fighting on the Western Front which excited his imagination and he became air mad. He was an engineering apprentice and, by the time he was 21, he had actually built his own plane. It wasn't a good one – it crashed.

He was unlucky. The Golden Age of Aviation was under way and he was missing out on all the plums. Pioneer flying took money or a sponsor with money and he had neither. In the late 1920s Alan Cobham was flying to the Far East, Australia and South Africa; in 1927 Lindbergh flew the Atlantic solo, and then Byrd brought off the North and South Pole double. Came the early 'thirties and Amy Johnson, Jim Mollison, Amelia Earhart and Wiley Post were breaking records wholesale and Billson hadn't had a look-in.

But he made it in the next phase. Breaking records was all very well, but now the route-proving stage had arrived which had to precede phase three – the regular commercial flight. Newspapers were cashing in on the public interest and organizing long-distance races such as the England-Australia Air Race of 1934, won by Scott and Campbell-Black. Billson came second in a race from Vancouver to Hawaii, and first in a mail-carrying test – Vancouver to Montreal. He was in there at last – a real heroic and intrepid birdman. It is hard to believe the adulation awarded those early fliers. Not even our modern astronauts are accorded the same attention.

It was about this time that some smart journalist gave him

the nickname of Flyaway Peter, echoing the nursery rhyme. It was good publicity and Billson went along with the gag even to the extent of naming his newborn son Paul and, in 1936, when he entered the London to Cape Town Air Race he christened the Northrop 'Gamma' he flew *Flyaway*. It was one of the first of the all-metal aircraft.

The race was organized by a newspaper which beat the drum enthusiastically and announced that all entrants would be insured to the tune of £100,000 each in the case of a fatality. The race began. Billson put down in Algiers to refuel and then took off again, heading south. The plane was never seen again.

Billson's wife, Helen, was naturally shocked and it was some weeks before she approached the newspaper about the insurance. The newspaper passed her on to the insurance company which dug in its heels and dithered. £100,000 was a lot of money in 1936. Finally it declared unequivocally that no payment would be forthcoming and Mrs Billson brought the case to court.

The courtroom was enlivened by a defence witness, a South African named Hendrik van Niekirk, who swore on oath that he had seen Billson, alive and well, in Durban four weeks after the race was over. It caused a sensation and no doubt the sales of the newspaper went up. The prosecution battered at van Niekirk but he stood up to it well. He had visited Canada and had met Billson there and he was in no doubt about his identification. Did he speak to Billson in Durban? No, he did not.

All very dicey.

The judge summed up and the case went to the jury which deliberated at length and then found for the insurance company. No £100,000 for Mrs Billson – who immediately appealed. The Appellate Court reversed the decision on a technicality – the trial judge had been a shade too precise in his instructions to the jury. The insurance company took it to the House of Lords who refused to have anything to do with it. Mrs Billson got her £100,000. Whether she lived happily ever after the writer of the article didn't say.

So much for the subject matter – the tone was something else. Written by a skilled journalist, it was a very efficient hatchet job on the reputation of a man who could not answer back – dead or alive. It reeked of the envy of a small-minded man who got his kicks by pulling down men better than himself. If this was what Paul Billson had read then it wasn't too surprising if he went off his trolley.

The article ended in a speculative vein. After pointing out that the insurance company had lost on a legal technicality, it went on:

> The probability is very strong that Billson did survive the crash, if crash there was, and that Hendrik van Niekirk did see him in Durban. If this is so, and I think it is, then an enormous fraud was perpetrated. £100,000 is a lot of money anywhere and at any time. £100,000 in 1936 is equivalent to over £350,000 in our present-day debased currency.

> If Peter Billson is still alive he will be 75 years old and will have lived a life of luxury. Rich men live long and the chances are that he is indeed still alive. Perhaps he will read these words. He might even conceive these words to be libellous. I am willing to risk it.

> Flyaway Peter Billson, come back! Come back!

I was contemplating this bit of nastiness when Charlie Malleson came into the office. He said, 'I've done a preliminary analysis of the consequences of losing the Whensley Group,' and smiled sourly. 'We'll survive.'

'Brinton,' I said, and tilted my chair back. 'He owns a quarter of our shares and accounts for a third of our business. We've got too many eggs in his basket. I'd like to know how much it would hurt if he cut loose from us completely.' I paused, then added, 'Or if we cut loose from him.'

33

Charlie looked alarmed. 'Christ! it would be like having a leg cut off – without anaesthetic.'

'It might happen.'

'But why would you want to cut loose? The money he pumped in was the making of us.'

'I know,' I said. 'But Brinton is a financial shark. Snapping up a profit is to him as mindless a reflex as when a real shark snaps up a tasty morsel. I think we're vulnerable, Charlie.'

'I don't know why you're getting so bloody hot under the collar all of a sudden,' he said plaintively.

'Don't you?' I leaned forward and the chair legs came down with a soft thud on to the thick pile carpet. 'Last night, in a conversation lasting less than four minutes, we lost fifteen per cent of Brinton's business. And why did we lose it? So that he can put the arm on Andrew McGovern who is apparently getting out of line. Or so Brinton says.'

'Don't you believe him?'

'Whether he's telling the truth or not isn't the point. The point is that our business is being buggered in one of Brinton's private schemes which has nothing to do with us.'

Charlie said slowly, 'Yes, I see what you mean.'

I stared at him. 'Do you, Charlie? I don't think so. Take a good long look at what happened yesterday. We were manipulated by a minority shareholder who twisted us around his little finger.'

'Oh, for God's sake, Max! If McGovern doesn't want us there's not a damn thing we can do about it.'

'I know that, but we could have done something which we didn't. We could have held the Whensley Group to their contract which has just under a year to run. Instead, we all agreed at the AGM to pull out in ten days. We were manœuvred into that, Charlie; Brinton had us dancing on strings.'

Charlie was silent.

I said, 'And you know why we let it happen? We were too damned scared of losing Brinton's money. We could have outvoted him singly or jointly, but we didn't.'

'No,' said Charlie sharply. 'Your vote would have downed him – you have 51 per cent. But I have only 24 to his 25.'

I sighed. 'Okay, Charlie; my fault. But as I lay in bed last night I felt scared. I was scared of what I hadn't done. And the thing that scared me most of all was the thought of the kind of man I was becoming. I didn't start this business to jerk to any man's string, and that's why I say we have to cut loose from Brinton if possible. That's why I want you to look for alternative sources of finance. We're big enough to get it now.'

'There may be something in what you say,' said Charlie. 'But I still think you're blowing a gasket without due cause. You're over-reacting, Max.' He shrugged. 'Still, I'll look for outside money if only to keep you from blowing your top.' He glanced at the magazine cutting on my desk. 'What's that?'

'A story about Paul Billson's father. You know – the accountant who vanished from Franklin Engineering.'

'What's the score on that one?'

I shook my head. 'I don't know. At first I had Paul Billson taped as being a little devalued in the intellect – running about eighty pence in the pound – but there are a couple of things which don't add up.'

'Well, you won't have to worry about that now. Franklin is part of the Whensley Group.'

I looked up in surprise. 'So it is.' It had slipped my mind.

'I'd hand over what you've got to Sir Andrew McGovern and wish him the best of British luck.'

I thought about that and shook my head. 'No – Billson disappeared when we were in charge of security and there's still a few days to the end of the month.'

'Your sense of ethics is too strongly developed.'

'I think I'll follow up on this one myself,' I said. 'I started it so I might as well finish it. Jack Ellis can stand in for me.

35

It's time he was given more responsibility.'

Charlie nodded approvingly. 'Do you think there's anything in Billson's disappearance – from the point of view of Franklin's security, I mean?'

I grinned at him. 'I'll probably find that he's eloped with someone's wife – and I hope it's Andrew McGovern's.'

Five

I went down to Fleet Street to look for Michael English, the journalist who had written the article on Peter Billson. His office thought he was at the Press Club, the Press Club invited me to try El Vino's. I finally ran him to ground in a pub off the Strand.

He was a tall, willowy, fair-haired man whom I disliked on sight, although what he had written about Billson might have influenced my feelings. He was playing poker dice with a couple of other journalists and looked at me doubtfully when I gave him one of my business cards to prick his curiosity.

'Security!' he said. There was a shade of nervousness.

I smiled reassuringly. 'I'd like to talk to you about Billson.'

'That little twit! What's he put you on to me for?' Apprehension surrounded English like a fog.

'You've seen him recently?'

'Of course I have. He came to the office making trouble. He threatened a law suit.' English snorted with unhumorous laughter. 'Our lawyer saw him off smartly on that one.'

I was deliberately obtuse. 'I'm surprised he bothered you. If your article was correct he stands a good chance of a jail sentence – although his grey hairs might save him, I suppose.'

English looked at me in surprise. 'It wasn't the old man. It was someone who claimed to be his son – said he was Paul Billson. He made quite a scene.'

I looked around and saw an empty corner table. 'I'd like to talk to you about it. Over there where it's quiet. What will you have?'

English hesitated, then shrugged. 'I don't mind. Make it a double scotch.'

As I ordered the drinks he said, 'I suppose you're investigating for the insurance company.' I made an ambiguous murmur, and he said, 'I thought they gave up years ago. Isn't there a time limitation on a crime like that?'

I smiled at him as he splashed water perfunctorily in his glass. 'The file is still open.'

English had been called into his editor's office the day after the article had appeared – the day before Billson went missing. He found the editor trying to cope with an angry and agitated man who was making incoherent threats. The editor, Gaydon, said in a loud voice, 'This is Mr English who wrote the article. Sit down, Mike, and let's see if we can sort this out.' He flicked a switch on the intercom. 'Ask Mr Harcourt if he can come to my office.'

English saw trouble looming ahead. Harcourt was the resident lawyer and his presence presaged no good. He cleared his throat and said, 'What's the trouble?'

Gaydon said, 'This is Mr Paul Billson. He appears to be disturbed about the article on his father which appeared in yesterday's issue.'

English looked at Billson and saw a rather nondescript man who, at that moment, was extremely agitated. His face was white and dull red spots burned in his cheeks as he said in a high voice, 'It was nothing but outright libel. I demand a retraction and a public apology.'

Gaydon said in a calming voice, 'I'm sure that Mr English wrote the truth as he saw it. What do you say, Mike?'

'Of course, you're right,' said English. 'Every matter of fact was checked against the original court records and the contemporary newspaper reports.'

'I'm not complaining about the facts,' said Billson. 'It's the damned inferences about my father. I've never read anything so scurrilous in my life. If I don't get a public apology I shall sue.'

Gaydon glanced at English, then said smoothly, 'It shouldn't come to that, Mr Billson. I'm certain we can come to some arrangement or agreement satisfactory to all parties.' He looked up as Harcourt entered the office and said with a slight air of relief, 'This is Mr Harcourt of our legal department.'

Rapidly he explained the point at issue, and Harcourt said, 'Do you have a copy of the article?'

He settled down to read the supplement which Gaydon produced and the office was uneasily quiet until he had finished. Gaydon tapped restlessly with his forefinger; English sat quite still, hoping that the film of sweat on his forehead didn't show; Billson squirmed in his seat as the pressure within him built higher.

After what seemed an interminable period Harcourt laid down the magazine. 'What exactly are you complaining about, Mr Billson?'

'Isn't it evident?' Billson demanded. 'My father has been blackguarded in print. I demand an immediate apology or I sue.' His finger stabbed at English. 'I sue him and the newspaper.'

'I see,' said Harcourt thoughtfully. He leaned forward. 'What do you believe happened to your father?'

'His plane crashed,' said Billson. 'He was killed – that's what I believe.' He slammed his hand on the magazine. 'This is just plain libel.'

'I believe that you will be unable to sue,' said Harcourt. 'You can sue only if your own reputation is at stake. You see, it's an established principle of law that a dead man cannot be libelled.'

There was a moment of silence before Billson said incredulously, 'But this man says my father is *not* dead.'

'But *you* believe he is dead, and *you* would be bringing the case to court. It wouldn't work, Mr Billson. You needn't take my word for it, of course; you can ask your own solicitor. In fact, I strongly advise it.'

'Are you telling me that any cheap journalist can drag my

father's name through the mud and get away with it?' Billson was shaking with rage.

Harcourt said gravely, 'I should watch your words, Mr Billson, or the shoe may be on the other foot. Such intemperate language could lead you into trouble.'

Billson knocked over his chair in getting to his feet. 'I shall certainly take legal advice,' he shouted, and glared at English. 'I'll have your hide, damn you!'

The door slammed behind him.

Harcourt picked up the magazine and flipped it to English's article. He avoided looking directly at English, and said to Gaydon, 'I suggest that if you intend to publish work of this nature in future you check with the legal department before publication and not after.'

'Are we in the clear?' asked Gaydon.

'Legally – quite,' said Harcourt, and added distastefully, 'It's not within my province to judge the moral aspect.' He paused. 'If the widow takes action it will be different, of course. There is a clear implication here that she joined with her husband in cheating the insurance company. How else could Peter Billson profit other than with his wife's connivance?'

Gaydon turned to English. 'What about the widow?'

'It's okay,' said English. 'She died a little over a year ago. Helen Billson married a Norwegian during the war and changed her name to Aarvik. It was when I stumbled over that fact that I decided to write up the story of Billson.'

Harcourt snorted and left, and Gaydon grinned at English. 'That was a bit close, Mike.' He picked up a pen. 'Be a good chap and pick up that chair before you leave.'

I bought English another drink. 'So Paul Billson didn't have a leg to stand on.'

English laughed. 'Not a hope. I didn't attack *his* reputation, you see. Christ, I'd forgotten the man existed.'

I said mendaciously, 'I'm not really interested in Paul Billson. Do you really think that Peter Billson faked his death to defraud the insurance company?'

'He could have,' said English. 'It makes a good story.'

'But do you believe it?'

'Does it matter what I believe?' He drank some scotch. 'No, of course I don't believe it. I think Billson was killed, all right.'

'So you were pretty safe in issuing that challenge to come forth.'

'I like to bet on certainties,' said English. He grinned. 'If he *did* defraud the insurance company he wasn't likely to rise to the bait, was he? I was on sure ground until his son popped up.'

I said, 'About that insurance. £100,000 is a hell of a lot of money. The premium must have been devilish high.'

'Not really. You must remember that by 1936 aeroplanes were no longer the unsafe string-and-sealing wax contraptions of the 'twenties. There wasn't a great deal of doubt that an aircraft would get to where it was going – the question was how fast. And this was at the time of a newspaper war; the dailies were cutting each other's throats to buy readers. Any premium would be a drop in the bucket compared with what they were spending elsewhere, and £100,000 is a nice headline-filling sum.'

'Did Billson stand a chance in the race?'

'Sure – he was a hot favourite. *Flyaway* – that Northrop of his – was one of the best aircraft of its time, and he was a good pilot.'

'Who won the race?'

'A German called Helmut Steiner. I think Billson would have won had he survived. Steiner only won because he took a hell of a lot of chances.'

'Oh! What sort of chances?'

English shrugged. 'I don't remember the times personally – I'm not that old – but I've read up on it. This was in the times of the Nazis. The Berlin Olympics were on and the Master Race was busy proving its case. German racing cars were winning on all the circuits because the Auto-Union was State subsidized; German mountaineers were doing damnfool things on every Alpine cliff – I believe some of them dropped off the Eiger at the time. It didn't prove they were good climbers; only that they were good Nazis. Germany had to beat everybody at everything, regardless of cost.'

'And Steiner?'

'Subsidized by the Hitler regime, of course; given a stripped military plane and a crackerjack support team seconded from the Luftwaffe. He was good, all right, but I think he knew Billson was better, so he took chances and they came off. He pressed his machine to the limit and the engine blew up on him as he landed in Cape Town. He was lucky it didn't happen sooner.'

I thought about that. 'Any possibility of Billson being sabotaged?'

English stared at me. 'No one has come up with that idea before. That really is a lulu.'

'What about it?'

'My God, the lengths to which insurance companies will go! What will you do if Billson was sabotaged? Sue the German government for £100,000? I doubt if Bonn would fall for that one.' He shrugged. 'Billson's plane was never found. You haven't a hope.'

I drained my glass. There wasn't much more I could get out of English and I prepared a sharp knife to stick into him. 'So you don't think you'll have any trouble from Paul Billson.'

'Not a chance,' he scoffed. 'Harcourt may be pious and sanctimonious but he tied Billson into knots. You can't libel a dead man – and Billson swears his father is dead.'

I smiled gently. 'A man called Wright once wrote about William Ewart Gladstone imputing that he was a hypocrite, particularly in sexual matters. This was in 1927 and Gladstone was long dead. But his son, the then Lord Gladstone, took umbrage and also legal advice. Like Paul Billson, he was told that the dead cannot be libelled, but he nailed

Wright to the cross all the same.'

English gave me a wet-eyed look. 'What did he do?'

'He libelled Wright at every opportunity. He called Wright a liar, a fool and a poltroon in public. He had Wright thrown out of his club. In the end Wright had to bring Gladstone to court to protect his reputation. Gladstone had Norman Birkett appear for him, and Birkett flayed Wright in open court. When the case was finished so was Wright; his professional reputation was smashed.' I slid the knife home. 'It could happen to you.'

English shook his head. 'Billson won't do that – he's not the man for it.'

'He might,' I said. 'With help.' I twisted the knife. 'And it will give me great pleasure to appear for him and to swear that you told me that you thought his father to be dead, in spite of what you wrote in your dirty little article.'

I rose and left him. At the door of the pub I stopped and looked back. He was sitting in the corner, looking as though someone had kicked him in the belly, knocking the wind out of him.

Six

I had an early lunch and then belatedly thought to ring Paul Billson's half-sister. I had expected to find her absent from home in the middle of the working day but the telephone was picked up on the third ring and a pleasant voice said, 'Alix Aarvik here.'

I told her who and what I was, then said, 'I take it you haven't heard from your brother, Miss Aarvik.'

'No, I haven't, Mr Stafford.'

'I'd like to talk to you about him. May I come round?'

'Now?' There was uncertainty in her voice.

'Time is of the essence in these matters, Miss Aarvik.' A platitude, but I find they tend to soothe people.

'Very well,' she said. 'I'll be expecting you.'

'Within the half-hour.' I rang off and took a taxi to Kensington.

With a name like hers I had envisaged a big, tow-headed Scandinavian, but she was short and dark and looked in her early thirties. Her flat was comfortable, if sparsely furnished, and I was interested to see that she was apparently moving out. Two suitcases stood in the hall and another on a table was open and half-packed.

She saw me looking around and said, 'You've caught me in the middle of packing.'

I smiled. 'Found another flat?'

She shook her head. 'I'm leaving for Canada. My firm has asked me to go. I'm flying tomorrow afternoon.' She made a gesture which was pathetically helpless. 'I don't know if I'm doing the right thing with Paul still missing, but I have my job to consider.'

'I see,' I said, not seeing a hell of a lot. Her mother had

come into a windfall of £100,000 but there was precious little sign of it around, either sticking to Paul Billson or Alix Aarvik. I made a little small talk while I studied her. She was not too well dressed but managed to make the most of what she had, and she didn't overdo the make-up. You could see thousands like her in the streets; a typical specimen of *Stenographica londiniensis* – the London typist.

When I married Gloria I had not a bean to spare and, during my rise to the giddy heights of success, I had become aware of all the subtle variations in women's knick-knackery from the cheap off-the-peg frock to the one-off Paris creation. Not that Gloria had spent much time in the lower reaches of the clothing spectrum – she developed a talent for spending money faster than I earned it, which was one of the points at issue between us. But I knew enough to know that Alix Aarvik was not dressing like an heiress.

I took the chair she offered, and said, 'Now tell me about Paul.'

'What do you want to know?'

'You can start by telling me of his relationship with his father.'

She gave me a startled look. 'You've got that far already?'

'It wasn't difficult.'

'He hero-worshipped his father,' she said. 'Not that he ever knew him to remember. Peter Billson died when Paul was two years old. You know about the air crash?'

'There seems to be a little doubt about that,' I said.

Pain showed in her eyes. 'You, too?' She shook her head. 'It was that uncertainty which preyed on Paul's mind. He wanted his father to be dead – rather a dead hero than a living fraud. Do you understand what that means, Mr Stafford?'

'You tell me.'

'I arranged for Paul to have psychiatric treatment. The psychiatrist told me that it was this that was breaking Paul in two. It's a dreadful thing to hero-worship a man – your father – and to wish him dead simultaneously.'

'So he had a neurosis. What form did it take?'

'Generally, he raged against injustice; the smart-aleck kind of injustice such as when someone takes credit for another's achievement. He collected injustices. Wasn't there a book called *The Injustice Collector*? That's Paul.'

'You say generally – how about specifically?'

'As it related to his father, he thought Peter Billson had been treated unjustly – maligned in death. You know about the court case?' I nodded, and she said, 'He wanted to clear his father's name.'

I said carefully, 'Why do you talk about Paul in the past tense?'

Again she looked startled and turned pale. 'I . . . I didn't know . . .' She intertwined her fingers and whispered, 'I suppose I think he's dead.'

'Why should you think that?'

'I don't know. But I can't think of any reason why he should disappear, either.'

'This neurosis about injustice – did he apply it to himself? Did he think that *he* was treated unjustly?'

She looked straight at me and said firmly, 'Never! He was always concerned about others. Look, Mr Stafford; I'll come right out and say that Paul wasn't – ' she caught herself – 'isn't too bright. Now you're in security at Franklin Engineering and I'll tell you that Paul isn't a thief or anything like that. He may not be an entirely balanced man, but he's honest.'

'I have no doubt about it, Miss Aarvik,' I said. 'My enquiries are as much on behalf of Paul as they are for Franklin Engineering. The management of Franklin are very much concerned about what happens to their employees.'

That was pious piffle which I hoped she'd swallow. Neither Stewart nor Isaacson had shown a whit of concern.

She said, 'Paul knew . . . knows he'll never make his way in the world, but he never showed resentment. I knew he found it hard to make out on only two hundred a month, but he never complained.'

I opened my mouth to contradict her and then closed it firmly. I waited the space of ten heart beats before I said, 'Is that all he got?'

'£2400 a year – it was all he was worth,' she said a little sadly. 'But you must have checked.'

'Yes,' I said bemusedly. 'The exact figure had slipped my memory.'

So Paul had been cheating on his sister. He had told her he earned £2400 a year when he got over three times as much, although according to Hoyland, and now his sister, that was probably as much as he was worth. You think you have a man taped, his life spread before you like a butterfly pinned in a showcase, and he surprises you with an inconsistency.

I said, 'Did you ever help him financially?'

She hesitated. 'Not directly.'

Slowly I coaxed the story from her. She had been supporting their mother in her last illness. Mrs Aarvik had been dying of cancer painfully and protractedly. Alix paid for a nurse and private hospital treatment and, towards the end, for the services of a specialist – all beyond the stark necessities of the National Health Service. It was very expensive and her savings ran out.

'Then Paul needed treatment,' she said. 'The psychiatrist I told you about.'

The psychiatrist was also in private practice and also expensive. Miss Aarvik had an understanding bank manager who allowed her a sizeable overdraft in spite of the prevailing credit squeeze. 'I'm paying it off as quickly as I can.' She smiled ruefully. 'That's why I'm pleased about the Canadian job; it's at a much higher salary.'

Paul Billson contributed nothing.

'I knew he couldn't save,' she said. 'So what else could I do?'

What else, indeed? I thought of the £12,000 tucked away in Paul's deposit account and marvelled at the curious quirks of mankind. Here was a man whom everybody

47

agreed to be a nonentity – a spineless, faceless creature hardly distinguishable from a jellyfish – and he was proving to be human, after all, just like the rest of us. Human enough to have an eye for the main chance and to batten mercilessly on his sister. Which may only go to show that my view of humanity is jaundiced, to say the least of it.

Anyway, it accounted for Miss Aarvik's sparsely furnished flat and for her neat but somewhat aged dress. If she was paying off a big overdraft she wouldn't be spending on luxurious fripperies. Which was a pity – she deserved better.

I said, 'Did the treatment do Paul any good?'

'I think so. He's been much quieter of late, until . . .'

Until English wrote his poisonous article and Paul blew up, nerved himself to tackle a newspaper editor, and then vanished.

'Think carefully,' I said. 'You probably know your brother better than anyone else. If he went off the rails for any reason, what would he be likely to do?'

'I can't think of anything. Unless . . .' She shook her head. 'No, that's silly.'

'It may not be,' I said encouragingly.

'Well, when he was a boy he used to dream of clearing his father's name by finding the aeroplane; actually going out to Africa and looking for it. It was never found, you know. Not a very practicable dream, I'm afraid; but Paul was never a practicable man.'

I thought about it. Somewhere south of the Mediterranean and north of the Congo. The Sahara. Not at all practicable.

'Of course, he gave up the idea long ago,' she said. 'Even Paul realized it was futile. It would need a lot of money, you see, and he never had the money.'

To tell her that her brother had his pockets stuffed with boodle would have been needlessly cruel. But now I had a lead, for what it was worth. '1936 is a long time ago,' I said. 'I doubt if there'd be anything to find now. What did your parents think of Paul's obsession?'

'My mother always said he'd grow out of it, but he never did. She lived with me and didn't see very much of him. She didn't like him talking so much about his father; she thought it was unhealthy. I suppose it was. He never knew his father, you see.'

'And *your* father – what did he think?'

She gave a wry smile. 'You must think we're an odd family. I never knew *my* father, either. He died before I was born. My mother married him during the war and he was killed in action. He was Norwegian, you know.'

'Your mother had a tough life,' I said. Two husbands killed leaving small children to bring up wasn't my idea of a bed of roses.

'Oh, she was always cheerful – right up to the end.'

'One thing puzzles me,' I said. 'Your mother was awarded £100,000 by the court. What happened to it? There must have been something left to keep her more comfortable in her old age.'

'I don't know,' said Miss Aarvik sombrely. 'I've wondered about that myself, but Mother never talked about it. You must realize that I only knew about it years afterwards when I was about thirteen. It didn't mean much then; children don't think of things that happened before they were born – the present is much more exciting.'

'But later – didn't you ask her?'

'I tried, but she would never talk about it.' She looked at me squarely. 'I think I take after my father, Torstein Aarvik; I never knew him, of course, so I can't be certain. But Paul took after Mother; they're alike in so many ways. She could be very silly and thoughtless at times. Not wilfully, you understand; but she did things without thinking too far ahead. Perhaps something happened that she was ashamed to talk about. She wasn't very bright, but I loved her very much.'

So Paul was the not too bright son of a not too bright

mother. That didn't get me far. I stood up. 'Well, thank you, Miss Aarvik, for all the information. You've been very frank.'

She rose with me. 'I must thank you for your interest, Mr Stafford.' She smiled wanly. 'You've certainly been more thorough in your inquiries than the police. Do you think you can find Paul?'

That put me in a moral dilemma. As far as Franklin Engineering was concerned the case was finished; Billson hadn't embezzled the petty cash nor had he breached security as far as I knew and I couldn't load further investigation costs on to the Franklin account. Nor could I load the costs on to Stafford Security Consultants Ltd – that wouldn't be fair to Charlie Malleson or Brinton who weren't in business for charity.

Neither was I. As far as I was concerned, Paul Billson was an unbalanced man whom I had discovered to be of an unscrupulous disposition and, as far as I could see, Alix Aarvik was better off without him. I decided to give what I had to the police and call it a day.

I said diplomatically, 'Your information will make it more likely.'

'If I give you a Canadian address will you write to me?' she asked. 'I've been wondering whether I should go at all while Paul is still missing.'

It struck me that Canada was the best place for her – somewhere away from the leeching of her brother. 'There's nothing you can do if you stay here,' I said. 'I'll certainly write to you.'

She scribbled an address on a stenographic note-pad. 'I don't have a home address yet, but that's the firm I'll be working for.'

I glanced at the sheet. Apparently she'd be with the Kisko Nickel Corporation of Vancouver; I'd never heard of it. I folded the paper and dutifully put it into my wallet as she escorted me to the door. Already the street lights were on as darkness descended. I thought of the quiet fortitude with which Alix Aarvik faced a not too happy life. She had not paraded her troubles before me; indeed, it had taken quite a bit of my not inconsiderable skill to extract many of the details from her. I hoped she'd be happy in Canada; she was good value.

I deliberated about the best way to go to find a taxi and turned in the direction of Kensington High Street. As I walked a man got out of a car parked by the kerb just ahead. He waited until I came abreast of him, then said, 'Your name Stafford?' He had a rough Cockney voice.

A door slammed on the other side of the car as someone else got out. 'Yes, I'm Stafford.'

'Got a message for yer, mate. Keep yer bleedin' nose outter fings wot don't concern yer. This'll 'elp yer remember.'

He suddenly drove his fist into my midriff, just below the sternum, and I gasped and doubled up, fighting for breath. I didn't have much of a chance after that. There were three of them and when I went down they got to work with their boots. It wasn't long before I passed out – but long enough to feel the pain.

Seven

A lot of people came to see me in hospital, some of whom surprised me by their appearance. The police came, of course, but they were followed by a man from the Special Branch checking on Billson because of the defence work done at Franklin Engineering. My wife didn't show up but she took the trouble to spend two minutes on the telephone ordering flowers to be sent to the hospital, which surprised me mildly.

Lord Brinton came, his hands behind his back. 'Don't want to drink this London water,' he said, and put a bottle of Malvern water on the bedside table. 'Spoils the taste of the scotch.' A bottle of Talisker joined the Malvern water.

I smiled – a painful process at the time. 'My doctor might not approve.'

'Better than bringing bloody grapes.' He pulled up a chair and sat warming his ancient and expensive bones at the wall radiator. 'Not as good as a real fire,' he grumbled.

'Hospitals don't like open fires.'

'Well,' he said. 'What the hell happened, Max?'

'I was beaten up,' I said patiently.

'So I see,' he said with a straight face. 'Why?'

'I don't know. It seems I was "poking my nose into fings wot don't concern me", to quote the spokesman of the assault committee. He neglected to be more specific.'

'Mistaken identity?'

I began to shake my head and hastily decided against it for fear it should fall off. 'He made sure he knew who I was first.'

'What were you doing in Kensington?'

'Following up on a case.' I told him about Billson and what

I had done. 'Miss Aarvik will be in Canada now,' I said.

'Good country,' observed Brinton. 'I was born there.' He said it as though the act of his being born there had conferred a distinction on Canada. 'I don't see how all this relates to your being beaten up.'

'Neither do I. Neither do the police or the Special Branch.'

His eyes sharpened. 'What's their interest?'

'Franklin Engineering makes bits and pieces of tanks.'

'And they're following up on Billson?'

'So it seems – but they're not pushing too hard. For all anyone can find out he hasn't committed a crime – yet.'

'You think he might?'

'Who knows what a man like Billson might or might not do. He's lived like a vegetable for fifteen years at least, and now he's gone charging off God knows where. He could be up to anything.'

'Well, you're out of it,' said Brinton. 'By the time you get out of here Andrew McGovern will have taken over responsibility for the security of Franklin Engineering.'

'How big a piece of the Whensley Group have you got?' I asked.

'About thirty per cent. Why?'

'Then you'll be a big enough shareholder to ask why Billson was paid three times as much as he's worth and why there's a mystery made of it.'

'I'll look into it,' said Brinton. 'Can't have the shareholders diddled like that. All right, if you weren't beaten up because of Billson, what else have you been doing recently to get you into trouble?'

'My life has been blameless.'

Brinton grunted in his throat. 'Don't try to con an old sinner. Nobody's life is blameless. You're sure you haven't been sleeping in any of the wrong beds?' I just looked at him and he said, 'Not that I'd blame you under the circumstances.'

Soon after that he went away.

Charlie Malleson came to see me. He inspected my assortment of bruises, and said, 'Better not go out into the streets just yet. Someone from the Race Relations Board might get you for trying to cross the colour line.'

I sighed. 'You can do better than that, Charlie. If you have to make jokes they'd better be good. How's business?'

'We're coping. How long do you think you'll be laid up?'

'Nobody tells me anything – you know what hospitals are like. From the way I feel now it'll be about six months, but I'll probably be back in a couple of weeks.'

'Take your time,' Charlie advised. 'Jack Ellis is trying on your shoes to see if they fit.'

'Good – but that will teach me to prophesy.' Charlie raised an eyebrow and I explained. 'I told Joyce that Jack was to take some of my work load. When she queried it I said that if I got knocked down in the street he'd have to take the lot. But this wasn't the sort of knocking down I had in mind.' I thought about Jack Ellis, then said, 'It's about time we made him a director, anyway. He's become very good and we don't want to lose him.'

'I agree,' said Charlie. 'And I think old Brinton will. Max, when did you last take a holiday?'

I grinned. 'That's a funny-sounding word. Maybe two years ago.'

'It's been four years,' he said positively. 'You've been knocking yourself out. My advice is to take some time off right now while you have a good enough excuse to fool your subconscious. Take a trip to the Caribbean and soak up some sun for a couple of months.'

I looked out of the window at the slanting rain. 'Sounds good.'

Charlie smiled. 'The truth is I don't want you around while Jack is finding his feet in a top job. You can be a pretty alarming bastard at times and it might be a bit inhibiting for him.'

That made sense, and the more I thought about it the better it became. Gloria and I could go away and perhaps we could paper over some of the cracks in our marriage. I knew that, when a marriage is at breaking-point, the fault is rarely solely on one side, and my drive to set up the firm had certainly been a contributing factor. Perhaps I could do something to stick things together again.

'I'll think about it,' I said. 'But I'd better see Jack. There are one or two things he ought to know before he gets his feet wet.'

Charlie's face cracked into a pleased smile which faded as he said, 'Who assaulted you, Max?'

We kicked the Billson case around for a while and got nowhere. So Charlie left, promising to send Jack Ellis to see me.

The really surprising visitor was Alix Aarvik.

I gaped as she came in and then said, 'Sit down, Miss Aarvik – you'll excuse me if I don't stand. I thought you were in Canada.'

She sat in the leather club chair which Brinton had had installed for his own benefit. 'I changed my mind,' she said. 'I turned down the job.'

'Oh! Why?'

She inspected me. 'I'm sorry about what happened to you, Mr Stafford.'

I laughed. By this time I was able to laugh without my ribs grinding together. 'An occupational hazard.'

Her face was serious. 'Was it because of your enquiries about Paul?'

'I can't see how it could be.'

'The police came to see me again. And some others who . . . weren't ordinary police.'

'Special Branch. Paul did work in a defence industry.'

'I didn't know what to think. They were so uncommunicative.'

I nodded. 'Their job is to ask questions, not to give

answers. Besides, they revel in an aura of mystery. May I ask why you turned down the Canadian job?'

She hesitated. 'About a quarter of an hour after you left my flat I went out to post a letter. There was an ambulance not far from the street door and you were being put into it.' She moistened her lips. 'I thought you were dead.'

I said slowly, 'It must have given you a shock. I'm sorry.'

There was a rigidity about her which betrayed extreme tension. She opened her mouth and swallowed as though the words would not come, then she made another attempt and said, 'Did you see who attacked you?'

The penny dropped. 'It wasn't your brother, if that's what you mean.'

She gave a long sigh and relaxed visibly. 'I had to know,' she said. 'I couldn't leave without knowing, and the police wouldn't tell me anything.'

I looked at her thoughtfully. 'If you thought your brother might attack anyone homicidally you should have warned me.'

'But I didn't think that,' she cried. 'Not when we talked together. It was only afterwards, when I saw you in the ambulance, that it occurred to me.'

I said, 'I want the truth. Have you seen Paul since he disappeared?'

'No, I haven't – I haven't.' Her face was aflame with her vehemence.

I said gently, 'I believe you.'

She was suddenly in tears. 'What's happened to Paul, Mr Stafford? What is he *doing*?'

'I don't know. Honestly, I don't know.' It took me some time to quieten her, and lying flat on my back didn't help. In order to divert her I said, 'You were being transferred to Canada. Will the fact that you turned down the offer affect your present job?'

'I don't think so,' she said. 'Sir Andrew was very good about it.'

A frisson ran down my back. 'Sir Andrew?'

'Sir Andrew McGovern. I'm his secretary.'

'You do mean the Chairman of the Whensley Group?'

'That's right. Do you know him?'

'I haven't had that pleasure. How did you come to work for him, Miss Aarvik?'

'I started work at Franklin Engineering eight years ago.' She smiled. 'In the typing pool. I like to think I'm good at my job – anyway I didn't stay long in the typing pool, and four years ago I was transferred to Group Head Office in London – that's Whensley Holdings Ltd.'

'I know,' I said. 'We handle the security.' But not for long I thought.

'Oh! You mean you employ the men who come around and make sure I've destroyed the executive typewriter ribbons?'

'Sort of. What made you start with Franklin Engineering? How did you get the job?'

'I was with a firm which went bust,' she said. 'I needed another job so Paul suggested Franklin. He'd been working there for quite a while and he said it was a good firm.'

So it was – for Paul Billson. Seeing that I'd started to open the can of worms it seemed a good idea to take the top right off. For instance, was Miss Aarvik's salary as inflated as her brother's? 'Do you mind telling me your present salary, Miss Aarvik?'

She looked at me with some surprise. 'I don't think so. I get £4200 a year – before tax.'

I sighed. That was fairly standard for a top secretary; certainly nothing out of the ordinary. And it was the most natural thing in the world to be introduced into the firm by Paul. 'Why the Canadian transfer?' I asked. 'Isn't it a bit odd for the secretary of the boss to be asked to move to another country? Or were you going with Sir Andrew?'

She shook her head. 'The way Sir Andrew put it, I was doing him a favour. The company I was going to – Kisko Nickel – is undergoing reorganization. I was to organize the office procedures, but only on loan for a year.'

'You must have been pleased about that. Wasn't it a step up? From secretarial to executive?'

'I was bucked about it,' she admitted. 'But then Paul . . .' Her voice tailed away.

'When were you offered the job?'

'It came up rather suddenly – last Monday.'

I wrinkled my brow. That was the day Hoyland rang to tell me of Billson's disappearance. There was something bloody funny going on but, for the life of me, I couldn't see how it hung together.

I smiled at her. 'Well, you see that I am very much alive. In the opinion of the police and of my associates at Stafford Security the attack on me had nothing to do with your brother.'

She looked at me squarely. 'What of your opinion?'

I lied. 'I am of the same opinion. If you want my advice you'll go straight to Sir Andrew McGovern and tell him you've reconsidered and you'll take the Canadian job after all.'

'And Paul?'

'There's nothing you can do about Paul, as I said before. He'll be found, but it's better for you to leave it to the professionals. I'll write to you in Canada.'

She nodded. 'Perhaps that would be the best thing to do.'

'One thing – I wouldn't mention to Sir Andrew that this is my advice, or that you've even seen me. My firm and Sir Andrew aren't on very good terms right now; he's fired Stafford Security and is setting up his own security organization for the Whensley Group, so I think any mention of me would be tactless, to say the least.'

Her eyes widened. 'Was this because of Paul?'

'Not at all. It happened before . . .' I stopped short. It hadn't happened before I knew about Billson. Brinton had sprung it on us at the board meeting on the afternoon when I had just returned from Franklin Engineering. I picked up quickly. 'Nothing to do with your brother at all, Miss Aarvik.'

When she had gone I stared at the ceiling for a long time. Then I opened the bedside cupboard, stripped the lead foil from Brinton's bottle of scotch, and poured myself three fingers. Brinton may have been right about it tasting better with Malvern water, but it tasted even better neat. I suddenly really needed that drink.

Eight

I soon became very damned tired of that hospital and especially of the food. I had just been served a so-called lunch which began with a watery soup which looked like old dishwater and ended with an equally watery custard which resembled nothing on God's earth when my doctor walked in, full of that synthetic bonhomie which is taught in medical schools as the bedside manner.

I thrust the tray under his nose. 'Would you eat that?'

He inspected it, his nose wrinkling fastidiously. 'What's wrong with it?'

'That wasn't the question,' I snarled.

His eyes twinkled. 'Well, possibly not,' he conceded.

'That's good enough for me,' I said. 'I'm discharging myself.'

'But you're not ready.'

'And I never will be if I have to eat this slop. I'm going home to get some decent food in my belly.' For all Gloria's faults she wasn't a half-way bad cook when she wanted to be.

'The food can't be all that bad if you're beginning to feel your oats.' I glared at him and he shrugged. 'All right, but the prescribed regimen is another week's rest and then I want you back here for inspection.'

I said, 'Where are my bloody trousers?'

So I went home by taxi and found Gloria in bed with a man. They were both naked and he was a stranger – I'd never seen him before to my knowledge but Gloria had a lot of odd friends. There weren't any fireworks; I just jerked my thumb at the bedroom door and said, 'Out!' He grabbed his clothes and disappeared, looking like a skinned rabbit.

In silence I looked at the heap of tousled bedclothes into which Gloria had vanished. Presently the front door slammed and Gloria emerged, looking aggrieved and a little scared. 'But the hospital said . . .'

'Shut up!'

She was stupid enough to ignore me. She informed me at length about the kind of man I was or, rather, the kind of man I wasn't. She embroidered her diatribe with all the shortcomings she could find in me, culled from seven years of married life, and then informed me that her bedfriend hadn't been the first by a long shot, and whose fault was that? In short, she tried to work up the familiar instant Stafford row to the nth degree.

I didn't argue with her – I just hit her. The first time I had ever hit a woman in my life. An open palm to the side of her jaw with plenty of muscle behind it. It knocked her clean out of bed so that she lay sprawling in a tangle of sheets by the dressing-table. She was still for a few moments and then shook her head muzzily as she pushed against the floor to raise herself up. She opened her mouth and closed it again as she caught my eye. Her fingers stroked the dull red blotch on her face and she looked at me unbelievingly.

I ignored her and walked to the wardrobe from which I took a suitcase from the top shelf and began to pack. Presently I broke the silence. 'You'll be hearing from my solicitor. Until then you can have the house.'

'Where are you going?' Her voice was soft and quiet.

'Do you care?'

She had nothing to say to that so I picked up the suitcase and left the bedroom. I went downstairs to my study and unlocked the bureau. As I took out my passport I was aware of Gloria standing by the door. 'You *can't* leave me,' she said desolately.

I turned my head and looked at her. 'For God's sake, go and put on some clothes,' I said. 'You'll die of pneumonia.'

When I put the passport and a few other papers into my

pocket and walked into the hall she was trudging disconsolately up the stairs. As I walked towards the front door she screamed, 'Come back, Max!'

I shut the door gently on her shout, closing an era of my life. *Sic transit Gloria mundi*. A lousy pun but a true one.

Nine

I suppose if I hadn't left Gloria I wouldn't have gone on with the Billson case. Billson himself had ceased to be a security matter and was merely a half-way maniac gone on an ancestor-worshipping bender. He was of no concern to anyone but himself and, possibly, Alix Aarvik.

But I had left Gloria, which put me in a somewhat ambiguous position. It had already been agreed that I would take a holiday, partly for my own benefit and partly to give free rein to Jack Ellis. The trouble was that I didn't feel like a holiday; I couldn't see myself toasting on the sands of Montego Bay, as Charlie had suggested. And so the devil found work for idle hands.

Besides, I *had* been assaulted, and if nothing else demanded that something should be done, company policy did.

So I asked Jack Ellis to come and see me at my club. Ellis had joined us four years earlier – young, bright and eager to learn. He was still young, but that didn't worry me; Napoleon was only twenty-six when he was General of the Army of Italy and licked hell out of the Austrians. Jack Ellis was twenty-seven, something that might hinder him when negotiating with some of the stuffier chairmen of companies, but time would cure that. In the meantime he was very good and getting better.

I took him aside into the cardroom which was empty in the afternoon. For a while we talked about his job and then I brought him up-to-date on the Billson story. He was puzzled as anyone about the whole affair.

'Jack,' I said. 'I want you to find Billson.'

He gave me an old-fashioned look. 'But he's not our pigeon any more. Apart from the fact that Whensley are

63

running their own show now, Billson is out of it.'

I said, 'When this firm was started certain rules were laid down. Do you remember Westlake, the security guard we had at Clennel Enterprises?'

Ellis's face was grave. 'I remember. It happened just after I joined the firm. Shot in the leg during a pay-roll snatch. He had to have it amputated.'

'But do you remember what happened to the man who shot him? We got to him before the coppers did. We handed him to the law intact, although I'd have dearly loved to break his leg. We also made sure that the story got around. And that's the rule, Jack – we look after our own. If any gun-happy bandit hurts one of our men he knows he has to cope with the police *and* our boys. And to coin a phrase – "we try harder". Got the picture?'

He smiled faintly and nodded. 'In this business it makes sense,' he acknowledged.

'The top-ranking coppers aren't too happy about it,' I said, 'because they don't like private armies. But we rub along with the middle level very nicely. Anyway, a member of Stafford Security Consultants Ltd has been assaulted, and the fact it was the boss makes no difference to the principle. I'm not on a personal vendetta but I want those boys nailed.'

'Okay – but Billson!'

'He's *got* to be connected somehow, so dig into him. The police aren't doing much because it's no crime to leave a job. They've got him on a list and if they come across him they'll ask him a few polite questions. I can't wait that long. All the villains in London know I've been done over, and they're laughing their heads off.'

'We should be able to get a line on Billson,' said Jack. 'It's not easy for a man to disappear into thin air.'

'Another thing; no one is to know any of this except me, you and the man you put on the job.'

'Not even Charlie Malleson?'

'Not even him. I suspect jiggery-pokery at high levels.' I saw the expression on Ellis's face, and said irascibly, 'Not

Charlie, for God's sake! But I want to cut out even the possibility of a leak. Some of our top industrialists are doing some queer things – Sir Andrew McGovern for one. Now, I want a thorough rundown on him; particularly a survey of any relationship he might have had with Paul Billson and with his secretary, Alix Aarvik.'

'Okay,' said Jack. 'I'll get it started right away.'

I pondered for a moment. 'Open a routine file on this. Your clients are Michelmore, Veasey and Templeton; send them the bills in the normal way.' As he raised his eyebrows I said shortly, 'They're my solicitors.'

'Right.'

'And good luck with the new job.' It wouldn't be fair to Jack if he got the idea that when I came back everything would be as it was before, so I said, 'If you don't drop too many clangers it's yours for good. I'm destined for higher things, such as busting into Europe.'

He went away a very happy man.

It's not easy for a man to disappear into thin air.

Those praiseworthy citizens who form and join societies dedicated to the preservation of civil liberties are quite right in their concern about the 'data bank' society. At Stafford Security we weren't a whit concerned about civil liberties; what we were doing was preserving the industrial secrecy of our clients, which doesn't amount to the same thing at all. As a corollary, because we protected against snooping we understood it, and were well equipped to do some snooping ourselves should the mood take us.

The bloodhounds were turned on to Paul Billson. No man living in a so-called civilized society can escape documentation. His name, and sometimes a number attached to his name, is listed on forms without end – driving licence, radio and TV licence, dog licence, income tax return, insurance applications, telephone accounts, gas and electricity accounts, passport applications, visa applications, hire purchase agreements, birth certificate, marriage certificate, death certificate. It seems that half the population is pushing around pieces of paper concerning the other half – and vice versa.

It takes a trained man with a hazy sense of ethics to ferret out another man's life from the confusion but it can be done, given the time and the money – the less time the more money it takes, that's all. Jack Ellis hoisted Michelmore, Veasey and Templeton's bill a few notches and the information started to come in.

Paul Billson applied for a passport the day after he disappeared, appearing in person at the London Passport Office to fill in the form. The same day he applied for an international driving licence. The following day he bought a Land-Rover off the shelf at the main London showroom, paid cash on the barrel and drove it away.

We lost him for a couple of weeks until he picked up his passport, then a quick tour of the consulates by a smooth operator revealed that he had applied for and been granted visas for Niger, Mali, Chad and Libya. That led to the question of what he was doing with the Land-Rover. He had got his green insurance card for foreign travel but a run around the shipping companies found nothing at all. Then our man at Heathrow turned up an invoice which told that a Mr Billson had air-freighted a Land-Rover to Algiers.

Whatever had happened to Paul had blown him wide open. After a lifetime of inactive griping about injustice, of cold internal anger, of ineffectual mumblings, he had suddenly erupted and was spending money as though he had a private mint. Air freight isn't cheap.

What Jack had dug up about Billson's finances was fantastic. The £12,000 in Paul's deposit account was but the tip of an iceberg, and he had nearly £65,000 to play around with. 'I don't know where the hell he got it,' said Jack.

'I do,' I said. 'He saved it. When he vanished he was on £8000 a year and spending about £2500. You do that for enough years and are careful with your investments and you'll soon rack up £65,000.'

66

Jack said, 'I'll tell you something, Max; someone else is looking for Billson. We've been crossing their tracks.'

'The police?'

'I don't think so. Not their style.'

'The Special Branch, then?'

'Could be. They move in mysterious ways their wonders to perform.'

I stretched out an arm for the telephone. 'I'll ask.'

Because some of our clients, such as Franklin Engineering, were into defence work, contact with the Special Branch was inevitable for Stafford Security. It was an uneasy relationship and we were tolerated only because we could take off them some of their work load. If, for example, we saw signs of subversion we tipped them off and were rewarded by being left alone. A strictly confidential relationship, of course; the trades unions would have raised hell had they known.

The man I rang was politely amused. 'Billson is no concern of ours. We checked back on what you told us; we even interviewed that bloody journalist – now there's a slimy bit of work. As far as we're concerned, Billson is a semi-paranoiac who has gone off the rails a bit. He might interest a psychiatrist, but he doesn't interest us.'

'Thanks.' I put down the telephone and said to Jack, 'He says they aren't interested, but would he tell me the truth?' I frowned as I turned the pages of the report. 'Algiers! Why didn't Billson apply for an Algerian visa?'

'He didn't need to. British citizens don't need visas for Algeria.' Jack produced another thin file. 'About Sir Andrew McGovern. Relationship with Billson – apart from the fact that they're remotely linked through Franklin Engineering – nil. Relationship with Alix Aarvik – nil. It's a straight master-and-servant deal – they're not even "just good friends". The Kisko Nickel Corporation *is* undergoing an internal reorganization due to a merger which McGovern engineered. But Alix Aarvik didn't go to Canada; she's still operating as McGovern's secretary.'

I shrugged. 'As I once said to Brinton, the best thing about advice is that you needn't take it.' I smiled sourly. 'It turned out that his advice was good, but that's no reason for Alix Aarvik to take mine.'

'Apart from that there's not much to get hold of in McGovern,' said Jack. 'He does seem to live in Brinton's pocket.'

'Not quite,' I said absently. 'Brinton has been having trouble with him. That's why we lost the Whensley account.' I was thinking of the Sahara; of how big and empty it was.

Jack sniffed. 'If they have quarrelled no one would notice it. McGovern entertained Brinton at his home two days ago.'

I said, 'If Brinton pats Andrew McGovern on the back it's just to find a good spot to stick the knife. Thanks, Jack; you've done a good job. I'll take it from here.'

When he had gone I rang Whensley Holdings and asked for Miss Aarvik. When she came on the line I said, 'Max Stafford here. So you didn't go to Canada, after all.'

'Sir Andrew changed his mind.'

'Did he? Miss Aarvik, I have some information about your brother which I think you ought to know. Will you have dinner with me tonight?'

She hesitated, then said, 'Very well. Thank you for your continued interest in my brother, Mr Stafford.'

'I'll call for you at your flat at seven-thirty,' I said.

After that I went down to the club library, took down *The Times Atlas*, and studied a map of the Sahara for a long time. It didn't take me as long as that to find out that the idea burgeoning in my mind was totally fantastic, utterly irresponsible and probably bloody impossible.

Ten

I picked up Alix Aarvik that evening and took her to a French restaurant, an unpretentious place with good food. It was only after we had chosen from the menu that I opened the subject over a couple of sherries. I told her where Paul Billson was.

'So he *is* trying to find the plane,' she said. 'But it's totally impossible. He's not the man to . . .' She stopped suddenly. 'How can he afford to do that?'

I sighed. Alix Aarvik was due to receive a shock. 'He's been holding out on you. Probably for a long time, judging by the cash he squirrelled away. He was getting £8000 a year from Franklin Engineering.'

It took a while for it to sink in, but as it did her face went pale and pink spots appeared in her cheeks. 'He could do *that*!' she whispered. 'He could let me pay his bills and not put up a penny for Mother's support.'

She was becoming very angry. I liked that; it was time someone got mad at Paul Billson. I wasn't so cool about him myself. I said, 'I'm sorry to have administered the shock, but I thought you ought to know.'

She was silent for a while, looking down into her glass and aimlessly rotating the stem between her fingers. At last she said, 'I just don't understand him.'

'It seems he didn't abandon his boyhood dream. He saved up his money to fulfil it.'

'At my expense,' she snapped. She gave a shaky laugh. 'But you must be wrong, Mr Stafford. I know what Paul was doing at Franklin Engineering. They wouldn't pay him that much.'

'That's another mystery. It seems they did. Your brother

had damn near £60,000 to his name when he pushed off –
and he turned it all into hard cash. If he's taken it with him
to Algiers he's put a hell of a crimp into the currency
regulations. I think Paul is now a law-breaker.'

'But this is ridiculous.'

'I agree – but it's also true; Paul has gone to look for his
father's plane. I can't think of any other reason why he
should shoot off to Algiers with a Land-Rover. He's looking
for a plane which crashed over forty years ago and that's a
hell of a long time. I was looking at a map this afternoon.
Do you know how big the Sahara is?' She shook her head
and I said grimly, 'Three million square miles – just about
the same size as the United States but a hell of a lot emptier.
It'll be like searching the proverbial haystack for the needle,
with the difference that the needle might not be there.'

'What do you mean by that?'

'Suppose Hendrik van Niekirk really did see Peter
Billson in Durban after he was supposed to have crashed.
You can lay ten to one that Billson wouldn't have left that
plane lying around for anyone to find. If he was a faker after
that insurance money my guess is that he'd ditch off-shore
in the Mediterranean. He'd row himself ashore in a col-
lapsible dinghy – they had those in 1936, I've checked – and
get himself lost. So Paul might be looking for something in
the desert that's not there.'

'I don't like that,' she said coldly. 'You're implying that
my mother was party to a fraud.'

'I'm sorry,' I said. 'I don't like it much myself, but it's a
possibility that has to be considered. I do it all the time in my
business, Miss Aarvik.'

A waiter interrupted us by bringing the first course. Over
the onion soup I said, 'Anyway, that's where your brother
is – somewhere in Algeria if he isn't already in Niger or Chad
or somewhere else as improbable.'

'He must be brought back,' she said. 'Mr Stafford, I don't
have much money, but is it at all possible for your detective
agency to look for him?'

'I don't run a detective agency,' I said. 'I run a security organization. Lots of people get the two confused. Frankly, I don't see why you want him back. You've just heard of how he's been deceiving you for years. I think you're better off without him.'

'He's my brother,' she said simply. 'He's the only family I have in the world.'

She looked so woebegone that I took pity on her. I suppose it was then the decision was made. Of course I hedged it about with 'ifs' and 'maybes' as a sop to my conscience should I renege, but the decision was made.

I said carefully, 'There's a possibility – just a possibility, mind you – that I may be going to North Africa in the near future. If I do, I'll ask around to see if I can find him.'

She lit up as though I'd given her the key to the Bank of England. 'That's very good of you,' she said warmly.

'Don't go overboard about it,' I warned. 'Even if I do find him your troubles aren't over. Supposing he doesn't want to come back – what am I supposed to do? Kidnap him? He's a free agent, you know.'

'If you find him send me a cable and I'll fly out. If I can talk to Paul I can get him to come back.'

'No doubt you can, but the first problem is to find him. But we have some things going for us. Firstly, there are large areas of the Sahara where he will *not* look for the aircraft.' I paused and then said acidly, 'Not if he has any sense, that is, which I beg leave to doubt.'

'Oh! Which areas?'

'The inhabited bits – the Sahara is not all blasted wilderness. Then there's the course Peter Billson intended to fly – that should give us a rough indication of where the plane is likely to be. Is there anyone who'd know such an odd item of information after forty years?'

She shook her head despondently, then said slowly, 'There's a man in the Aeronautical Section of the Science Museum – Paul used to talk to him a lot. He's some sort of aeronautical historian, he has all sorts of details in his records. I don't remember his name, though.'

'I'll check,' I said. 'The other point in our favour is that in a relatively empty land a stranger tends to stand out. If Paul is buzzing about remote areas in a Land-Rover he'll leave a pretty well-defined trail.'

She smiled at me. 'You're making me feel better already.'

'Don't raise your hopes too high. When . . . if I go to North Africa I'll send you an address where you can contact me.'

She nodded briefly and we got on with the meal.

I took her home quite early and then went back to the club to bump into Charlie Malleson who was just coming out. 'I thought I'd missed you,' he said. 'I was just passing and I thought I'd pop in to see you.'

I glanced at my watch. 'The bar's still open. What about a drink?'

'Fine.'

We took our drinks to an isolated table and Charlie said, 'I rang you at home but no one was in, so I took a chance on finding you here.' I merely nodded, and he cleared his throat uncomfortably. 'Is it true what I hear about you and Gloria?'

'Depends what you've heard, but I can guess what it is. Bad news gets around fast. It's true enough. Where did you hear it?'

'Brinton was saying something yesterday. Gloria's been talking to him.'

'Getting her version in first, no doubt. She won't impress Brinton.'

'Well, I'm truly sorry it happened this way. Are you starting a divorce action?'

'It's in the hands of my solicitor now.'

'I see,' he said slowly. I don't know what he saw and I didn't really care. 'How are you feeling otherwise?' he asked. 'You're not long out of hospital.'

I looked at him over the edge of my glass. 'Have you ever

been beaten up, Charlie? Given a thorough going-over by experts?'

'I can't say that I have.'

'It's the most degrading thing that can happen to a man,' I said flatly. 'It isn't so much what they do to the body; that can stand a lot of punishment. It's the feeling of utter helplessness. You're no longer your own man – you're in the hands of others who can do with you what they like. And you ask me how I feel.'

'You're bitter about it, aren't you, Max? You know, I didn't expect that of you.'

'Why not?'

'Well, you have the reputation of being a pretty cold fish, you know. You run your end of the business like a computer.'

'There's nothing wrong with being logical and acting logically,' I said.

'No.' There was a pause before Charlie said, 'I suppose the divorce will keep you in England.'

I drained my glass. 'I don't see why it should. I'm thinking of taking your advice to soak up some sun. I'll be glad to get away from London for a while.'

Charlie looked pleased. 'It'll do you good; you'll come back like a new man.'

'How is Jack Ellis settling in?'

'Very well. I'm glad you said what you did to him about the job; it's cleared the air and makes things easier all round. How long do you expect to be away?'

'I don't really know. Hold the fort, double the profits and bank the proceeds. Expect me when you see me.'

We talked idly for a few more minutes and then Charlie took his leave. I had an obscure feeling that he had not 'dropped by in passing' but had come for a reason, to get some question answered. About the divorce? About my health? I went over the conversation and wondered if he had got his answer.

I had an uneasy night. I thought of myself as seen by others –

Max Stafford, the cold fish. I hadn't known Charlie had thought of me in that way. We had always been personal friends as well as getting on well with each other in the business. To get a flash of illumination on oneself through the eyes of another can sometimes come as a shock.

I slept and woke again after having bad dreams of vaguely impending doom. I lay with open eyes for a long time and then, finding sleep impossible, I turned on the bedside light and lit a cigarette.

I prided myself on thinking and acting logically, but where in hell was the logic of goose-chasing to Algiers? The sexual bounce, maybe, from Gloria to Alix Aarvik? The desire to be the parfit, gentil knight on a white charger going on a quest to impress the maiden? I rejected that. Alix Aarvik was a nice enough girl but there was certainly no sexual attraction. Maybe Max Stafford was a cold fish, after all.

What, then?

Maybe it was because I thought I was being manipulated. I thought of Andrew McGovern. He had tried to send Alix to Canada. Why? In the event he didn't send her. Why? Was it because I had been a bit too quick and caught her and talked to her the day before she was supposed to leave? If the damage had been done there would be no reason to send her away. I had been beaten up immediately after I had seen her. If McGovern had been responsible for that I'd have to think up some new and novel punishment for him.

Was McGovern deliberately putting pressure on me through Brinton? Brinton, on the day of the board meeting, had said he was under pressure from McGovern. What sort of a hold could McGovern have over a shark like Brinton? And if McGovern was doing the squeezing, why was he doing it?

Then there was Paul Billson. Before he entered my life I had been moderately happy, but from the moment Hoyland rang me up to have his hand held there had been nothing but trouble. Everything seemed to revolve around Paul, a man obsessed.

Logic! If everything revolved around Paul Billson, maybe he was the person to talk to. Maybe going to Algiers wasn't such a bad idea, after all.

I put out the light and slept.

Three days later I flew to Algiers.

Eleven

Algiers is the only city I know where the main post office looks like a mosque and the chief mosque looks like a post office. Not that I spent much time in the mosque but I thought I had made a major error when I entered the post office for the first time to collect letters from poste restante. I gazed in wonder at that vast hushed hall with its fretted screens and arabesques and came to the conclusion that it was an Eastern attempt to emulate the reverential and cathedral-like atmosphere affected by the major British banks. I got to know the post office quite well.

Getting to know the whereabouts of Paul Billson was not as easy. Although my French was good, my Arabic was non-existent, which made it no easier to fight my way through the Byzantine complexities of Algerian bureaucracy, an amorphous structure obeying Parkinson's Law to the nth degree.

The track of my wanderings over Algiers, if recorded on a map, would have resembled the meanderings of a demented spider. At the twentieth office where my passport was given the routine fifteen-minute inspection by a suspicion-haunted official for the twentieth time my patience was nearly at snapping point. The trouble was that I was not on my own ground and the Algerians worked to different rules.

My hotel was in Hamma, in the centre of town near the National Museum, and when I returned, early one evening, I was dispirited. After a week in Algiers I had got nowhere, and if I couldn't track Billson in a city what hope would I have in the desert? It seemed that my cutting edge had blunted from lack of practice.

As I walked across the foyer to collect my room key I was

accosted by a tall Arab wearing the ubiquitous *djellaba*.
'M'sieur Stafford?'

'Yes, I'm Stafford.'

Wordlessly he handed me an envelope inscribed with my
surname and nothing else. I looked at him curiously as I
opened it and he returned my gaze with unblinking brown
eyes. Inside the envelope was a single sheet of paper, un-
headed and with but two typewritten lines:

> I believe you are looking for Paul Billson.
> Why don't you come to see me?

There was a signature underneath but it was an in-
decipherable scrawl.

I glanced at the Arab. 'Who sent this?'

He answered with a gesture towards the hotel entrance.
'This way.'

I pondered for a moment and nodded, then followed him
from the hotel where he opened the rear door of a big
Mercedes. I sat down and he slammed the door smartly and
got behind the wheel. As he started the engine I said, 'Where
are we going?'

'Bouzarea.' After that he concentrated on his driving and
refused to answer questions. I gave up, leaned back in
cushioned luxury, and watched Algiers flow by.

The road to Bouzarea climbed steeply out of the city and I
twisted to look through the back window and saw Algiers
spread below with the Mediterranean beyond, darkening
towards the east as the sun set. Already strings of lights were
appearing in the streets.

I turned back as the car swung around a corner and
pulled up against a long wall, blank except for a small door.
The Arab got out and opened the car door and indicated
the door in the wall which was already swinging open. I
walked through into a large walled garden which appeared
to be slightly smaller than Windsor Great Park, but not
much. In the middle distance was a low-slung, flat-roofed

77

house which rambled inconsequently over the better part of an acre. The place stank of money.

The door behind closed with the snap of a lock and I turned to confront another Arab, an old man with a seamed, walnut face. I didn't understand what he said but the beckoning gesture was unmistakable, so I followed him towards the house.

He led me through the house and into an inner courtyard, upon which he vanished like a puff of smoke into some hidden recess. A woman lay upon a chaise-longue. 'Stafford?'

'Yes – Max Stafford.'

She was oldish, about sixty plus, I guessed, and was dressed in a style which might have been thought old-fashioned. Her hair was white and she could have been anyone's old mother but for two things. The first was her face, which was tanned to the colour of brown shoe leather. There was a network of deep wrinkles about her eyes which betokened too much sun, and those eyes were a startling blue. The blue eyes and the white hair set against that face made a spectacular combination. The second thing was that she was smoking the biggest Havana cigar I've ever seen.

'What's your poison? Scotch? Rye? Gin? You name it.' Her voice was definitely North American.

I smiled slowly. 'I never take drinks from strangers.'

She laughed. 'I'm Hesther Raulier. Sit down, Max Stafford, but before you do, pour yourself a drink. Save me getting up.'

There was an array of bottles on a portable bar so I went and poured myself a scotch and added water from a silver jug. As I sat in the wicker chair she said, 'What are you doing in Algiers?'

She spoke English but when she said 'Algiers' it came out as '*el Djeza'ir*'. Then she was speaking Arabic. I said, 'Looking for Paul Billson.'

'Why?'

I sipped the scotch. 'What business is it of yours?'

78

She offered me a gamine grin. 'I'll tell you if you tell me.'

I looked up at the sky. 'Is it always as pleasant here in winter?'

She laid down her cigar carefully in a big ashtray. 'So okay, Stafford; you're a hard trader. But just tell me one thing. Are you here to hurt Paul?'

'Why should I want to hurt him?'

'For Christ's sake!' she said irritably. 'Must you always answer a question with a question?'

'Yes, I must,' I said sharply. 'Until you declare your interest.'

'So, all right; let's quit fencing.' She swung her legs off the chaise-longue and stood up. Her build was stocky and she was a muscular old bird. 'I was a friend of Paul's father.'

That sounded promising, so I gave measure for measure. 'His sister is worried about him.'

Her voice was sharp. 'His sister? I didn't know Peter Billson had a daughter.'

'He didn't. His widow remarried during the war to a Norwegian who was killed. Alix Aarvik is Paul's half-sister.'

Hesther Raulier seemed lost in thought. After a while she said, 'Poor Helen; she sure had a tough time.'

'Did you know her?'

'I knew them both.' She went over to the bar and poured a hefty slug of neat rye whisky. She downed the lot in one swallow and shuddered a little. 'Paul told me Helen had died but he said nothing about a sister.'

'He wouldn't.'

She swung around. 'What's that supposed to mean?'

'He treated her pretty badly. People don't talk about those to whom they've been unkind. I'll tell you this much – Paul wasn't much help to his mother in her last years.' I picked up my glass again. 'Why should you think I'd hurt Paul?'

She gave me a level stare. 'I'll have to know a lot more about you before I tell you that, Max Stafford.'

'Fair enough,' I said. 'And I'll need to know a lot more about you.'

She smiled faintly. 'Seems we're going to have us a real gabfest. You'd better stay to dinner.'

'Thanks. But tell me something. Where is Paul now?'

'Come with me,' she said, and led me into the garden where she pointed to the south at a low range of hills just visible in the twilight. 'See those? Those are the foothills of the Atlas. Paul Billson is way to hell and gone the other side.'

By the time we went in to dinner our stiff-legged attitude had relaxed. I was curious about this elderly, profane woman who used an antique American slang; any moment I expected her to come out with 'twenty-three, skidoo'. I gave her a carefully edited account and ended up, 'That's it; that's why I'm here.'

She was drinking whisky as though she ran her own distillery at the bottom of the garden but not one white hair had twitched. 'A likely story,' she said sardonically. 'A big important man like you drops everything and comes to Algiers looking for Paul. Are you sweet on Alix Aarvik?'

'I hardly know her. Besides, she's too young for me.'

'No girl is too young for any man – *I know*. You'll have to do better than that, Max.'

'It was a chain of circumstances,' I said tiredly. 'For one thing I'm divorcing my wife and I wanted to get out of it for a while.'

'Divorcing your wife,' she repeated. 'Because of Alix Aarvik?'

'Because the man in her bed wasn't me,' I snapped.

'I *believe* you,' she said soothingly. 'Okay, what's your percentage? What do you get out of it?'

'I don't know what you mean.'

A cold blue eye bored into me. 'Look, buster; don't give me any of that Limey blandness. You tell me what I want to know or you get nothing.'

I sighed. 'Maybe I don't like being beaten up,' I said, and told her the rest of it.

She was silent for a moment, then said, 'That's a hell of a

concoction – but I believe it. It's too crazy to be a spur-of-the-moment story.'

'I'm glad to hear you say that,' I said feelingly. 'Now it's my turn. How do you happen to live in Algiers – for starters.'

She looked surprised. 'Hell, I was born here.' It seemed that her father was of French-Arab mixture and her mother was Canadian; how that unlikely match came about she didn't say. Her mother must have been a strong-minded woman because Hesther was sent to school in Canada instead of going to France like most of the children of the wealthy French colonists.

'But I haven't been back in years,' she said. That would account for her outdated slang.

She had met Peter Billson in Canada. 'He was older than I was, of course,' she said. 'Let's see; it must have been 1933, so I'd be seventeen.'

And Billson was thirty. Hesther was on vacation, visiting the home of a schoolfriend, when Billson came into her life. She was the guest of McKenzie, a wealthy Canadian who was interested in the development of air travel, particularly in the more remote parts of Canada. Billson had begun to make a name for himself, so McKenzie had invited him for a long weekend to pick his brains.

Hesther said, 'It was like meeting God – you know what kids are. These days they go nuts over long-haired singers but in those days the fliers were top of the heap.'

'What sort of a man was he?'

'He was a man,' she said simply. She stared blindly back into the past. 'Of course he had his faults – who hasn't? – but they were the faults of his profession. Peter Billson was a good pilot, a brave man ambitious for fame, an exhibitionist – all the early fliers were like that, all touting for the adulation of the idiotic public.'

'How well did you get to know him?'

She gave me a sideways look. 'About as well as a woman can get to know a man. 1933 was the year I lost my virginity.'

It was hard to imagine this tough, leathery woman as a seventeen-year-old in the toils of love. 'Was that before Billson married?'

Hesther shook her head. 'I felt like hell when I had to talk to Helen over the coffee cups. I was sure I had guilt printed right across my forehead.'

'How long did you know him?'

'Until he died. I was supposed to come back here in 1934 but I managed to stretch out another year – because of Peter. He used to see me every time he was in Toronto. Then in 1935 I had to come back because my mother threatened to cut off the funds. The next time I saw Peter was when he landed here during the London to Cape Town Air Race of '36. I saw him take off from here and I never saw him again.' There was a bleakness in her voice when she added, 'I never married, you know.'

There wasn't much to say to that. After a few moments I broke the uncomfortable silence. 'I hope you won't mind telling me a bit more about that. Did you know his flight plan, for instance?'

'I don't mind,' she said a little wearily. 'But I don't know much. I was a girl of twenty, remember – and no technician. He had that beefed-up Northrop which was a freight carrier. Jock Anderson had installed extra gas tanks in the cargo space and the plan was to fly south from Algiers to Kano in Nigeria. The desert crossing was going to be the most difficult leg, so Jock came here with a team to give the plane a thorough check before Peter took off.'

'Jock Anderson – who was he?'

'The flight mechanic. Peter and Jock had been together a long time. Peter flew the planes and pushed them hard, and Jock kept the pieces together when they threatened to bust apart. They made a good team. Jock was a good engineer.'

'What happened to him afterwards?'

'When Peter disappeared he broke up. I've never seen a man get drunk so fast. He went on a three-day splurge, then he sobered-up and left Algiers. I haven't seen him since.'

I pondered on that but it led nowhere. 'What do you think of Paul Billson?'

'I think he's a nut,' she said. 'Hysterical and crazy. Totally unlike his father in every way.'

'How did you get to know him?'

'Same way as I got to know you. I have ears all over this city and when I heard of a man looking into Peter Billson I was curious so I sent for him.'

'All right,' I said. 'Where is he?'

'Gone looking for his Daddy. By now he'll be in Tammanrasset.'

'Where's that?'

Hesther gave me a crooked smile. 'You go south *into* the desert until you're going *out* of the desert. That's Tammanrasset, in the Ahaggar about two thousand kilometres south of here. Plumb in the middle of the Sahara.'

I whistled. 'Why there?'

'If you're looking for something in the Ahaggar, Tam is a good place to start.'

'What's the Ahaggar like?'

Hesther looked at me for a moment before she said, 'Mountainous and dry.'

'How big?'

'Christ, I don't know – I haven't measured it lately. Wait a minute.' She went away and returned with a book. 'The *Annexe du Hoggar* – that's the administrative area – is 380,000 square kilometres.' She looked up. 'I don't know what that is in square miles; you'll have to figure that yourself.'

I did, and it came to nearly 150,000 square miles – three times the area of the United Kingdom. 'Paul Billson *is* crazy,' I said. 'What's the population?'

Hesther consulted the book again. 'About twelve thousand.'

'There doesn't seem much to administer. People are thin on the ground out there.'

'If you go there you'll find out why,' she said. 'Are you thinking of going after him?'

'The idea has crossed my mind,' I admitted. 'Which makes me as crazy as he is, I suppose.'

'Not really. You should find him easy enough. Getting to Tammanrasset is no problem – there are a couple of flights a week.'

'If I can fly that does make it easier.'

She nodded. 'Then all you have to do is to wait in Tammanrasset until he shows up. If he's in the Ahaggar and wants more gas there's no place he can get it except Tam.' She considered for a moment. 'Of course, if you want to chase after him, that's different. You'd need a guide. Luke Byrne is usually in Tam at this time of year – he might fancy the job.'

'Who's he?'

She laughed. 'Another crazy man. It would tickle his fancy to go looking for a lunatic.' She lit an after-dinner cigar. 'If you're going to Tam you'll need a permit. If you try to get one yourself it'll take two weeks – I can get you one in two days. What will you do when you find Paul Billson?'

I shrugged. 'Persuade him to go back to England if I can.'

'You'll find it hard cutting through that obsession.'

'His sister might stand a better chance, and she said she'd come out. Would you help her, as you're helping me?'

'Sure.'

'What do you believe?' I asked. 'Is Peter Billson's body out there somewhere?'

'Sure it is – what's left of it. I know what you mean; I read about that South African son-of-a-bitch who said he'd seen Peter in Durban. I've often wondered how big a bribe the bastard took. I'll tell you this, Max; Peter Billson wasn't an angel, not by a long way, but he was honest about money. And Helen was the next thing to an angel and no one's going to tell me that she perjured herself for half a million bucks. It just wasn't their style.'

She sighed. 'Let's quit talking about it now, shall we? It's not been my practice to look too deeply into the past, and

84

I'm not ready to start now.'

'I'm sorry,' I said. 'Perhaps I'd better go.'

'Hell, no!' she said. 'Stick around and have some more brandy and I'll match you for dirty stories.'

'All right,' I said obligingly, and told her the limerick about the Bishop of Chichester who made all the saints in their niches stir.

I didn't see Hesther again at that time, but she certainly had some pull because I was ready to leave in a day and a half complete with permit and a seat booked on the plane at her expense delivered to my hotel by her Arab chauffeur. In a covering note she wrote:

I hope you don't mind about the plane ticket; it's just that I'd like to do my bit towards the memory of P.B. If you do find that idiot, Paul, club him on the head, put him in a sack and ship him back to Algiers.

I wired Luke Byrne and he'll be expecting you. You'll find him at the Hotel Tin Hinan. Give him my regards.

I don't know if it means anything but someone else is looking for Paul – a man called Kissack. I don't know anything about him because he blew town before I could check on him.

Best of luck, and come back for another visit.

Twelve

I didn't know what to expect of Tamman-rasset but it was certainly different from Algiers. From the air it was a scattering of houses set in a mist of green at the foot of barren hills. Transport from the airstrip was by truck along an asphalted road which led between tall, square pillars which were the entrance to the town. They looked like the decor for a fifth-rate B-movie about the Foreign Legion.

I called it a town, but it would be more appropriate to call it a village. Be that as it may, it was the metropolis of the Ahaggar. The main street was wide, shaded by acacia trees, and bordered by single-storey houses apparently made of dried mud which looked as though they'd wash away in a half-way decent shower of rain. The truck driver blared his horn to clear a path through the pedestrians, tall men dressed in blue and white who thronged the centre of the street as though the internal combustion engine hadn't been invented.

The truck drew up outside the Hotel Tin Hinan where there was a tree-shaded courtyard filled with spindly metal tables and chairs at which people sat drinking. From a loudspeaker above the hotel entrance came the nasal wail of an Eastern singer. I went inside into a dusty hall and waited until someone noticed me. There was no reception desk.

Presently I was noticed. A dapper man in none too clean whites asked in massacred French what he could do for me. I said, 'There should be a reservation. My name is Stafford.'

His eyebrows lifted. 'Ah, M'sieur Stafford! M'sieur

Byrne awaits you.' He steered me to the door and pointed. '*Voilà!*'

I stared at the man sitting at the table. He was dressed in a long blue robe and a white turban and he looked like nobody who could be called Byrne. I turned back to the receptionist only to find that he had gone back into the hotel, so I walked over to the table and said hesitantly, 'Mr Byrne?'

The man hesitated with a glass of beer half way to his lips and then set it down. 'Yes,' he said, and turned to face me. Under shaggy white eyebrows blue eyes stared out of a deeply tanned face which was thin to the point of emaciation so that the nose jutted out like a beak. Beneath the nose was a wide mouth with thin lips firmly compressed. I could not see his chin because a fold of his turban had somehow become wrapped about his neck, but his cheeks were bearded with white hair. He loooked like Moses and twice as old.

I said, 'My name is Stafford.'

'Sit down, Mr Stafford. Have a beer?' He spoke in English with an American accent which, under the circumstances, was incongruous.

As I sat down he beckoned to a waiter. '*Deux bières.*' He turned back to me. 'Hesther told me about you. She said you might need help.'

'I might. I'm looking for a man.'

'So? Most men look for women.'

'His name is Billson. He's around here somewhere.'

'Billson,' Byrne repeated thoughtfully. 'Why do you want him?'

'I don't know that I do,' I said. 'But his sister does. He's looking for a crashed aeroplane. Are there any of those about here?'

'A couple.'

'This one crashed over forty years ago.'

Byrne's expression didn't change. 'None as old as that.' The waiter came back and put down two bottles of lager and two glasses; Byrne nodded at him briefly and he went away. It seemed that Byrne had a line of credit at the Hotel Tin Hinan.

I poured the beer. 'I'm told the Ahaggar is a big place – very mountainous. A wrecked plane may not have been found.'

'It would be,' said Byrne.

'But, surely, with the thin population . . .'

'It would be found.' Byrne was positive. 'How did Billson get here? By air?'

'He has a Land-Rover.'

'How long has he been here?'

I shrugged. 'I don't know. A week – maybe two.'

Byrne stared into the street without moving his eyes and was silent for some time. I leaned back in the chair and let him think it over. This was a man I found hard to assess because I had no notion of the springs which moved him. He was as alien to me as any of the men dressed like him who strolled in the street, in spite of the fact that he spoke English.

Presently he asked, 'How well do you know Hesther Raulier?'

'Hardly at all. I met her only two days ago.'

'She likes you,' he said. 'Got a bag?'

I jerked my thumb in the direction of the hotel entrance. 'In there.'

'Leave it lay – we'll pick it up later. I'm camped just outside Tam; let's take a walk.' He arose and did something complicated with his head cloth, making quite a production of it. When he had finished his face was hidden, and the cloth left only a slit at eye-level through which he looked.

We left the hotel and walked along the main street of Tammanrasset in a direction away from the airstrip. Byrne was a tall man, yet no taller than any of the other men who, similarly dressed, walked languidly in the street. It was I who was the incongruous figure in that place.

'Do you always dress like an Arab?' I asked.

'Not if I can help it. I don't like Arabs.'

I stared at him because his answer was incomprehensible.
'But . . .'

He bent his head and said, with some amusement, 'You
have a lot to learn, Stafford. These guys aren't Arab, they're
Imazighen – Tuareg, if you prefer.'

Byrne's camp was about two miles outside the village. It
consisted of three large leather tents set in a semi-circle, their
backs to the wind. The sand in front of them had been swept
smooth and, to one side, a small fire crackled, setting off
detonations like miniature fireworks. In the middle distance
camels browsed.

As we approached, a man who had been squatting next to
the fire stood up. 'That's Mokhtar,' said Byrne. 'He'll look
after you while I'm away.'

'Where are you going?'

'To snoop around. But first you tell me more about
Billson.'

Byrne strode over to the fire and the two men had a brief
conversation. Mokhtar was another tall man who wore the
veil. Byrne beckoned me to join him in the middle tent where
we sat on soft rugs. The inner walls of the tent were made of
reeds.

'Right; why does Billson want to find a forty-year-old
crash?'

'It killed his father,' I said, and related the story.

I had just finished when Mokhtar laid a brass tray before
Byrne; on it was a spouted pot and two brass cups. 'You like
mint tea?' asked Byrne.

'Never had any.'

'It's not bad.' He poured liquid and handed a cup to me.
'Would you say Billson was right in the head?'

'No, I wouldn't. He's obsessed.'

'That's what I figured.' He drank from his cup and I
followed suit. It was spearminty and oversweet. 'How does
Hesther come into this?'

'She knew Billson's father.'

'How well?'

I looked him in the eye. 'If she wants you to know she'll tell you.'

He smiled. 'Okay, Stafford; no need to get sassy. Did you learn this from Hesther herself?' When I nodded, he said, 'You must have got right next to her. She don't talk much about herself.'

I said, 'What chance has Billson of finding the plane?'

'In the Ahaggar? None at all, because it isn't here. Quite a few wrecks scattered further north, though.' He laughed suddenly. 'Hell, I put one of them there myself.'

I glanced at him curiously. 'How did that happen?'

'It was during the war. I was in the Army Air Force, flying Liberators out of Oran. We got jumped by a gang of Focke-Wolfs and had the hell shot out of us. The cockpit was in a mess – no compass working – we didn't know where the hell we were. Then the engines gave up so I put down. I guess that airplane's still where I put it.'

'What happened then?'

'I walked out,' said Byrne laconically. 'Took a week and a half.' He stood up. 'I'll be back in a couple of hours.'

I watched him walk away with the smooth, almost lazy stride I had already noticed was common to the Tuareg, and wondered what the hell he was doing in the desert.

Presently Mokhtar came over with another tray of mint tea together with small round cakes.

It was three hours before Byrne came back, and he came riding a camel. The sun was setting and the thorn trees cast long shadows. The beast rocked to its knees and Byrne slid from the saddle, then came into the tent carrying my bag. The camel snorted as Mokhtar urged it to its feet and led it away.

Byrne sat down. 'I've found your boy.'

'Where is he?'

He pointed north. 'Out there somewhere – in the mountains. He left five days ago. He applied at Fort Lapperine for a *permis* but they wouldn't give him one, so he left anyway. He's a goddamn fool.'

'That I know,' I said. 'Why wouldn't they give him a *permis*?'

'They won't – not for one man in one truck.'

'He'll be coming back,' I said. 'Hesther said Tam was the only place he can get fuel.'

'I doubt it,' said Byrne. 'If he was coming back he'd be back by now. Those Land-Rovers are thirsty beasts. If you want him you'll have to go get him.'

I leaned back against the reed wall of the tent. 'I'd like that in more detail.'

'Paul Billson is an idiot. He filled his tank with gas and went. No spare. Five days is overlong to be away, and if he has no spare water he'll be dead by now.'

'How do I get there?' I said evenly.

Byrne looked at me for a long time, and sighed. 'If I didn't know Hesther thought something of you I'd tell you to go to hell. As it is, we start at first light.' He grimaced. 'And I'll have to go against my principles and use a stink-pot.'

What he meant by that I didn't know, but I merely said, 'Thanks.'

'Come on,' he said. 'Let's help Mokhtar get chow.'

'Chow' proved to be stringy goat, hard on the teeth and digestion, followed by a strong cheese which I was told was made of camel's milk. Byrne was taciturn and we went to sleep early in readiness for an early start. I lay on my back at the entrance to the tent, staring up at a sky so full of stars it seemed I could just reach up an arm to grab a handful.

I wondered what I was doing there and what I was getting into. And I wondered about Byrne, who spoke almost as archaic a slang as Hesther Raulier, a man who referred to his food by the World War Two American army term of 'chow'.

Thirteen

Byrne's 'stinkpot' turned out to be a battered Toyota Land Cruiser which looked as though it had been in a multiple smash on a motorway. Since there wasn't a motorway within two thousand miles, that was unlikely. Byrne saw my expression and said, 'Rough country,' as though that was an adequate explanation. However, the engine ran sweetly enough and the tyres were good.

We left in the dim light of dawn with Byrne driving, me next to him, and Mokhtar sitting in the back. Jerricans containing petrol and water were strapped all around the truck wherever there was an available place, and I noted that Mokhtar had somewhat unobtrusively put a rifle aboard. He also had a sword, a thing about three feet long in a red leather scabbard; what the devil he was going to do with that I couldn't imagine.

We drove north along a rough track, and I said, 'Where are we going?'

It was a damnfool question because I didn't understand the answer when it came. Byrne stabbed his finger forward and said briefly, 'Atakor,' then left me to make of that what I would.

I was silent for a while, then said, 'Did you get a *permis*?'

'No,' said Byrne shortly. A few minutes went by before he relented. 'No fat bureaucrat from the Maghreb is going to tell me where I can, or cannot, go in the desert.'

After that there was no conversation at all, and I began to think that travelling with Byrne was going to be sticky; extracting words from him was like pulling teeth. But perhaps he was always like that in the early morning. I thought of what he had just said and smiled. It reminded me of my own reaction to Isaacson's treatment of Hoyland. But that had been far away in another world, and seemed a thousand years ago.

The country changed from flat gravel plains to low hills, barren of vegetation, and we began to climb. Ahead were mountains, such mountains as I had never seen before. Most mountains begin rising gently from their base, but these soared vertically to the sky, a landscape of jagged teeth.

After two hours of jolting we entered a valley where there was a small encampment. There was a bit more vegetation here, but not much, and there were many sheep or goats – I never could tell the difference in the Sahara because the sheep were thin-fleeced, long-legged creatures and I began to appreciate the Biblical quotation about separating the sheep from the goats. Camels browsed on the thorny acacia and there was a scattering of the leather tents of the Tuareg.

Mokhtar leaned forward and said something to Byrne, who nodded and drew the truck to a halt. As the dust drifted away on the light breeze Mokhtar got out and walked over to the tents. He was wearing his sword slung across his back, the hilt over his left shoulder.

Byrne said, 'These people are of the Tégéhé Mellet. Mokhtar has gone to question them. If a Land-Rover has been anywhere near here they'll know about it.'

'What's the sword for?'

Byrne laughed. 'He'd feel as undressed without it as you would with no pants.' He seemed to be becoming more human.

'The Teg-whatever-it-is-you-said . . . is that a tribe of some kind?'

'That's right. The Tuareg confederation of the Ahaggar consists of three tribes – the Kel Rela, the Tégéhé Mellet and the Taitoq. Mokhtar is of the Kel Rela and of the noble clan. That's why he's gone to ask the questions and not me.'

'Noble!'

'Yeah, but not in the British sense. Mokhtar is related to the

Amenokal – he's the boss, the paramount chief of the Ahaggar confederation. All you have to know is that when a noble Kel Rela says, "Jump, frog!" everybody jumps.' He paused, then added, 'Except, maybe, another noble Kel Rela.' He shrugged. 'But you didn't come out here to study anthropology.'

'It might come in useful at that,' I said.

He gave me a sideways glance. 'You won't be here long enough.'

Mokhtar came back, accompanied by three men from the camp. All were veiled and wore the long, flowing blue and white gowns that seemed to be characteristic of the Tuareg. I wondered how they kept them so clean in that dusty wilderness. As they came close Byrne hastily adjusted his own veil so that his face was covered.

There were ceremonial greetings and then a slow and casual conversation of which I didn't understand a single word, and I just sat there feeling like a spare part. After a while Byrne reached into the back of the truck and produced a big round biscuit tin. He took out some small packages and handed them round, and Mokhtar added his own contribution. There was much graceful bowing.

As he started the engine Byrne said, 'Billson came through here four days ago. He must have been travelling damned slow.'

'I don't wonder,' I said. 'He's more used to driving on a road. Which way did he go?'

'Towards Assekrem – or further. And that's not going to be any joke.'

'What do you mean?'

He gave me a considering look. 'Assekrem is a Tamachek word – it means, "The End of the World".'

The truck jolted as he moved off. The Tuareg waved languidly and I waved back at them, glad to offer some contribution to the conversation. Then I sat back and chewed over what Byrne had just said. It wasn't comforting.

Presently I said, 'What did you give those men back there?'

'Aspirin, needles, salt. All useful stuff.'

'Oh!'

Three hours later we stopped again. We had been moving steadily into the mountains which Byrne called Atakor and had not seen a living soul or, indeed, anything alive at all except for thin grasses burnt by the sun and the inevitable scattered thorn trees. The mountains were tremendous, great shafts of rock thrusting through the skin of the earth, dizzyingly vertical.

And then, at a word from Mokhtar, we stopped in the middle of nowhere. He got out and walked back a few paces, then peered at the ground. Byrne looked back, keeping the engine running. Mokhtar straightened and walked back to the truck, exchanged a few words with Byrne, and then took the rifle and began to walk away into the middle distance. This time he left his sword.

Byrne put the truck into gear and we moved off. I said, 'Where's he going?'

'To shoot supper. There are some gazelle close by. We'll stop a little further on and wait for him.'

We drove on for about three miles and then came across a ruined building. Byrne drew to a halt. 'This is it. We wait here.'

I got out and stretched, then looked across at the building. There was something strange about it which I couldn't pin down at first, and then I got the impression that it wasn't as much ruined as intended to be that way. It had started life as a ruin.

Byrne nodded towards the tremendous rock which towered three thousand feet above us. 'Ilamen,' he said. 'The finger of God.' I started to walk to the building, and he said sharply, 'Don't go in there.'

'Why not? What is it?'

'The Tuareg don't go much for building,' he said. 'And they're Moslem – in theory, anyway. That's a mosque, more elaborate than most because this is a holy place. Most desert mosques are usually just an outline of stones on the ground.'

'Is it all right if I look at it from the outside?'

'Sure.' He turned away.

The walls of the mosque were of stones piled crazily and haphazardly one upon the other. I suppose the highest bit of wall wasn't more than three feet high. At one end was a higher structure, the only roofed bit, not much bigger than a telephone box, though not as high. The roof was supported by stone pillars. I suppose that would be a sort of pulpit for the imam.

When I returned to the truck Byrne had lit a small fire and was heating water in a miniature kettle. He looked up. 'Like tea?'

'Mint tea?'

'No other kind here.' I nodded, and he said, 'Those stone pillars back there weren't hand-worked; they're natural basalt, but there's none of that around here for twenty miles. Someone brought them.'

'A bit like Stonehenge,' I commented, and sat down.

Byrne grunted. 'Heard of that – never seen it. Never been in England. Bigger, though, isn't it?'

'Much bigger.'

He brought flat cakes of bread from the truck and we ate. The bread was dry and not very flavoursome but a little camel cheese made it eatable. It had sand mixed in the flour which was gritty to the teeth. Byrne poured a small cup of mint tea and gave it to me. 'What are you?' he asked. 'Some sort of private eye?' It was the first time he had shown any curiosity about me.

I laughed at the outdated expression. 'No.' I told him what I did back in England.

He looked towards the mosque and Ilamen beyond. 'Not much call for that stuff around here,' he remarked. 'How did you get into it?'

'It was the only thing I know how to do,' I said. 'It was what I was trained for. I was in the Army in Intelligence, but when I was promoted from half-colonel to colonel I saw the red light and quit.'

He twitched his shaggy eyebrows at me. 'Promotion in your army is *bad*?' he enquired lazily.

'That kind is. Normally, if you're going to stay in the line of command – field officer – you're promoted from lieutenant-colonel to brigadier; battalion CO to brigade CO. If you only go up one step it's a warning that you're being shunted sideways into a specialist job.' I sighed. 'I suppose it was my own fault. It was my pride to be a damned good intelligence officer, and they wanted to keep me that way. Anyway, I resigned my commission and started the firm I've been running for the last seven years.'

'Chicken colonel,' mused Byrne. 'I never made more than sergeant myself. Long time ago, though.'

'During the war,' I said.

'Yeah. Remember I told you I walked away from a crash?'

'Yes.'

'I liked what I saw during that walk – never felt so much alive. The other guys wouldn't come. Two of them couldn't; too badly injured – and the others stayed to look after them. So I walked out myself.'

'What happened to them?' I asked.

He shrugged. 'I gave the position of the plane and they sent a captured Fiesler Storch to have a look. Those things could land in fifty yards. It was no good; they were all dead.'

'No water?'

He shook his head. 'Goddamn Arabs. They wanted loot and they didn't care how they got it.'

'And you came back here after the war?' I asked.

He shook his head. 'I let the war go on without me. During the time I was walking through the desert I got to thinking. I'd never seen such space, such openness. And the desert is clean. You know, you can go without washing for quite a time here and you're still clean – you don't stink. I liked the place. Couldn't say as much for the people, though.' He poured some more mint tea. 'The Chaamba Arabs around El Golea aren't too bad, but those bastards in the Maghreb would skin a quarter and stretch the skin into a dollar.'

'What's the Maghreb?'

'The coastal strip in between the Mediterranean and the Atlas.' He paused. 'Anyway, early in '43 I got a letter to say my Pop was dead. He was the only family I had, so I had no urge to go back to the States. And General Eisenhower and General Patton and more of the top brass were proposing to go to Italy. I didn't fancy that, so when the army went north I came south looking for more favourable folks than Arabs. I found 'em, and I'm still here.'

I smiled. 'You deserted?'

'It's been known as that,' he admitted. 'But, hell; ain't that what a desert's for?'

I laughed at the unexpected pun. 'What did you do before you joined the army?'

'Fisherman,' he said. 'Me and my Pop sailed a boat out o' Bar Harbor. That's in Maine. Never did like fishing much.'

Fisherman! That was a hell of a change of pace. I suppose it worked on the same principle that the best recruiting ground for the US Navy is Kansas. I said, 'You're a long way from the sea now.'

'Yeah, but I can take you to a place in the Ténéré near Bilma – that's down in Niger and over a thousand miles from the nearest ocean – where you can pick up sea-shells from the ground in hundreds. Some of them are real pretty. The sea's been here and gone away. Maybe it'll come back some day.'

'Ever been back to the States?'

'No; I've been here thirty-five years and like to die here,' he said peacefully.

Mokhtar was away a long time, nearly five hours, and when he came back he had the gutted carcass of a gazelle slung across his shoulders. Byrne helped him butcher it, talking the while.

Presently he came over to me and squinted into the sun. 'Getting late,' he said. 'I reckon we'll stay here the night. Billson is either between here and Assekrem or he ain't. If he is, we'll find him tomorrow. If he ain't, a few hours won't make no difference.'

'All right.'

'And we've got fresh meat. Mokhtar tells me he stalked that gazelle for twenty kilometres and downed it in one shot.'

'You mean he walked twenty kilometres!'

'More. He had to come back. But he circled a bit, so say under thirty. That's nothing for a Targui. Anyway, Mokhtar's one of the old school; he learned to shoot with a muzzle-loader. With one of those you have to kill with one shot because the gazelle spooks and gets clear away before you can reload. But he likes a breech-action repeater better.'

And so we stayed under the shadow of Ilamen that night. I lay in the open, wrapped in a *djellaba* provided by Byrne, and looked up at those fantastic stars. A sickle moon arose but did little to dim the splendour of those faraway lights.

I thought of Byrne. Hesther Raulier had compared him with Billson, calling him, 'another crazy man'. But the madness of Byrne was quite different from the neurotic obsession of Billson; his was the madness that had struck many white men – not many Americans, mostly Europeans – Doughty, Burton, Lawrence, Thesiger – the lure of the desert. There was a peacefulness and a sanity about Byrne's manner which was very comforting.

I thought in wonder of the sea-shells to be picked up from the desert a thousand miles from the sea but had no fore-shadowing that I would be picking them myself. The night was calm and still. I suddenly became aware of the startling incongruity of Max Stafford, hot-shot businessman from the City of London, lying in a place improbably called Atakor beneath the Finger of God which was not far from the End of the World.

Suddenly London ceased to matter. Lord Brinton and Andrew McGovern ceased to matter; Charlie Malleson and Jack Ellis ceased to matter; Gloria and Alix Aarvik ceased to matter. All the pettifogging business of our so-called civilization seemed to slough away like an outworn skin and I felt incredibly happy.

I slept.

I woke in the thin light of dawn conscious of movement and sound. When I lifted my head I saw Byrne filling the petrol tank from a jerrican – it was that metallic noise that had roused me. I leaned up on one elbow and saw Mokhtar in the desert mosque; he was making obeisances to the east in the dawn ritual of Islam. I waited until he had finished because I did not want to disturb his devotions, then I arose.

Thirty minutes later after a breakfast of cold roast venison, bread and hot mint tea we were on our way again, a long plume of dust stretching away behind us. Slowly the majestic peak of Ilamen receded and new vistas of tortured rock came into view. According to Byrne, we were on a well-travelled road but to a man more accustomed to city streets and motorway driving that seemed improbable. The so-called road was vestigial, distinguishable only by boulders a shade smaller than those elsewhere, and the truck was taking a beating. As for it being well-travelled I did not see a single person moving on it all the time I was in Atakor.

Nearly three hours later Byrne pointed ahead. 'Assekrem!'

There was a large hill or a small mountain, depending on how you looked at it, on the top of which appeared to be a building. 'Is that a house?' I asked, wondering who would build on a mountain top in the middle of a wilderness.

'It's the Hermitage. Tell you about it later.'

We drove on and, at last, Byrne stopped at the foot of the mountain. There seemed to be traces of long-gone cultivation about; the outlines of fields and now dry irrigation ditches. Byrne said, 'Now we climb to the top.'

'For God's sake, why?'

'To see what's on the other side,' he said sardonically. 'Come on.'

And so we climbed Assekrem. It was by no means a mountaineering feat; a track zig-zagged up the mountain, steep but not unbearably so, and yet I felt out of breath and panted for air. Half way up Byrne obligingly stopped for a breather, although he did not seem in discomfort.

I leaned against the rock wall. 'I thought I was fitter than this.'

'Altitude. When you get to the top you'll be nine thousand feet high.'

I looked down to the plain below where I saw the truck with Mokhtar sitting in its shade. 'This hill isn't nine thousand feet high.'

'Above sea level,' said Byrne. 'At Tam we were four and a half thousand high, and we've been climbing ever since.' He rearranged his veil as he was always doing.

'What's this about a Hermitage?'

'Ever hear of Charles de Foucauld?'

'No.'

'Frenchman, a Trappist monk. In his youth, so I hear, he was a hellion, but he caught religion bad in Morocco. He took his vows and came out here to help the Tuareg. I suppose he did help them in his way. Anyway, most of what the outside world knows about the Tuareg came from de Foucauld.'

'When was this?'

'About 1905. He lived in Tam then, but it wasn't much of a place in those days. In 1911 he moved here and built the Hermitage with his own hands. He was a mystic, you see, and wanted a place for contemplation.'

I looked at the barren landscape. 'Some place!'

'You'll see why when we get to the top. He didn't stay long – it damn near killed him; so he went back to Tam and that did kill him.'

'How so?'

'In 1916 the Germans bribed the Libyan Sennousi to stir up trouble with the desert tribes against the French. The Tuareg of the Tassili n' Ajjer joined with the Sennousi and sent a raiding party against Tam. De Foucauld was caught and shot with his hands bound – and it was an accident. An excitable kid of fifteen let a gun go off. I don't think they meant to kill him. Everyone knew he was a *marabout* – a holy man.' He shrugged. 'Either way he was just as dead.'

I looked at Byrne closely. 'How do you know all this?'

He leaned forward and said gently, 'I can read, Stafford.' I felt myself redden under the implied rebuke, but he laughed suddenly. 'And I talked to some old guys over in the Tassili who had been on the raid against Tam in 1916. Some of the books I read sure are wrong.' He half-turned as if about to set off again, but stopped. 'And there was someone else in Tam not long ago like de Foucauld – but a woman. English, she was; name of Daisy Wakefield. Said she was related to some English lord – something to do with oil. Is there a Lord Wakefield?'

'There is.'

'Then that must be the guy.'

'Did you know her?'

'Sure, Daisy and I got on fine. That's how I caught up with the news; she subscribed to the London *Times*. A mite out-of-date by the time it got here but that didn't matter.'

'What happened to her?'

'She got old,' he said simply. 'She went north to El Golea and died there, God rest her soul.' He turned. 'Come on.'

'Byrne,' I said. 'Why are we climbing this mountain?'

'To see a guy at the top,' he said without turning.

I trudged after him and thought: *My God! Wakefield oil!* This damned desert seemed littered with improbable people. In fact, I was following one of them. Maybe two, counting Paul Billson.

The building at the top of Assekrem was simple enough. Three small rooms built of stone. There were two men there who ushered us inside. They were dark-skinned men with Negroid features. Byrne said casually, 'Don't handle any of the stuff here; it's de Foucauld's stuff – holy relics.'

I looked about with interest as he talked with the men. There was a simple wooden table on which were some books, a couple of old-fashioned steel pens and a dried-out ink-well. In one corner was a wooden cot with an inch-thick mattress which looked about as comfortable as concrete. On a wall was a picture of the Virgin.

Byrne came over to me. 'Billson went through three days ago, I think. Or it could have been two days because another truck went through the day after, and I'm not sure which was Billson. But that truck came out again yesterday.'

'We didn't see it.'

'Might have gone out the other way – through Akar-Akar.' He rubbed his jaw reflectively and looked at me. I noticed he hadn't bothered to keep up his veil in the presence of these men. He said abruptly, 'I want to show you something frightening – and why de Foucauld built here.'

He turned and went outside and I followed. He walked across the natural rock floor of a sort of patio to a low stone parapet, and then pointed north. 'That's where your boy is.'

I caught my breath. Assekrem was a pimple on the edge of a plateau. Below the parapet were vertiginous cliffs, and spread wide was the most awe-inspiring landscape I had ever seen. Range after range after range of mountains receded into the blue distance, but these were none of your tame mountains of the Scottish Highlands or even the half-tamed Swiss Alps. Some time in the past there had been a fearsome convulsion of the earth here; raw rock had ripped open the earth's belly with fangs of stone – and the fangs were still there. There was no regularity, just a jumble of lava fields and the protruding cores of volcanoes for as far as the eye could see, festering under a brassy sun. It was killer country.

'That's Koudia,' said Byrne. 'The land beyond the end of the world.'

I didn't say anything then, but I wondered about de Foucauld. If he chose to meditate here – did he worship God or the Devil?

Fourteen

Byrne was still talking to the dark-skinned men who had come out to join us. There was much gesticulating and pointing until, at last, Byrne got something settled to his satisfaction. 'These guys say they saw something burning out there two days ago.'

'Christ!' I said. 'What is there to burn?'

'Don't know.' He fumbled in the leather pouch which depended from a cord around his neck and took out a prismatic compass. He looked at me and said with a grin, 'I'm not against all scientific advance. Mokhtar, down there, thinks I'm a genius the way I find my way around.' He put the compass to his eye to take a sight.

'How far away?'

'Don't know that, either. They say it was a column of smoke – black smoke.'

'In the daytime?'

There was astonishment in Byrne's eyes as he looked at me. 'Sure; how the hell else could they see smoke?'

'I was thinking about the Bible,' I said. 'The Israelites in the wilderness, guided by a pillar of smoke by day and a pillar of fire by night.'

'I don't think you've got that right,' he said mildly. 'I read it as a pillar of cloud.' He turned back to take another sight. 'But I guess we'd better take a look. I make it just about due north of here, on a compass bearing. I don't bother none about magnetic variation, not on a short run.'

'What do you call short?'

'Anything up to fifty kilometres. Magnetic deviation is another thing. These goddamn hills are full of iron and you've got to check your compass bearing by the sun all the time.'

He put the compass away, and from another bag he took a couple of small packages which he gave to the two men. There was a ceremonial leave-taking, and he said, 'Salt and tobacco. In these parts you pay for what you get.'

As we set off down the steep path I said, 'There is something that's been puzzling me.'

Byrne grunted. 'Hell of a lot of things puzzle me, too, from time to time. What's your problem?'

'That veil of yours. I know it's Tuareg dress, but sometimes you muffle yourself up to the bloody eyebrows and other times you don't bother. For instance, you didn't bother up there; you let them see your face. I don't understand the rationale.'

Byrne stopped. 'Still on your anthropological kick, huh? Okay, I'll tell you. It's the politeness of the country. If you're in a place and you don't do as everybody does in that place, you could get yourself very dead. Take a Targui and set him in the middle of London. If he didn't know he had to cross the street in a special place, and only when the light is green, he could get killed. Right?'

'I suppose so.'

Byrne touched his head cloth. 'This thing is a *chech*; it's a substitute for the real thing, which is a *tagelmoust*, but you don't see many of those around except on high days and holidays. They're very precious. Now, nobody knows why the Tuareg wear the veil. I don't know; the anthropologists don't know; the Tuareg don't know. I wear mine because it's handy for keeping the dust out of my throat and keeps a high humidity in the sinuses on a dry day. It also cuts down water loss from the body.'

He sat down on a convenient rock and pointed downwards. 'You've seen Mokhtar's face?'

'Yes. He doesn't seem to bother about me seeing it.'

'He wouldn't – he's a noble of the Kel Rela,' said Byrne cryptically. 'Society here is highly class-structured and a ceremonial has grown up around the veil. It's polite to hide your face from your superiors and, to a lesser extent, from your equals. If Mokhtar met the *Amenokal* you'd see nothing of him except his eyelashes.'

He jerked his thumb upwards. 'Now, those guys up there are Haratin, and the Haratin were here thousands of years ago, long before the Tuareg moved in. But the Tuareg conquered them and made slaves of them, so they're definitely not my superior, so the veil don't matter.'

'But you're not a Tuareg.'

'The male singular is Targui,' said Byrne. 'And I've been a Targui ten years longer than I was an American.' He jabbed his finger at me. 'Now, you'll see lots of Tuareg faces, because you're a no-account European and don't matter. Got it?'

I nodded. 'I feel properly put in my place.'

'Then let's get the hell out of here.'

If I had thought Atakor was bad it was hard to make a comparison with Koudia; I suppose the only comparison could be between Purgatory and Hell. I soon came to realize that the high road I had anathematized in Atakor was a super highway when compared to anything in Koudia.

I put it to Byrne and he explained. 'It's simple. People make roads when they want to go places, and who in God's name would want to come here?'

'But why would anyone want to be in Atakor except a mystic like de Foucauld?'

'The Hermitage is a place of pilgrimage. People go there, Moslem and Christian alike. So the going is easy back there.'

After leaving Assekrem and plunging into the wilderness of Koudia I don't suppose we made more than seven miles in the first two hours – walking pace in any reasonable country. Koudia was anything but reasonable; I don't think there was a single horizontal bit of land more than five paces across. If we weren't going up we were going down, and if we weren't doing either we were going around.

The place was a litter of boulders – anything from head size to as big as St Paul's Cathedral, and the springing of the

Toyota was suffering. So was I. We bounced around from rock to rock and I rattled around the cab until I was bruised and sore. Byrne, at least, had the wheel to hold on to, but I don't think that made it any better for him because it twisted in his hands as though it was alive. As for Mokhtar, he spent more of his time out of the truck than in.

Apart from the boulders there were the mountains themselves, and no one could drive up those vertical cliffs so that was when we went around, Byrne keeping his eyes on his compass so as not to lose direction in all the twisting and turning we had to do. He stopped often to take a reciprocal sighting on Assekrem to make sure we were on the right line.

As I say, Mokhtar spent more time on the ground than in the truck, and it wasn't too hard for him to keep up. He had a sharp eye for signs of passage, and once he stopped us to indicate tyre marks on a patch of sand. He and Byrne squatted down to examine them while I investigated my bruises. When we were about to start again Byrne said, 'Superimposed tracks. One vehicle going in and another, later, coming out.'

I had casually inspected those tracks myself but I couldn't have trusted myself to tell which way the vehicles were going. As a Saharan intelligence officer I was a dead loss.

About seven miles in two hours, then we stopped for a rest and food. There was no vegetation in Koudia at all but Mokhtar had thoughtfully gathered a bundle of acacia twigs while waiting for us at Assekrem and soon had a fire going to boil water for the inevitable mint tea. I said to Byrne, 'Don't you ever drink coffee?'

'Sure, but this is better for you in the desert. You can have coffee when we get back to Tam. Expensive, though.'

The sun was past its height and sinking towards the west as we sat in the shade of the Toyota. This was the hottest part of the day and, in Koudia, that meant really hot. The bare rocks were hot enough to fry eggs and the landscape danced in a constant heat shimmer.

I remarked on this to Byrne, and he grinned. 'This is

winter – would you like to be here in summer?'

'Christ, no!'

'This is why they wouldn't give Billson a *permis*. And come nightfall the temperature will drop like a rock. You leave water exposed out here and you'll have half an inch of ice on it by three in the morning. If Billson is lost he'll either have burned to death or frozen to death.'

'I like a cheerful man,' I said acidly.

Mokhtar had disappeared about his private business but suddenly he appeared on top of a boulder about two hundred yards away. He gave a shrill whistle which attracted our attention, and waved both his arms. 'He's found something,' said Byrne, scrambling to his feet.

We went over to Mokhtar and that took us more than ten minutes in that ankle-breaking terrain. When we were fifty yards away Mokhtar shouted something, and Byrne said, 'He's found a truck. Let's see if it's a Land-Rover.'

As we scrambled on top of the boulder, which was as big as a moderate-sized stately home, Mokhtar pointed downwards, behind him. We walked over and stared to where his finger was pointing. There was a vehicle down there behind the boulder, and it was a Land-Rover. Or, at least, it had been – it was totally burnt-out. There was no sign of Billson or anyone else, and I suddenly realized that I wouldn't know Billson if I saw him. I was a damn fool for not having a photograph.

Byrne said, 'The black smoke would come from the burning tyres. Let's get down there.'

Going down meant going back the way we had come and walking around the boulder. As we came in sight of the Land-Rover, Byrne, in the lead, spread his arms to stop us. He spoke rapidly to Mokhtar who went on ahead, peering at the ground. Presently he waved and Byrne walked over to him, and they had a brief discussion before Byrne beckoned to me.

'There's been another truck here; its tracks are on top of those of the Land-Rover, and it went that way.' He pointed back in the general direction of the Toyota.

'Where's Billson?' My mouth was dry.

Byrne jerked his head at the Land-Rover. 'Probably in there – what's left of him. Let's see.'

He stood up and we walked over to the Land-Rover. It was a total wreck – a burnt-out carcass; it sat on the ground, the wheel rims entangled in the steel reinforcing wires of what had been tyres. There was still a lingering stench of burning rubber in the air.

The window glass had cracked and some of it had melted, and the windscreen was totally opaque so that it was difficult to see inside. Byrne reached out and tugged at the handle of the door on the driver's side and cursed as it came away in his hand. He walked around and tried the other door. He jerked it open and looked inside, with me looking over his shoulder.

The inside was a mess. The upholstery had burned, releasing blackened coil springs, and even the plastic coating of the driving wheel had burnt away, leaving bare metal. But there was no body, either in front or on the rear seats.

We went around to the back and got the tailgate open, to find scant remnants of what appeared to be two suitcases. Again, no body. I said, 'The other truck must have taken him away.'

'Maybe,' said Byrne noncommittally. He poked around a bit more in the ruined Land-Rover, then he straightened up. 'Did Paul Billson have any enemies?'

'He may have had.' I went cold as I realized we were speaking of Billson in the past tense just as his half-sister had done. I said, 'I hardly think he'd have the kind of enemy who would follow him to the middle of the Sahara to kill him.'

'Mmm.' Byrne made a nondescript noise and continued his examination. 'I've seen lots of burnt-out trucks,' he said. He picked up a jerrican lying to one side, snapped open the cap, and sniffed. 'He had gas in here. He must have been carrying it in the back there, because he had no cans strapped on the side when he left. This is empty now.'

'Perhaps there was an accident when he was refilling the main tank.'

'Then where's the body?'

'As I say – the other truck rescued him.'

Byrne stood back and looked at the Land-Rover, then talked more to himself than to me. 'Let's see; twenty-eight gallons in the main tank plus about four in the can – that's thirty-two. He'd need at least twenty to get here, so he was in trouble without a fire – he didn't have enough gas to get back to Tam. That leaves twelve gallons – eight in the tank and four in this can, I'd say.'

'How do you know the can wasn't empty? He could have refilled his main tank anywhere – even before Assekrem.'

'There's been gas in the can until quite recently – it smells too strong. And when I picked it up the cap was still closed. Now, if that can had been full of gas during the fire it would have exploded – but it hasn't.'

Byrne seemed to be arguing in circles. 'So he put it in the main tank,' I said exasperatedly.

'No,' said Byrne definitely. 'I've seen a lot of burnt-out trucks in the desert, but never one like this – not with all four tyres gone like that, not with so much fire damage up front.' He bent down to examine the petrol tank, and then crawled under.

When he emerged he stood up and tossed something in his hand. 'That was lying on the ground.' It was a small screw cap with a broken wire hanging from it. 'That's the drain cap for the gas tank. The wire which is supposed to stop it unscrewing has been cut. That makes it certain. Someone doused this truck with gas from the can, then decided it would be a good idea to have more. So he drained another four gallons from the tank – maybe eight – to do a really good job of arson. You don't get auto tyres burning all that easily. Then he tossed in a match and went away, and the guy who would do that wouldn't be rescuing Billson.'

'So where's Billson?'

'Don't know. Maybe we'll find his body around here some place.'

I remembered something. 'The man I put on Billson's track back in England seemed to think that someone else was also looking for him.' I frowned. 'And then Hesther Raulier . . .' I pulled out my wallet and found the note she had enclosed with the air ticket. I scanned it and handed it to Byrne.

He read it through, then said, 'Know this guy, Kissack?'

'Never heard of him.'

'Neither have I.' He gave me back the note.

'Another thing,' I said. 'Billson might have had a lot of money with him. I think he smuggled it out of the UK.'

'What do you call a lot of money?'

'The thick end of £60,000.'

Byrne whistled. 'I'd call that a lot, too.' He swung around and rooted in the back of the Land-Rover where all that was left of two suitcases were the locks, hinges, metal frames and a pile of ashes. He said, 'Whether Billson's money was in here when the fire bust out we'll never know without a forensic laboratory, and those are a mite scarce around here. Was it common knowledge that Billson would be carrying so much loose dough?'

'I shouldn't think so,' I said. 'It's really only a guess on my part.'

'You don't have a monopoly on guesses,' said Byrne. 'And a lot of guys have been killed for less than that.'

As we walked away from the Land-Rover I said, 'Funny that the chap who did this should close the cap on that empty jerrican; especially as he was going to leave it.'

'Probably automatic,' said Byrne. 'I do it myself. Good habit to have.'

'I'd still like to know what Billson was doing here,' I said.

'He was looking for a wrecked airplane, like you said. And he'd have found it, too – it's about five miles further north of here. I was going to head there if we hadn't found this. Billson must have heard about it back in Tam so he came for a look-see, the goddamned fool!'

'It couldn't be . . .' I began.

'Of course it couldn't be his father's plane,' said Byrne tiredly. 'It's a French military airplane that force-landed back when they were getting ready to blow an atom bomb up at Arak. They got the crew out by chopper, then went back to take out the engines and some of the instruments. Then they left the carcass to rot.'

He went to talk to Mokhtar, and I sat on a rock feeling depressed. Billson must have been the biggest damned fool in the history of the Sahara. He had probably read the Land-Rover's Owner's Manual and taken the manufacturer's fuel consumption claim as gospel, but it's one thing tooling along a motorway and another fighting your way through Koudia. I doubt if we'd been getting more than five miles to the imperial gallon since we left Assekrem and perhaps ten or twelve in Atakor. I don't think it's disrespectful to British Leyland to suggest that the Land-Rover was averaging about the same.

But Billson had probably measured straight lines on a map and set out on that basis. But that was water under the bridge or, more accurately, vapour through the carburettor. What we had now was an entirely different set of circumstances in which Billson's idiocy didn't figure because, if we found his body it would be because he had been murdered by a man, and the man was possibly called Kissack.

It was then that I made the discovery. Mokhtar or Byrne would probably have done it, but they didn't – I did, and it brought back some of my self-respect as a working member of this crazy expedition and made me feel something less of a hanger-on while others did the work.

I was looking down idly at the rock on which I sat when I noticed a small brown stain over which an ant was scurrying. For a moment I wondered how even an ant could live in Koudia, and then I noticed another and then another. There was quite a trail of them going backwards and forwards between a crack in the rock and the stain.

I stood up, looked at the Land-Rover, took a line on it, and then explored further away. Sure enough ten yards further on there was another stained rock, and a little way along there was another. I turned. 'Hey!'

'What is it?'

'I think I've found something.' Byrne and Mokhtar came up and I said, 'Is that dried blood?'

Mokhtar moistened the tip of his little finger and rubbed it on the stain, then he sniffed his fingertip delicately, looked at Byrne, and said one word. 'Yeah,' said Byrne. 'It's blood.'

'There's a line of it coming from the Land-Rover.' I turned and pointed towards a narrow ravine. 'I think he went up there.'

'Okay – Mokhtar goes first; he's better at this than we are. He can see a sign you wouldn't know was there.'

Billson, if it was Billson's blood, had gone up the ravine but fairly soon it became obvious that he hadn't travelled in a straight line. Not because of the difficulty of the terrain because he had dodged about quite a bit when he had no obvious need to, and on occasion he had reversed his course. And the blood splashes got bigger.

'Hell!' I said. 'What was he doing? Playing hide-and-seek?'

'Maybe he was at that,' said Byrne grimly. 'Maybe he was being chased.'

We found him at last, tumbled into a narrow crack between two rocks where there was shade. Mokhtar gave a cry of triumph and pointed downwards and I saw him sprawled on sand which was bloodstained. His face wasn't visible so Byrne gently turned him over. 'This Billson?'

'I wouldn't know,' I said. 'I've never seen him.'

Byrne grunted and felt about the body. The face of the man was puffy and swollen and his skin was blackened. Incongruously, he was wearing a normal business suit – normal for England, that is. At least I had had the sense to visit a tailor to buy what was recommended as suitable attire for the desert, even if the tailor had been wrong to the point of being out of his mind. The probability rose that this was indeed Billson.

Byrne said, 'Whoever the guy is, he has a hole in him. He's been shot.' He held out his fingers, red with liquid blood.

'He's alive!' I said.

'Not for long if we don't do something.' Byrne spoke to Mokhtar, who went away fast. He then turned the man over so that he lay more easily and put his hand inside his jacket to withdraw a passport and a wallet from the inside breast pocket. He flipped open the passport one-handedly. 'This is your boy; this is Paul Billson.' He gave me the passport and wallet.

I opened the wallet. It contained a sheaf of Algerian currency, a smaller wad of British fivers, and a few miscellaneous papers. I didn't bother to examine them then, but put the passport and the wallet into my pocket.

'We're in trouble,' said Byrne. He indicated Billson. 'Or he is. If he stays another night he'll die for sure. If we try to take him out he'll probably die. You know how rough it'll be getting back to Assekrem; I don't know if he can take it in his condition.'

'It's a question of the lesser of two evils.'

'Yeah. So we try to take him out and hope he survives.' He looked down at Billson. 'Poor, obstinate bastard,' he said softly. 'I wonder how well Hesther knew his old man? She said in her note to you that she'd wired me. I didn't tell you it was a ten-page cable, and she was pretty firm and detailed in her instructions.'

'Has the flow of blood stopped?' I asked.

'Yeah; I have the tail of his shirt wadded into the hole. We can't do much until Mokhtar gets back. He won't be long.'

'You must have known about Paul Billson before I arrived.'

'Sure I did, but he'd taken off by then.'

I said, 'If you hadn't waited for me you could have got here earlier.'

'Not much. I got Hesther's cable the morning you came. I don't know when she sent it, but the communications in this country aren't noted for reliability.'

'But you did lead me a little way up the garden path.' It seemed odd to be making conversation over the body of a man who was probably dying.

Byrne said, 'I wanted time to size you up. I don't like to travel with people I can't trust. Hereabouts it can be fatal.'

'So I passed the examination,' I said flatly.

He grinned. 'Just by a hair.'

A shadow fell athwart us. Mokhtar had come back. He had brought cloth for bandages, water, and a couple of sand ladders. The sand ladders, as Byrne had earlier explained, were to put under the wheels of the Toyota if we got stuck in sand. They were about six feet long and of stout tubular steel. 'Only stinkpots need them,' Byrne had said. 'Camels don't.'

Byrne tore off a strip of cloth, soaked it in water and put it in Billson's mouth; being careful not to choke him. Then he proceeded to dress the wound while Mokhtar and I lashed the sand ladders together to make an improvised stretcher.

It took us over an hour to get Billson the comparatively short distance back to the Toyota.

Fifteen

We had travelled two hours' worth into Koudia but it took us four hours to get out from the time Byrne started the engine until we drove beneath the peak of Assekrem. He picked his way as delicately as he could through that rocky desolation but, even so, Billson took a beating. Fortunately, he knew nothing of it; he was unconscious. I tended him as best I could, cushioning his body with my own, bathing his face, and trying to get some water into him. He did not move voluntarily nor did he make a sound.

I had expected Byrne to stop at Assekrem where perhaps we could have got help from the Haratin at the Hermitage, but he drove past the beginning of the path up the cliff and we camped about three miles further on. Mokhtar took a roll of cloth from the back of the Toyota and very soon had a windbreak erected behind which we laid Billson. It was now dark so Byrne redressed the wound in the acid light of a glaring pressure lantern.

He sat back on his heels and watched Mokhtar administer a salve to Billson's blackened face. 'If we can get some water into him he might survive,' he said. 'That's only a shoulder wound and the bullet went right through without hitting bone. Weakening but not killing. He's suffered more from exposure than the wound.'

I said, 'Why didn't you stop at Assekrem? They might have had something to help him.'

'Not a chance.' He nodded towards the Toyota. 'I have more stuff in my first aid kit than there is in the whole of the Ahaggar, if you except the hospital at Tam. Besides . . .' His voice tailed away, which was odd in Byrne because he was usually pretty damned decisive.

'What's the matter?'

'Do you know anything about Algerian law?'

'Not a thing.'

'Well, Billson broke one of them. He came out here without a *permis*.'

'So did you.'

'But I didn't apply for one – he did. You can be sure that when he disappeared from Tam they knew where he'd gone. There are police posts on all the main tracks out of Tam and when he didn't show up at any of those they'd be sure. So when he shows up in Tam he'll be arrested.'

'At least he'll get hospital treatment,' I said. 'And when he's out of hospital I'll stand bail.'

'You'll be lucky,' said Byrne drily. 'Because this guy is going to show up with a bullet hole in him and Algerian cops are no different than any other cops – they don't like mysterious bullet wounds. It's going to be a mess.'

He held up a finger. 'One – Billson has broken the law, and it's a serious offence. The Algerians are nuts on security and they don't like foreign nationals floating around the desert tribes unobserved. That could mean prison and I wouldn't wish my worst enemy in an Algerian prison.' A second finger joined the first. 'Two – he comes back with a bullet wound and that the cops won't like either. It's not an offence to be shot but it means someone else ought to be in jail, and that means trouble where there ought to be no trouble.' A third finger went up. 'Three – the guy who was shot is a foreigner and that brings Algiers into the act complete with a gaggle of diplomats. As far as I know Britain broke off diplomatic relations with Algeria years ago. I don't know who represents British nationals here – could be the Swiss – but that means a three-cornered international hassle, and no one is going to like that.'

'I begin to see the problems,' I said thoughtfully.

'Four,' said Byrne remorselessly. 'And this is the big one. Supposing we take Billson into Tam and he goes into hospital. It's only a small place and within twelve hours everybody is going to know about the man in hospital who was shot – including the guy who shot him . . .'

'. . . and who thinks he's dead,' I chipped in.

'. . . and whom Billson can identify. What's to stop him having another crack and finishing the job?'

'If he's still around.'

'What makes you think he won't be?' Byrne stood up and looked down at Billson. 'This guy is giving everybody a pain in the ass – including me.' He shook his head irritably. 'If it wasn't for Hesther . . .' His voice tailed away again.

'Is there an alternative to Tam?'

'Yeah.' He kicked at the sand. 'But I'll have to think about it.'

He went over to the truck and came back with the rifle, then spoke to Mokhtar who took a full magazine from the pouch hung on his neck. Byrne slipped it into the rifle with a metallic click, worked the action to put a bullet up the spout, and carefully set the safety-catch. 'I suppose you know how to use one of these, Colonel, sir?'

'I have been known to.'

'You might have to use it. It shoots a shade to the left and upwards; say, two inches at ten o'clock at a hundred yards. We'll stand watches tonight.'

I frowned. 'Expecting trouble? I'd have thought . . .'

He broke in. 'Not really, but Billson will have to be watched throughout the night.' He held up the rifle. 'This is for unexpected trouble.'

I stood the middle watch in order to give both Byrne and Mokhtar an uninterrupted run of sleep; I didn't know where we were going if it wasn't Tammanrasset, but wherever it was they would have to take me there, so they were more important than me.

Billson was unmoving but still breathing, and I thought he looked a shade better than he had. For one exasperated moment that evening I had thought of quitting and going back to London. As Byrne had said – though less politely – Billson was nothing but trouble for everyone who came near him, and I did think of leaving him to stew in his own juice.

But the thought of going back and telling Alix Aarvik about all this made my blood run cold. Besides, it wouldn't be fair on Byrne and Mokhtar who had gone to a great deal of trouble to help a man they didn't know. Also, I would have to be on hand when Billson recovered because someone had to get him out of the country as he had very little money left. And London was far away and receding fast, and I found I quite enjoyed the desert in a masochistic way.

I took the rifle and looked at it in the dim light of the fire. it was an old British Lee-Enfield .303 and, judging by its low number, it had seen service in the First World War, as well as the Second. I took out the magazine and worked the action to eject the round in the breech, then looked down the barrel into the fire. It was as clean as a whistle and any hardened sergeant would have had to give Mokhtar full marks. He had looked after it well. I reloaded and laid the rifle aside, then checked Billson again.

Towards the end of my watch he began to stir and, just before I woke Byrne, he had begun to mutter, but his ramblings were incoherent. I put my hand to his brow but he did not seem to be running a temperature.

I woke Byrne. 'Billson's coming to life.'

'Okay; I'll tend to him.' Byrne looked at the sky to get the time. He wore no watch. 'You get some sleep. We start early; our next camp is at Abalessa.'

I wrapped myself in my *djellaba* because it was very cold, and lay down. I wasted no time wondering about Abalessa but fell asleep immediately.

Billson was obviously better in the morning, but he was dazed and I doubt if he knew where he was or what was happening to him. We bedded him down in the back of the Toyota on the camel hair cloth that had served as a windbreak and on a couple of *djellabas*. 'We can get some camel milk once we're out of Atakor,' said Byrne. 'And maybe scare up some hot soup. That'll bring him around better than anything else.'

We travelled fast because Byrne said we had a long way to go. Coming out of Atakor we encountered the Tuareg camp we had passed on the way in. They were packing up to go somewhere but found some warm camel milk for Mokhtar. Byrne had thrown a *djellaba* casually into the back of the truck, covering Billson, and stood guard. 'There's no need for anyone to see him.'

We left the camp and stopped for a while a little later while we spooned milk into Billson. He seemed even better after that, even though the skin was peeling from his face and the backs of his hands in long strips. Mokhtar applied more salve and then we set off again, with Byrne really piling on the speed now that the country was much better.

These things are relative. Coming from the green land of England, I would have judged this place to be a howling wilderness. All sand, no soil, and the only vegetation an occasional clump of rank grass and a scattering of thorn trees which, however desirable they may have been to a camel, did nothing for me. But I had not just come from England; I had come from Koudia and Atakor and what a hell of a difference that made. This country was beautiful.

We travelled hard and fast, making few stops, usually to top up the tank with petrol from the jerricans. Billson finished the milk and was able to drink water which put a bit more life into him, although he still wandered in his wits – assuming he had any to begin with. Once Byrne stopped and sent Mokhtar on ahead. He disappeared over a rise, then reappeared and waved. Byrne let out the clutch and we went ahead at a rush, topping the rise and down the other side to cross what, for the Sahara, was an arterial highway.

'The main road north from Tam,' said Byrne. 'I'd just as soon not be seen crossing it.'

'Where are we going?'

'We're going round Tam to the other side – to Abalessa.'

He fell silent and concentrated on his driving.

Abalessa, when we got there, was a low hill on the horizon. We didn't drive up to it but made camp about a mile away. There was still some gazelle meat left so Mokhtar seethed it in a pot to make soup for Billson before putting on the kettle for the mint tea. Byrne grunted. 'You can have your coffee when we go into Tam tomorrow. Me, I'm looking forward to a cold beer.'

'But I thought . . .'

'Not Billson,' said Byrne. 'He stays here with Mokhtar. Just you and me. We've got to make you legal.'

I scratched my chin. I hadn't shaved during the past few days and it felt bristly. Maybe I'd grow a beard. I said, 'You'll have to explain that.'

'Strictly speaking, you should have reported at the *poste de police* at Fort Lapperine as soon as you got into Tam. Your name will have been on the airplane manifest, so by now the cops will be wondering where you are.'

'Nobody told me that. Specifically, you didn't tell me.'

'You'd have been told if you'd registered at the hotel. Anyway, I just told you.' He pointed to the hill in the distance. 'That's your alibi – the Tomb of Tin Hinan.' He paused. 'Mine, too.'

'The previous owner of the hotel, I suppose.'

He grinned. 'The legendary ancestress of the Tuareg. I did see a camera in your bag, didn't I?'

'Yes; I have a camera.'

'Then tomorrow we climb up there and you take a whole raft of photographs and we take them into Tam to be developed. That proves we have been here if anyone gets nosey. I don't want anyone getting the idea we went the other way – up into Atakor. Not immediately, anyway.'

'How long do we stay in Tam?'

'As long as it takes to satisfy that fat little guy behind the desk that we're on the level – no longer. The story is this; you came into Tam, got talking to me, and asked about the Tomb of Tin Hinan – you'd heard about it – it's famous. I said I'd take you there and we left immediately, and we've been here ever since while you've been rootling around like an archaeologist. *But* you don't bear down on that too heavily because to do real archaeology you need a licence. Only, tonight I discovered you hadn't registered with the cops so I've brought you back to get things right. Got the story?'

I repeated the gist of it, and Byrne said, 'There's more. The fat little guy will ask about your future plans, and you tell him you're going south to Agadez – that's in Niger.'

I looked at him blankly. 'Am I?'

'Yeah.' He pointed at Billson. 'We've got to get this guy out of Algeria fast. Clear out of the country.'

I scratched my bristles again. 'I have no Niger visa. First, I didn't have time to get one, and secondly I had no intention of going. Looking at this place from England, I decided that there's a limit to what I could do.'

'You'll get by without a visa if you stick with me.'

'Have you got a visa for Niger?'

'Don't need one – I live there. Got a pretty nice place in the Aïr ou Azbine, to the north of Agadez. I come up to Tam once a year to look after a couple of things for Hesther. She's got interests here.'

Mokhtar served up mint tea. I sat down, feeling comfortably tired after a long day's drive. 'How did you come to know Hesther?' I sipped the tea and found I was coming to like the stuff.

'When she was younger she used to come down to the Ahaggar quite a lot; that was when the French were here. One time she got into trouble in the Tademaït – that's about 700 kilometres north of here. Damn place fries your brains out on a hot day. Wasn't bad trouble but could have gotten worse. Anyway, I helped her out of it and she was grateful. Offered me a job in Algiers but I said I wasn't going to the damned Maghreb, so she asked me to help her out in Tam. That went on for a couple of years, then once, when she came down to Tam, we got to talking, and the upshot was that she staked me to my place in the Aïr, down in Niger.'

'What do you do down there?' I asked curiously. Byrne had to earn a living somehow; he just couldn't go around helping strangers in distress.

'I'm a camel breeder,' he said. 'And I run a few salt caravans across to Bilma.'

I didn't know where Bilma was and a salt caravan sounded improbable, but the camel breeding I could understand. 'How many camels have you got?'

He paused, obviously calculating. 'Pack animals and breeding stock together, I'd say about three hundred. I had more but the goddamn drought hit me hard. Seven lean years, just like in the Bible. But I'm building up the herd again.'

'Who is looking after them now?'

He smiled. 'If this was Arizona you'd call Mokhtar's brother the ranch foreman. His name is Hamiada.' He stretched. 'Got film for your camera?'

'Yes.'

'That's okay then. I reckon I'll go to sleep.'

'Aren't you going to eat?'

'We'll eat well in Tam tomorrow. There's just enough chow left to feed Mokhtar and Billson until we come back. Wake me at midnight.' With that he rolled over and was instantly asleep.

So I went hungry that night but I didn't mind. I looked around and saw that Mokhtar was asleep, as was Billson. It seemed as though I had been elected to stand first watch.

At about eleven Billson awoke and was coherent for the first time. He muttered a little, then said clearly, 'It's dark. Why is it dark?'

'It's night time,' I said softly.

'Who are you?' His voice was weak but quite clear.

'My name is Stafford. Don't worry about it now, Paul; you're quite safe.'

He didn't say anything for some time, then he said, 'He shot me.'

'I know,' I said. 'But you're all right now. Go to sleep and we'll talk tomorrow.'

He fell silent and when I looked at him closely five minutes later I saw that his eyes were closed and that he was breathing deeply and evenly.

At midnight I woke Byrne and told him about it, then went to sleep myself.

Sixteen

We didn't have much time for Billson in the morning because Byrne wanted to get back to Tam and we still had to go to the mound of Abalessa to take photographs, and so we had time to exchange only a few words. Mine were consoling – Byrne's were more in the nature of threats.

Billson was very weak, but rational. He had some more of the soup that Mokhtar prepared and managed to eat a few bits of the meat. As I knelt next to him he said, 'Who are you?'

'I'm Max Stafford. Your sister sent me to find you.'

'Alix? How did she know where I'd gone?'

'It wasn't too hard to figure,' I said drily. 'I suppose you know you did a damn silly thing – bolting like that.'

He swallowed. 'I suppose so,' he said reluctantly. He looked past me. 'Who are those Arabs?'

'They're not Arabs. Now listen, Paul. You made a bigger mistake when you went into Atakor without a permit. Did you know that you didn't have enough petrol to get back to Tam?' His eyes widened a little and he shook his head. 'And then you were shot. Who shot you – and why?'

His face went blank and then he frowned and shook his head. 'I don't remember much about that.'

'Never mind,' I said gently. 'All you have to do is to get well. Paul, if the police find you they'll arrest you and you'll go to prison. We are trying to stop that happening.'

I turned as Byrne called, 'Are you ready?' There was impatience in his voice.

'Coming.' I stood up and said to Billson, 'Rest easy.'

Byrne was more forthright. A Tuareg in full fig can be pretty awe-inspiring but, to the recumbent Billson, Byrne towering over him must have seemed a mile high. There is also something particularly menacing about a man who utters threats when you can't see his face.

Byrne said, 'Now, listen, stupid. You stay here with this man and you don't do a goddamn thing. If you step out of line just once Mokhtar will cut your crazy head off. Hear me?'

Paul nodded weakly. I noted that Mokhtar was wearing his sword and that the rifle was prominently displayed. Byrne said, 'If you do one more screwball thing we'll leave you for the vultures and the fennecs.' He strode away and I followed him to the Toyota.

On top of the mound of Abalessa were the ruins of a stone building, very unTuareglike. 'French?' I asked. 'Foreign Legion?'

'Hell, no!' said Byrne. 'Older than that. There's one theory that this was the southernmost post of the Romans; it has a likeness to some of the Roman forts up north. Another theory is that it was built by the remnants of a defeated legion that was driven down here. The Romans did lose a couple of legions in North Africa.' He shrugged. 'But they're just theories.'

'What's this about Tin Hinan?'

'Over here.' I followed him. 'She was found down there.' I peered into the small stone chamber which had obviously been covered by a hand-worked stone slab that lay nearby. 'It's still a mystery. The Tuareg have a story that a couple called Yunis and Izubahil were sent from Byzantium to rule over them; that would be about the year 1400. Some of the jewellery found on her was East Roman of that period, but some of the coins dated back to the fifth and sixth century. And there were some iron arm rings which the Byzantines didn't wear.'

He changed his tone and said abruptly, 'We're not here for a history lesson – get busy with your snapshots. Put me in one of them, and I'll do the same for you. Fool tourists are always doing that.'

So I ran off a spool of pictures and Byrne took a couple of me and we went away although I should have liked to have stayed longer. I have always liked a good mystery which, I suppose, was the reason I was in the Sahara anyway.

Abalessa was about sixty miles from Tammanrasset and we made it in just about two and a half hours, being helped during the last stretch by the asphalted road from the airstrip to Tam. That ten-mile bit was the only paved road I saw in the whole Sahara and I never found out why it had been put there.

Byrne pulled up outside the Hotel Tin Hinan. 'Go in and make your peace,' he said. 'I'm going to nose around. I'll meet you back here in, maybe, an hour. You can have a beer while you're waiting.'

'Am I staying here tonight?'

'No, you'll be with me. But you'll probably have to pay for your room reservation. Give me your film.'

So I took the film from the camera, gave it to him and got out, and he drove away blasting the horn. There was the predictable confusion in the hotel with reproaches which I soothed by paying the full room charge even though I had not used it. The manager's French was bad but good enough for me to hear that the police had been looking for me. I promised faithfully to report to the *poste de police*.

Then I went into the courtyard, sat at a table, and ordered a beer, and nothing had ever tasted so good. Nothing had changed in Tammanrasset since the day I had flown in and seen it with new eyes. The Tuareg walked down the sandy street in their languid, majestic manner, or stood about in small groups discussing whatever it was that Tuareg discuss. Probably the price of camels and the difficulty of shooting gazelle. A lot of them wore swords.

Of course, there was no reason why Tam should have changed. It was I who had changed. Those few days in Atakor and Koudia had made the devil of a difference. And now it seemed I was to go down to Niger – to a place called

Agadez and where was it? Ah yes; the Aïr ou something or other. I didn't know how far it was and I wondered if I could buy a map.

There were other things I needed. I looked down at myself. The natty tropical suiting the London tailor had foisted on me was showing the strain of desert travel. I gave the jacket an open-handed blow and a cloud of dust arose. With those travel stains and my unshaven appearance I probably looked like a tramp; any London bobby would have run me in on sight. But I saw no chance of buying European-style clothing in Tam. I'd ask Byrne about that.

I finished the beer and ordered a coffee which came thick and sugary and in very small quantity, which was just as well, and I decided I'd rather stay with the mint tea. I was half way through the second beer when Byrne pitched up. His first act was to order a beer and his second to drain the glass in one swallow. Then he ordered another, and said, 'No one called Kissack has been around.'

'So?'

He sighed. 'Don't mean much, of course. A guy can change his name. There's a party of German tourists going through.' He laughed. 'Some of them are wearing *Lederhosen*.'

I wasn't very much amused. In the desert *Lederhosen* weren't any more ridiculous than the suit I was wearing. I said, 'Have you any maps? I'd like to know where I'm going.'

'Don't use them myself, but I can get you one.'

'And I can do with some clothes.'

He inspected me. 'Wait until we get further south,' he advised. 'Nothing much here; better in Agadez. Your prints will be ready in an hour; I put the arm on the photographer.' He drained his glass. 'Now let's go tell the tale to the cops.'

Outside the entrance to the *poste de police* he said, 'Got your passport?'

I pulled it out of my pocket and hesitated. 'Look, if I say I'm going to Niger it's going to look funny when he finds no Niger visa in here.'

'No problem,' said Byrne. 'He won't give a damn about that. Niger is another country and it's not his worry what trouble you find yourself in there. He'll be only too happy to get you out of Algeria. Now go in and act the idiot tourist. I'll be right behind you.'

So I reported to the plump uniformed policeman behind the desk, and laid down my passport. 'I've been waiting for you, M'sieur Stafford,' he said coldly. 'What kept you?' He spoke heavily accented French.

'*Merde!*' said Byrne. 'It was only a couple of days.' I supposed I shouldn't have been surprised that Byrne spoke French, but I was. It was ungrammatical but serviceable.

'Three and a half, M'sieur Byrne,' said the policeman flatly.

'I thought he'd reported – I only found out last night, and we came straight in.'

'Where were you?'

'Abalessa.' He added something in a guttural language totally unlike that in which he spoke to Mokhtar. I took it to be Arabic.

'Nowhere else?'

'Where else is there to go out there?' asked Byrne.

I said, 'I suppose it's my fault. I jumped at the chance to go out there as soon as I met Mr Byrne. I didn't know I had to report here until he told me last night.' I paused, and added, 'It's quite a place out there; I'm not sure it's Roman, though.'

The policeman didn't comment on that. 'Are you staying in Tammanrasset long, M'sieur Stafford?'

I glanced at Byrne. 'No; I'm going down to Agadez and the Aïr.'

'With M'sieur Byrne?'

'Yes.'

He suddenly seemed more cheerful as he picked up my passport. 'We have much trouble with you tourists. You don't understand that there are strict rules that you must follow. There is another Englishman we are looking for. It all wastes our time.' He opened the passport, checked me against the photograph, and flicked the pages. 'There is no visa for Algeria here,' he said sharply.

'You know it's not necessary,' said Byrne.

'Of course.' The policeman's eyes narrowed as he looked at Byrne. 'Very good of you to instruct me in my work.' He put his hands flat on the table. 'I think a lot about you, M'sieur Byrne. I do not think you are a good influence in the Ahaggar. It may be that I shall write a report on you.'

'It won't get past the Commissioner of Police in Algiers,' said Byrne. 'You can depend on that.'

The policeman said nothing to that. His face was expressionless as he stamped my passport and pushed it across the desk. 'You will fill out *fiches* in triplicate. If you do not know how I am sure M'sieur Byrne will instruct you.' He indicated a side table.

The *fiche* was a small card, somewhat smaller than a standard postcard and printed in Arabic and French. I scanned it, then said to Byrne, 'Standard bureaucratic stuff – but what the hell do I put down under "Tribe"?'

Byrne grinned. 'A couple of years ago there was a guy here from the Isle of Man. He put down Manx.' He wilted a little under my glare and said, 'Just put a stroke through it.'

I filled in all three *fiches* and put them on the policeman's desk. He said, 'When are you leaving for Niger?'

I looked at Byrne, who said, 'Now. We just have to go to Abalessa to pick up some gear.'

The policeman nodded. 'Don't forget to report at the checkpoint outside town. You have an unfortunate habit of going around it, M'sieur Byrne.'

'Me? I never!' said Byrne righteously.

We left and, just outside the office, passed a man carrying a sub-machine-gun. Once in the street I said, 'He doesn't like you. What was all that about?'

'Just a general principle. The boys in the Maghreb don't like foreigners getting too close to the Tuareg. That guy is an Arab from Sidi-bel-Abbès. It's about time they recruited their police from the Tuareg.'

'Can he get you into trouble?'

'Fat chance. The Commissioner of Police lives in Hesther Raulier's pocket.'

I digested that thoughtfully, then said, 'What did you say to him in Arabic?'

Byrne smiled. 'Just something I wouldn't want to say to your face. I told him you were a goddamn stupid tourist who didn't know which end was up. I also managed to slip in that we were waiting for a roll of film to be developed. With a bit of luck he'll check on that.'

We went shopping. Byrne seemed well known and there was a lot of good-natured chaffing and laughter – also a lot of mint tea. He bought salt, sugar and flour, small quantities of each in many places, spreading his custom wide. He also bought a map for me and then we went back to the hotel for a final beer.

As we sat down he said, 'No trace of Kissack, but the word is out to look for him.'

The map was the Michelin North and West Africa, and the scale was 40 kilometres to the centimetre, about 63 miles to the inch. Even so, it was a big map and more than covered the small table at which we were sitting. I folded it to more comfortable proportions and looked at the area around Tammanrasset. The ground we had covered in the last few days occupied an astonishingly small portion of that map. I could cover it with the first joint of my thumb.

I observed the vast areas of blankness, and said, 'Where are we going?'

Byrne took the map and put his finger on Tammanrasset. 'South from here, but not by the main road. We take this track here, and as soon as we get to Fort Flatters we're in Niger.' He turned the map over. 'So we enter the Aïr from the north – through Iferouane and down to Timia. My place is near there. The Aïr is good country.'

I used my thumb to estimate the distance. It was a crow's

flight of about four hundred miles, probably six hundred on the ground and, as far as I could see, through a lot of damn all. The Aïr seemed to be mountainous country.

I said, 'What's an *erg*?'

Byrne clicked his tongue. 'I guess it's best described as a sea of sand.'

I noted with relief that there was no *erg* on the route to the Aïr.

We drank our beer leisurely and then wandered down the street to pick up the photographs. Suddenly Byrne nudged me. 'Look!' A policeman came out of a doorway just ahead and crossed the road to go into the *poste de police*. 'What did I tell you,' said Byrne. 'He's been checking those goddamn pictures.'

'Hell!' I said. 'I didn't think he'd do it. A suspicious crowd, aren't they.'

'Keeping the Revolution pure breeds suspicion.'

We collected the photographs, picked up the Toyota at a garage where it had been refuelled and the water cans filled, and drove back to Abalessa.

Mokhtar reported no problems, but Billson suddenly became voluble and wanted to talk. He seemed a lot stronger and, since he hadn't been able to talk to Mokhtar, it all came bursting out of him.

But Byrne would have none of it. 'No time for that now. I want to get out of here. Let's go.'

Again we picked up speed as we hit the asphalted section of road and, because we had to go through Tam, Billson was put in the back of the truck and covered with a couple of *djellabas*. The road to the south left Tam from Fort Lapperine and, as we turned the corner, I was conscious of the man standing outside the *poste de police*, cradling a submachine-gun in his arms, and sighed with relief as we bumped out of sight.

About four miles out of town Byrne stopped and went to the back of the truck where I joined him. He uncovered

Billson, and said, 'How are you?'

'I'm all right.'

Byrne looked at him thoughtfully. 'Can you walk?'

'Walk?'

Byrne said to me, 'There's a police checkpoint just around the corner there. I bet that son of a bitch back there has told them to lay for me.' He turned to Billson. 'Yes, walk. Not far – two or three kilometres. Mokhtar will be with you.'

'I think I could do that,' said Billson.

Byrne nodded and went to talk to Mokhtar. I said to Billson, 'You're sure you can do it?'

He looked at me wanly. 'I can try.' He turned to look at Byrne. 'Who is that man?'

'Someone who saved your life,' I said. 'Now he's saving your neck.' I went back and got into the cab. Presently Byrne got in and we drove on. I looked back to see Billson and Mokhtar disappear behind some rocks by the roadside.

Byrne was right. They gave us a real going-over at the checkpoint, more than was usual, he told me afterwards – much more. But you don't argue with the man with the gun. They searched the truck and opened every bag and container, not bothering to repack which Byrne and I had to do. They pondered over my passport for a long time before handing it back and then we had to fill in more *fiches*, again in triplicate.

'This is damn silly,' I said. 'I did this only this morning.'

'Do it,' said Byrne shortly. So I did it.

At last we were allowed to go on and soon after leaving the checkpoint Byrne swerved off the main track on to a minor track which was unsignposted.

'The main road goes to In Guezzam,' he said. 'But it would be tricky getting you over the border there. Fort Flatters will be better.' He drove on a little way and then stopped. 'We'll wait for Mokhtar here.'

We got out of the truck and I looked at the map. After a few minutes I said, 'I'm surprised they're not here by now. We were a fair time at the checkpoint and it doesn't take long to walk three kilometres.'

'More like eight,' said Byrne calmly. 'If I'd told him the truth he might have jibbed.'

'Oh!'

Presently Mokhtar emerged on to the side of the road. He was carrying Billson slung over his shoulder like a sack. We put him in the back of the truck and made him as comfortable as possible, revived him with water, and then drove on.

Seventeen

We drove to the Aïr in easy stages, doing little more than a hundred miles a day. It was during this period that I got to know Paul Billson, assuming that I got to know him at all because he was a hard man to fathom. I think Byrne got to know him a lot better than I did.

In spite of his garrulity at Abalessa, he felt a lot less like talking after passing out while going around the checkpoint, but he was a lot better that evening when we made camp. We now had tents which were carried on a rack on top of the truck, and while Byrne and Mokhtar were erecting them I dressed Billson's wound. It was clean and already beginning to heal, but I puffed some penicillin powder into it before putting on fresh bandages.

He was bewildered. 'I don't know what's going on,' he said pathetically. 'Who are you?'

'I told you – Max Stafford.'

'That means nothing.'

'If I said that I was responsible for security at Franklin Engineering would that mean anything?'

He looked up. 'For God's sake! You mean you've chased all the way out here because I left Franklin's in a hurry?'

'Not entirely – but you get the drift. There's a lot you can tell me.'

He looked around. We were camped on the lee side of a ridge almost at the top. I had queried that when Byrne picked the spot; camping on the flats at the bottom of the ridge would have been better, in my opinion. Byrne had shaken his head. 'Never camp on low ground. More men die of drowning in the Sahara than die of thirst.' When I expressed incredulity he pointed to mountains in the north-east. 'You could have a thunderstorm there and not know it. But a flash flood sweeping through the wadis could come right through here.' I conceded his point.

Billson said, 'Where are we?'

'About fifty miles south-east of Tammanrasset.'

'Where are we going?'

'Niger. We're getting you out of Algeria; the police are looking for you. You bent the rules.'

'Why are you doing this for me?'

I put the last knot in the bandage and snipped off the loose ends. 'Damned if I know,' I said. 'You've certainly proved to be a bloody nuisance. Niger is probably the last place in the world I want to go to.'

He shook his head. 'I still don't understand.'

'Have you remembered anything about the man who shot you?'

'A bit,' said Billson. 'I stopped because one of the tyres was going soft and I thought I might have to change a wheel. I was looking at it when this other car came along.'

'Car or truck?' A car seemed improbable in Koudia.

'A Range-Rover. I thought he might help me so I waved. He came up and stopped about ten yards away – then he shot me.'

'Just like that?'

'Just like that. I felt this blow in my shoulder – it knocked me down. It didn't hurt; not then.'

I looked at Billson speculatively. This sounded an improbable story, but then, Billson collected improbabilities about him as another man might collect postage stamps. And I never forgot for one moment that I had been badly beaten up in a quiet street in Kensington.

'Did you see the man?'

'Yes. He – they chased me.'

'How many?'

'Two of them.'

'Were they locals? I mean, were they Arabs or Tuareg?'

'No, they were white men, like you and me.'

'Didn't he say anything before he shot you?'

'No. As I said, the car just stopped and he shot me.'

I sighed. 'So what happened then?'

'Well, when I fell down they couldn't see me because I was behind the Land-Rover. Close by there was a gap between two rocks and I nipped in there. I heard them getting out of their car so I went between the rocks and up a sort of cleft and ran for it.'

He fell silent so I prompted him. 'And they chased you. Did they shoot at you again?'

He nodded. 'Just the one man. He didn't hit me.' He touched his shoulder. 'Then this started to hurt and I became dizzy. I don't remember any more.'

He had collapsed and fortunately fallen out of sight down a cleft in the rocks. The men had probably searched for him and missed him, not too difficult in Koudia. But burning his Land-Rover was another way of killing him; I couldn't imagine a man with a gunshot wound and no water walking out of Koudia.

'How did you find me?' he asked.

'We were looking for you.'

He stared at me. 'Impossible. Nobody knew where I'd gone.'

'Paul, you left a trail as wide as an eight-lane motorway,' I said. 'It wasn't difficult for me, nor for someone else, evidently. Do you have any enemies? Anyone who hates you badly enough to kill you? So badly that they'd follow you to the middle of the Sahara to do it?'

'You're mad,' he said.

'Someone is,' I observed. 'But it's not me. Does the name of Kissack mean anything to you?'

'Not a thing.' He brooded a moment. 'What happened to my Land-Rover? Where is it?'

'They burned it.'

He looked stricken. '*They burned it!*' he whispered. 'But what about . . .' He stopped suddenly.

'How much money did you have in those suitcases?' I

asked softly. He didn't answer, so I said, 'My assessment is about £56,000.'

He nodded dully.

'Whether they searched those cases before dousing them with petrol or not doesn't matter. You've lost it.' I stood up and looked down at him. 'You're a great big law-breaker, Paul. The British can nail you for breaking currency regulations, and now the Algerians are looking for you. If they find you with a bullet hole in you that'll bring more grief to someone. Jesus, you're a walking disaster.'

'Sorry to have been the cause of trouble,' he mumbled. His hand twitched, the fingers plucking at his jacket.

I contemplated that piece of understatement with quiet fury. I bent down and stuck my finger under his nose. 'Paul, from now on you don't do a single thing – not a single bloody thing, understand, even if it's only unzipping your fly – without consulting either me or Byrne.'

His head jerked towards Byrne. 'Is that him?'

'That's Byrne. And walk carefully around him. He's as mad at you as I am.'

They had finished putting up the tents and Mokhtar had a fire going. I told Byrne what I had got from Billson, and he said contemplatively, 'Two Europeans in a Range-Rover. They shouldn't be hard to trace. And they shot him just like that? Without even passing the time of day?'

'According to Paul – just like that.'

'Seems hard to believe. Who'd want to shoot a guy like that?'

I said tiredly, 'He was driving around with 56,000 quid in British bank notes packed in his suitcase. I shouldn't think it went up in flames in the Land-Rover. He probably opened his mouth too wide somewhere along the line, and someone got greedy.'

'Yeah, you could be right. But that doesn't explain Kissack.'

'I don't believe he exists.'

'If Hesther says he was looking for Paul Billson, then he

exists,' said Byrne firmly. 'Hesther don't make mistakes.'

We had mutton that night because Mokhtar had bought a sheep that morning from a passing Targui at Abalessa. He grilled some of it kebab-style over the fire and we ate it with our fingers. It was quite tasty. Byrne pressed Billson to eat. 'I'm trying to fatten you up,' he said. 'When we get to Fort Flatters you've got to walk some more.'

'How much more?' asked Billson.

'Quite a piece – maybe thirty kilometres. We've got to get you round the Algerian border post.' He turned to me. 'You'll have a walk, too; around the Niger border post.'

I didn't look forward to it.

The next night I tackled Paul again, this time not about what he'd been up to in North Africa, but about the puzzling circumstances of his life in England. I could have questioned him as we drove but I didn't want to do it in front of Byrne. Paul might unburden himself to a single interrogator but he might not before an audience.

I dressed his wound again. It was much better. As I re-wrapped the bandage I said, 'How much did you earn at Franklin Engineering, Paul?'

'£200 a month.'

'You're a damned liar,' I said without heat. 'But you always have been, haven't you? You were on £8000 a year – that's nearly four times as much. Now, tell me again – how much did you earn?' He stayed sullenly silent, and I said, 'Tell me, Paul; I want to hear it from you.'

'All right. It was £8000 a year.'

'Now, here comes the £8000 question,' I said. 'Do you consider that you were worth it to Franklin Engineering?'

'Yes – or they wouldn't have paid it to me.'

'You don't really believe that, do you?' Again he maintained silence. 'Do you know that Mr Isaacson wanted to fire you ten years ago, but the managing director wouldn't agree?'

'No.'

'Do you know that Mr Stewart wanted to fire you when he arrived from Glasgow to reorganize the accounts office, and again the managing director wouldn't have it?'

'No.'

'Who is your guardian angel, Paul?'

'I don't know what you mean.'

'For God's sake!' I said. 'You were doing work that any sixteen-year-old office boy could do. Do you think that was worth eight thousand quid a year?'

He avoided my eye. 'Maybe not,' he muttered.

'Then how come you were paid it? There must have been some reason. Who were you blackmailing?'

That got him angry. 'That's a damnable thing to say,' he spluttered. 'You've no right . . .'

I cut in. 'How did you get the job?'

'It was offered to me. I got a letter.'

'When was this? How long ago?'

Billson frowned in thought, then said, 'Must have been 1963.'

'Who sent the letter?'

'A man called McGovern. He was managing director of Franklin.'

McGovern! Then managing director of Franklin Engineering, later Chairman of the Board, now Chairman of the entire Whensley Group and knighted for his services to industry. Sir Andrew McGovern, who ran like a thread through Billson's life and who wanted to run his own security operation as soon as Billson disappeared.

I said, 'What was in the letter?'

'McGovern offered me a post at £2000 a year.' Billson looked up. 'I grabbed it.'

He would! £2000 wasn't a bad salary back in 1963 when the average pay was considerably less than £1000. 'Didn't you wonder why McGovern was offering that?'

'Of course I did.' Billson stared at me. 'But what did you expect me to say? I wasn't going to turn it down because it was too much.'

I had to smile at that. Billson might be stupid, but not stupid enough to say, 'But, Mr McGovern; I'm not worth half that.' I said, 'So you just took the money and kept your mouth shut.'

'That's right. I thought it was all right at first – that I'd have to earn it. It worried me because I didn't know if I could hold down that sort of job. But then I found the job was simple.'

'And not worth £2000 then or £8000 now,' I commented. 'Now tell me; why was McGovern grossly overpaying you?'

'I don't know.' Billson shrugged and said again, almost angrily, 'I tell you – I don't know. I've thought about it for years and come to no answer.' He glowered at me. 'But I wasn't going to ask McGovern.'

No, he wouldn't; he'd be frightened of killing the goose that laid the golden eggs. I laid that aspect aside and turned to something else. 'How did Alix come to work for Franklin Engineering?'

'There was a vacancy in the typing pool,' said Billson. 'I told her about it and she applied. She got the job but she wasn't in the typing pool long. She became McGovern's secretary and he took her with him when he moved to London. Alix is a clever girl – she has brains.'

'Did McGovern know she's your half-sister?'

'I don't know. I didn't tell him.' He gave a deep sigh. 'Look, it was like this. I hardly *saw* McGovern. I wasn't in the kind of job where you hob-nob with the managing director. During the first six years I don't think I saw McGovern as many times, and I haven't seen him at all since. That's when he moved to London.'

Very curious indeed! I said, 'Now, it's a fact that you kept your enhanced pay a secret from your sister. Why did you do that?'

'Oh, hell!' Billson suddenly grabbed a handful of sand. 'I've just told you – Alix is smart. If she knew she'd ask me why – and I couldn't tell her. Then she'd dig into it and perhaps find out.' He wagged his head. 'I didn't want to know.'

He was afraid that Alix would shake all the leaves off the money tree. Billson might be a stupid man in many ways but he had cunning. Before he started work for Franklin Engineering he had already lived for many years at low pay and was quite content to continue to do while he amassed a small fortune. But to what end?

'You've acted the bastard towards Alix, haven't you, Paul?' I said. 'You must have known she was in financial difficulties and had to borrow money from the bank. And it was to help you, damn it!'

He said nothing. All he did was to pour fine sand from one hand to the other. I suppose a psychologist would call that a displacement activity.

'But the psychiatrist didn't help much, did he? You had a sudden brainstorm.'

'What the hell do you know about it?' he said petulantly. 'You don't know why I'm here. No one does.'

'Do you think I'm a damned fool?' I demanded. 'You've come out here to find your father's aeroplane.'

His jaw dropped. 'How do you know that? You couldn't . . . no one could.'

'Jesus, Paul; you're as transparent as a window-pane. You read that article by Michael English in the Sunday supplement and it sent you off your rocker. I talked to English and he told me what happened in the editor's office.'

'You've seen English?' He dropped the sand and dusted off his hands. 'Why have you been following me? Why come out here?'

It was a good question. My original idea had just been to ask a few questions in Algiers and let it go at that. I certainly hadn't expected to be on my way to Niger in the company of one Targui, one pseudo-Targui and one man who was half way round the bend. It had been a chain of circumstances, each link not very important in itself, excepting perhaps when we found Billson half dead.

I said wearily, 'Let's say it's for Alix and leave it at that, shall we?' It was the truth, perhaps, but only a fraction of it.

'She worries about you, and I'm damned if you deserve it.'

'If I hadn't been shot I'd have found it,' he said. 'The plane, I mean. I was within a few miles of it.' He drove his fist into the sand. 'And now I'm going in the opposite direction,' he said exasperatedly.

'You're wrong,' I said flatly. 'That crashed aircraft in Koudia is French. Byrne knows all about it. Ask him. You went at that in the way you go about everything – at half-cock. Will you, for once in your life, for God's sake, stop and think before you take action? You've been nothing but a packet of trouble ever since you left Franklin.'

I didn't wait for an answer but got up and left him and, for once, I didn't confide my findings to Byrne. This bit really had nothing to do with him; he knew nothing of England or of London and could contribute nothing.

I walked out of camp a couple of hundred yards and sat down to think about it. I believed Billson – that was the devil of it. I had told him that he was as transparent as glass, and it was true. Which brought me to McGovern.

I thought about that pillar of British industry for a long time and got precisely nowhere.

Eighteen

And so we travelled south.

At the Algerian border post Mokhtar guided Billson on foot around it while Byrne and I went through. There were more *fiches* to fill in – in triplicate, but we didn't get the full treatment we had had at the police post outside Tammanrasset. We went on and waited for Billson in the no-man's-land between the Algerian post and Fort Flatters in Niger, then it was my turn to walk, and Mokhtar took me on a long and circuitous route around the fort. If the two border posts compared notes, which Byrne doubted they would, then two men would have gone through both.

When Mokhtar and I rejoined the truck beyond Fort Flatters Byrne seemed considerably more cheerful. I was footsore and leg-stretched and was glad to ease myself down creakily into the seat next to him. As he let out the clutch he said gaily, 'Nice to be home.'

We were eighty miles into Niger when we camped that night and the country hadn't changed enough to justify Byrne's cheeriness, but thereafter it became better. There was more vegetation – thorn trees, it's true – but there was also more grass as we penetrated the mountains, and I saw my first running water, a brook about a foot across. According to Byrne, we had left the desert but, as I have said, these things are relative and this was still a wilderness to the untutored eye.

'The Aïr is an intrusion of the Sahel into the desert,' said Byrne.

'You've lost me,' I said. 'What's the Sahel?'

'The savannah land between the desert and the forest in the south. It's a geographer's word. Once they called it the

Sudan but when the British pulled out they left a state called the Sudan so the geographers had to find another word because they didn't want to mix geography and politics. They came up with Sahel.'

'Doesn't look much different from desert.'

'It's different,' said Byrne positively. 'These uplands get as much as six inches of rain a year.'

'That's a lot?'

'A hell of a lot more than Tam,' he said. 'There've been periods of up to ten years when it hasn't rained there at all.'

We stopped at a small village called Iferouane which must have been important in the Aïr because it had an airstrip. Although the people here were Tuareg there was a more settled look about them. 'Still nomadic,' said Byrne. 'But there's more feed around here, so they don't have to move as far or as often.'

There were more animals to be seen, herds of camels, sheep and goats, with a few hump-backed cattle. The Tuareg seemed to be less formal here than in the north and some of the faces I saw were decidedly Negroid. I mentioned that to Byrne, and he shook his head. 'Those people are either Haratin or slaves.'

'Slaves!'

'Sure. The Tuareg used to go raiding across the Niger Bend to bring back slaves.'

'Is there still slavery?'

'Theoretically – no. But I wouldn't bet on it. A few years ago a British novelist bought a slave in Timbouctou just to prove that it could be done. Then he set the man free which was a damnfool thing to do.' He saw my frown. 'He had no land, so he couldn't grow anything; he had no money so he couldn't buy anything – so what was the poor bastard to do? He went back to his old master.'

'But slavery!'

'Don't get the wrong idea,' said Byrne. 'It's not what you think and they don't do too badly.' He smiled. 'No whips, or anything like that. Here, in the Aïr, they grow millet and cultivate the date palms on a share-cropping basis. Theoretically they get a fifth of the crop but a smart guy can get as much as half.'

Byrne seemed well-known and popular in Iferouane. He talked gravely with the village elders, chaffed the young women, and distributed sweets and other largesse among the children. We stayed there a day, then pushed on south over rougher country until we arrived at Timia and Byrne's home.

Ever since we had left Fort Flatters Billson had avoided me. He couldn't help being close in the truck but he didn't talk and, out of the truck, he kept away from me. I suppose I had not hidden my contempt of him and, naturally enough, he didn't like it. I had penetrated his thick skin and wounded whatever *amour propre* he had, so he resented me. I noticed that he talked a lot with Byrne during this time and that Byrne appeared to show interest in what he was saying. But Byrne said nothing to me at the time.

Byrne was unTuareg enough to have built himself a small house on the slopes of what passed for a pleasantly-wooded valley in the Aïr. The Tuareg in the area lived, not in leather tents as they did in the desert to the north, but in reed huts, cleverly made with dismountable panels so that they could be collapsed for loading on the back of a pack camel. But Byrne had built a house – a minimal house, it is true, with not much in the way of walls – but a house with rooms. A permanent dwelling and, as such, foreign to the Tuareg.

We arrived there late and in darkness and I didn't see much that night because we ate and slept almost immediately. But next morning, Byrne showed me around his kingdom. Close by there was something which, had it been permanent, would have been called a village and Byrne talked to a man whom he told me was Hamiada, Mokhtar's brother. Hamiada was tall, even for a Targui, and his skin, what little I could see of it above his veil, was almost as white as my own.

Byrne said to me, 'Most of the herd's grazing out towards

Telouess – about twenty kilometres away. I'm going out there tomorrow. Like to come?'

'I'd like that,' I said. 'But what about Billson?' Billson was not with us; when we had left that morning he was still asleep.

Byrne looked troubled. 'I want to talk to you about him – but later. Now I want to show you something.'

Hamiada had gone away but he returned a few minutes later leading a camel. It was one of the biggest beasts I had seen and looked to be about ten feet high at the hump, although it could hardly have been that. It was of a colour I had never seen before, a peculiar smokey-grey. Byrne said, 'This is my beauty – the cream of my herd. Her name is Yendjelan.'

He spoke with such obvious pride that I felt I had to echo it even though I was no expert on the finer points of camel-breeding. 'She's a very fine animal,' I said. 'A racing camel?'

He chuckled. 'There's no such thing. She's a Mehari – a riding camel.'

'I thought they raced.'

'Camels don't run – not unless they're urged. And if they run too far they drop dead. Fragile animals. When you come with me tomorrow you'll be riding one. Not Yendjelan, though; she's mine.'

Yendjelan looked at me in the supercilious way of a camel, and her lip curled. She thought as much of the idea of me riding a camel as I did.

We looked at some more of Byrne's herd, the few that were browsing close by. As I watched them chewing up branches of acacia, three-inch thorns included, I wondered how in hell you controlled a camel. Their mouths would be as hard as iron.

We accepted Hamiada's hospitality – cold roast kid, bread and camel milk. Byrne said abruptly, 'About Billson.'

'Yes.'

'What was your intention?'

I sighed. 'I don't quite know. I thought if we could get

him further south into Nigeria, then I could get him on to a plane back to England.'

Byrne nodded. 'Yes, south to Kano, a plane from there to Lagos, and so home.' He paused, chewing thoughtfully like one of his own camels. 'I don't know if that would be such a good thing.'

'Why not?'

'The guy's unstable enough as it is. He's come out here and made a bust of it so far. If he goes home now he knows he'll never be able to come back, and that might knock him off his perch entirely. He could end up in a looney-bin. I don't know that I'd like that. Would you?'

I thought of the biblical bit about being one's brother's keeper. Also the Chinese bit to the effect that if you save a man's life you are responsible for him until he dies. Also the Sinbad bit about the Old Man of the Sea. 'What's he to you?' I asked.

Byrne shrugged. 'Not much. Something to Hesther, though.'

I wondered, not for the first time, about the exact relationship between Byrne and Hesther Raulier. She'd said she'd never married but that did not necessarily mean much between a man and a woman. I said, 'What are you suggesting? That we indulge him in his fantasies?'

'Fantasies? Oh, sure, they're fantasies as far as Billson is concerned. I mean, it's fantastic for Billson to suppose that he could come out here and find that airplane unaided. But, as far as the plane itself is concerned, I've been talking to him and what he says makes a weird kind of sense.'

'You mean he's talked you into believing that the plane's still here?'

'Must be,' said Byrne simply. 'It was never found.'

'Not necessarily so,' I said. 'Not if Billson did defraud the insurance company.'

'I thought Hesther had talked you out of that way of thinking.'

'Maybe – but for Christ's sake, the Sahara is a bloody big

149

place. Where the hell would we start?'

Byrne drained a bowl of camel milk. 'Billson really studied that last flight of his father. He's got all the details at his fingertips. For instance, he knew that when his old man took off from Algiers he intended to fly a great circle course for Kano.' He chuckled. 'I borrowed your map and traced that course. It's been a few years since I had to do spherical trigonometry but I managed.'

'And what conclusion did you come to?'

'Okay; the distance is 2800 kilometres – about 1500 nautical miles, which is the unit he'd work in for navigational purposes. It would take him over the Ahaggar about 150 kilometres east of Tam. It would take him right over here, and smack bang over Agadez. Paul wasn't all that crazy when he went to look at an airplane in the Ahaggar. 'Course he should have checked with someone first – me, for instance – but the idea was good.'

'Where is all this leading?'

Byrne said, 'All the planes in that race took the great circle course because a great circle is the shortest distance between two points on the earth's surface. Now, Agadez lies *exactly* on that course and so it made a good aiming point. Furthermore, it was a condition of that leg of the race that the planes had to fly low over Agadez – it was a sort of checkpoint. Every plane except two buzzed Agadez and was identified. One of the planes that wasn't seen at Agadez was Billson's.'

'And the other?'

'Some Italian who got a mite lost. But he arrived in Kano, anyway.'

'Maybe Peter Billson had weather trouble,' I said. 'Forced down.'

'He was forced down all right,' agreed Byrne. 'But not by weather. Paul has checked that out; got meteorological data for the time of flight. He's been real thorough about this investigation. The weather was good – no sandstorms.'

'Obsessionally thorough.'

'Yeah,' said Byrne. 'But thorough all the same. Now, when Peter Billson went down it would be likely to be to the north of Agadez, and one thing's for sure – it wasn't in the Aïr. There are too many people around here and the plane would have been found. The same applies anywhere north of the Ahaggar. If it went down there it would have been found by some Chaamba bedouin.'

'So that leaves the Ahaggar and you're certain it's not there. You're talking yourself into a corner.'

He said, 'When the French were getting ready to blow that atom bomb at Arak they lost three planes in the Ahaggar. I've told you about one of them. They gave the Ahaggar a real going-over, both from the air and on the ground. They found three planes which was all they expected to find. I'm pretty sure that if Billson's plane had been there the French would have found it.'

'Perhaps they did,' I said. 'And didn't bother to mention it.'

Byrne disagreed. 'It would have made big news. You don't suppose Billson was the only record-breaking airman lost in the Sahara, do you? There was a guy called Lancaster went down in 1933 south of Reggan in the Tanezrouft. He wasn't found until 1962 and it made the headlines.'

I worked it out. 'Twenty-nine years.'

'He was still with the plane, and he left a diary,' said Byrne. 'It made bad reading. Paul knows all about Lancaster; he *knows* how long a crashed plane can remain undetected here. That's why he thinks he can still find his father.'

'This place where Lancaster crashed – where is it?'

'In the Tanezrouft, about 200 kilometres south of Reggan. It's hell country – *reg*, that's gravel plain for as far and farther than you can see. I know a bit of what happened to Lancaster because I read about it back in '62 and Paul has refreshed my memory. Lancaster was flying a light plane and put down at Reggan to refuel. He took off, got into a sandstorm and lost direction; he flew *east* damn near as far as In Salah before he put down at Aoulef to find out where

151

he was. He'd intended to fly to Gao on the Niger Bend and that was due south, but he'd used up too much fuel so he went back to Reggan. He left next day and after a while his engine quit. So he crashed.'

'Didn't they search for him?'

'Sure they did – by air and ground. I don't know how good their air search was back in 1933, but they did their best. Trouble was they were looking mostly in the wrong place, towards Gao. Anyway, he had two gallons of water and no more, because he had an air-cooled engine. He died eight days later, and was found twenty-nine years later. That's the story of Lancaster.'

'Who found him?'

'A routine French patrol working out of Bidon Cinq. What the hell they were doing in the Tanezrouft I don't know. Probably on a vehicle-testing kick – I can think of no other reason for going into that hell hole.'

'All right,' I said. 'You've made a point. So Peter Billson and his plane can still be in the desert. Are you proposing that we go look for it in this place – the Tanezrouft?'

'Not goddamn likely,' said Byrne. 'I think it possible that Billson went off course. When he disappeared there was a search but, just like Lancaster, he wasn't found because they weren't looking in the right place.'

'And you know the right place, I suppose.'

'No, but think of this. Lancaster's plane was found by the French. For all we know it might have been seen much earlier by, say, some Hartani or even a Targui. But why would they want to report it? It would mean nothing to them. Don't forget, this plane crashed only three years after the final battle between the French and the Tuareg when the French got the upper hand at last. The Tuareg felt they didn't owe the French a goddamn thing. Sure, if they'd found Lancaster alive they'd have brought him out, but they wouldn't care much about a dead guy in a dead plane.'

'All right,' I said. 'Spit it out. What are you getting at?'

Byrne said, 'Would you put up, say, five camels to help

find Paul's old man?'

The question was so unexpected that I blinked with astonishment and I suppose I was testy. 'What the devil do you mean?'

'I mean put up the price of five camels.'

'How much is a camel worth?' I asked suspiciously.

Byrne scratched his jaw through his veil. 'An ordinary pack camel will go for about a hundred pounds sterling. A reasonable Mehari will fetch between a hundred fifty and two hundred.' He laughed. 'You couldn't buy Yendjelan for a thousand. Okay, let's say five hundred.'

'You want me to put up £500,' I said carefully. 'To find Paul's father.'

'I'd put up the same,' he said. 'In camels.'

'So now we have ten camels,' I said. 'How do they help? Do we ride them spaced a hundred yards apart in a sweep of the bloody Sahara?'

'No,' said Byrne calmly. 'They're a reward for a sighting of a plane that crashed in 1936 – payable when we're taken to see it.'

It was a good idea provided I was willing to fork out £500 to help Paul Billson, which wasn't a cast-iron certainty. A good idea but for one thing – the time element. I said, 'For God's sake! How long will it take for news of this reward to get around? Two months? Three months? I don't have that much time to spend here, and if I go, then Billson goes, even if I have to do what Hesther suggested – club him and put him in a sack.'

Byrne laughed quietly. 'You don't know much about the desert. There are trucks going up from Agadez to Tam every day – two days' journey at the most. Those truck drivers waste no time in sight-seeing; they've seen it already. From Tam to In Salah – another day. From Agadez east to Bilma – two days. From Bilma to Djanet in the Tassili n' Ajjer – two more days driving fast. In six days minimum I can get news to all the important oases in the desert. The whole Sahara is a big sounding-board if the news is important enough.'

I was sceptical. 'Word of mouth?'

'Word of mouth – hell!' Byrne snorted. 'Ten thousand leaflets handed out. Printed in Arabic, of course. Those who can't read will go to the public letter-writers for a reading as soon as they hear of a ten-camel reward.'

'You're crazy,' I said. I looked around at the thorn trees and the browsing camels. 'Where the blazes are you going to get ten thousand leaflets printed here?'

'I'll draw it up tonight,' he said. 'Then have them Xeroxed in Agadez. They have a machine in the bank.' He leaned forward and peered at me. 'Something the matter?' he enquired gently.

'No,' I said weakly. 'Nothing the matter. It's just the idea of blanketing the Sahara with leaflets seems a bit weird. You've never worked for J. Walter Thompson, have you?'

'Who's he?'

'A small advertising agency back in the States – and elsewhere.'

'Never heard of him.'

'If you ever leave the desert I'd apply for a job with him. You'd do well.'

'You're nuts!' he said. 'Well, what about it?'

I started to laugh. Between chuckles I said, 'All right . . . I'll do it . . . but it won't be for Paul Billson. It'll be worth it just to say I've done a saturation advertising campaign in the Sahara.'

Byrne wagged his head. 'Okay – I don't care why you do it so long as you do it.'

'What do I do?' I said. 'Give you a cheque?'

'Now what in hell would I do with a cheque?' he asked. 'I'll put up your half and you get the cash to Hesther in Algiers as and when you can.' He paused. 'Pity we don't have pictures of the plane. Paul had some but they went up with the Land-Rover.'

'I can help there. I got some photocopies from the Aeronautical Department of the Science Museum in London. Not Billson's plane but one exactly like it.'

'Good,' said Byrne. 'We'll put those on the hand-out. Or maybe drawings might be better.' He adjusted his veil and stood up. 'There's one thing you maybe haven't thought of.'

'What's that?'

'If the guy who shot Paul is still around he might get to know of these leaflets if he has local connections. If he does he'll be drawn down here like a hornet to a honey-pot. It might turn out real interesting.'

It might indeed!

Nineteen

When Paul Billson heard what we were going to do he took it as his due. He didn't even thank us, and I could have picked him up and shaken him as you would try to shake sense into a puppy. But that was the man, and he wasn't going to change. Byrne settled down to draw up his leaflet and I wandered away to think about things – mostly about Byrne, because I was fed up with thinking about Paul.

From what I had seen of Byrne's camels he seemed to take pride in breeding a superior animal. If his information on the price of camels was correct and a pack camel would cost £100, then it would be reasonable to assume that his might average, say, £150. That would make him worth £45,000 in stock alone, regardless of his other interests. He had said he ran salt caravans; I didn't know if that was profitable but I assumed it was. Then there was whatever he got from Hesther Raulier for looking after her affairs in the desert, and there were probably other sources of income.

It seemed likely that Byrne was a wealthy man in his society. I don't know how far the Tuareg had been forced into a cash economy – I had seen very little money changing hands – but even on a barter basis Byrne would be rich by desert standards.

Next day Byrne and I went into Agadez, Paul staying behind on Byrne's insistence. 'I don't want you seen in Agadez,' he said. 'You'd stand out like the Tree of Ténéré. You spend the day here – and stay put. Understand?'

Paul understood. It wasn't what Byrne said, it was the way he said it that drove it home into Paul's skull.

As we drove away Byrne said, 'And Hamiada will see that

he stays put.' There was a touch of amusement in his voice.

I said, 'What was that you said about a tree?'

'The Tree of Ténéré?' He pointed east. 'It's out there. Only tree I've ever heard of being put on the maps. It's on your map – take a look.'

So I did, and there it was – *L'Arbre du Ténéré*, about a hundred and sixty miles north-east of Agadez in the *Erg du Ténéré*, an area marked yellow on the map – the colour of sand. 'Why should a tree be marked?'

'There's not another tree in any direction for about fifty kilometres,' said Byrne. 'It's the most isolated tree in the world. Even so, a fool French truck driver ran into it back in 1960. It's old – been there for hundreds of years. There's a well there, but the water's not too good.'

So the map indicated – *eau très mauvaise à 40 m.*

It was a little over a hundred miles to Agadez over roughish country. Even though we were able to pick up speed over the last forty miles of reasonable track it took us five hours, averaging twenty miles an hour for the whole trip.

Agadez seemed a prosperous little town by Saharan standards. It even had a mosque, something I had not seen in Tam. We parked the truck outside the Hotel de l'Aïr and went inside to have a beer, then Byrne went to the bank to have his leaflets printed. Before he left he said, 'You might like to do some shopping; it's better here than in Tam. Got any money?'

It occurred to me that Byrne was laying out considerable sums during our travels and he would need recompense. I dug out my wallet and checked it. I had the equivalent of about a hundred pounds in Algerian currency, another four hundred in travellers' cheques and a small case stuffed with credit cards.

Byrne looked at my offerings and said, 'None of that is much use here. You give anyone a strange piece of paper or a bit of plastic and he'll laugh at you.' He produced a small wad of local currency. 'Here. Don't worry, I'll bill you when you leave, and you can settle it with Hesther in Algiers.'

And I had to make do with that.

I walked along the dusty street and found that American influence had even penetrated as far as Agadez – there was a supermarket! Not that an American would have recognized it as such but it was passable, although the stock of European-style clothing was limited. I bought a pair of Levi's and a couple of shirts and stocked up with two cartons of English cigarettes. Then I blinked at an array of Scotch whisky, not so much in astonishment that it was there at all but at the price, which was two-thirds the London price. I bought two bottles.

I took my booty and stowed it in the Toyota, then had another beer in the hotel while waiting for Byrne. When he came back we took the Toyota to a filling station to refuel and there, standing next to the pumps, was a giraffe.

I stared at it incredulously. 'For God's sake! What the hell . . .'

The giraffe bent its neck and looked down at us with mild eyes. 'What's the matter?' asked Byrne. 'Haven't you seen a giraffe before?'

'Not at a filling station.'

Byrne didn't seem in the least surprised. 'I'll be a little while here. This is where we start the distribution of our message.'

I nodded wordlessly and watched the giraffe amble away up the main street of Agadez. As Byrne opened the door I said, 'Hang on. Satisfy my curiosity.'

'What about?'

I pointed. 'That bloody giraffe.'

'Oh, that. It's from the zoo. They let it out every morning, and it goes back every night to feed.'

'Oh!' Well, it *was* an explanation.

We arrived back at Byrne's place in the Aïr the next day, having camped on the way. I was getting to like those nightly camps. The peace was incredible and there was nothing more arduous to think about than the best place to make the fire and the best place to sleep after testing the wind direction. It was a long way from the busy – and now meaningless – activities of Stafford Security Consultants Ltd.

At that particular camp I offered Byrne a scotch, but he shook his head. 'I don't touch the hard stuff, just have the occasional beer.'

I said, 'I can't get over the fact that it's cheaper than in England.'

'No tax on it,' he said. 'In England you need a lot of money to build essentials like Concorde airplanes so your taxes are high.' His tone was sardonic. 'Out here who needs it?' He picked up the bottle. 'This stuff is brought up from Nigeria, mostly for the tourist trade. Same with the cigarettes. Might even have come up on the back of a camel.'

The whisky tasted good, but after the first I found I didn't want another. I said, 'The most incredible thing today was that bloody giraffe.'

'Civilized people hereabouts,' said Byrne. 'Don't like to keep things in cages. Same with camels.'

'What do you mean?'

'Well, a Tuareg-trained camel is worth more than one trained by an Arab, all other things being equal. A Targui is kinder about it and the camel responds. Real nice people.'

Looking up at the stars that night I thought a lot about that.

After that nothing very much happened except that I got a new suit of clothes and learned how to ride a camel, and the two were connected. Byrne was going out to inspect his herd, and when I arrived for my camel-riding lesson in jeans he shook his head solemnly. 'I don't think so,' he said. 'I really don't think so.'

And so I dressed like a Targui – loose, baggy trousers in black cotton cloth fitting tight around the ankles, a white *gandoura*, the Tuareg gown, and another blue *gandoura* on top of that. There was a *djellaba* too, to be worn in cold weather or at night. Literally topping it off was the *chech*, twenty feet of black cotton, about eighteen inches wide, which Byrne painstakingly showed me how to arrange.

When I was dressed in all my finery I felt a bit of a fool and very self-conscious, but that wore off quickly because no one else took any notice except Billson and I didn't give a damn for his opinion. He wouldn't change his clothing nor ride a camel; I think he had slightly Empire notions about 'going native'.

A camel, I found, is not steered from the mouth like a horse. Once in the saddle, the Tuareg saddle with its arm-chair back and high cross-shaped pommel, you put your bare feet on the animal's neck and guide it by rubbing one side or the other. Being on a camel when it rises to its feet is the nearest thing to being in an earthquake and quite alarming until one gets used to it.

Byrne, Hamiada and I set out with two pack camels for the grazing grounds near Telouess and were going to be away for over a week, Byrne commenting that he could not reasonably expect any reaction from his leaflet campaign for at least a fortnight. He had arranged with the owner of the filling station for the distribution of the leaflets in packets of 500 to the twenty most important oases south of the Atlas mountains.

'And it'll take that time to bring Paul up to the mark,' he said. 'Because one thing is certain – if we find that airplane it's going to be in some of the lousiest country you've ever seen, else the French would have found it years ago.'

What Billson did while we were away I don't know. I never found out and I didn't ask.

Looking back, I think those days spent wandering in the Aïr was the most idyllic time of my life. The pace was slow, geared to the stride of a camel, and the land was wide and empty. One fell into an easy rhythm, governed not by the needs of other men but by the passage of the sun across the sky, the empty belly, the natural requirements of the beast one was riding.

We found Byrne's herd and he looked at the animals and found their condition good. They were looked after by a family of Tuareg headed by a man called Radbane. 'These people are of the Kel Ilbakan,' said Byrne. 'A vassal tribe from south of Agadez. They graze their stock here in the winter and help me with mine.'

We accepted Radbane's hospitality and stayed at his camp for two days, and then struck west, skirting the base of a mountain called Bagzans. We were striking camp on the ninth day out of Timia when Hamiada gave a shout and pointed. We had visitors; three camels were approaching, two with riders. As they came closer Byrne said, 'That's Billson.'

He frowned, and I knew why. It would need something urgent to get Billson up on to a camel.

They came up to the camp and I noted that Billson's camel was on a leading rein held by the Targui who accompanied him. The camels sank to their knees and Billson rocked violently in the saddle. He slid to the ground painfully, still incongruously dressed in his city suit, now worn and weary. His face was grey with fatigue and he was obviously saddle-sore. I had been, too, but it had worn off.

I said, 'Come over here, Paul, and sit down.' Byrne and Hamiada were talking to the Targui. I dug into my saddle-bag and brought out the bottle of whisky which was still half full. I poured some into one of the small brass cups we used for mint tea and gave it to Paul. It was something he appreciated and, for once, he said, 'Thanks.'

'What are you doing out here?' I asked.

'I saw him,' he said.

'Who did you see?'

'The man who shot me. He was in Timia asking questions, and then came on to Byrne's place.' He paused. 'In the Range-Rover.'

'And you saw him? To recognize him?'

Paul nodded. 'I was bored – I had no one to talk to – so I went down among the Tuareg. There's a man who can speak a little French, about as much as me, but we can get on. I was outside his hut when I saw the Range-Rover coming so I ducked inside. The walls are only of reeds, there are plenty of cracks to look through. Yes, I saw him – and I knew him.'

'Was he alone?'

'No; he had the other man with him.'

'Then what happened?' I looked up. Byrne had come over and was listening.

'He started to talk to the people, asking questions.'

'In Tamachek?' asked Byrne abruptly.

'No, in French. He didn't get very far until he spoke to the man I'd been with.'

'That would be old Bukrum,' said Byrne. 'He was in the Camel Corps when the French were here. Go on.'

'They just talked to the old man for a bit, then they went away. Bukrum said they asked him if there were any Europeans about. They described me – my clothes.' His fingers plucked at his jacket. 'Bukrum told them nothing.'

Byrne smiled grimly. 'He was told to say nothing – they all were. Can you describe these men?'

'The man who asked the questions – the one who shot me – he was nearly six feet but not big, if you see what I mean. He was thin. Fair hair, very sunburned. The other was shorter but broader. Dark hair, sallow complexion.'

'Both in European clothes?'

'Yes.' Paul eased his legs painfully. 'Bukrum and I had a talk. He said he'd better send me to you because the men might come back. He said you'd be where wheels wouldn't go.'

I looked at the jumble of rocks about the slopes of Bagzans. Bukrum had been right. I said, 'I've asked this question before but I'll ask it again. Can you think of any reason – any conceivable reason – why two men should be looking for you in the Sahara in order to kill you?'

'I don't know!' said Paul in a shout. 'For Christ's sake, I don't know!'

I looked at Byrne and shrugged. Byrne said, 'Hamiada and I will go to Timia and nose around. We'll make better time on our own.' He pointed to the Targui who was talking to Hamiada. 'His name is Azelouane; he's Bukrum's son. He'll take you to a place in the hills behind Timia and you stay there until I send for you. There's water there, so you'll be all right.' He looked at the three camels which Azelouane had brought. 'You stay here today; those beasts need resting. Move off at first light tomorrow.'

Within ten minutes he and Hamiada were mounted and on their way.

It took us two days to get to the place in the hills behind Timia so, with the day's enforced rest, that was three days. There was a pool of water which Azelouane called a *guelta*. He, too, had a small smattering of French so we could talk in a minimal way with the help of a lot of hand language. We were there for three more days before Byrne came.

During this time Billson was morose. He was a very frightened man and showed it. Having a hole put in you with intent to kill tends to take the pith out of a man, but Paul had not really been scared until now. Probably he had reasoned that it was a case of mistaken identity and it was over, his attacker having given him up for dead after burning the Land-Rover. The knowledge that he was still being pursued really shook him and ate at his guts. He kept muttering, 'Why me? Why *me*?' He found no answer and neither did I. He also got rid of the rest of my whisky in short order.

Byrne arrived late at night, riding tall on Yendjelan and coming out of the darkness like a ghost. Yendjelan sank to her knees, protesting noisily as all camels do, and he slid from the saddle. Azelouane unsaddled her while I brewed up some hot tea for Byrne. It was a cold night.

He sat by the fire, still huddled in his *djellaba* with the hood over his head, and said, 'You making out all right?'

'Not bad.' I pointed to where Billson was asleep. 'He's not

doing too well, though.'

'He's scared,' said Byrne matter-of-factly.

'Find anything?'

'Yeah. Two guys – one called Kissack, a Britisher; the other called Bailly. He's French, I think. They're scouring the Aïr looking for Billson.' He paused. 'Looking for me, too. They don't know about you.'

'How do they know about you?'

'My name had to go on that leaflet,' he said. 'That's how I figured it. No point in issuing a reward unless you give the name and place of the guy offering it.'

'Where are they now?'

'Gone to Agadez to fill up with gas. I think they'll be back.'

I thought about it, then said slowly, 'That tells us something. They're not just looking for Billson; they're after anybody who is looking for that bloody plane. Billson's name wasn't on the leaflet, was it?'

'No,' said Byrne shortly.

'That does it,' I said. 'It must be the plane.' I put my hand on his arm. 'Luke, you'd better watch it. They put a bullet into Billson on sight. They could do the same to you.' I realized that I had addressed him by his given name for the first time.

He nodded. 'That's what I thought.'

'Christ, I'm sorry to have got you into this.'

'Make never no mind,' he said. 'I'm not going to stick my head up as a target. And you didn't get me into this. I did.'

I said, 'So it's Peter Billson's plane. But why? Why should somebody want to stop us finding it?'

'Don't know.' Byrne fumbled under his *djellaba* and his hand came out holding a piece of paper. 'First results have started to come in. Maybe we should have just offered one camel; they're reporting every goddamned crashed airplane in the desert. Fifteen claimants so far. Five are duplications – reporting the same plane – so that cuts it down to ten. Six of those I know about myself, including that French plane in

Koudia I told you of. That leaves four. Three of those are improbable because they're in areas where any crash should have been seen. That leaves one possible.'

'Where is it?'

'Up on the Tassili n' Ajjer. Trouble is it's way off Peter Billson's great circle course.'

'How far off?'

'About fifteen degrees on the compass. I know I argued that Billson must have been off course – that's why the search didn't find him. But fifteen degrees is too much.' He accepted a cup of tea.

'So what do we do now?'

'Sit tight and wait for more returns to come in.' He sipped the tea and added as an afterthought, 'And keep out of Kissack's way.'

'Couldn't we do something about him?'

'Like what?'

'Well, couldn't Paul go to the police in Agadez and lay a charge of attempted murder?'

Byrne snorted. 'The first thing they'd ask is why he didn't tell the Algerian authorities. Anyway, the cops here wouldn't be too interested in a crime that happened in Algeria.' He was probably right; I doubted if there'd be any Interpol co-operation in the Sahara. He said, 'I'm tired,' and rolled over and went to sleep in his sudden way.

I beat my brains out wondering why Kissack and Bailly should want to kill anyone searching for an aircraft that had crashed over forty years before. Presently I stopped thinking. I wasn't aware of it. I was asleep, too.

Byrne had brought us some provisions. Millet to be pounded in a mortar and boiled to a thin gruel before having crushed dates added, and flour and salt to make flapjacks. Azelouane went off somewhere and returned with a goat kid which he killed by slitting its throat, so we had fresh meat.

And so we sat tight in the hills, half a day's journey from Timia.

Three days later Byrne went back, leaving early in the morning and returning the same night. He reported that Kissack was still active. 'He's really scraping the bottom of the barrel,' he said. 'Tassil Oued, Grup-Grup, El Maki – all the little places. But Timia seems to attract him. He knows I live near there. He was in Timia again at midday today.'

'Hell!' I said. 'Be careful.'

He laughed. 'I was standing six feet from him and I was just another Targui. How was he to know different unless someone told him, and my people wouldn't give him a drink of water in the Tanezrouft.' There was a tinge of pride in the way he said 'my people'.

I thought that the Tuareg veil certainly did have its advantages, as did the fact that all the Tuareg dress alike in blue and white.

He said, 'There's another batch of sightings from hopefuls who'd like to win ten camels each. Twenty-two. Most of them duplicating the first lot.'

'Any possibles?'

He shrugged. 'Just that one on the Tassili n' Ajjer. Let's go talk to Paul. Where is he?'

'Down by the *guelta*. He spends a lot of time just looking at the water.'

So we went looking for Paul and found him, as I thought we would, sitting on the little sandy beach by the pool. Byrne sat on a rock and said, 'Paul, I want to talk to you.'

'What about?'

'I reckon you know more about your father's last flight than anyone in the world. I'd like your opinion on some-thing.' He clicked his fingers at me. 'The map.'

The sun was dipping behind the hills but there was still enough light to see by. Byrne spread the map on the sand and traced a line with his finger. 'Algiers to Kano – that's the great circle course your father intended to fly. Right?'

Paul examined the line Byrne had drawn. 'Yes, that's about it.'

'It's not *about* anything,' said Byrne. 'That's the line.' He took the stub of pencil from the wallet which hung from his neck. 'Now we have one possibility – and it's here.' He marked the map with a cross.

Paul turned the map around. 'No,' he said firmly.

'Why not?'

'My father was a good pilot. He'd never have gone so far off course.'

Byrne said, 'Remember I was a flier, too, so I know what I'm talking about. What time of day did he take off from Algiers?'

Paul said, 'He landed in Algiers just after midday. He didn't refuel immediately because his mechanic wanted to check the plane. That woman in Algiers said . . .'

'You mean Hesther Raulier?'

'Yes.'

'Then call her by her name,' said Byrne harshly. 'She is *not* "that woman in Algiers". Go on.'

Paul flinched. 'Hesther Raulier said there was an argument about that. My father wanted to refuel immediately and take off, but the mechanic wouldn't have it. He said he wanted to have the plane just right.'

I said, 'Paul, in this race was time on the ground deducted from the elapsed time, or was it a case of whoever got to Cape Town first had won?'

'Whoever got to Cape Town first won outright.'

I said to Byrne, 'Then every minute Peter Billson spent on the ground was a minute lost. It's not surprising he argued for a quick take-off.'

Byrne nodded. 'Who won the argument?'

'Must have been the mechanic,' said Paul. 'The wo – Hesther Raulier said she took my father to an hotel where he got some sleep.'

'Then when did he take off?'

'At five that afternoon.'

'That time of year it would be dark at six,' said Byrne. 'He was making a night flight. He wouldn't be able to tell from the ground whether he was on course or not. He couldn't see the ground.'

'Hesther Raulier said it worried my father,' said Paul. 'Not the night flying, but he'd be landing at Kano in the dark. He didn't know if the airstrip would be illuminated.'

'Yeah,' said Byrne. 'That Northrop cruised at 215 mph, but he'd be pushing it a bit. Say eight hours to Kano landing at one in the morning. But he didn't get that far.'

It was now too dark to see the map clearly. I said, 'So what's the next move?'

'That's up to Paul,' said Byrne. 'I still think the plane was off course, and now I know it was a night flight that makes it certain to my mind.' He tapped the map. 'This could be Peter Billson's plane.'

I said, 'You'd be willing to take us there?'

'If that's what Paul wants.'

I looked towards Paul. I couldn't see his face but his movements showed indecision. At last he said hesitantly, 'Yes. All right.' Again no mention of thanks.

Byrne clapped his hands together lightly. 'We leave at dawn.'

Twenty

We arrived at Byrne's house at eleven next morning, Byrne having scouted ahead to see if it was safe to go in. Once there he wasted no time. 'I thought Paul would make that decision,' he said to me. 'We have to go through Agadez to tank up on gas, but Paul mustn't – not with Kissack about. I've sent Hamiada on ahead. He'll be waiting with camels this side of Agadez to take Paul around.'

That reminded me of something. 'I haven't seen Mokhtar around. He just seemed to evaporate as soon as we got here from Algeria.'

Byrne laughed. 'He'll be half way to Bilma by now. He's my *madugu*.'

'What's that?'

'Caravan master. He's taking millet to Bilma and bringing back salt. We should catch up with him the other side of Fachi.'

'We're going to Bilma?'

'Through Bilma,' corrected Byrne. 'And away to hell and gone the other side.'

I went to study my invaluable map, and I didn't much like what I saw. We'd be crossing the *Erg du Ténéré* and there was no track marked. And beyond that was the *Grand Erg du Bilma*. It seemed that I was going to see the Tree of Ténéré, very bad water at forty metres included.

When I next saw Byrne he was cleaning and oiling an automatic pistol and another lay by his side. 'You're an old army man; take your pick,' he invited.

They were both German; one was a Walther and the other a Luger. I said, 'Where did you get those?'

'There was a bit of trouble up north, if you remember,' he

said. 'The trouble I walked away from. A lot of guns, too; and quite a few came south.'

I nodded. Both the pistols were standard German side-arms, officers for the use of. I picked the Walther and Byrne nodded approvingly. I said, 'I wouldn't give one of these to Paul.'

Byrne looked at me disgustedly. 'Think I'm crazy? If I'm going to be shot it had better be by the right guy.' He handed me a packet of ammunition and a spare magazine. 'Load up.'

I loaded the magazines and slipped one into the butt of the pistol. Then I had a problem; I didn't know where to put the damned thing. There was an inside pocket in the breast of the *gandoura* but it wasn't good enough to take anything as heavy as an automatic pistol. Byrne watched me with a sardonic eye, then said, 'There's a belt and holster in the closet behind you.'

There was a pocket built into the holster to take the spare magazine. I strapped the belt around my waist under the *gandoura*. There was no problem of access because the arm-holes of a *gandoura* are cut very low and one can withdraw one's arms right inside. A *djellaba* is made the same way, and on a cold night among the Tuareg one could be excused for thinking one was among a people without arms.

We left within the hour, just Byrne, Billson and myself in the Toyota, heading for Agadez. Four hours later Byrne swung off the track and we found Hamiada camped in a grove of doum palms. 'This is where you leave us,' Byrne said to Paul. 'Hamiada will take you to the other side of Agadez. We'll join you later tonight.' He had a few words with Hamiada, then we left them and rejoined the track.

We filled up with petrol and water at the filling station in Agadez and I noticed Byrne paying special attention to the tyres. He talked briefly with the owner and then we set off again. Byrne said, 'There's another batch of sightings but they're all duplicate.'

Going by the mosque we were held up for a moment by

the giraffe which was strolling up the street. Byrne nudged me. 'Look there.' He nodded towards the Hotel de l'Aïr. A Range-Rover was parked outside.

'Kissack?'

'Could be. Let's find out.' He swung across the dusty street and parked next to the Range-Rover. We got out and he studied it, then produced a knife and bent down to the rear wheel.

'What are you doing?'

He straightened and put the knife away. 'Just put my mark on a tyre,' he said. 'It'll be comforting to know if Kissack's around or not.' He looked at the hotel entrance. 'Let's go talk to him.'

'Is that wise?'

'He's looking for me, ain't he? And I know it. It would be the neighbourly thing to do. If this is Kissack he has a bad habit of shooting folks without as much as a word of greeting. If a guy's going to shoot at me I'd like to get to know him before he does. That's what I didn't like about the Army Air Force – you got shot at by strangers.'

I said, 'You're the boss.'

'Damn right,' he said. 'Now, pull up your veil, and when we go in there don't sit down – just stand behind me. And don't say a goddamn word under any circumstances.' He reached into the back of the Toyota and pulled out a sword. 'Put that on.'

I slung on the sword in the way I had seen Mokhtar wear his, and followed Byrne into the hotel. So I was a Targui, a good enough disguise. I wasn't worried about my colour; all anyone could see of me were my eyes and my hands, and the backs of my hands were deeply tanned. Anyway, many of the Tuareg were lighter coloured than I was.

Byrne went up to the bar and questioned the barman who jerked a thumb towards an inner room. We went in to find it deserted except for two men sitting at a table. Paul had described them well. Kissack was a tall, thin man with fair hair who was not so much tanned as burned, the way the sun often affects fair-skinned people. Strips of skin were peeling from his forehead. Bailly was swarthy and the sun wouldn't affect him much.

Byrne said, 'I'm Byrne. I hear you've been looking for me.'

Kissack looked up and his eyes widened. '*You* are Byrne?'

'Yeah.' Byrne lowered his veil. I wondered if Kissack knew that was a mark of contempt.

Kissack smiled. 'Sit down, Mr Byrne. Have a drink?' He was English, probably a Londoner to judge by his accent.

'Thanks.' Byrne sat down. 'I'll have a beer.' Kissack's eyes wandered past him to rest on me thoughtfully. Byrne jerked his thumb at me. 'He don't drink; it's against his religion. He'll have a lemonade.'

Kissack held up his arm and a waiter came and took the order. 'My name is Kissack. This is M'sieur Bailly.'

Bailly merely grunted, and Byrne nodded shortly. Kissack said, 'I understand you are interested in aeroplanes, Mr Byrne.'

'Yeah.'

'Crashed aeroplanes.'

'Yeah.'

Kissack narrowed his eyes as he studied Byrne. He was getting the answers he wanted, but they were too monosyllabic for his taste. 'May I ask why?' he said smoothly.

'Guess it's because I used to be a flier myself.'

'I see. Just a general interest.'

'Yeah.'

Kissack's eyes flickered to Bailly, who grunted again. It was a sound of disbelief. 'Any particular aircraft you're interested in.'

'Not really. They're all interesting.'

'I see. What's the most interesting aeroplane you've come across so far?'

The waiter came back. He put a beer on the table and handed me a glass of lemonade. Byrne didn't answer immediately but picked up his glass and studied the bubbles.

'I guess it's the wreck of an Avro Avian up in the Tanezrouft. Got quite a history. Name of *Southern Cross Minor*. Owned by Kingsford-Smith who flew it from Australia to England in 1931. Then a guy called Lancaster bought it to try to beat Amy Mollison's record to Cape Town.' He drank some beer, then added drily, 'He didn't.'

Kissack seemed interested. 'When was this?'

'1933. The wreck wasn't found until 1962. The desert hides things, Mr Kissack.'

'Any other old aeroplanes?'

'None as old as that – far as I know.'

Byrne was playing with Kissack, teasing him to say outright what he wanted. I pushed the glass of lemonade under my veil and sipped. It was quite refreshing.

'Any about as old?'

'Well, let's see,' said Byrne reflectively. 'There are a couple of dozen wrecks from the war littered about in places too difficult to get them out. I wrecked one of those myself.'

'No – from before the war?'

'Not many of those. What's *your* interest, Mr Kissack?'

'I'm a reporter,' said Kissack. 'Investigative stuff.'

'In the Sahara?' queried Byrne sardonically.

Kissack spread his hands. 'Busman's holiday. I'm just touring around and I guess my journalistic instincts got the better of me.'

Byrne nodded his head towards Bailly. 'He a reporter, too?'

'Oh no. M'sieur Bailly is my guide.'

Bailly looked more suited to be a guide to the murkier regions of the Kasbah in Algiers. Byrne said, 'Is that all you wanted me for?' He drained his glass.

Kissack stretched out his hand. 'How long have you lived here, Mr Byrne?'

'Thirty-five years.'

'Then please stay. I'd like to talk to you. It's nice to be able to talk to someone again in my own language. I have very

173

little French and M'sieur Bailly has no English at all.' H
was a damned liar; Bailly was taking in every word. Kissack
said, 'Have another beer, Mr Byrne – that is, if you're not in
a hurry.'

Byrne appeared to hesitate, then said, 'I'm going no place.
All right, I'll have another beer. You want to pick my
brains, that's the payment.'

'Good,' said Kissack enthusiastically, and signalled for a
waiter. 'You'll be able to fill me in on local colour – it's
hard for Bailly to get it across.'

'I'll do my best,' said Byrne modestly.

The waiter took the order and I gave him my empty glass.
Kissack said casually, 'Ever come across a man called
Billson?'

'Know of him. Never did get to meet him.'

'Ah!' Kissack was pleased. 'Do you know where he is?'

'He's dead, Mr Kissack,' said Byrne.

'Are you sure of that?'

'Well, I can't say I am,' admitted Byrne. 'There was no
death certificate. But I reckon he's dead, all right.'

Kissack frowned. 'How do you know?'

'Hell!' said Byrne. 'He must be. His airplane crashed over
forty years ago. You don't suppose he's still walking across
the desert like the children of Israel?'

Kissack said in a choked voice, 'That's not the Billson I
meant.'

'No?' said Byrne. 'I thought you were still on the airplane
kick.' The waiter put a beer in front of him and he picked it
up.

'Your Billson,' said Kissack softly. 'When did that happen?'

'Was in 1936 during the London to Cape Town Air Race.'
He shrugged. 'And he's not my Billson.'

'Do you know where *that* aeroplane is?'

'Nobody knows where it is,' said Byrne. 'I told you – the
desert hides things. Hell, you could hide an air fleet in three
million square miles.' He drank some beer. 'Not that I

wouldn't be interested in it if someone found it.'

'You wouldn't be looking for it?' asked Kissack.

'Why in hell would I be doing that? I've better things to do with my time. When that airplane is found it'll be in a goddamn nasty part of the desert, else it would have shown up by now. I've better things to do than risk my neck like that.'

Kissack put his hand to his breast pocket. From it he extracted a piece of paper which he unfolded and laid on the table. It was one of Byrne's leaflets. 'I'm unable to read this myself but Bailly translated it for me,' he said. 'I found it remarkably interesting.'

'Yeah, I suppose a reporter might.'

'And you still say you're not looking for that aeroplane?'

'Not specifically – no.' Byrne pointed to the leaflet. 'That's something I distribute every three-four years – more in hope than anything else. I told you, I was a flier during the war. Flying in North Africa, too. I'm interested in desert airplanes, especially since I put one there myself. Might write a book about them.'

'A scholarly monograph, no doubt,' said Kissack sarcastically. '*Some Aspects of Air Disasters in the Sahara.*'

'I know it sounds nutty,' said Byrne. 'But it's my hobby. Most folks' hobbies seem nutty to someone or other. Ever thought how crazy stamp collecting is?'

'Expensive, too,' said Kissack. 'Ten camels must be worth a lot of money.'

'Might seem so to you.' Byrne shrugged. 'I breed them.' He grinned at Kissack. 'Get them at cost price, as you might say. And it ain't much, spread over three or four years.'

Kissack wore a baffled look. The yarn Byrne was spinning was just mad enough to be true. He took a deep breath, and said, 'The man I'm looking for is Paul Billson.'

'*Paul* Billson.' Byrne tasted the word along with some beer. '*Paul* Billson.' He shook his head. 'Can't say I've heard of him. Any relation?'

'I don't know,' said Kissack flatly. He prodded the leaflet

with his forefinger. 'Get any results from that?'

'Not so far. Just the same goddamn list I got last time I put it out.'

Kissack looked at him for a long time wordlessly. Byrne stirred, and said, 'Anything more you'd like to know?'

'Not for the moment,' said Kissack.

Byrne stood up. 'Well, you know where to find me again if you want me. Up near Timia. Nice to have visited with you, Mr Kissack. Hope I've been of help.' He nodded pleasantly to Bailly. '*Bonjour, M'sieur Bailly.*'

Bailly grunted.

As we drove away from the hotel I said, 'Well, now we know.'

'Yeah,' said Byrne laconically. After a while he said, 'That guy gives me a real creepy feeling.'

'Why should he be looking for Paul? He must have written him off as dead.'

'It must have come as a hell of a shock to him,' said Byrne. 'He knocks off Paul, then the whole goddamn Sahara is flooded with questionnaires about crashed airplanes – and coming from Niger, for God's sake! He must have been a confused boy.'

'But he was quick off the mark.' I thought about it. 'Good thing we didn't bring Paul into town.' I laughed. 'That was a crazy yarn you spun him.'

'It won't hold him long,' said Byrne. 'He'll ask around and find I've never done a damnfool thing like that before. I'm hoping he'll go up to Timia – that'll give us some space between us. If he wastes his time on Timia we'll be the other side of Bilma before he finds out he's lost us.'

Twenty-One

We drove east out of Agadez for about five miles, then left the track to rendezvous with Hamiada at the place appointed. Hamiada had already made camp and had a tent erected. We stayed there the night and slept early in preparation for an early start to cross the Ténéré.

Next morning I gave Billson the jeans and shirts I had bought. 'You can't wander around the Sahara in a business suit,' I said. 'You'd better wear these. I think they'll fit.'

He rejected them and I said, 'Paul, you're a damned fool! Kissack, back there, has your description and he knows what you're wearing.' I shrugged. 'But please yourself.'

Paul changed his clothing fast.

I noticed that Hamiada had cut a lot of acacia branches which he tied in bundles and put in the back of the truck. When I asked Byrne about this he said, 'If we want hot food we have to have fuel.' He nodded towards the east. 'There's nothing out there.'

Hamiada left, taking the camels and going back to Timia. We went in the opposite direction, at first due east, and then curving to the north-east. For the first fifty miles it wasn't too bad; the track was reasonably good and we were able to hold an average speed of about thirty miles an hour. But then the track petered out and we were on rough ground which gradually gave way to drifts of sand, and finally, the sand dunes themselves.

'So this is what you call an *erg*,' I said.

Byrne laughed shortly. 'Not yet.' He indicated a crescent-shaped dune we were passing. 'These are barchan dunes. They're on the move all the time, driven by the wind. Not very fast – but they move. All the sand is on the move, that's why there's no track here.'

Presently the isolated barchan dunes gave way to bigger sand structures, rolling hills of sand. The mountains of the Aïr had long disappeared below the horizon behind us. Byrne drove skilfully, keeping to the bottom of the valleys and threading his way among the dunes. I wondered how he knew which way to go, but he didn't seem worried. As we went he discoursed on the different types of sand.

'This ain't too bad,' he said. 'At least you can stop without getting into trouble. *Fech-fech* is the worst.'

'What's that?'

'Sometimes you get times of high humidity – high for the desert, anyway. At night in winter the moisture freezes out of the air and forms dew on the surface of the sand. That makes a hard crust on the top with soft sand underneath. Driving on that is okay if you keep moving, but if you stop you're likely to break through and go down to your axles.' He paused and said reflectively, 'Don't bother a camel none, though.'

Another time he said, 'A few years ago I was up north, round about Hassi-Messaoud where the oil-wells are. I came across a big truck – could carry a hundred tons. Russian, it was; used for carrying oil rigs about. The guys who were driving it were Russians, too, and they showed me how it worked. It had eight axles, sixteen big balloon tyres and you could let air out and pump air in by pressing buttons in the cab. They reckoned that with a full load they could jiggle things so that the weight on the ground per square inch was no more than that of a camel. A real nice toy it was.'

'Ingenious.'

'Yeah.' He laughed. 'But they were sloppy about it. They had five of the tyres on wrong way around. Anyway, a few weeks later I heard what happened to it. They were driving along and decided to stop for the night. So they stopped, had something to eat, and went to sleep. But they stopped on *fech-fech* and during the night the truck broke through. The

Russians were sleeping underneath it and it killed them both. They never did get it out.'

A nice illustrative and macabre story of the dangers of the desert. Byrne said, 'Lousy stinkpots! Never have liked them except when I'm in a hurry, like now.'

After a while the sand dunes levelled off into a plain of sand, and presently Byrne said, 'The Tree!' On the far horizon ahead was a black dot which might well have been an optical illusion – a speck of dust on the eyeball – but which proved to be a solitary wide-spreading thorn tree. There was a well near the tree and the ground all about was littered with the olive-shaped pellets of camel dung. There were also several skeletons of camels, some still covered with hide, mummified in the dry, hot desert air.

Byrne said, 'We'll stop here for something to eat – but not near the well. Too many biting bugs.'

As we drove past, Paul, behind me, said, 'There's someone standing by the tree.'

'So there is,' said Byrne. 'Just one man. That's unusual here. Let's go see who he is.'

He pulled over the wheel and we stopped just by the tree. The man standing there was not a Targui because he wore no veil and his skin was darker, a deep rich brown. He was shorter than the average Targui and not as well dressed. His *gandoura* was black and his head cloth in ill array.

Byrne got out and talked to the man for a few minutes, then came back to the truck. 'He's a Teda from the Tibesti. He's been hanging around here for three days waiting for someone to come along. He's heading east and he can't do the next stretch alone.'

'How did he get here?'

'Walked. Only just made it, too. Did the last two days without water. Do you mind if we give him a lift as far east as we're going?'

'It's your truck,' I said. 'And you're the boss.'

Byrne nodded and waved to the man, who came over to

the Toyota. He was carrying a shaggy goatskin bag which Byrne said was a *djerba*, used for holding water. Byrne tapped the bag and asked a question, pointing to the well. The man answered and then, at a command from Byrne, emptied the contents of the bag on the ground.

'It's okay to drink that stuff if you have to,' said Byrne. 'But not unless. An addax antelope fell into the well a few years ago and it's been no goddamn good since.'

As we drove away I said, 'What's his name?'

'He didn't say. He said his name used to be Konti.'

I frowned. 'That's a funny thing to say.'

'Not really,' said Byrne. 'It means he's a murderer.' He seemed unperturbed.

I twisted around to look at the man in the back of the truck, whose name used to be Konti. 'What the hell . . .'

'It's okay,' said Byrne. 'He won't kill us. He's not a professional murderer. He probably killed somebody in a blood feud back home and had to take it on the lam. Maybe he reckons it's now safe to go back or he's got word his family has paid the blood money.'

He stopped the truck about a mile the other side of the Tree. 'This will do.' We got out. From the back of the truck Byrne took what appeared to be a length of metal pipe. 'Help me fill this.'

There was a brass cap on the top which he unscrewed. I held a funnel while Byrne filled the contraption with water from a jerrican. As he did so he said, 'This is a volcano – the most economic way of boiling water there is.'

It was simple, really, consisting of a water jacket, holding about two pints, around a central chimney. Byrne poked a lighted spill of paper into a hole in the bottom, added a few twigs of acacia and, when the fire had taken hold of those, popped in a handful of pellets of dried camel dung which he had picked up near the tree. They burned fiercely, but with no smell. Within five minutes we had boiling water.

We lunched on bread and cheese and mint tea, our

murderer joining in. 'Ask him his name,' I said. 'I can't keep on referring to him as the man who used to be Konti.'

As Byrne talked to the man Paul said, 'I'm not going to ride with any murderer. Nobody asked me if he could come along.'

Byrne stopped abruptly and turned to Paul. 'Then you'll walk the rest of the way, either forward or back.' He jerked his head. 'He's probably a better man than you. And the reason you weren't asked is that I don't give a good god-damn what you like or what you don't like. Got it?' He didn't wait for a reply but went back to talking in guttural tones.

I looked at Paul, whose face was as red as a boiled beet. I said softly, 'I told you to walk carefully around Byrne. You never learn, do you?'

'He can't talk to me like that,' he muttered.

'He just did,' I pointed out. 'And what the hell are you going to do about it? I'll tell you – you're going to do noth-ing, because Byrne is the only thing standing between you and being dead.'

He lapsed into a sulky silence.

Byrne finished his interrogation and turned back to me. 'He says it's okay for you to call him Konti now. I don't speak his lingo well, but he has some Arabic – and I was just about right. He killed a man three years ago in the Tibesti and ran away. He's just learned that the blood money has been paid so he's going back.' He paused. 'Blood camels, really; there's not much hard cash in the Tibesti.'

'How many camels are worth a man's life?'

'Five.'

'Half a 1930s aeroplane,' I commented.

'You could put it that way,' he said. 'The change of name is a pure ritual, of course. You know what he'd do when he ran away? He'd kill an antelope, take a length of its large intestine, and pull it on to his feet like socks. Then he'd jump up and down till it broke. Symbolic breaking of the trail, you see.'

'Weird,' I said.

'Yeah; funny people, the Teda. Related to the Tuareg but a long ways back.' He looked up at the sun. 'Let's go. I want to be the other side of Fachi before nightfall.'

We pressed on and entered an area where again there were large dunes, some of them several hundred feet high. I realized that Byrne was doing all the driving and offered to spell him but he rejected the idea. 'Later, maybe; but not now. You'd get us stuck. There's an art in driving in soft sand, and you have to hit these rises at just the right angle.'

Once I glimpsed an animal with large ears scurrying over the edge of a dune. Byrne said it was a fennec. 'Desert fox. Gets its moisture from eating insects and jerboas. Jerboas make water right in their own bodies. Least, that's what a guy told me who was out here studying them. That fennec wouldn't show himself in daytime in summer; too goddamn hot.'

Fachi was a small, miserable oasis a little over a hundred miles from the Tree of Ténéré. The people were Negroid and the women wore rings in their noses. 'These people are Fulani,' said Byrne with an edge of contempt in his voice. 'The Tuareg don't like 'em, and they don't like the Tuareg. We're not staying here – they'd steal us blind.'

We stopped only long enough to fill the water cans and to buy a goat kid which Byrne efficiently killed and butchered, then we went on for ten miles and camped just as the sun was setting. We cooked a meal, then ate and slept, and were on our way again at dawn next day.

We drove mile after rolling mile among the dunes and sometimes over them when there was no other recourse. Once I said to Byrne, 'How the devil do you know which way to go?'

'There's an art in that, too,' he said. 'You've got to know what the prevailing wind was during the last few months. That sets the angle of the dunes and you can tell your direction by that. It don't change much from year to year but enough to throw you off and get you lost. And you keep an eye on the sun.'

It was nearly midday when we rose over the crest of a dune and Byrne said, 'There's the *azelai.*'

'What?'

'The salt caravan Mokhtar is taking to Bilma. He's two days out of Fachi.'

That gave me a clue as to the difference between the speed of a camel and that of a Toyota. 'How long from Agadez to Bilma?'

'Four weeks. Two or three weeks in Bilma to rest up, then back again with the salt. Best part of three months for the round trip.'

The caravan consisted of about three hundred camels and perhaps twenty camel drivers. 'Fifty of these are mine,' said Byrne, and hailed Mokhtar. He came towards the truck with the slow, lazy saunter of the Tuareg, looked at me in surprise, and then laughed and said something to Byrne who chuckled and said, 'Mokhtar thinks I've got a convert. He wants to know if I'm setting up in competition with the Prophet.'

He examined his animals and expressed satisfaction at their condition, and then we went on, and the caravan, plodding its slow three-miles-an-hour pace, was soon left behind.

It was at about three that afternoon when the offside front tyre burst and the steering-wheel slewed violently in Byrne's hands. 'Goddamn!' he said, and brought us to a halt.

There was a whipcrack at my ear and the windscreen shattered. I had been shot at in Korea and I knew a bullet when I heard one, even without the evidence of the broken windscreen. 'Everyone out,' I yelled. 'We're under fire.'

I jerked at the door handle and jumped out. The bullet had come from my side, so I ran around the truck to get into cover. As I did so a fountain of sand spurted a yard ahead of me. Paul was still in the truck, not being quick enough off the mark, and I found Byrne hauling him out. I discovered that I was holding the Walther pistol in my hand although I couldn't remember drawing it.

The shooting was still going on, sharp cracks in the dead, dry air. I judged it to be a rifle. But no bullets were coming anywhere near us. Byrne nudged me. 'Look!' He pointed upwards to the dune behind us.

Konti, the Teda, was running up the dune and was already three-quarters of the way to the top, which was about sixty feet. His *gandoura* fluttered in the breeze of his passage, and bullets sent the sand flying about his feet. At the top, silhouetted against the sky, he seemed to stumble, then he fell rather than jumped over the other side of the dune and was gone from sight. The shooting stopped.

'Think he was hit?'

'Don't know,' said Byrne, and opened the rear door of the Toyota. He put his arm inside and withdrew the Lee-Enfield rifle. 'I think Kissack got ahead of us.' He took a full magazine from the pouch at his neck and loaded the rifle.

There was another shot and a thump, then the metallic howl of a ricochet off metal. The truck quivered on its springs. 'The bastards have us pinned down,' said Byrne. 'If we try to make a run for it now we'll be dead meat.' He looked up at the dune behind us. 'That guy only got away because he did the unexpected. I guess he's been shot at before.'

'If he did get away.'

Another bullet slammed into the side of the truck.

'Yeah.'

I looked around for Billson and found him scrunched up behind the rear wheel, making himself as small as possible. Byrne followed my glance. 'He won't be much help,' he said flatly. 'We can count him out.'

'So what do we do?'

'Shoot back.'

There was a *thunk* and a soft explosive blast of air as

184

another tyre went. Byrne said, 'He does that once more and we're stuck. I only have two spares. See if you can locate the son of a bitch.'

Carefully I raised my head, looking through the windows of the Toyota. I stared at the dune I saw which was about a hundred feet high, and ran my eye along the line of the crest. There was another shot which hit the truck and then I saw a slight movement.

I ducked down. 'He's on top of the dune and about twenty degrees to the left.'

'How far?'

'Hard to say. Two fifty to three hundred yards. It'll be an uphill shot.'

'Uh-huh!' Byrne adjusted the sight on the rifle. 'Now let the dog see the rabbit. And, for Christ's sake, keep that handgun ready and watch our flanks.'

I stood back at a crouch as Byrne pushed the barrel of the rifle through the open window in the door of the truck. I glanced from side to side but nothing moved. 'I see him,' said Byrne softly. They fired together and Byrne ducked. The truck shivered on its springs. 'I think I put some sand in his eyes,' he said.

There was silence broken only by metallic creakings from the cooling engine and a soft liquid gurgling noise. I was beginning to think Byrne was right when there came another shot and a bullet went right through both open windows of the truck, breaking the sound barrier about six inches above my head with a vicious crack.

Byrne said, 'I'll bet he moved. If I can do that again be ready to make a break for it. Then try to out-flank them. If we don't do something we'll be shot to bits just standing here.'

'All right.'

He raised his head and looked up at the dune. 'Yeah, he moved. Now where in hell is he?' Another bullet came our way with disastrous effect. It slammed into the tyre on the wheel behind which Billson crouched and there was a *whoosh* as the air escaped.

'That's buggered it!' said Byrne. Paul was whimpering and trying to burrow his way into the soft sand. 'We won't get far on three wheels, but I've got the bastard spotted.'

He brought up the rifle again and prepared to fire. I said, 'Hold it, Luke!' and put all the urgency I could into my voice.

He lowered his head. 'What is it?'

I knew what that gurgling noise had meant. 'He's either got the petrol tank or one of the fuel cans. Can't you smell it?' Byrne sniffed the stink of petrol. I said, 'You shoot that thing and we could go up in flames in a big way. It only needs a spark.'

'Jesus!' He withdrew the rifle and stared at me, and the same thing was in both our minds. It would need only a spark from a ricochet off metal to fire the vapourizing petrol.

I said, 'I made that mistake in Korea, and I've got burned skin to prove it.'

'I wondered about that puckering on your chest. We'd better run for it then. Different directions. I think there's only one guy shooting; he won't get us both.'

'What about Paul?'

'He can do what the hell he likes.'

A bullet smashed into a headlight and glass flew.

'All right,' I said. 'Immediately after the next shot.'

Byrne nodded.

There was no next shot – not from the rifle, but faintly in the distance someone screamed, an ululating noise of pure agony which went on and on. I jerked, torn from the tension of waiting to run into a greater tension. I stared at Byrne. 'What's that?'

The scream still went on, now broken into sobbing screeches as someone fought for breath. 'Someone's hurting, that's for sure,' he said. There were distant shots, not from the rifle but from pistols in my judgement. Then the screaming stopped and again there was silence.

We listened for a long time and heard nothing at all. After a while I said, 'I think . . .'

'Quiet!' snapped Byrne.

In the distance was the unmistakable noise of a balky starter turning an engine over. It whined a few more times and then the quieter engine must have fired because the noise stopped. Byrne said, 'Maybe they're leaving.'

'Maybe it's a trick to get us in the open.' He nodded at that so we stayed there.

After perhaps ten minutes there was a shout and I looked up at the dune, careful to keep cover. Standing up there was Konti and he was shouting and waving. Byrne took a deep breath. 'I'll be goddamned! Let's go see.'

We climbed the dune and Konti started to jabber at Byrne with much gesticulation. He was very excited and understandably so; it had been an exciting fifteen minutes. He pointed down to the valley on the other side of the dune and he and Byrne walked down with me following because I wanted to know what was going on.

There were tyre tracks down there and someone had shed a lot of blood, perhaps a pint or more. Byrne squatted down and pointed to where a tyre had gone over blood-dampened sand. 'Kissack,' he said. 'That's the mark I put in his rear tyre.'

'What happened?'

'What happened is that you can thank God we picked up Konti yesterday. He probably saved our lives.'

'How?'

Byrne talked to Konti for a few minutes then said to me, 'He says there were three men here. From the description he gives they were Kissack, Bailly and another guy, probably an Arab. Kissack and the Arab were up top on the dune with Kissack doing the shooting. Bailly was standing here by the car. So Konti came around here and threw a knife at him.'

'A knife!' I said blankly. 'And that was what all the screaming was about?' I couldn't think why. A man with a knife in him didn't usually make that kind of row, but of course it would depend where the knife hit him. I looked around, then said, 'How did Konti get close enough to throw a knife? There's no cover.'

'You ain't seen the knife,' said Byrne. 'After it hit Bailly it buried itself in the sand. Konti picked it up before he called us.'

He said something to Konti and held out his hand. Konti fumbled about his person and produced the knife, which was like no knife I'd ever seen before. It was about eighteen inches long and made out of a single piece of flat steel an eighth of an inch thick. The handle was a foot long but the rest of it is hard to describe. It curved in a half-circle and two other blades projected at right-angles with hooks on the end. There seemed to be a multiplicity of cutting edges, each as sharp as a razor. It was very rusty.

'That's a *mouzeri*,' said Byrne. 'The Teda throwing knife. It's thrown horizontally from below waist level and it'll stop a horse going at full gallop. It's used for hunting addax and oryx but it'll also chop a man off at the ankles at sixty yards. Bailly didn't know what hit him, but Konti says it damn near took his left foot right off and badly injured his right ankle.'

I looked at the rusty blades. 'If he doesn't die of loss of blood it'll be by blood-poisoning,' I observed. What this thing had done to Bailly was enough to make anyone scream.

'I hope so,' said Byrne harshly. He took the queer-shaped knife and gave it back to Konti, who grinned cheerfully. 'Konti says it's the same knife he used to kill his enemy with in the Tibesti.' He looked down at the blood on the sand and shrugged. 'Let's go see what the damage is.'

The damage was bad. Three tyres shot to pieces and only two spares. But that wasn't the worst, because the petrol tank had a hole in it. We had refilled from the jerricans not long before the shooting and there wasn't nearly enough petrol to take us to Bilma even if we had good tyres.

I said, 'Well, we've got plenty water and food. All we have to do is to sit tight until Mokhtar comes along, then we can hitch a ride on a camel.'

'Yeah,' said Byrne. 'Good thinking – but for one thing. He ain't coming this way.'

Twenty-Two

Billson had still not got over his fit of the quivers. I couldn't say that I blamed him; being shot at takes different men in different ways, and Paul had not been the most stable man to begin with. And there was something else that Paul had to contend with which did not obtain under war conditions. He lived with the knowledge that he was being hunted personally, that someone malevolent was pursuing him with intent to kill. Every bullet that came our way had Paul's name engraved upon it.

And so he was in no shape to take an immediate part in the discussion. Konti, while being wise in desert ways, knew little about the Ténéré; it was not his stamping ground. The same applied to me except the bit about desert ways, and so most of the decisions were made by Byrne.

After the flat statement that Mokhtar was not coming our way I merely said, 'Oh!' and waited for what he'd say next. What he did say was: 'That *djerba* is going to come in useful. We're going to walk a piece.'

'How far?'

He said, 'I came this way because it's a short cut and okay for a truck. The camel trail is fifteen miles to the south.'

After leaving Fachi I would have sworn that Byrne had navigated from camel skeleton to camel skeleton but I had seen none in the last few miles. And he had just given the reason why. 'Fifteen miles,' I said, feeling relieved. 'That's not far.'

Byrne said, 'We'll need to take water – as much as we can carry.'

'To walk fifteen miles?'

Byrne took me by the elbow and walked me out of Paul's

hearing. He said, 'It'll take us the rest of today and all day tomorrow. You ever walked in soft sand?'

'Not far.' I looked up the valley. 'But it doesn't seem too difficult.'

He followed my glance. 'The camel trail to Bilma is successful because it follows the grain of the country. You can go up the long valleys between the dunes. We'll be walking against the grain; you'll be going up and down dunes until you're dizzy. It's fifteen miles across country plus five miles of climbing up and another five miles going down. And there are other things to keep in mind.'

'Such as?'

He shook his head. 'I'll tell you if it's necessary. No point in you worrying about what may not happen. Let me do the worrying.'

He only succeeded in making me uneasy.

The first thing we did was to fill the *djerba* with water from a jerrican, then Byrne looked me up and down. 'How much weight do you reckon you can carry?'

I remembered army route marches which were not so much for use in these mechanized days as to toughen the men. Officers were supposed to do better than the men. I picked a figure, then hastily revised it downwards as I thought of climbing interminably in soft sand. 'Forty pounds.'

Byrne shook his head. 'Too much. A jerrican half-full for you and Paul; that's about thirty pounds each. Konti can take his *djerba*; he's used to it.'

We took a full jerrican and split it between two, then made slings so the jerricans could be back-packed, taking care to put in plenty of padding to avoid chafe. Byrne made us take the *djellabas*. 'It gets cold at night.' I noted that the jerrican he picked to carry himself was full. That would be a killing load for a man on the wrong side of sixty if what he had said about our journey was true, but I said nothing about it. He knew what he was doing.

We then ate and stuffed what was left of the bread and cheese and a few scraps of meat into the breast pockets of our *gandouras.* 'Drink hearty,' advised Byrne. 'Water is better in you than out. Any camel knows that.'

When Byrne had spoken of water in the past he had referred to litres or gallons interchangeably, but his gallons were American. I estimated that we moved away carrying eight and a half imperial gallons in jerricans plus what was in the *djerba* which was difficult to estimate – say, nearly twelve gallons in all. It seemed a lot of water to take for a fifteen-mile hike and I wondered what possibilities were lurking in Byrne's mind.

My memories of the journey I seldom care to reflect upon. The most insistent thing that comes to mind is the soft, yet gritty, sand. A building contractor would have delighted in it because it would be ideal for making high-quality cement and concrete and, no doubt, some sharp entrepreneur will find some way of shipping it out and making a profit. God knows, there's enough of it. But I can never now look upon an expanse of sand without feeling, in imagination, the cruel tug of that damned jerrican on my back.

We passed the place where Konti had hamstrung Bailly, crossed the valley and climbed another of the dunes which, in that place, were running from sixty to a hundred feet high. I suppose we were lucky in a way because the forward slopes which we had to climb were not as steep as the reverse slopes. Had we been going north instead of south it would have been much worse.

I watched Byrne going ahead of me across a valley floor and it came to me that there was some significance to that languid, gliding walk of the Tuareg – it came from much walking in sand, using the most economical means possible. I tried to imitate it without much success; you had to have been born with it or trained by the years like Byrne. My feet were more accustomed to city pavements.

We climbed another dune, feet digging into the sand against insistent pull of the back packs, and sometimes slipping backwards. On the crest I paused for breath and looked around. Byrne had well described an *erg* as a sea of sand. The Ténéré was like a still picture of a storm at sea, the waves frozen in mid-heave. But these waves were bigger than any wave of water and stretched interminably as far as I could see.

The sun was setting, casting long shadows into the troughs, and the crest of the dune on which I was standing wound sinuously for many miles until it dipped out of sight. The dunes themselves were soft and smooth, sculptured by the wind, unmarked by footprint, whether of man or animal.

Byrne gestured impatiently and we went slipping and sliding down the other and steeper side. Many times during that awful journey I lost control during these descents. The jerrican on my back would seem to push and I would lose my balance and fall headlong. Luckily the sand was soft and cushiony, but not so soft in individual grains that it wasn't also abrasive, and the skin of my hands became tender.

If I was suffering like that, what of Billson? I had lived a sedentary city life but had tried to temper myself and keep in condition by gymnastics and fencing. Paul had worked for fifteen years in the same dreary office in Luton and, from what I had gathered during the course of investigating his life he hadn't done much to keep fit. But the odd thing was that during this time he didn't complain once. He stolidly climbed and just as stolidly picked himself up when he slipped and fell, and kept up the same speed as the rest of us, which wasn't all that slow with Byrne setting the pace.

I was slowly coming to a conclusion about Paul. Some men may be sprinters, good in the short haul and competent in a crisis. Paul might prove to be the reverse. While not handling crises particularly well he was tenacious and stubborn, as proved by his lifelong obsession about his father, and this stroll across the Ténéré was bringing out his best qualities. Be that as it may, he did as well as anyone on that journey, ill-conditioned though his body was for it.

We stopped on top of a dune just as the sun was dipping

below the horizon, and Byrne said, 'Okay; you can take off your packs.'

It was a great relief to get rid of that jerrican which had seemed to increase in weight with every step I took. Billson slumped down and in the red light of the setting sun his face was grey. I remembered that he had been shot in the shoulder not many weeks before, and said gently, 'Here, Paul; let me help you.' I helped him divest himself of his back pack, and said, 'How's your shoulder?'

'All right,' he said dully.

'Let me look at it.' His chest was heaving as he drew panting breaths after that last climb and he made no move, so I unbuttoned the front of his shirt and looked at his shoulder before it became too dark to see. The wound, which had been healing well, was now inflamed and red. It would seem that the pull of the jerrican on the improvised harness was chafing him. I said, 'Luke, look at this.'

Byrne came over and inspected Paul. He said, 'We drink the water out of his can first.'

'And perhaps we can transfer some into my can.'

'Maybe,' he said noncommittally. 'Let's eat.'

Our dinner that night was cold and unappetizing. The stars came out as the light ebbed away in the west and the temperature dropped. Byrne said, 'Better wear *djellabas*.'

As I put mine on I asked, 'How far have we come?'

'Mile and a half – maybe two miles.'

'Is that all?' I was shattered. It seemed more like five or six.

'More'n I expected.' Byrne nodded towards Billson. 'I thought he'd hold us up. He still might. I suggest you take some of his water. Do it now before we leave.'

'Leave! You're not going on in the dark?'

'Damn right I am. We're in a hurry. Don't worry; I have a compass and the moon will rise later.'

I put half of Billson's water into my jerrican, reflecting that Byrne was still carrying a full one. He gathered us together.

'We're moving off now. So far you've not done much talking. That's good because you needed your breath. But now you talk because it's dark – you don't lose contact with anyone and you don't let them lose contact with you. It'll be slow going but we need every yard we can make.'

He said something to Konti, probably repeating what he'd told us, then we descended from the top of the dune. It was damned difficult in the dark, and Byrne kept up a constant grunting, 'Ho! Ho! Ho!', sounding like a demented Santa Claus. But it was enough to let us know where he was, and I was encouraged to raise my own voice in song.

At the bottom he rounded us up and we set off across the valley floor under those glittering stars. I sang again; a ditty from my army days:

> 'Uncle George and Auntie Mabel
> Fainted at the breakfast table.
> Let this be an awful warning
> Not to do it in the morning.'

I paused. 'Billson, are you all right?'

'Yes,' he said wearily. 'I'm all right.'

From the left Konti made a whickering noise. He sounded like a horse. Byrne grunted, 'Ho! Ho! Ho!'

> 'Ovaltine has put them right,
> Now they do it morn and night;
> Uncle George is hoping soon
> To do it in the afternoon.
> Hark the Herald Angels sing,
> "Ovaltine is damned good thing."'

Billson made the first attempt at a witticism that I had heard pass his lips. 'Were you a Little Ovaltiney?'

I bumped into Byrne. 'Now we've had the commercial,' he said acidly. 'Let's get climbing.'

So up we went – slowly.

I didn't know then how long we stumbled along in the dark but it seemed like hours. Later Byrne said he'd called a halt just before midnight, so that meant a six-hour night march at probably not more than half a mile an hour. He stopped unexpectedly when we were half way up a slope, and said, 'This is it. Dig in.'

Thankfully I eased the jerrican from me and massaged my aching shoulders. In the light of the moon I saw Billson just lying there. I crawled over to him and helped him out of his harness, then made sure his *djellaba* was wrapped around him, and built up a small rampart of sand on the downhill side of him to prevent him rolling to the bottom in his sleep. Before I left him he had passed out.

I crawled over to Byrne and demanded in an angry whisper, 'What the hell's the flaming hurry? Paul's half dead.'

'He will be dead if we don't get to where we're going by nightfall tomorrow,' said Byrne unemotionally.

'What do you mean?'

'Well, an *azelai* don't stop at sunset like we've usually been doing. Mokhtar will push on until about eleven every night. 'Course, it's easy for them, they're going along the valley bottoms.'

'How does he navigate?'

'Stars,' said Byrne. 'And experience. Now, I figure to get to where he'll be passing through before sundown, and I also figure that he'll be passing through some time during the night. Camels don't have headlights and tail lights, you know; and an *azelai* moves along goddamn quiet, like. At night a caravan could pass within two hundred yards of you and you wouldn't know it, even though in daylight it would be in plain sight. That's why I want to get there when I can see.'

'See what?'

'I'll figure that out when I get there. Now go to sleep.'

I was about to turn away when I thought of something.

'What happens if we miss the caravan?'

'Then we walk to Bilma – that's why we brought all the water. Konti and I would make it. You might. Billson wouldn't.'

That was plain enough. I dug out a trench in the side of the dune to lie in, and hoped it didn't look too much like a grave. Then I pulled the *djellaba* closer around me, and lay down. I looked up at the pock-marked moon for a long time before I went to sleep. It must have been all of three minutes.

We drank all of Billson's remaining water the following morning and abandoned his jerrican. 'Soak yourselves in it,' advised Byrne. 'Get as much water into you as you can hold.'

Breakfast in the light of dawn was frugal and soon done with. I cleaned out the last few crumbs from my pocket, hoisted the jerrican on to my back with distaste, and was ready to go.

Billson said, 'Stafford, why don't we put half your water in here?' He kicked the discarded jerrican with a clang. 'I could carry it.'

I looked at him in surprise. That was the first time he had offered to do anything for anyone so far. Maybe there was hope of reclaiming him for the human race, after all. I said, 'Better put that to Byrne; his can is full.'

Byrne stepped over to Billson. 'Let's see your shoulder.' He examined it and shook his head. 'You couldn't do it, Paul. More abrasion and more sand in there and you'll get gangrene. Keep it wrapped up. Let's move.'

And so we set off again – 'Up the airy mountain, down the rushy glen' – the mountain bit was real enough and it was certainly airy on that cold morning, but there were no rushes and the valleys were anything but glen-like, although welcome enough because they gave a brief respite for level walking.

I pictured us as four ants toiling across a sand-box in a children's playground. At mid-morning, when we stopped to take on water, I said, 'To think I liked building sand castles when I was a kid.'

Byrne chuckled. 'I remember a drawing I once saw, a cartoon, you know. It was in a magazine Daisy Wakefield had up in Tam. There was a detachment of the Foreign Legion doing a march across country like this, and one guy is saying to the other, "I joined the Legion to forget her, but her name is Sandra." I thought that was real funny.'

'I'm glad you're keeping your sense of humour.'

Billson was doing all right. He didn't say much, but kept up with us just in front of Konti. I had the idea that Byrne had detailed Konti as rearguard to keep an eye on Paul. Although he kept up with us I doubt if he'd have been able to if he still had water to carry. His wound was troubling him; not that he complained about it, but I noticed he favoured his right arm when he took a tumble and fell.

There wasn't much point in stopping long at midday because we had nothing to eat and only needed to drink water. Byrne said, 'Okay, Max; take off your pack.'

We had drunk from my jerrican at the mid-morning stop, so I said, 'No; you take off yours.'

The wrinkles about his eyes deepened as he stared at me, but then he said obligingly, 'Okay.' So we lightened his load by a few pounds between us.

That day I found I was glad to be wearing the Tuareg veil and the rest of the fancy dress. I could see that Paul, apart from anything else, was beginning to suffer from exposure whereas I was protected.

The rest of the day until sunset passed in a blur of exhaustion. Up one side, down the other, and still another one to come. Against the grain of the land, Byrne had said. It was a good descriptive phrase and I was now really beginning to find how good it was.

I fell into a blind, mindless rhythm and a chant was created in my mind – what the Germans call an 'earworm' – something that goes round and round in your head and you can't get rid of it. *One bloody foot before the next bloody foot. One bloody dune after the next bloody dune. One bloody foot before the next bloody foot. One bloody dune after the next bloody dune. One bloody* . . . It went on and on and on . . .

Maybe it helped me.

And so it went on for hour after hour until I staggered into Byrne who had stopped. So did my bloody foot. 'We made it just in time.' He looked at the sun. 'Three-quarters of an hour to nightfall.'

'We're there?' I said thickly, and looked down the side of the dune. The valley bottom didn't look much different than any of the others we'd crossed.

'Yeah. Mokhtar will be coming along there.'

I looked around. 'Where's Billson?'

'Maybe a quarter-mile back. Konti's looking after him. Let's go down.'

When we got to the bottom I looked up and saw Paul and Konti silhouetted against the sky at the top of the dune. 'You mean we can rest now?'

'No,' said Byrne relentlessly. He started to walk up the valley so I followed. I was tired but at least this was reasonably level ground and I didn't have to go up and down. The dunes began to close in on either side and then the valley widened. Byrne stopped. 'This is the place. How wide would you say this valley is?'

'Quarter of a mile.'

'More. Six hundred yards. I want three trenches dug going up and down the valley. Each maybe ten yards long but I'd like more.'

That sounded like work and I wasn't in the mood for it. 'How deep?'

'Not much; just so that your feet can recognize it in the dark. We're all going to stand sentry tonight.'

The idea was simple and good. The trenches divided the width of the valley into four equal parts and the four of us would patrol back and forth, each on our 150-yard stretch. When our feet encountered a trench we'd know it was time to turn around smartly and go back, just like a sentry in front of Buck House. If the caravan was coming through, then statistically it was highly likely that one of us was going to run into a camel. And the walking would keep us awake.

I began to dig where Byrne indicated, heaping the soft sand aside with my hands because I had nothing else to dig with. But first I unloaded the jerrican and had some water. Billson and Konti came down and were put to work, and by nightfall we had done all we could do, not to Byrne's satisfaction but that couldn't be helped.

Then came the patrolling back and forth across the width of the valley, each in our own sector. I was weary and the slow trudge in the thick sand didn't help. Every so often my feet encountered the edge of the trench and I turned to go back. Say three hundred yards for the round trip, about six to the mile. I wondered how many miles I was going to walk that night. Still, it was better than the bloody dunes.

On a couple of occasions at a trench I met Byrne and we exchanged a word before we turned and went our opposite ways. If we could have synchronized our speeds we could have met every time, but there was no way of doing that in the darkness.

The night wore on and my pace became slower. I was desperately tired and it was only because I had to walk that I kept awake, although sometimes I wonder if at times I wasn't walking in my sleep. But the walking and a few hunger pangs kept me going.

I encountered Byrne again, and he said, 'Have you seen Konti?'

'We met a couple of patrols ago. He's awake, if that's what's worrying you.'

'It's not. I should be finding Billson, and I'm not.'

I sighed. 'He's had a harder day than most of us. He's clapped out.'

'It leaves a hole in the line. I'll feel better when the moon comes up.'

We didn't have to wait that long. There was a yell from Konti and a startled cry of '*Hai! Hai! Hai!*' as someone strove to quieten a plunging camel. Then a couple of Tuareg came up from *behind* us, from up the valley. Half of that caravan had got past us without anyone knowing until Konti had bumped into someone.

I sat down, exactly where I was. 'Luke,' I said. 'I'm going to sleep.'

Twenty-Three

And so I went into Bilma by camel. Paul did, too, but Byrne walked after the first day. Konti walked all the time. These men were seemingly indestructible. Mokhtar had camped where he found us, but we continued the next day and, as Byrne had said, well into the darkness before we camped again.

Then Byrne began to walk, as did all the Tuareg, and I noted his feet were bare. He walked lithely by the side of the camel I rode. I said, 'Is it normal to walk?'

'Yeah.'

'All the way from Agadez to Bilma?'

'And back.' He looked up. 'We're all humble camel drivers – like the Prophet.'

I thought about it, thinking how quickly we had traversed that fastness in the Toyota. 'I would have thought it would be more efficient to use trucks.'

'Oh, sure.' He pointed ahead. 'Bilma produces 4000 tons of salt a year. The whole export job could be done with twenty 20-tonners. If this was Algeria they'd use trucks. The bastards in the Maghreb are nuts on efficiency when it's profitable.'

'Then why not here?'

'Because the Niger government is sensible. A camel can carry a seventh of a ton so, to shift a year's salt you need 28,000 camels. Like I said, a camel is a fragile animal – for every day's work it must have a day's rest. So – three months on the salt trail means another three months' resting-up time and feeding. That's six months, which takes care of the winter season. No one comes across here in summer. So you do have to have 28,000 camels because each makes but one journey. At $180 each that's a capital investment of better than five million dollars. Add harness, wrappings, drivers' pay and all that and you can make it six million.'

'God!' I said. 'It would certainly pay to use trucks.'

'I haven't finished,' said Byrne. 'A camel can last four years in the business, so that means 7000 new animals needed every year. Somebody has to breed them; guys like me, but more usually like Hamiada. What with one thing and another there's two million dollars going to the breeders from the Bilma salt trade. And Bilma's not the only source of salt. In the Western Sahara there's Taoudenni which supplies Timbouctou and the whole Niger Bend area – that's much bigger than the Bilma trade.' He looked up at me. 'So it's illegal to carry salt on trucks. It would ruin the traditional economy and destroy the structure of the desert tribes if trucks were allowed.'

'I see,' I said thoughtfully. 'Humanitarianism versus efficiency.' It made sense, but I doubt if a hard-headed City businessman would have agreed.

'Look,' said Byrne. 'The Kaouar.'

Stretching across the horizon was a wall of mountains, blue-hazed with distance. 'Bilma?'

'Bilma,' he said with satisfaction.

Half a day later I could see welcome tints of green, the first sight of vegetation since leaving Fachi, and soon I could distinguish individual date palms. Byrne hastened ahead to talk to Mokhtar, then came back. 'We won't go into Bilma – not yet,' he said. 'Kissack might be there and so we have to go in carefully. We'll stop at the salt workings at Kalala.'

Kalala proved to be a plain with heaps of soil thrown up from the salt workings. There were many men and more camels as several other caravans were in residence. Our camels were unloaded of their cargo and Byrne pointed out the sights. He indicated the group of men around Mokhtar. 'More Tuareg from the Aïr. I guess they'll be going back tomorrow. They look ready.' He swung around. 'Those guys, there, are Kanuri up from Chad. Salt is the most important substance in Africa. If the animals don't get it they go sick. The Kanuri from Chad are cattlemen, so they need salt. So are the Hausa from around Kano in Nigeria.'

'How long has this been going on?'

'I wouldn't know. A thousand years – maybe more. You stay here, Max; see that Paul doesn't wander. I'm going into Bilma to borrow a truck – I want to retrieve the Toyota. Also to see if Kissack is here.'

'Be careful.'

'I'm just another Targui,' he said. 'The veil is useful.'

He went away and I collected Billson and we went to look at the salt workings. Billson had improved a lot. Although a long camel ride is not popularly regarded as being a rest cure, there is no doubt that it is when compared to running up and down sand dunes. Mokhtar had provided an ointment of which Byrne approved, and the angry inflamation around Paul's wound had receded.

Paul had improved in spirit, too, and for a man who normally kept a sulky silence he became quite chatty. Maybe the desert had something to do with it.

Looking down at the salt pans was like viewing a less salubrious section of Dante's Inferno. Salt-bearing earth was dug from pits and thrown into evaporating pans where an impure salt was deposited on the surface as the water evaporated under the hot sun. This, laboriously scraped away, was packed into moulds and shaped into pillars about three feet high.

Paul said suddenly, 'You know, it's the first time that bit of the Bible has made sense – about Lot's wife being turned into a pillar of salt. I've never understood about a pillar of salt until now.'

I thought of the caravan trails across the Sahara and wondered if salt from Bilma had found its way to ancient Israel. It was improbable – the Dead Sea was saltier than other seas – but the method of manufacture was probably oid.

We went back to the caravan and rested. The camels were resting, too, and some of them were lying flat on their sides after they had been unloaded. I had never seen camels do that. I was studying one of them when Mokhtar passed. He saw my interest and struggled for words. After a lot of thought he came out with 'Fatigué – très fatigué.'

I nodded. If I'd walked for a month, sixteen hours a day, I'd be bloody tired, too. But Mokhtar had walked and he looked as fresh as a daisy. The camel's ribs were showing through its hide. I said, 'It's thin – maigre.' I patted my own flank, and repeated, 'Maigre.'

Mokhtar said something in Tamachek which I couldn't understand. Seeing my incomprehension, he took the camel's halter and brought it to its feet. He beckoned, so I followed him as he led the camel about a quarter of a mile to a stone trough which was being laboriously filled with water from a well.

The camel dipped its head and drank. It drank for ten minutes without stopping and filled out before my eyes. It must have drunk more than twenty gallons of water and when it had finished it was as plump and well-conditioned a beast as I'd seen.

Byrne did not come back until mid-morning of the next day, but he came in the Toyota. Apart from the smashed windscreen it looked no different than before it had been shot up, but then, it had looked battered to begin with. A few holes were neither here nor there, and a difference that makes no difference is no difference.

Billson and I were well rested – a good night's sleep does make a difference – but for the first time Byrne looked weary. I said, 'You need sleep.'

He nodded. 'I'll rest this afternoon and sleep tonight, but we have something to do first. Get in.'

I climbed into the Toyota and Byrne let out the clutch. As we drove away a breeze swept through the cab. 'It's going to be draughty from now on,' I said. 'Where are we going?'

'To waylay a gang of tourists,' he said to my surprise. 'How's your German?'

'Adequate – no more.'

'Maybe it'll do. Kissack's in Bilma. He took Bailly to what passes for a hospital and spun a yarn about an auto accident to explain Bailly's foot. It passed because there's no doctor. Bailly is being flown out tomorrow.'

'He could hardly report being assaulted – not after what he did to us. But why don't we report to the police?'

'And how would we explain you? You're in Niger illegally.' Byrne shook his head decisively. 'Hell, we'd be tied up for months, with or without you. Besides, I'd like to settle with Kissack myself and in my own way.'

'So where do German tourists come in?'

'It struck me that Kissack doesn't know about you.'

I thought about that and found it was probably true. I hadn't told anyone in England where I was going. As far as anyone knew I was sunning myself in Jamaica, as Charlie Malleson had suggested, instead of doing the same in an improbable place like Bilma. And even though I had been close enough to Kissack to touch him he only knew me as an anonymous Targui. The only times he had seen me were in the Hotel de l'Air and over the sights of a rifle in the Ténéré.

Byrne said, 'I want to put you next to Kissack. Find out what he's doing.'

'But the German tourists?'

'I was talking to a Ténéré guide, a Targui I know called Rhossi. He says there's a German crowd coming in from the north and they should be hitting Bilma this afternoon – he's going to take them across the Ténéré. It's a government regulation that all tour groups must have a guide in the Ténéré.'

I wasn't surprised. 'So?'

'There aren't many Europeans in Bilma so you can't just walk in to chat with Kissack. The local law would spot you and want to see your papers. But if you arrive with a gang of

Germans you can merge into the background. I'm going to drop you about five miles out of Bilma and you can bum a lift.'

It would work. Any party of Europeans would give a lone European hitch-hiker a lift for a few miles. 'What do I tell them?'

'Hell, tell them anything you like. No. There's some rock carvings about seven miles out just off the road. Tell them that you walked out of Bilma to look at them, but now you're tired and you'd appreciate a lift back.' He thought for a moment. 'You'd better see the carvings.'

So we went to look at rock carvings up the rough track north of Bilma. I suppose they were more engravings than carvings, cut into the vertical sides of rocks but not too deeply. The subjects were interesting; there were many cattle with spreading horns, a rider on a horse which was unmistakably a stallion though the rider was depicted as a mere stick figure, and, surprisingly, an elephant drawn with a fluent line which Picasso would have been proud of.

'An elephant?'

'Why not?' asked Byrne. 'Where do you suppose Hannibal got the elephants to cross the Alps?'

That question had never troubled me.

Byrne said, 'The North African elephant went extinct about two thousand years ago. I've seen skeletons, though. They were midgets – about half the size of an Indian elephant.'

I looked at the barren waste around us; there wasn't enough vegetation to support a half-sized rabbit. I looked back at the engraving. 'How old?'

'Maybe three thousand years. Not as old as the paintings in the Tassili.' He pointed to a series of marks – crosses, circles, squares and dots. 'That's more recent; it's Tifinagh, the written form of Tamachek.'

'What does it say?'

'I wouldn't know; I can't read it.' He smiled. 'Probably something like "I love Lucy", or "Kilroy was here". You'd better change your clothes.'

So I reverted to being a European and the clothing seemed oddly restricting after the freedom of a *gandoura*. As Byrne drove back to the track he said, 'The tour leader will probably collect all the passports and take them into the fort for inspection. He won't ask for yours, of course. Just mingle with the group enough so it looks as though you're one of them. They'll split up to have a look at Bilma pretty soon and that gives you your chance to hunt up Kissack.'

'That's all right as long as the cops don't do a head count.' Byrne shook his head at that. 'Where am I likely to find Kissack?'

'Anywhere – look for the Range-Rover – but there's a broken-down shack that calls itself a restaurant. You might find him there. Anyway, it's a chance to have a beer.'

He dropped me by the side of the track and drove away after thoughtfully leaving a small canteen of water which looked as though it had started life in the British army.

The German group pitched up three hours later, eighteen people in four long-wheelbase Land-Rovers. I stood up and held out my hand as the first Land-Rover came up, and it drew to a halt. My German, learned when I was with the Army of the Rhine, was about as grammatical as Byrne's French, but just as serviceable. No foreigner minds you speaking his language badly providing you make the attempt. Excepting the French, of course.

The driver of the first Land-Rover was the group leader, and he willingly agreed to take me into Bilma if I didn't mind a squash in the front seat. He looked at me curiously. 'What are you doing out here?'

'I walked out from Bilma to look at some rock engravings.' I smiled. 'I'd rather not walk back.'

'Didn't know there were any around here. Plenty up north at the Col des Chandeliers. Where are they?'

'About three kilometres back, just off the track.'

'Can you show me? My people would be interested.'

'Of course; only too glad.'

So we went back to look at the engravings, and I reflected that it was just as well that Byrne had taken me there. We spent twenty minutes there, the Germans clicking away busily with their Japanese cameras. They were a mixed lot ranging from teenagers to old folk and I wondered what had brought them into the desert. It certainly wasn't the normal package deal.

Less than half an hour after that we were driving up the long slope which leads to the fort in Bilma. The Land-Rovers parked with Teutonic precision in a neat rank just by the gate and I opened the door. 'Thanks for the lift.'

He nodded. 'Helmut Shaeffer. Perhaps we will have a beer in the restaurant, eh?'

'I'm Max Stafford. That's a good idea. Where is the restaurant?'

'Don't you know?' There was surprise in his voice.

'I haven't seen much of Bilma itself. We got in late last night.'

'Oh.' He pointed down the slope and to the right. 'Over there; you can't miss it.'

As Byrne had predicted, he began collecting passports. I lingered, talking with a middle-aged man who discoursed on the wonders he had seen in the north. Shaeffer took the pile of passports into the fort and the group began to break up. I wandered off casually following a trio heading in the general direction of the restaurant.

It was as Byrne had described it; a broken-down shack. The Germans looked at the sun-blasted sign and the peeling walls and muttered dubiously, then made up their minds and went inside. I followed closely on their heels.

It was a bare room with a counter on one side. There were a few rough deal tables, a scattering of chairs, and a wooden bench which ran along two sides of the room. My hackles rose as I saw Kissack sitting on the bench at a corner table next to a man in local dress – not a Targui because he did not wear the veil. That would be the Arab Konti had seen. Kissack was eating an omelette.

He looked up and inspected us curiously, so I turned and started to talk in German to the man next to me, asking if he thought the food here would be hygienically prepared. He advised me to stick to eggs. When I looked back at Kissack he had lost interest in us and seemed more intent on what was on his plate.

That gave me an idea. I crossed the room and stood before him, and asked in German if he recommended the omelette.

He looked up and frowned. 'Huh! Don't you speak English?'

I put a smile on my face and it felt odd because I didn't feel like smiling at this assassin. 'I was asking if you could recommend the omelette. Sorry about that, but I've been travelling with this crowd so long that the German came automatically.'

He grunted. 'It's all right.'

'Thanks. That and a beer should go down well.' I sat at the next table quite close to him.

He turned away and started to talk in a low voice to the Arab. The sun was not dealing kindly with Kissack. His face was burned an angry red and the skin was still peeling from him. I was glad about that; he wasn't earning his murderer's pay easily.

As a waiter came to take my order an aircraft flew over quite low. Kissack made a sharp gesture and the Arab got up and walked out. I ordered beer and an omelette, then I twisted and looked through the window behind me. The Arab was walking towards the fort.

Presently a bottle of beer and a not too clean glass was put in front of me. As I poured the beer I wondered how to tackle Kissack. It was all right for Byrne to talk airily about putting me next to Kissack – that had been done – but what next? I could hardly ask, '*Killed any good men recently?*'

But I had to make a start and old ploys are best, so I said,

'Haven't we met before?'

He grunted and looked at me sideways. 'Where have you come from?'

'Up north. Over the Col des Chandeliers.'

'Never been there.' His eyes returned to his plate.

I persisted. 'Then it must have been in England.'

'No,' he said flatly without looking up.

I drank some beer and cursed Byrne. It had seemed a good idea at the time; fellow countrymen meeting on their travels are usually glad to chat, but Kissack was bad-tempered, grouchy and uncommunicative. I said, 'I could have sworn . . .'

Kissack turned to me. 'Look, chum; I haven't been in England for ten years.' He put a lot of finality in his voice, indicating quite clearly that the subject was closed.

I drank some more beer and waited for my omelette. I was becoming annoyed at Kissack and was just about to put in the needle when someone called, 'Herr Stafford!' I froze, then looked up to see Shaeffer who had just come in. I glanced sideways at Kissack to see if the name had meant anything to him, but apparently it didn't and I breathed easier.

'Hi, Helmut,' I said, hoping he wouldn't show surprise at easy familiarity with his given name from a casual acquaintance. 'Have a beer.' As he sat down I immediately regretted my invitation. Shaeffer could unknowingly drop a clanger and reveal that I was not a part of his group. The only thing going for me was that his English was not too good.

'Everything all right at the fort?' I asked in German.

He shrugged. 'They're too busy to bother with us now. A plane came in from Agadez to take an injured man to hospital. I left the passports; I'll pick them up later.'

The waiter put an omelette in front of me and I ordered a beer for Shaeffer. Kissack ordered another beer for himself so he'd be staying a while. I turned to him. 'You know, I *have* seen you before.'

'For Christ's sake!' he said tiredly.

'Wasn't it in Tammanrasset? You were driving a Range-Rover.'

That got through to him. He went very still, a glass half way to his lips. Then he turned and looked at me with stony eyes. 'What are you getting at, chummy?'

'Nothing,' I said coolly. 'It's just that a thing like that niggles me. Nice to know I wasn't mistaken. You were in Tam, then.'

'And what if I was? What's it to you?'

I tackled my omelette. 'Nothing.' I turned to Shaeffer and switched to German. 'I forgot to tell you. Rhossi, your guide, is here in Bilma. Someone told me he was waiting for a German party so I assume it's you. Have you seen him?' Out of the corner of my eye I saw Kissack staring at me. I hoped his lack of German was complete.

Shaeffer shook his head. 'He'll be camped at Kalala near the salt workings.'

I turned back to Kissack. 'I was just asking Helmut, here, if he's seen the guide yet. You need a guide to cross the Ténéré.'

'When were you in Tammanrasset?' Kissack asked suddenly.

'Evidently when you were,' I said. 'Oh, by the way; did you hear anything about that chap who disappeared? Another Englishman. There was a devil of a brouhaha going on about it when I left.'

Kissack moistened his lips. 'What was his name?'

'Wilson,' I said. 'No, that's not right. Williamson? No, not that, either. My memory really is playing me up – first you, now this chap.' I frowned. 'Billson!' I said in triumph. 'That was his name. Billson. The police were really in a stew about him, but you know what Algerians are like. Bloody bureaucrats with sub-machine-guns!'

The waiter put a bottle of beer and a glass in front of Shaeffer and another bottle before Kissack. He ignored it. 'What happened to this Billson?' His voice was over-controlled.

I didn't answer immediately but popped a slice of omelette into my mouth. I'd got Kissack interested enough to ask questions and that was progress, and the omelette was quite good. I swallowed and said, 'He went up into Atakor without asking permission and didn't come back. There were a hell of a lot of rumours floating around when I left.'

'What sort of rumours?'

'Oh, the usual stuff that goes around when anything like that happens. Unbelievable, most of it.'

I had Kissack hooked because he asked, 'Such as?'

I shrugged. 'Well, for instance, someone said his Land-Rover had been found burnt out the other side of Assekrem. You know those parts?'

'Not well,' said Kissack tightly.

'This is a damned good omelette,' I observed. 'Anyway, someone else said his body had been brought out and he'd died of exposure. But then there was a buzz that he'd been brought out alive but he'd been shot. I told you – unbelievable stuff. Those things don't happen these days, do they? The desert is pretty civilized now.'

'What are you talking about?' asked Shaeffer. He grinned. 'My Tamachek is better than my English – I heard Tammanrasset and Atakor and Assekrem.'

'Oh, just about an Englishman who vanished near Tam.'

Kissack was looking bleak. He said, 'Any rumours about what finally happened to Billson?'

'The last I heard was that he was in hospital in Tam with a police guard – sort of house arrest. Just another bloody rumour, though.'

Kissack fell silent and poured his beer. He was thinking hard; I could almost see the damned wheels going round. I turned to Shaeffer and started to chat about the problems of crossing the Ténéré, all in German. After a while Kissack said, 'Stafford . . . it is Stafford, isn't it?'

I turned. 'Yes?'

'How did you get from Tam to here?'

That was a stumer; a damned good question. I visualized

the Michelin map I had pored over, and said lightly, 'Flew across to Djanet from Tam, then came south. I was already booked into the party. Why?'

'What were you doing in Tam?'

I frowned. 'Not that it's any of your business but I'm interested in Charles de Foucauld. I wanted to see where and how he lived.'

Kissack said, 'I think you're a damned liar.' He nodded towards Shaeffer. 'Any tour group coming down from Djanet is going to go through Tammanrasset anyway. Why should you want to go there twice?'

I stood up. 'Because I'm leaving the group at Agadez and going south to Kano. That's why. Now get up off that damned bench. No man calls me a liar.'

Kissack looked up at me but didn't move. Shaeffer said, 'What's the matter?' He hadn't understood what was said but the changed atmosphere needed no language to understand.

'This man called me a liar.' I was suddenly infuriated with Kissack and I wanted to belt hell out of him. I stooped, grabbed his shirt, and hauled him to his feet. The table went flying and a glass smashed on the floor. Kissack made a grab for the inside of his jacket so I rammed my elbow into his side and felt the hardness of a gun.

Then Shaeffer grabbed me from behind and hauled me away. 'Herr Stafford; this is no place to make trouble,' he said, his mouth close to my ear. 'The prison here is not good.'

Kissack had his hand inside his jacket. I shook off Shaeffer's hands and stuck a finger at Kissack. 'You don't want the coppers here, either – not with what you have there. You'd have too much explaining to do.'

The barman came from behind the bar carrying a foot-long bar of iron, but stopped as Shaeffer said something in Arabic. Kissack withdrew his hand and it came out empty. 'I don't know what you mean.' His eyes flickered towards the barman. 'Hell; this is a lousy place, anyway.' He dipped his hand into his pocket and tossed a couple of bank notes on to the floor, then walked towards the door.

From a distance someone said in German, 'Brawling Englishmen – I bet they're drunk.'

I said to Shaeffer, 'Tell the owner I'll pay for any damage. Your Arabic sounds better than his French.'

He nodded and rattled off some throat-scratching Arabic. The barman nodded curtly without smiling, picked up the money, and returned to the bar. Shaeffer said, 'You should not cause fighting here, Herr Stafford.' He shook his head. 'It is not wise.'

'I was provoked.' I looked through the window and saw Kissack walking towards the mud-coloured huddle of houses that was Bilma. I had blown it. I hadn't got a damned thing out of him that was of any use. What's more, I had probably given him grounds for suspicion.

But perhaps something could be retrieved if I was quick about it. I went to the bar and laid a bank note down. The barman looked at me unblinkingly so I put down another. I had to add two more before he nodded curtly. Then I went out fast, looking for Kissack. If I could get him alone he was going to tell me quite a few things, gun or no gun.

Twenty-Four

Bilma is constructed on something like the lines of Daedalus's Labyrinth; no streets, just a warren of alleys and passages, and if I had met the Minotaur I wouldn't have been particularly surprised. It was difficult keeping up with Kissack and twice I lost him and had to cast about. Not that he was being evasive – he didn't look behind him to see if he was being followed or anything like that. In fact, I think he was lost himself at times, not very difficult in Bilma, and I swear we passed the same corner three times.

I followed him deeper and deeper into the maze. There were very few people about and those I encountered regarded me incuriously. They looked to be the same kind that I had seen at Fachi and whom Byrne had called Kanuri. Every so often I would pass a more or less open space where sheep or goats were penned or where chickens scratched, but in general there were just mud walls set with secretive doors every so often. A good shower of rain would have dissolved Bilma in one night, sending it back to the earth from which it had arisen.

At last I peered around a corner to see Kissack open a door and vanish inside. I walked up and looked at the door and then at the expanse of windowless wall. It wouldn't be too difficult to climb but doing the burglar bit in broad daylight would be unwise – even a blank-minded Kanuri would regard that as anti-social, and I was uncomfortably aware of an old toothless crone who had stopped at the end of the alley and was looking at me.

While I was debating the next step my mind was made up for me by a voice saying in French, 'Why didn't he wait at the restaurant?' It floated from the corner I had just turned.

That did it. There was just one thing to do so I opened the door and slipped inside. I found myself in a courtyard just big enough to hold Kissack's Range-Rover and very little else. Around the sides of the courtyard were hovels made of the ubiquitous mud.

Behind me, on the other side of the door, the voice said, 'Is this it?' There wasn't much else to do but what I did. I hurled myself forward and dived under the Range-Rover, being thankful for the generous ground clearance. I was only just in time because the door opened wide just as I got hidden and several men came into the courtyard. I twisted my head, counted feet, and divided by two – four men.

'Where is Kissack?' said the man who had queried about the restaurant. He still spoke French. '*Kissack!*' he bellowed.

'In here.' Kissack's voice came from one of the mud buildings.

The French-speaker switched to English. 'You come out here.' A door slammed and Kissack's feet came into view. 'If you think I'm going into that flea-ridden kennel you're mistaken.' The tone was distasteful and the accent standard BBC grade announcer's English.

'Hello, Lash,' said Kissack.

'Don't hello me,' said Lash acidly. 'And it's Mr Lash to you.' He went back into French. 'You lot get lost for the next half-hour but then be findable.'

'How about the restaurant?' someone asked.

'That's all right – but stay there so I can find you.' Three men went away and the door slammed. Lash said, 'Now just what in hell have you been doing, Kissack?'

'Just doing what I was told,' said Kissack sullenly.

'Like hell you have!' said Lash explosively. 'There's a contract out on Billson and he's still alive. Why?'

'Christ, I don't know,' said Kissack. 'He should be dead. I shot him in some of the most God-awful country you've ever seen. He *couldn't* have walked out.'

'So he was helped, and the next thing is someone is advertising for that bloody aeroplane. Advertising, by God!

217

Leaflets all over the bloody desert! The idea, Kissack, was not to draw attention to that aeroplane but, because you're ham-fisted, everybody and his bloody Arab uncle is looking for it.'

'That's not my fault,' yelled Kissack. 'I didn't know about Byrne.'

'He's the man who put out the leaflets?'

'Yes. He's a sodding Yank who's gone native.'

'I'm not going to stand here and fry my brains out,' said Lash. 'Get in the car.'

The Range-Rover rocked on its springs as they got in, and I took the opportunity of easing my position because a stone was digging into my hip. The arrival of Lash changed everything. Kissack having failed twice had sent for reinforcements – and the boss had arrived. From what I heard, Lash was certainly more incisive than Kissack.

And I could still hear them because they had the windows down. Lash said, 'When we heard about the leaflets I told you to stay put in Agadez. So what happens? I arrive to find you've gone into the damned desert. Then we get a message that Bailly's been in a motor smash. What happened to him?'

'It wasn't a smash,' said Kissack. He told Lash of how he had ambushed us. 'I had them nailed down, all but one who got away – and I reckoned he couldn't get far on foot. They didn't have a chance. Then Bailly started to scream his bloody head off.'

'What happened?'

'Christ knows! This Arab did something to him. What or how I don't know, but he's going to lose his foot. There was Bailly wriggling around on the sand and yelling fit to bust, and the Arab was dodging away among the dunes. We chased him a bit but he got away.'

'You were scared,' said Lash flatly.

'You'd be bloody scared if you'd seen what he did to Bailly,' Kissack retorted. 'He wouldn't stop screaming. I had to slug him to shut him up.'

'So then you put him in this car and brought him to Bilma. Kissack, you're stupid.'

'What else was there to do?'

'You could have killed Bailly to shut him up and then attended to the others. You said you had them nailed down.'

'Jesus, you . . .' Kissack's voice caught. 'You're a cold-hearted bastard.'

'I'm a realist,' said Lash. 'Now, who were these men you were shooting at?'

'One of them was Byrne, the Yank who got out the leaflets. He spun me a yarn back in Agadez but I saw through it. Another I'm pretty sure was Billson. The other two were Arabs.'

'Arabs or Tuareg?'

'Who cares? They're all the same to me.'

'I repeat, and I don't like repeating myself – you're stupid, Kissack. Did they wear veils?'

'Byrne did – and one of the others. The one who did for Bailly had no veil.' There was a pause while Lash digested that, and Kissack said defensively, 'What's the difference? Christ, I hate this bloody desert.'

'Shut up!' Lash was silent for a while, then said, 'What happened to them?'

'I don't know. They aren't here. I shot up that Toyota pretty good; got three of the tyres. And no one is going to walk out of all that sodding sand out there, Mr Lash.'

'You said that before about Billson, and you were wrong.' Lash was contemptuous. 'And I'm betting you're wrong again because you're stupid. Before I flew down from Algiers I took the trouble to find out about this American, Byrne. He's been in the desert thirty-five years, Kissack. The Algerians don't like him much but he has friends with political clout so he still hangs around. Anyway, he spends most of his time here in Niger. If you didn't kill him, then I'm saying he's going to get out because he knows how. Did you kill him?'

'No,' said Kissack sullenly.

'Tomorrow you take me and show me that shot-up Toyota. If it's not there you're going to wish you were Bailly.'

'It'll be there, Mr Lash. I know where I put the bullets.'

'Don't bet on it,' said Lash coldly. 'Because I'm assuming it's not there. Now I told you to stay in Agadez and wait for me. Why the hell didn't you?'

Kissack had an access of courage. 'Remember what you said when you came in here. You said there was a contract out on Billson and you asked why he was still alive. I was just doing the job.'

'Good God Almighty!' said Lash violently. 'Those bloody leaflets changed all that. Even a cretin like you should have realized that. Whether Billson is alive or dead, that plane is going to be found now. If it is, then my principal is going to be up a gum tree and he's not going to like that.'

'If I'd got Byrne there'd be nobody to give the reward. That's why I had a crack at him.'

'I don't deal in damned ifs,' snapped Lash. 'I want certainties. And you're wrong. If that crashed plane is worth maybe a thousand pounds to Byrne, then anyone who finds it will figure it's worth something to someone else, whether Byrne is around or not. I tell you, that plane is going to be found and talked about.'

'What's so bloody special about it?' asked Kissack.

'None of your business.' Lash fell silent. Presently he said, 'Any idea why Byrne and Billson suddenly took off in this direction? Do you know where they were going?'

'I didn't ask.'

'Working in the dark as usual,' said Lash acidly. 'Now this is how we work it from now on. I'm betting that Byrne and Billson are still around – so we find them. And when we do you don't lay a bloody finger on them. What's more, if they're in trouble you get them out of it. Understand?'

'Hell! One minute you want to know why they're not dead, and the next you want me to pick 'em up and dust 'em off.' Kissack was disgusted.

Lash was heavily patient. 'We don't know where that plane is, do we? But Byrne might have a good idea by now – he's the one who's been advertising for it. So we let him find it and, if necessary, we help him. Then, when we've got Byrne, Billson and the plane all in one place . . .'

'Bingo!' said Kissack.

'And I'll be along to see you don't make a balls-up of it,' said Lash. 'Now, is there anything else you think I ought to know? It doesn't matter how insignificant it is.'

'Can't think of anything, except there's been some funny rumours going round Tammanrasset.'

'What rumours?'

'Well, I heard that Billson was in some sort of hospital jail in Tam. But he couldn't be, could he? Not if he was in the Ténéré.'

'When did you hear this?'

'Today – in the restaurant. A British tourist travelling with a German crowd was shooting his mouth off. Billson dead of exposure, Billson alive with a bullet in him, Billson alive and in jail. But all just rumours, this chap Stafford said.'

'*What!*'

'He said they were just rumours; nothing certain.'

'What did you say the name was?'

'Whose name?'

'The British tourist, for Christ's sake! Who else are we talking about?'

'Oh! He called himself Stafford. No, he didn't; but his German mate called him Stafford.'

'Good God Almighty!' said Lash softly.

'And he answered to Stafford when I talked to him. Is he important?'

'Did he say where he'd come from? He's been in Tammanrasset, you say.'

'He came down from Djanet with a German tour group. Said he'd flown to Djanet from Tam. I thought that was a bit funny but he explained it. Said he was leaving the tour at Agadez and going down to Kano.'

'And he had a German friend?' Lash sounded puzzled.

'That's right. They jabbered a lot in German. I think he was the tour leader. They were talking about a guide to take them across the Ténéré.'

'Coming down from the *north* with Germans? But how . . .' Lash cut himself short. 'When was this?'

'Not long ago. I came straight here from the restaurant and then you pitched up a couple of minutes later.'

'Then he might still be there?'

'He was there when I left.' There was a hint of a shrug in Kissack's voice. 'We had a bit of a barney; he was getting on my wick.'

'How?'

'All his talk about Billson in Tam was making me edgy.'

'So you do have some imagination, after all. Come on; let's see if he's there.'

'So who is he?'

They got out of the Range-Rover and walked across the courtyard. Lash said, 'Trouble!'

The door slammed.

Twenty-Five

I got out from under the Range-Rover and looked about. A minor puzzlement which had been a fugitive at the back of my mind during that interesting conversation had been how they had got the Range-Rover into that courtyard. It couldn't be driven through Bilma, not through alleys four feet wide at the most. The puzzle was solved by the sight of a big pair of double doors, so I opened one and found myself on the edge of the town, clear the other side from the restaurant.

I did the three miles to Kalala at a jog-trot, my mind busy with the implications of what I had heard, the most interesting one being that Lash knew me – or of me – and he had been very surprised to hear that I was in Bilma. That, and a phrase that had been dropped a couple of times, made it almost certain that it had been Lash who had me beaten up in Kensington. I owed him something for that.

When I got back to the resting caravan Byrne was asleep but Billson was around. He said, 'Where have you been? Where did he take you?' He looked me up and down, examining my English tailoring. 'And why did you change? Byrne wouldn't tell me anything when he came back.'

If Byrne had decided to keep mum then so would I. Paul had been improving during the last few days, but if he knew what I had just found out he might blow his top. It was the final proof positive that someone wanted him dead and would go to any length to kill him. And expense was no object, so it seemed. Touring half a dozen men around the Sahara by road and air isn't the cheapest pastime in the world, especially if they're killers – guns for hire.

I said casually, 'I've just been wandering around Bilma to

see what I could see.'

'Did you find the Range-Rover?'

'If it's there it must be hidden.' That was true enough.

'What about Kissack?' he said fretfully.

I remembered that Byrne and I had not said anything to Paul about meeting Kissack and Bailly in Agadez. I lied. 'I wouldn't know Kissack if I stood next to him. And he wouldn't know me. Relax, Paul; you're safe enough here.'

I went to the Toyota, got out my Tuareg gear, and changed, feeling the better for it. The clothing worn in any area has been refined over the years and is suited to the conditions. It made sense to wear Tuareg clothes and I no longer felt on my way to a fancy dress ball but, instead, cool and free.

That night, when Paul was asleep, I woke Byrne and told him my story. When I got to Lash's suggestion to Kissack about what he ought to have done about Bailly he said ironically, 'This Lash is a really nice guy.'

'He calls himself a realist,' I said, and carried on.

When I had finished he said, 'You did right well, Max; but you were goddamn lucky.'

'That's true enough,' I admitted. 'I made a mess of tackling Kissack from the start.'

'Luck runs both ways. Take Billson, now; he's lucky you followed him from England. He'd be dead otherwise, up in Koudia.'

I smiled. 'We're both of us lucky to have you along, Luke.'

He grunted. 'There's one thing I don't understand. You said something about a contract. What sort of contract?'

'You've been away from civilization too long. It's under-world jargon imported from the States. If you want a man killed you put out a contract on him on a fee contingency basis.'

'You call that civilization? Out here if a guy wants another man dead he does his own killing, like Konti.'

I smiled but this time it was a bit sour. 'It's called the division of labour.'

'Which brings us back to the big question,' said Byrne. 'Who would want Paul dead? And a bigger question, at least to my mind – who would want me dead?'

'I rather think I'm on the list now,' I said. 'I don't know, Luke; but a name that springs to mind is Sir Andrew McGovern.'

'A British sir!' Byrne said in astonishment.

'I haven't told you much about the English end of this,' I said. 'But now you've got yourself on Lash's list I think you ought to know.' So I told him what I knew, then said, 'I think Lash must have had me beaten up. All contracts aren't for killing. They wanted to discourage me.'

'And this guy McGovern?'

'Everything seems to lead back to him.' I ticked off points on my fingers. 'He employed Paul in the first place and saw that he's been grossly overpaid ever since. As soon as Paul had his brainstorm and disappeared McGovern pulled my firm out of security of the Whensley Group. He couldn't just do it for Franklin Engineering, you see – that would have looked fishy. He didn't want me looking too deeply into Paul and his affairs and that was the only way he could stop me. Then he tried to get Paul's sister out of the way before I could see her by sending her to Canada. That didn't work so he called off that plan and kept her in England. It was about that time when I was beaten up and warned off. Everything goes back to McGovern.'

'Okay,' said Byrne. 'Now tell me why. Why should a titled Britisher get into an uproar about an airplane that crashed in 1936?'

'I'm damned if I know. But Andrew McGovern is going to answer a lot of questions to my satisfaction when I get back to London.'

'You'd better change that to *if* you get back to London,' said Byrne wryly. 'How old is McGovern?'

I hadn't thought of that. 'I don't know. Maybe fifty-five – pushing sixty.'

'Let's take the top figure. If he's sixty now he'd be eighteen in 1936.'

Or thirteen on the lower figure. I said, 'This makes less and less sense. How could a teenager be involved?'

Byrne moved his hand in a dismissive gesture. 'Let's stick to the present. Did you get a look at Lash?'

I shook my head. 'Only his feet. I was flat on my belly under that Range-Rover. I didn't see any of the others, either; except Kissack, of course, and his Arab friend.'

'But there are now five of them?' I nodded, and he said, 'Must have come in on the airplane that's taking Bailly back to Agadez. And Lash's plan now is to do nothing until we find that airplane?'

'As of now it is. He could change his mind.'

'That we'll have to risk. Now, we know what he's going to do, but he doesn't know we know, so that gives us an edge. He wants to help us along until we locate that airplane. Okay, that's fine with me and I propose to let him help, and to do that he'll have to show himself.'

'Maybe. Perhaps he'll be master-minding in the background.'

'I don't think so,' said Byrne. 'He won't use Kissack because he knows I've seen Kissack, and Kissack knows I tried to screw him so Lash knows it too. And from what you tell me, the other guys along with him are hired muscle from Algiers.'

'Or hired guns,' I said glumly.

'Could you recognize him by voice?'

'I think so, unless he's smart enough to change it.'

'Good enough.' I couldn't see Byrne in the darkness but there was a smile in his voice. 'You know, Max; if these guys follow us and help us on our way I wouldn't be surprised if they got in real trouble. The desert can be a dangerous place, especially when it has help.'

I said, 'How much of this do we tell Paul?'

'Are you out of your mind?' he said. 'We don't tell him a goddamn thing. He's just along for the ride.'

We left early next morning with Konti still with us. 'We'll take him as far as Djado,' said Byrne. 'Then he'll head east, back home to the Tibesti.'

We drove openly around Bilma and past the fort. I didn't see Kissack or anyone who might be Lash. Then we took the track due north, skirting the ramparts of the Kaouar mountains, sheer cliffs for mile after mile. Just after leaving Bilma Byrne said, 'About forty kilometres ahead there's the military post at Dirkou; I'll have to stop there for gas. But not you – they'd want to see your papers and you got none. So I'll park you just outside with Konti. He don't like soldiers, either.'

When we came into sight of distant palm groves he stopped and pointed. 'Head that way as straight as you can. That'll bring you to the road the other side of the post but out of sight. Wait for me there.'

Konti and I got out. Byrne was about to start off again but he paused. 'You got a spare bottle of whisky?'

'In my bag in the back. Why?'

'There's a guy in Dirkou who likes his booze. A sweetener makes life run easier around Dirkou.' He drove off.

Konti and I set off across the desert which, thank God, was flat thereabouts. Presently I stooped and picked up something. Byrne had been right – there were sea-shells in the desert near Bilma.

After about half an hour's trudge we reached the track and waited, being careful to stand behind a convenient rock and not in plain sight. Soon we heard the grind of gear-changing and I looked out to see the Toyota approaching, so we stepped out and Byrne stopped just long enough for us to climb in.

He jerked his thumb back to Dirkou. 'Would you say Lash is a big man?'

'His feet were middling size.'

'There's a Britisher back there. Came in twenty minutes behind me.'

'Don't tell me,' I said. 'In a Range-Rover.'

'No; in an old truck nearly as beat-up as mine. He's pretty tall, pretty broad, dark hair.'

'Anyone with him?'

'Two guys. From the way they spoke Arabic together I'd say they're from the Maghreb – Algiers, most likely. The Britisher don't speak Arabic, he talks to them in French which they don't understand too good.'

'It fits,' I said.

'They'll be more than twenty minutes behind us when they leave Dirkou,' said Byrne with a grin. 'I had a talk with the guy who likes his booze. Right now he's turning them inside out and the English feller is swearing fit to bust a gut. Won't do him no good, though. Seems that whisky has its uses.'

'That might be useful,' I said thoughtfully. 'If your whisky drinker is turning them over that thoroughly he might find guns. He wouldn't like that, would he?'

'That passed through my mind,' agreed Byrne cheerfully. 'Let us not smooth the way of the transgressor.' He laughed at my expression. 'Lots of good things in the Bible.'

From the seat behind me Billson said, 'What are you talking about? Who was that man back there?'

'Just a guy,' said Byrne. 'Maybe nothing to do with Kissack but I like to play safe.'

I said, 'Don't worry about it, Paul.'

The track was bad and got steadily worse. Every so often we would pass a village with the inevitable grove of date palms. There was evidently water under the tall cliffs of the Kaouar mountains. But the villagers hadn't tried to make life easier for themselves by maintaining the track.

We travelled steadily all day and not only the track deteriorated but so did the weather. A wind arose, lifting the sand in a haze which dimmed the sun, and dust filtered everywhere in the truck. It was then that I found the true efficacy of the Tuareg veil and pulled it closer about my face.

Disaster struck in the late afternoon. There was a grinding noise from somewhere at the back of the Toyota and we came to a shuddering halt in soft sand. Byrne said, 'Goddamn it! That's something wrong with the transmission.'

So we got out to look at the damage. The rear wheels were sunk nearly to the axle in the fine sand and I could see it was going to be a devil of a job to get out even if there was nothing wrong with the transmission. And if the transmission had gone we could be stuck there forever. Byrne didn't seem too worried; he merely dug out two jacks from the back of the truck and laid them on the sand. 'Here's where the hard work starts,' he remarked. 'We'll need the sand ladders from up top.'

Paul and I got down the sand ladders. Byrne regarded Paul thoughtfully. 'Would you do me a favour?'

'Of course. What is it?'

'Go to the top of that rise back there and keep your eyes open. If you see anyone coming let us know fast.'

Paul looked at Konti. 'What about him?'

'I need him,' said Byrne briefly.

'Oh! All right.' Paul started off back down the track.

Byrne laughed shortly. 'Paul will keep a better look-out than any of us. He seems to value his skin more.'

'I don't know,' I said. 'I'm pretty attached to mine.'

An hour later we knew the worst, and it was bad. 'The differential gears are pretty near all stripped,' said Byrne. 'No wonder it sounded like my old man's coffee-grinder back home in Bar Harbor. It never could grind coffee worth a damn.'

I regarded the jacked-up Toyota gloomily. 'What do we do? Walk?'

'There's a place called Seguedine a piece up the road – maybe ten kilometres. Not that there's much there, but maybe we could use a team of camels to haul us out.'

'And then what? The differential's busted. There wouldn't

229

be a service station in Seguedine?'

Byrne laughed. 'Not likely. But I've got a spare differential in the back of the truck. The bastards are always stripping so I've made it a habit to keep a spare. But I'd like to get in cover before replacing it. It's going to blow a son of a bitch tonight and this damned sand gets in everywhere. Not good for differentials.'

'Well, who goes? I can't speak the language.'

Byrne grinned. 'I sent Konti on ahead half an hour ago. I was pretty sure of what I'd find.'

I looked around and, sure enough, Konti was missing. But Billson was running towards us at full tilt. 'Someone coming!' he yelled. 'They'll be here in five minutes or less.'

He skidded to a halt in front of us. 'Any idea who it is?' asked Byrne calmly.

'It looked like the truck we saw in Dirkou.'

Byrne's right arm disappeared inside his *gandoura* and when it reappeared he was holding a fistful of gun. He worked the action and set the safety-catch, then put it away again. Paul watched him wide-eyed. 'Go and sit in the front seat, Paul,' said Byrne.

Billson scurried around the truck and I saw to my own pistol. Byrne said, 'If this is Lash we'll pretty soon find out how genuinely he wants to help. Keep your veil up and your mouth shut.' He stooped and put an oil-can upright on the ground. 'If you recognize his voice kick that over, accidental like.'

We waited, the hot desert wind driving at us and flicking grains of sand into our faces. It was as much to protect my face as to hide it when I drew up and tightened the veil in the way Byrne had shown me. Then I stood with my arm inside my *gandoura* hanging straight down with the pistol in my hand; it couldn't be seen and I would waste no time in drawing from the holster.

The truck came over the rise two hundred yards away, travelling fast and trailing a long plume of dust which was blown to one side by the wind. As it approached it slowed, and then drew to a halt abreast of us. The driver was obviously not a European but the man who got out of the front passenger seat was. He was as Byrne had described him, fairly big and with dark hair. His eyes flickered towards Byrne and me, then he looked at Paul in the front seat and said, 'Are you in trouble? Perhaps I can help.'

I didn't hear what Paul answered because I took half a pace to one side and knocked over the oil-can with a metallic clatter. Byrne raised his voice. 'Yeah, you can say we're in trouble. Lousy differential's bust.'

Lash turned his head and stared at Byrne, then came to the back of the truck. 'You an American?' He filled his voice with well-simulated incredulity.

'We get around.'

'You don't look like one,' said Lash in an amused tone. He nodded at me. 'I suppose he's American, too.'

'Nope,' said Byrne. 'He's British like you.'

Lash raised his eyebrows but said nothing. I suppose Byrne had done the right thing. Lash knew I was around and there was no point in me hiding; and it would be difficult to maintain the deception unless I pretended I was deaf and dumb.

He stooped and looked under the Toyota, then said, 'Yes, I'd say you're in trouble.' He straightened. 'By the way, my name is Lash – John Lash.'

'I'm Luke Byrne. This here is Max Stafford and the feller up front is Paul Billson.' I was afraid that Lash would offer to shake hands which would have been difficult with me holding the pistol, but he merely nodded. Byrne said, 'The differential don't matter – I have a spare; but I'd sure appreciate a tow out of this sand and a few kilometres up the road.'

'That shouldn't be too difficult,' said Lash, and turned away and began to talk to the men in his truck. From the intonation he was speaking French although I didn't get the words. I noted he did not introduce them.

Byrne took his right arm from his *gandoura* and his hand

was empty. If he was willing to take a chance then so was I, so I unobtrusively holstered the pistol and did the same. He said, 'We'll put in the sand ladders before we let the jacks down; it'll be easier with them.'

Lash's two companions got out of their truck. I walked to the cab of the Toyota. Paul said in a low voice, 'That's the man who was at Dirkou.'

'So?'

'So wasn't Byrne suspicious of him?'

'Hell!' I said. 'He's just a Good Samaritan come to get us out of trouble. Don't be paranoiac, Paul. Get out and help.'

We put the sand ladders under the rear wheels, then let the Toyota down on to them and took away the jacks. Lash didn't have a towing chain but Byrne did, and we were ready to go within ten minutes. It was then I noticed that one of Lash's men had disappeared.

Lash and the other man got into their truck and the engine fired. In a low voice I said to Byrne, 'Where's the other thug?'

'Gone back over the rise – and I know why.'

'Why, for God's sake?'

'It ain't because he's shy of exposing himself,' Byrne said sardonically. 'My guess he's gone back to flag down Kissack and stop him. The Range-Rover won't be far behind.'

It made sense. Lash wouldn't want us to see Kissack. I said, 'One thing – don't talk about Lash while we're being towed or you'll spook Paul.'

'I'll watch it.' He raised his voice. 'Paul, you stand on this side and Max on the other. If you think we're getting deeper into trouble, then yell.' He got behind the wheel and waved at Lash, who revved his engine.

There was no trouble. Lash's truck was more powerful than it looked and pulled us out of the sand easily, though what it did to one of the sand ladders was indescribable. Byrne threw away that twisted bit of junk as being unusable and we collected the few tools that were lying around. As we did so, the missing man came walking at a smart pace up the road. He saw us looking at him and zipped up the fly of his trousers. Byrne looked at me and grinned faintly.

So the man who was going to kill us towed us into Seguedine, which wasn't much of a place, but there was a ruin with three standing walls and a decrepit roof which was enough to shelter the Toyota from the wind. Lash helped us push it in. 'Mind if I stay the night here with you?' he asked. 'Perhaps I could help you strip the transmission.'

'No call for that,' said Byrne. 'I can manage.'

Lash smiled. 'And I don't feel like driving on in a sandstorm. A man could lose his way. I have a feeling that could be bad.'

'Sure could,' Byrne agreed. 'You could get dead. You want to stay, you stay. It's a free country. Thanks for your help, Mr Lash; you got us out of a nasty hole, but there's no call for you to get your hands dirty.'

But Lash helped us anyway. I suppose he thought it in his own interest to put us on our way as fast as possible. His henchmen disappeared, probably to tell Kissack what was happening. Lash wasn't all that much of a help, though, and his aid was confined to handing over tools when asked, as indeed was mine. Byrne could have done the job quite handily himself and, for a man who professed hatred of 'stinkpots' he was American enough to understand them well.

Paul came and went restlessly. Once, in Lash's absence, Byrne said to him enthusiastically, 'Lash is a real nice guy, don't you think? Him getting us out of the sand and helping us like this and all.'

I said, 'Yes; a Good Samaritan, Paul.' I looked over Byrne's shoulder and saw Lash come slowly out of the shadows, and wondered if Byrne had known that Lash was behind him, listening. Probably he had known; there were no flies on Luke Byrne.

We finished the job in the glare of a pressure lantern after nightfall, then cleaned up and prepared a meal just as Konti showed up. Byrne talked to him for a moment then said to me, 'He walked as far as here, found no one, so he went up the track a long ways with no success. Walking fools, these Teda.'

Lash contributed a bottle of whisky for after-dinner drinks. I accepted a tot, and so did Paul, but Byrne refused politely. 'Where are your friends, Mr Lash?'

Lash raised his eyebrows. 'Friends? Oh, you mean . . . They're just showing me around. Professional guides.' I glanced at Byrne who didn't bat an eyelid at that preposterous statement. 'They prefer to eat their own food.' Lash looked around in the darkness. 'What is this place?'

'Seguedine? Used to be people here – three or four families of Kanuri. Must have moved out since I was here last. The Tassili Tuareg come from the north when the feed gives out there. Where are you heading?'

Lash shrugged. 'Nowhere in particular. Just looking around.' That was supposed to give him an excuse for popping up out of nowhere at any time and occasioning no surprise, but it was a stupid thing to say. Even a tyro like myself had observed that desert crossings were most carefully prepared with times and distances collated and fuel and water carefully metered. No one in his right mind would flutter hither and yon like a carefree butterfly. To risk running out of fuel or water was dangerous.

Lash sipped his whisky. 'And you?'

'Pretty much the same,' said Byrne uninformatively.

I would have thought Lash might have pursued the subject of our further travels, but he didn't. He made desultory conversation, telling us he was the managing director of a firm in Birmingham which specialized in packaging and that this was the first real holiday he'd had in seven years. 'I decided to do something different,' he said.

He tried to draw me out on what I did in England so I told him the truth because he knew all about me anyway and to lie would arouse his suspicions. 'Recuperating from an illness,' I said, then added, 'And getting over a divorce.'

Both statements were true; he'd probably been the cause of the 'illness' and the bit about Gloria could confuse him by its truth. The truth can be a better weapon than lies.

After a while he excused himself, after getting nowhere with Billson, and went to his truck where he bedded down. Soon thereafter Konti came out of the darkness and spoke to Byrne, who questioned him closely. Paul said to me, 'Inquisitive, isn't he?'

'Not abnormally so. Chit-chat between ships that pass in the night.'

'I don't like him.' Paul pulled his *djellaba* closer about him. 'I don't think he's what he says he is.' I *knew* it, but Paul was showing an acuity which surprised me. Perhaps it was the sixth sense of the hunted animal.

A few minutes later, out of Paul's hearing, Byrne said, 'Kissack is camped about a mile from here. I sent Konti to scout him out.' He chuckled. 'I don't think Kissack will be comfortable out there. The wind's still rising.'

'Do we stand watches?'

Byrne shook his head. 'Konti will watch all night.'

'Bit hard on him, isn't it?'

'Hell, no! He'll sleep in the Toyota tomorrow. For a Teda to sleep while on the move is sheer unaccustomed luxury.'

Next morning the storm had blown itself out and Lash had gone together with his truck. 'Went just before dawn,' said Byrne. 'Sudden guys, these friends of yours. Kissack shoots folks without saying a word and Lash goes, just like that. Unneighbourly, I call it.'

'So what now?'

'On to Chirfa and Djanet.'

Chirfa was nearly a hundred and fifty kilometres north of Seguedine and consisted of a Tuareg camp and one deserted Foreign Legion fortress which might have stood in for Fort Zinderneuf in *Beau Geste* but for one thing – there was an anchor carved above the main gate. Because we were about as far away from the sea as a human being can get on this planet I stared at this improbable emblem and asked Byrne about it.

'I wouldn't know. Maybe it was built by French marines.'

The Tuareg seemed different from those I had met before, being more shabbily dressed. Byrne said they were of the Tassili Tuareg. From them he bought a donkey, which he gave to Konti. 'This is where he leaves us,' he said. 'He'll go east, past Djado and on to the Tibesti.'

'How far to the Tibesti?'

'Maybe five hundred kilometres; it's over in Chad.'

'Walking all the way?'

'Yeah. But the donkey'll help.'

'My God!' I watched Konti walk out of sight, towing the donkey.

As he walked back to where the Toyota was parked Byrne said, 'We've been followed most of the way here, but I lost sight of them about an hour ago. Two trucks.'

'Lash and Kissack.'

'I guess so. Wish I hadn't lost them; they're a couple of guys I like to keep my eye on.'

Twenty-Six

About ten kilometres out of Chirfa we climbed the pass that is called the Col des Chandeliers for no apparent reason because I didn't see anything that looked like a candlestick. At the top Byrne stopped under a cliff on which was a huge engraving about twenty feet high of a barbaric figure holding a spear. He ignored it, having seen many rock engravings before, and climbed up a little way to where he could get a good view of the way we had just come.

Presently he came down again. 'No one in sight.' He seemed disappointed. 'I'd just as lief know where that bastard is.'

'I knew it,' said Paul. 'You mean Lash.'

Byrne shrugged. 'You're a big boy now, Paul. Yeah, I mean Lash.'

'Who is he? I felt there was something wrong with him.'

I sighed. 'He might as well know, Luke.' I looked at Paul and said deliberately, 'Lash is Kissack's boss.'

He was hurt. 'Why didn't you tell me before?'

'Because we didn't know how you'd take it,' I said. 'You're apt to go off half cock. We found out about him back in Bilma.'

'But who is he?'

'I don't know, but he's in the packaging industry like I'm a candidate for the *Playboy* centrefold. My guess is that he's a big noise in the London underworld.'

'Why would anyone like th—'

'For God's sake, Paul! I don't know. Stop asking unanswerable questions.' I turned to Byrne. 'Let's go.'

He shook his head. 'Either they're behind us or they're ahead of us. If they're ahead, then we'll run into them

237

sooner or later. If they're behind, I'd just as soon know it. We'll wait here awhile. Paul, climb up there and keep watch.'

Paul hesitated, then nodded briefly and climbed up to where Byrne indicated. Byrne said, 'We'll give them an hour.' He turned and walked away and I fell into step beside him. 'You wouldn't be holding out on me, would you, Max? I mean, there isn't anything you haven't told me.'

'You know as much as I do.'

'Then maybe it's Paul. We may have to talk to him seriously.'

I shook my head. 'I've done that – filleted him. He knows nothing.'

Byrne gave a soft exclamation, then stooped and picked up something. He examined it then handed it to me. 'A souvenir of the Sahara.'

It was a small blade carved from stone and about an inch long and half an inch wide. It was beautifully polished and the cutting edge was still keen. 'A small chopper,' he said.

'Tuareg?'

'Hell, no!' He pointed upwards at the engraving of the giant with the spear. 'His people. If you keep your eyes open you can find dozens of things like that around here. Three thousand years old – maybe more.'

I passed my finger over the polished stone. *Three millennia!* It seemed to put me and my doings into an oddly dwindled perspective. Three-quarters of an hour later when Paul shouted I had found another, larger, axe-head and a couple of arrow-heads. I hastily pocketed them and ran for the Toyota.

Byrne was up on the cliff. 'Maybe six kilometres back,' he reported when he got down. 'Both trucks – that suits me fine. Let's go.' So off we went, bouncing down the other side of the Col des Chandeliers and heading north-west.

I kept an eye to the rear and presently saw the faint dots trailing dust plumes like comet tails. They kept an even distance behind, not dropping back and not catching up, and we went on like that for perhaps a couple of hours. Then we came to a beacon by the side of the track. Byrne said, 'Balise 593. Check the odometer – I want exactly fifty kilometres on top of what we've got now.'

I kept an eye on the odometer, watching the kilometres roll by. None of us talked much. Byrne because he was concentrating on his driving, me because I had nothing much to say, and Paul, I suspect, because his thoughts were occupied by the trucks behind. When fifty kilometres had been added on to the score I said, 'This is it.'

'Not quite,' said Byrne, and drove on for another half kilometre before he stopped. He got out and swung himself up on top of the Toyota where he stood gazing back. Then he got back into the cab and remarked, 'I wouldn't want them to lose us now.'

'Why not?'

He pointed off to the left. 'That, believe it or not, is supposed to be a track, and that's the way we're going. We'll soon find out how professional Lash's guides are.' He waited five minutes and then moved off, swinging on to the track which was hardly distinguishable.

The country changed and we lost sight of the mountains, being on an immense gravel plain as flat as a billiard table from horizon to horizon. 'This is called *reg*,' he said. 'Not bad for travelling on if you don't mind the monotony. I guess it was sea bottom at one time.'

Monotonous it certainly was and I began to become sleepy. I looked back at Paul and saw that weariness had conquered whatever terrors he had of Lash and Kissack. He was heavily asleep. The kilometres and miles flowed away beneath our wheels and still the view was unchanged. At one time I said, 'This must be the biggest plain in the desert.'

'Hell, no!' Byrne said. 'That's the Tanezrouft – about as big as France. Makes this look like a postage stamp. It'll be changing in a while – for the worse.'

And it did. First there were isolated barchan dunes, yellow crescents against the black gravel, then bigger patches of sand which Byrne avoided. Finally there was more sand than gravel and he couldn't avoid it. He said conversationally, 'In desert driving this is what separates the men from the boys. This is *fech-fech* – remember what I told you about it?'

I remembered the macabre tale of the big truck breaking through. 'Now you tell me!'

He turned his head and grinned. 'It's okay if you keep up your speed – sort of skim along the surface. Trouble might come if you slow down. I'm betting that those goons of Lash's don't know that.'

'You knew it was here?'

'Yeah. I was stuck here myself once about twenty years back. There's usually *fech-fech* here at this time of year.'

I said, 'It looks like ordinary sand to me.'

'Different colour. And if you look back you'll see we're not kicking up as much dust. One thing's for certain – we don't stop to find out for sure.'

Presently, after about an hour, he changed direction and soon after came to a stop. He climbed again on to the top of the cab and looked around, and when he got back he was grinning. 'Not a sign of them. Mr Lash might have helped us back at Seguedine but I don't think we should help him now. We join the main track to Djanet over there. That's Balise Berliet 21. Know what Djanet means?'

'I don't even know what Balise Berliet 21 means.'

'The Berliet Motor Company tested their heavy trucks out here and signposted the desert. And Djanet is Arabic for Paradise.'

Twenty-Seven

       Paradise was built partly on the desert floor and partly on a rocky hillside and provided more amenities than most oasis towns. The hotel was spartan but clean and better than most; bedroom accommodation was in *zeribas*, grass huts with the walls hung with gaily-coloured blankets, and there were showers which actually worked. As I sponged myself down I reflected that Byrne had been right – the desert is a clean place and a man doesn't stink. This was the first shower I'd had in nearly a month.

Byrne had left the Toyota in the hotel compound and had gone looking for his informant, the putative lucky winner of ten camels. He came back some time later with two Tuareg whom he introduced as Atitel and his son, Hami. 'Have you got those photocopies of the Northrop?'

'Sure.' I dug into my bag and gave them to him.

He unfolded them. 'Where did you get these?'

'The Science Museum in London – they're from Jane's *All the World's Aircraft*, 1935 edition.'

He spread the photocopies on the table and began to interrogate Atitel, pointing frequently to the photograph of the Northrop 'Gamma'. This particular specimen must have been one of the first aircraft to be used by Trans-World Airlines because the TWA emblem was on the fuselage near the tail. It was a stylishly designed plane, long and sleek, with the cockpit set far back near the tail. It had, of course, been designed in the days when aircraft had cockpits and not flight decks, and it had a non-retracting undercarriage with the struts and wheels enclosed in streamlined casings. The caption described it as a freight and mail-carrying monoplane.

At last Byrne straightened. 'This could be it. He says there's a metal bird of the *Kel Ehendeset* up on the Tassili about three days' march in from Tamrit.'

'How far is that, and what the devil is a *Kel* whosit?'

'Maybe seventy kilometres. The *Kel Ehendeset* are you and me – anyone who knows about machines.' He turned to Atitel and they talked briefly, then he said, 'He says the *Kel Ehendeset* have power over the *angeloussen* – the angels – and it's the *angeloussen* who make the trucks move and lift the air-planes.'

'Sounds logical. If it's three days' march then it's about six hours by *angeloussen* power.'

Byrne looked at me disgustedly as though I ought to know better. 'We won't get the Toyota on to the plateau. When we go we walk.' He tapped the photograph. 'Atitel seems pretty certain that the wreck on the Tassili is just like this. He insists there are no engine nacelles on the wings and that the fuselage is cylindrical up front just like in the picture. That's the big radial engine there.'

'Then it may be Billson's?'

'Could be.' Byrne shook his head. 'But the Tuareg don't go much for pictures – like all Moslems. Against their religion, so they have no experience of pictures. I've known a guy hang a picture on the wall of his tent in imitation of what he's seen Europeans do in their houses. It was something he'd cut out of a magazine because he liked it. He'd put it upside-down.' He smiled. 'It was a picture of a square-rigger in full sail, but he'd never seen a ship or even the goddamn sea, so all it made was a pretty pattern which maybe looked just as well upside-down.'

'But if Atitel *has* seen a plane, then he should be able to compare it with a picture.'

'I wouldn't bet my life on it, but I suppose we'll have to take the chance. We didn't come all this way for nothing.'

'When do we start?'

He began to dicker with Atitel and a lot of palavering went on with Hami putting in his tuppence-worth from time to time. It was fifteen minutes before Byrne said, 'He says he can't start until late tomorrow or, maybe, early the day after. He's got to round up some donkeys that have strayed. The plane is about fifty kilometres from Tamrit – that's on the edge of the plateau at the top. We won't be doing much more than fifteen kilometres a day up there so it means taking water for at least a week, preferably ten days. That means baggage animals and more donkeys than he can lay his hands on right now.'

He turned back to Atitel and money changed hands. When the Tuareg had gone I said, 'That money was Algerian.'

Byrne looked at me in surprise. 'Yeah; because we're in Algeria.'

'When did that happen?'

He grinned. 'Remember the detour we took to lose Lash? Well, it took around the border posts, too. You're okay, Max; you're legal in Algeria.'

'But Billson may not be.'

He grunted. 'Relax. There's a hell of a lot of desert between here and Tam; the word may not have filtered through.' He held up the photocopies. 'Mind if I hang on to these? I have some figuring to do.' I nodded. 'Where's Paul?'

'Still in the shower.'

He laughed. 'I told you a guy could drown in the desert.' Then he sat at the table, took out his stub of pencil and began making calculations on the back of one of the photocopies, referring constantly to the specifications of the Northrop 'Gamma'.

We didn't start next day or even the day after, but the day after that. Byrne grumbled ferociously. 'Sometimes these people give me a pain in the ass.'

I grinned. 'I thought you were one of them – a proper Targui.'

'Yeah; but I revert to type at times. I'm thinking of Lash and Kissack. I don't know how badly they were sanded in, but it won't take them forever to get out. I want to get clear before they get here.'

'What makes you think they'll come to Djanet?'

'Only place they can get gas.'

But it gave me the chance of unwinding and relaxing after the heavy pounding in the Toyota. And I slept in a bed for the first time since leaving Algiers – the hotel mattress wasn't much harder than the sand I'd become accustomed to. And we all had a few welcome beers.

On the third day after arrival we drove out of Djanet in the Toyota and we still hadn't seen Lash. I said, 'Perhaps he's still out there where you stranded him.'

'My heart bleeds for him,' said Byrne. He cocked his head and looked back at Paul. 'What do you think?'

'I hope he rots,' said Paul vindictively. 'Kissack, too. All of them.'

Paul was becoming bloodthirsty, but it wasn't too surprising. It's hard to be charitable towards people who shoot at you without telling you why.

We drove towards the mountains, towards steep cliffs which reared up like a great stone barrier. At last we bumped to a halt in a grove of tamarisk trees among which donkeys were grazing. Atitel and Hami waved in greeting as we got out. Byrne grunted in disgust. 'Those goddamn animals should have been loaded by now.'

'Where are we going?'

His arm rose forty-five degrees above the horizontal as he pointed and I got a crick in my neck as I looked up. 'Up there.'

'My God!' The cliffs rose vertically for about two thousand feet and Byrne was pointing to a cleft, a ravine which cut into them, leaving a v-shaped notch at the top which looked like a gunsight. 'I'm no bloody mountaineer.'

'Neither is a donkey and any man can go where a donkey can. It's not as steep as it looks.' He cocked an eye at the sun. 'Let's get started. I want to be at the top before nightfall.'

He chivvied Atitel and Hami into loading the donkeys.

The goatskin *djerbas* of the Tuareg were kinder to the animals than the jerricans which held the rest of our water supply because they caused less chafe, but there weren't enough *djerbas* and so the jerricans had to be used. Most of the load was water for man and animal.

'I'm figuring on ten days,' said Byrne. ''Course we may be lucky and find a *guelta* – that's a rock pool – but we can't depend on it. Now you see 'em, now you don't.'

So we loaded water and food for five men and seven donkeys for ten days, and Byrne added a cloth-wrapped parcel which clinked metallically. He also added the Lee-Enfield rifle to the top of one load, being careful to strap it tight. 'I'll be back in ten minutes,' he said, and got into the Toyota and drove away.

I watched him out of sight, then turned to Paul. 'What about this? Think you can make it?'

He looked up at the cliffs. 'I think I can; I won't be carrying anything. Not like when we were crossing the dunes in the Ténéré.'

His face was drawn and pale in spite of the tan he had acquired. I don't think he had been a fit man even when he left England because his life had been sedentary. Since then he had been shot and nearly died of exposure, and what we had been doing since had been no rest cure. I said, 'Maybe it would be better if you stayed. I'll talk to Byrne about it.'

'No,' he said sharply. 'He'd agree with you. I want to come. There may be – ' he swallowed – 'may be a body.'

The obsession which had driven him all his life was nearing its culmination. Within only a few days he had the chance of finding out the truth about his father, and he wasn't going to give up now. I nodded in agreement and looked up at the cliffs again. It still looked a killer of a climb.

Byrne came back on foot. 'I've put the truck where it won't be found easily. Let's move.'

I drew him on one side. 'Have you been up there before?'

'Sure. I've been most places.'

'What's the travelling like once we get on top?'

245

'Not bad – if we stick to the water-courses.'

'Water-courses!' I said incredulously.

'You'll see,' he said with a grim smile. 'It's the damnedest country you're ever likely to see. Like a maze – easy to get lost. What's your point?'

'I'm thinking of Paul.'

Byrne nodded. 'Yeah, he's been on my mind, too. But if he can get to the top here he'll be okay.'

'*Tassili n' Ajjer*,' I said thoughtfully. 'What does that translate as?'

'The Plateau of Goats – not that I've ever seen any. A few wild camels, though.' He shook his head irritably. 'Let's move, for God's sake!'

And so we started. It wasn't bad at first because we were on gently rising ground approaching the base of the cliffs. When we got to the ravine it was bigger than it looked at first, maybe half a mile wide at the bottom and narrowing as it rose. There was a path of sorts which zig-zagged from side to side so that for every hundred yards of forward travel we walked perhaps six hundred. And climbed, of course, but not as much.

It was a steady toil which put a strain on the calf muscles and on to the heart and lungs, a battle for altitude. It wasn't any kind of a mountaineering feat, just damned hard work which went on and on. There was no sound but the steady rasping of breath in my throat, the occasional clatter as a stone was dislodged to go bounding down the ravine, and the clink of a jerrican as it hit a rock. Sometimes a donkey would snort but no one had breath for talking.

I think we would have made the top quicker had it not been for Paul who held us back. We stopped frequently for him to catch up, and waited while he rested. It gave me time to rest my own lungs, for which I was thankful. Atitel and Hami didn't seem worried by the effort; they would smoke a half-cigarette and carefully put away the stubs before resuming the climb. As for Byrne, he was all whipcord and leather, as usual, but his nose was beakier and his cheeks more sunken than I had noticed before.

So it was that it took us over four hours to climb two thousand feet and I doubt if the ground distance we had covered would be more than a mile and a half when measured on a map. As soon as the ground began to level we stopped and within minutes Atitel and Hami had the inevitable miniature Tuareg camp fires going and water on the boil to make tea. I said breathlessly, 'Are we there?'

'Nearly. The worst is over.' Byrne pointed towards the setting sun. 'I reckon you can see over eighty kilometres from here.'

The view was fantastic – dun-coloured hills close by changing to blue and purple in the distance. Byrne pointed towards a jumble of dunes. 'The *Erg d'Admer*; all that sand was washed down from the plateau. Must have been one of the biggest waterfalls in the world right here – a fall of two thousand feet.'

'Waterfall!' I said weakly.

'Sure; the Tassili was well watered at one time. Real big rivers. And it was good cattle country with plenty of feed. Long time ago, of course.'

Of course!

I sipped sweet tea from a small brass cup and regarded Paul, who was lying flat on his back and seemed completely exhausted. He'd made it but only just. I went over to him. 'Have some tea, Paul.'

His chest heaved. 'Later,' he gasped.

'Max!' said Byrne. His voice was soft but there was a snap of command in it. I looked up and he jerked his head so I went and joined him where he stood looking down the ravine. He pointed to the desert floor and there, two miles away and nearly half a mile below was a movement of sand.

'Dust devils?' They were familiar in the desert; miniature whirlwinds caused by the convection currents stirred up by the heat.

Byrne looked up at the sun. 'Not at this hour. I think we've got company. There are two.'

'How the hell would Lash know we came here?'

Byrne shrugged. 'Anyone going up to the Tassili from Djanet would come this way. No other way as easy.' Easy! 'He'll have been asking around in Djanet; it would have been no trick to trace us – just a few enquiries at the hotel.'

'We ought to have been more discreet.'

'It wouldn't have worked. No one can hire men and animals in Djanet without the word getting round. Lash's men might speak Tamachek, but even if they have only Arabic they'd have no trouble in finding out what they wanted to know.'

I looked down the cliffside and there was no movement to be seen. 'So we're in trouble.'

'Not too much,' said Byrne unperturbedly. 'They won't climb up here in the dark, and the sun will set in an hour. I guess they'll wait until tomorrow. That gives us a chance to get lost.' He looked back at Paul. 'We'll give him time to rest up then push on.'

'Where to?'

'Over the rise there – to Tamrit and Assakaô.'

Never could I have imagined a landscape such as that of the Tassili n' Ajjer. We walked in the beds of long-gone rivers which, when in flood, had carved deeply into the soft sandstone, making what were now canyons, the walls of which were scalloped into whole series of shallow caves on all sides. When desiccation set in and the water had gone the wind had continued to work on the Tassili, abrading the sandstone for thousands of years and sculpturing the rock into pillars and pinnacles of fantastic shape, some towering two hundred or more feet, others undercut at the base and felled as a woodsman would fell a tree.

· The land had a baked appearance like an ill-made pie left too long in the oven and, indeed, the Tassili had been under the furnace of the sun for too long without the amelioration of vegetative cover. The sandstone was blackened and covered with a patina of what Byrne called desert varnish. 'You get dew on the stone some nights,' he said. 'And it draws iron and manganese to the surface. Next day the dew evaporates and the iron and manganese oxidize. Have that happening for a few hundred or thousand years and you get a good coating of varnish.'

As he had said, it was a maze, the canyons that had been water-courses joining, linking and separating. I had the feeling that this had been some sort of delta, the end of a journey for a mighty river, once fast but now slow and heavy with silt like the delta of the Nile. But then it had come to Tamrit and the edge of the Tassili to plunge two thousand feet to the land below, taking the silt to what were now the huge dunes of the *Erg d'Admer*. And now there was no water. The land was dry as a camel bone found in the Ténéré, but not bleached – rather sun-scorched and hardened like a mummified corpse.

That I saw during the first hour before the sun set and then, at Byrne's insistence, we continued, aided by the lamp of a full moon, until nine that night when he relented and we made camp. By this time Paul was near collapse and I was wearier than I'd been since our stroll through the Ténéré. Too tired to eat, I crawled into one of the shallow caves in the rock and fell asleep huddled in my *djellaba*.

I awoke in daylight to find a man looking down at me. He was dark-skinned and wore nothing but a loincloth and, in his right hand, he carried a spear. Behind him was a herd of cattle, healthy-looking beasts with piebald hides and wide-spreading horns. And beyond them was a group of hunters carrying bows, some with arrows nocked to the string.

I blinked in surprise and sat up and stared. The man was nothing but paint on the wall of the cave, and so were the cattle and the hunters. I jerked my head around and saw Byrne squatting outside the cave, feeding the water-boiling contraption he called a volcano. Behind him Hami was loading *djerbas* on to a donkey.

'Luke,' I said, 'have you seen this?'

He looked up. 'Time you were awake. Sure, I've seen it – one of the Tassili frescoes.'

I turned back to stare at it. The colours seemed as fresh as though it had been painted the week before and there was a fluency and elegance of line in the drawing of the cattle which any modern painter would envy. 'How old is this?'

Byrne came into the cave. 'The cattle? Three thousand years, could be four.' He moved along the wall of the cave until he came to the end. 'This is older – this mouflon.' I scrambled to my feet and joined him. The wild sheep was more crudely executed. 'Eight thousand years,' said Byrne. 'Maybe more, I wouldn't know.'

I began to examine the wall more carefully, looking for more treasures, but he said brusquely, 'No time for that. We've a long way to go. Wake Billson.'

Reluctantly I turned away, woke Paul, and then helped to make our breakfast. Not more than half an hour after I had woken we were on our way again, threading the canyons of the Tassili. An hour later I saw the green of trees, big ones lofting more than fifty feet. The branches were wide spread but twisted and gnarled.

I said, 'There must be water here,' and pointed.

'Cypress,' said Byrne. 'Those can have a tap root a hundred feet long and going straight down. And they're older than Methuselah; maybe they were here at the time the guy was painting those cattle back there in the cave.'

We left the trees behind and marched in silence and again all was silence except for the clatter of stones and the snorting of the donkeys and an occasional word passing between Atitel and Hami. There wasn't much to say about what we were looking for – everything had been said to exhaustion. And there wasn't much to say about Lash, either. If he was coming up behind he'd either catch us or he wouldn't.

We stopped briefly at midday to eat, and again at sunset, and then pressed on into the moonlit night. I thought it unsafe and said so, but Byrne was confident that Atitel knew what he was doing, more confident than I. Again we stopped at about nine and I found another cave. To my surprise I was not as tired as I had expected to be, and Paul was better, too. I looked at him as he unslung a jerrican from a donkey and thought of what Isaacson, back in Luton, had called him. A *nebbish*! The total nonentity.

It was true! Hours had gone by at a time when, even in Paul's presence, I had not given him a thought. When we drove in the Toyota he always sat in the back and wasn't under my eye. On this, and other, desert marches he always brought up the rear. He said little, never commenting on what he saw, however wondrous, but just stubbornly put one foot in front of the other. And he never complained, no matter how he felt. It was something to say for Paul but, all the same, he might just as well not have been there. The *nebbish*!

As for Luton – that was a million miles away, on another planet.

We fed on dates and dried mutton and I asked Byrne what progress we were making. He chewed vigorously, then swallowed. 'Not too bad. Atitel reckons on less than a day and a half. He says he'll see a landmark he knows before dark tomorrow.'

'What about Lash?' I said. 'And Kissack?'

'What about them? At Tamrit we left them at least eight hours behind, and you can add another three hours tonight because they won't be moving at night. I guess we're a full day ahead. And they don't know where we're going.'

'We've been leaving tracks. I've noticed. Prints in the sand and donkey droppings.'

He nodded. 'Sure. But we've also been moving a lot on rock and leaving no trail. They can follow us if they know how but it'll take up a lot of time, casting around and all. That puts us another day ahead, maybe two.' He took another bite of mutton and said casually, 'We might run into them on the way back.'

'That's nice.'

He grinned. 'I'll ask Atitel to take us back another way.'

When I awoke the next morning I eagerly scanned the wall of the cave but, to my disappointment, it was bare rock. Hami had baked bread in the hot sand under a fire, and it was crunchy in the crust and very tasty if you ignored the gritty sand. After breakfast we set off again, Atitel leading the way through the shattered wastes of the Tassili n' Ajjer.

The worst thing that could possibly have happened occurred at mid-afternoon. We were picking our way through a particularly bad patch where, for some reason or other, the wind action on the sandstone columns had been accentuated. The grinding action of sand-laden wind against the bases of the columns had felled a lot of them and, in their fall they had smashed and broken, leaving a chaos of debris through which it was difficult to negotiate our way.

Suddenly the donkey which Atitel was leading brayed vigorously and plunged, butting him in the back so that he fell. He gave a cry and Byrne ran up and stamped at something on the ground. When I got to him I saw it was a snake. 'Horned viper,' said Byrne, and ground its head to pulp under his heel. 'It scared the donkey.'

It had done more than that because Atitel was sitting up holding his leg and groaning. Byrne examined it and looked up at me. 'It's broken,' he said flatly.

'Christ!' I said. 'What do we do now?'

'Make a splint for a start.'

That wasn't as easy as it sounded because we had nothing suitable for a splint other than the barrel of the rifle. Un-expectedly, it was Paul who came up with a good idea. He tapped a jerrican which was hanging on the flank of a donkey and it rang hollowly. 'This empty?'

'Yeah.'

'We can bash it with rocks,' said Paul. 'Flatten it. We ought to be able to make some sort of rigid splint.'

'We can do better than rocks,' said Byrne, and went to a

donkey and unpacked the cloth-covered bundle he had brought. From it he produced a hammer and a cold chisel. 'Get that can on the ground.'

It took time and the desert rang with the sound as it echoed from column to column but eventually we splinted Atitel's leg, padding it first and then binding the metal with strips ripped from a *gandoura*. He had stopped groaning and looked on interestedly as we did it.

When we had finished Byrne squatted next to him and uttered the first words of what proved to be a long conversation. I said to Paul, 'God knows what we'll do now. From what Byrne told me last night we're ten or twelve kilometres from where the old man said he saw the plane.'

'We'll go on.' Paul's face was set in stubbornness.

'Be reasonable.' I waved my hand at the chaos all about us. 'How the hell can we find it without a guide? This, Paul – this bloody Godforsaken land – is the reason it wasn't found in the first place. You could walk within ten yards and never see it.'

'We'll go on,' he said. 'And we'll find it.'

I shook my head and looked to where Atitel was drawing with his finger in the sand. Byrne was asking questions. I shrugged and went to help Hami adjust the harness on one of the donkeys where the edge of a jerrican had chafed and worn a sore spot in its hide.

Half an hour later Byrne stood up. 'Okay; Atitel and Hami are going back. The old man can ride a donkey and Hami will lead another with enough food and water for the two of them. He'll take Atitel to Tamrit and then go down into Djanet for help.'

I said, 'They might run into Lash.'

'I've told them about Lash. They know enough to keep clear of him. Hami will go back a different way.' He laughed shortly. 'I said it's a blood feud; they understand that.'

'And us?'

'We go on.' I looked at Paul, who was grinning. 'Atitel's landmark is unmistakable, according to him. It's a big rock

253

column about two hundred feet high and split from the top to half way down as though someone has driven a wedge into it – you know, like splitting timber. He says all we have to do is to keep going the way we are now and we should see it in a couple of hours.'

'And the plane?' Paul's voice was shrill.

'Is about three kilometres north-west of the split column.'

It was chancy. Atitel's idea of north-west might not co-incide with Byrne's compass, and I didn't like the sound of that '*about* three kilometres' – it could be anything from two to four, more or less. I figured we might have to search five or six square kilometres. Still, it was better than the situation I had envisaged when talking to Paul.

I said, 'Can you guide us back to Tamrit? I don't know that I could.'

'Yeah. I've been taking compass bearings.' Byrne looked from me to Paul. 'Well, what about it?'

Paul nodded vigorously, so I shrugged. If it was a question of taking a vote I was out-voted. I said, 'It's all right with me as long as Atitel will be okay. It's a long way back to Tamrit and then he'll have to wait alone while Hami goes down that bloody ravine and on into Djanet. Do you think it's fair on him?'

'It's his idea,' said Byrne. 'He don't mind the broken leg just as long as he can get it set properly. He says he's broken that leg before. What he's really worried about is his ten goddamned camels. He wants them.'

'Then tell him to pray to Allah that this is the aeroplane we're looking for.'

We redistributed loads on the donkeys and then the two Tuareg went back, with Atitel riding a donkey led by Hami, his splinted leg sticking out grotesquely at right-angles. Then there were just the three of us left with five donkeys. I led two and so did Paul, while Byrne coped with one so that he could have a hand free for his compass.

I was mildly surprised when we saw Atitel's landmark after a two-hour march. It didn't seem possible that things could go right for us – I had half expected that we'd have to search for the damn thing – but there it stood unmistakably as Byrne had described it, a tall tower which looked as though a giant had taken a swipe at it with an axe and had cleft it from the top.

We camped at its base. Paul was all for going on the further three kilometres to the north-west but Byrne wouldn't have it. 'It's late,' he said. 'I didn't mind night marches with Atitel; I trusted him. But any one of us could bust a leg in the dark. We'll leave it until morning.'

So we left it until morning and breakfasted before dawn, then set out as soon as it was light enough to see clearly. In all my years, even in the army, there was never a period during which I made as many dawn starts as in the desert. We marched three kilometres, Byrne setting the direction and pacing us. That took an hour. Then we stopped in the middle of nowhere and unloaded the donkeys and hobbled them so they wouldn't stray.

The landscape was anarchic; a disorder of rock columns, a hugger-mugger of hiding places. Peter Billson's plane could be within a hundred yards but there was no way of knowing. I said into the silence, 'It could have burnt out.'

'No,' said Byrne. 'Atitel said it was intact. He's seen planes before at the airstrip at In Debiren and he said that this plane still had its wings on. He said it was *exactly* like the plane in the picture.'

'That's incredible! You mean Billson landed in the middle of all this in the dark without bending anything. I don't believe it.'

'He was a good pilot,' protested Paul.

'I don't care if he could fly as well as the Archangel Gabriel – it still seems bloody impossible.'

'Maybe the *angeloussen* helped him,' said Byrne. 'Now, we've got to do this real careful. No one goes off alone. We keep in sight or sound of each other. If you're out of sight keep hollering.' He stared at Paul. 'In this mess a guy can get lost awful easy so mind what I say.'

Paul mumbled assent. He was quivering like an eager dog who wanted to go and chase rabbits. I said, 'I didn't look at those photocopies too closely. How big is this Northrop?'

'Forty-eight feet wingspan,' said Paul. 'Length, thirty-two feet. Maximum height, nine feet.'

It was bigger than I had assumed. We were looking for something in an area of, say, fifteen hundred square feet. I felt a bit better, but not much.

'We spread out in a line, Paul in the middle,' said Byrne. 'And you take your direction from me.'

And so began the search. We quartered the area in overlapping sweeps so as not to miss anything, and it was damned hard work. This was not a mere matter of making a march; we had to cover and inspect an area, which meant scrambling over rocks and looking behind every column in that broken wilderness.

We searched all day without finding anything but rocks.

That night Paul was dispirited. He huddled in his *djellaba* and aimlessly tossed a stone from one hand to the other while staring blankly with unmoving eyes. I didn't feel too good myself and said to Byrne, 'What do you think?'

He shrugged. 'Maybe Atitel was out in his distance and direction. We'll look again tomorrow. Get some sleep.'

'God!' I said. 'Talk about needles in haystacks. And there's that proverb about leaving no bloody stone unturned.'

Byrne grunted. 'If it was easy to see it would have been found years ago. Atitel says he came on it only by chance four years ago. He'd come up here trying to trap wild camel foals and got himself lost.'

'Why didn't he report it when he got back to Djanet?'

'It didn't mean that much to him. If there had been a body he might have, but he said there was no body near.'

'Do you think Billson tried to walk out?'

'He was a damned fool if he did.'

Paul came alive. 'He wouldn't try that,' he said positively. 'He knew the rules about that. All the pilots in the race were told to stay by the plane if they came down.'

'Yeah,' said Byrne. 'It's the sensible thing to do and, from what I've heard of him, Peter Billson was a sensible guy.' He paused. 'Sorry to bring this up, Paul; but when Atitel told me there was no body I had my doubts about this being the right airplane. What in hell would a good flier like your old man be doing way over here anyway? He'd be off course by nearly two hundred miles.'

'Atitel identified the plane,' said Paul obstinately.

'Yeah, but when I first suggested the Tassili you said yourself your father was too good a pilot to be fifteen degrees out.'

It was all very depressing.

We found it next morning only ten minutes after restarting the search. I found it, and it was infuriating to think that if Byrne hadn't called off the search the previous night another ten minutes would have done it.

I scaled the side of a pillar of rock that had fallen intact and walked across it to see what was on the other side. There, in a sixty-foot-wide gully was an aeroplane looking as pristine as though it had just been delivered from the manufacturer. It stood in that incongruous place as it might have stood on the tarmac outside a hangar.

'Luke!' I yelled. 'Paul! It's here!'

I scrambled down to it, and they both arrived breathless. 'That's it!' shouted Paul. 'That's my father's plane.'

I looked at Byrne. 'Is it?'

'It's a Northrop "Gamma",' he said, and passed his hand almost reverentially over the fuselage. 'Yeah, this is Peter Billson's plane. Look!'

Over forty years of wind-driven sand had worn away the painted registration marks but on the fuselage one could still detect the outline of the letters which made up a word – *Flyaway*.

'Oh, God!' said Paul, and leaned on the trailing edge of the wing. Suddenly he burst into tears. All the pent-up emotion of a lifetime came out of him in one rush and he just stood there and wept, racked with sobs. To those brought up in our stiff-upper-lip society the sight of a man in tears is apt to be unnerving, so Byrne and I tactfully walked away until Paul could get a grip on himself.

We walked a little way down the gully away from the plane, then Byrne turned and said, 'Now how in hell did he put it down there?' There was wonder in his voice.

I saw what he meant. There was not much clearance at the end of each wingtip and beyond the plane the gully narrowed sharply and if the aircraft had rolled a few feet further the wings would have been ripped off. I said as much.

'That's not what I mean,' said Byrne. He turned and studied the terrain with narrowed eyes. 'This airplane is in a goddamn box.' He pointed to the wall of rock at the wider end of the gully. 'So how did it get in the box?' He shook his head and looked up at the sky. 'He must have brought it down like a helicopter.'

'Is that possible?'

'Unlikely. Look, the guy is in trouble; it's night time and something has gone wrong, so he has to put down. He can't see worth a damn, his landing speed is sixty miles an hour, and yet he sets that thing down right way up on its wheels in a space that should be impossible.'

I looked around. 'No wonder it wasn't found. Who'd look on the Tassili anyway? And if they did it's in an impossible place.'

'Let's go get the gear,' he said. 'We'll set up camp here.'

He called out, telling Paul to stay there, and we went to round up the donkeys, load them, and take them back to the plane. It was difficult to find a way in but we found a cleft big enough to take one donkey at a time, and unloaded and set up camp in the clear space just behind *Flyaway*. After that the donkeys were taken out again, hobbled, and turned loose to feed on what sparse vegetation they could find.

When we got back Paul had recovered, although his eyes

were still red. 'Sorry about that.'

'That's all right, Paul,' I said. 'I didn't expect an icy calmness.'

Byrne was pacing the distance from the rock wall at the end of the gully to the tail of the plane. I walked towards him. 'Sixty yards,' he said, and blew out his cheeks expressively. 'I still don't believe it. Paul okay?'

I nodded and put my hand up to touch the rudder. 'She looks ready to fly.'

'You'd have to lift her out of here with a crane,' said Byrne. 'And then build a runway. But there's more. Look!' He pointed down to the tail wheel which was flat. When he kicked it, it fell apart in a powdery heap. 'That's the weak link. The airplane is fine – all metal. 24ST Alclad according to the specification, and the desert wouldn't hurt that. The engine will be fine, too; it'll just need the dried oil cleaning out and it'll run as sweetly as new. But all the sealings will have gone, and all the gaskets, and anything made of rubber. And I guess any plastic parts, too. I hear those early plastics weren't too stable chemically.' He sighed. 'No, she'll not fly again – ever.'

As Paul joined us Byrne said, 'Mind if I take a look in the cockpit?' Paul looked puzzled, as well he might, because this was the first time Byrne had asked his permission to do anything. Byrne explained, 'I guess this is your airplane – by inheritance, Paul.'

Paul swallowed, and I saw the glisten of tears in his eyes. 'No,' he said huskily. 'I don't mind.'

Byrne walked around the tailplane and put his foot on the step on the wing fillet, then swung himself up to look into the cockpit. The cockpit cover was slid back and he looked down and said, 'Fair amount of sand in here.'

I left him to it and walked back to get my camera. I spent some time cleaning the lens, which wasn't easy because the air was dry and the static electricity such that you could see the fine dust jumping on to the surface of the lens under its attraction. I did my best and then loaded the camera with a film and went back to take pictures.

Byrne had got into the cockpit and was fiddling around with the controls. The rudder moved, but with a squeaking and grating noise, and then the ailerons went up and down with less disturbance. Paul was standing on one side, doing nothing but just looking at *Flyaway*. I have never seen a man look so peaceful, and I hoped he would now be cured of what ailed him, because there was no doubt that he had been a man badly disturbed to the point of insanity.

I used up the whole roll of film, taking pictures from various angles, including two of the faded name on the side of the fuselage. Then I rewound the film into its cassette and packed it away with my unused shaving gear.

Presently Byrne called me and I went back to the plane. He was still in the cockpit. 'Come up here.'

I put my foot on the step and hoisted myself up. He had his pocket prismatic compass in his hand. 'Look at this!' He tapped an instrument set at the top of the windscreen.

'What is it?'

'The compass. It reads one hundred eighty-two degrees.' He held up the prismatic compass so I could see it. 'Mine reads one hundred seventy-five.'

'Seven degrees difference. Which is right?'

'Mine's not wrong,' he said evenly.

'An error of seven degrees wouldn't account for Billson being fifteen degrees off course.'

'Maybe not.' He handed me the prismatic compass. 'I want you to go back there – well away from the airplane. Take a sighting on the rudder; I want you lined up exactly the way the airplane is. Then take a reading and come back and tell me what it is.'

I nodded and climbed down, then went back as far as I had left the baggage. I sighted on the rudder and got a reading of 168°. I thought I'd made an error so I checked my position and tried again and got the same result. I went back to Byrne. 'A hundred and sixty-eight.'

He nodded. 'Fourteen degrees difference – that would be

about right to put him here.' He tapped the aircraft compass again. 'Look, Billson is flying at night, right? So he's flying by compass. Let's say he sets a course of one eighty degrees. He's actually going one sixty-six and way off course.'

'His compass was that much out?'

'Looks like it. And it must have gone wrong in Algiers because he got that far without trouble.'

I said, 'Why did your compass give different readings in here and out there?'

'Magnetic deviation,' he said. 'Remember what I told you at Assekrem about iron in the mountains causing trouble? Well, there's a lot of iron here. Up front there's a goddamn hunk of iron called an engine. That affects the compass reading. Now, that's a Wright Cyclone with nine cylinders and, in flight, all the spark plugs are busy sparking and sending out radiation. They tell you they can be screened but I've never seen anyone do a good job of screening yet. And there'll be other bits of iron about the airplane – the oleo struts, for instance.' He tapped the metal of the fuselage. 'This don't matter – it's aluminum.'

I said, 'What are you trying to tell me?'

'I'm getting to it.' Byrne stared thoughtfully at the compass. 'Now, you build an airplane, and you take a perfectly good compass and put it in that airplane and it gives you a wrong reading because of all the iron around. So you have to adjust it to bring it back to what it was before you put it in the airplane.' He pointed to the compass. 'Built in back of there are some small magnets put in just the right places to compensate for all the other iron.'

'And you think one of them fell off? Because of vibration, perhaps?'

'Nope,' he said shortly. 'They're not built to fall off; they're screwed in real tight. And there's something else – any compass, no matter how good, will give a reading that's a bit off when you're flying on different courses. You see, the needle is always pointing in the same direction, to magnetic north; so when you change course you're swinging all your iron around the needle.'

'It's getting more complicated.'

'This is the real point. Every compass in every airplane is tested individually because all airplanes have different magnetic characteristics – even the same models. The airplane is flown along different known courses and the compass readings are checked. Then a compass adjuster does his bit with his magnets. It's a real skilled job, more of an art than a science. He works out his calculations and maybe adds in the date last Tuesday, then he makes out a deviation card for the residual errors he can't get rid of on various courses. I've been looking for Billson's deviation card and I can't find it.'

'Not surprising, after forty-two years. What are you really getting at, Luke?'

'You can bet your last cent that Billson would have had his compass checked out real good before the race. His life depended on it.'

'And it let him down.'

'Yeah; but only after Algiers. And compasses don't go fourteen degrees wrong that easy.'

I stared at him. '*Sabotage!*'

'Could be. Can't think of anything else.'

My thoughts went back to English, the journalist who had set fire to Paul. 'That idea has come up before,' I said slowly. 'A German won the race – a Nazi. I don't suppose he could have done it personally, but a friend of his might.'

'I'd like to take this compass out,' said Byrne. 'There's a screwdriver in that kit of tools I brought.'

'I wondered about that,' I said. 'Were you expecting this?'

'I was expecting something. Don't forget there's a son of a bitch who is willing to kill to prevent this plane being found.'

'I'll get the screwdriver.'

As I dropped to the ground Byrne said, 'Don't tell Paul.' Paul was sitting on the ground in front of *Flyaway* just looking at her. I walked away, got the screwdriver and came back, concealing it in the folds of my *gandoura*. Byrne attacked the first of the four screws which held the compass in place. It seemed locked solid but an extra effort moved it and then it rotated freely.

He took out all four screws and gently eased the compass out of place and turned it over in his hands. 'Yeah,' he said. 'You see these two brass tubes here? Inside those are small pole magnets. This screw here makes the tubes move like scissor blades – that's how the compass adjuster gets his results. And this is a locking nut to make sure the tubes can't move once they're set.'

He tested it with his fingers. 'It's locked tight – which means . . .'

'. . . that if the compass is fourteen degrees out of true it was done deliberately?'

'That's right,' said Byrne.

Twenty-Eight

Sabotage! An ugly word. An uglier deed.

I said, 'How long would it take to do it?'

'You saw how easy it was to take out this compass. To make the change and put back the compass wouldn't take long. A maximum of fifteen minutes for the whole job.'

'I'm taking that compass back to England with me,' I said. 'Just as it is. I'm beginning to develop peculiar ideas.'

'It only tells half the story,' said Byrne. 'We have to solve the other half – why did he come down? I have ideas on that. I want to look at the plumbing of this airplane.'

'I'll leave you to it.' I climbed down from the wing and joined Paul. 'Well, Paul, this is it – journey's end.'

'Yes,' he said softly. He looked up. 'He wasn't a cheat. That South African was lying.'

'No, he wasn't a cheat.' I certainly wasn't going to tell Paul that the compass had been gimmicked – that would really send him round the twist. I said carefully, 'Byrne is trying to find out what was wrong with *Flyaway* to make her come down. Do you mind?'

'Of course not. I'd like to know.' He rubbed his shoulder absently. 'That newspaper back in England. Do you think the editor will publish an apology?'

'An apology? By God, Paul, it'll be more than that. It will be headline news. There'll be a complete vindication.' But it would be better if we could find the body, I thought.

I looked around and tried to put myself in Billson's place. He had either tried to walk out or he hadn't, and both Paul and Byrne were fairly certain that he'd do the right thing and stick close to *Flyaway*; it was standard operating procedure. He must have known that an air search would be laid on and that an aeroplane is easier to spot than a man on foot. What he didn't know was that no one dreamed of searching the Tassili area.

So if he hadn't walked out where was he? Atitel had said he hadn't seen a body, but had he searched?

I said nothing to Paul but walked away and climbed the side of the fallen rock pillar from which I first saw *Flyaway*, and began to walk along it. It was my idea that Billson would want to get out of the sun, so I was looking for a cave.

I found the remains of the body half an hour later. It was in one of the shallow scooped-out caves peculiar to the Tassili and the walls were covered with paintings of men and cattle and hunting scenes. I use the word 'remains' advisedly because scavengers had been at the body after Billson had died and there were pieces missing. What was left was half covered in blown sand, and near by was the dull gleam of a metal box which could have been a biscuit tin.

I touched nothing but went back immediately. Paul hadn't moved but Byrne was on top of *Flyaway* and had opened some kind of a hatch on the side of the fuselage. As I climbed up he said, 'I think I've got it figured.'

'Never mind that,' I said. 'I've found the body.'

'Oh!' He turned his head and looked at Paul, then turned back to me. 'Bad?'

'Not good. I haven't told Paul yet. You know what he's like.'

'You'll have to tell him,' said Byrne definitely. 'He'll have to know and he'll have to see it. If he doesn't he'll be wondering for the rest of his life.' I knew he was right. 'But don't tell him yet. Let's get this figured out first.'

'What have you found?'

'If you look in the cockpit you'll see a brass handle on the left. It's a sort of two-way switch governing the flow of gas to the engine. In the position it's set at now it's drawing fuel from the main tank. It was in that position when I found it. Turn it the other way and gasoline is drawn from an auxiliary tank which has been built into the cargo space here. Got the picture?'

'He was drawing from his main tank when he crashed.'

'That's it.' He fumbled in his *gandoura* and came out with the photocopies I had given him. 'According to this, the main tank holds 334 gallons which gives a range of seventeen hundred miles at three-quarters power – that's cruising. But Billson was in a race – he wouldn't be cruising. I reckon he'd be flying on ninety per cent power, so his range would be less. I figure about fifteen hundred miles. It's eighteen hundred from Algiers to Kano, so that's a shortfall of three hundred miles.'

'Hence the auxiliary tank.'

'Yeah. So he needs another three hundred miles of fuel – and more. He'd need more because he might run into head winds, and he'd need a further reserve because he wouldn't want to do anything hairy like finding Kano in the dark and coming in on his last pint of gas. At the same time he wouldn't want this auxiliary tank to be full because that means weight and that would slow him down. I've been trying to figure like Billson and I've come up with the notion that he'd put a hundred fifty gallons in this tank. And you know what?'

'Tell me.'

'That's just about enough to bring him from Algiers to here on the course he was heading.'

'You mean when he switched over from the auxiliary to the main tank his engine failed. Empty main tank?'

'Hell, no! Billson wasn't an idiot – he'd supervise the filling himself. Besides, there are gauges in the cockpit. The engine quit all right, but it wasn't because the tank was empty. I'd like to find out why.'

'How?'

'I'd like to open up the main tank. Think Paul would mind?'

'I'll ask him.'

Paul said he didn't mind; in fact, he developed an interest as Byrne stood with hammer in one hand and cold chisel in the other surveying *Flyaway*. 'I've been tracing the gas lines and I'd say the main tank is in this mid-section here – might even extend into the wing fillets. I'll start there.'

He knelt down, laid the cutting edge of the chisel against the fuselage, and poised the hammer. 'Wait!' said Paul quickly. 'You might strike a spark.'

Byrne turned his head. 'So?'

'The petrol . . .'

'There ain't no petrol – no gasoline – in here, Paul. Not after forty-two years. It'll have evaporated.'

'From a sealed tank?' said Paul sceptically.

'No fuel tank is sealed,' said Byrne. 'There's a venting system. You try to pull gas from a tank without letting air in and you'll get nowhere. It's okay, Paul; there's no fuel in here now.'

There was a clang as he struck the head of the chisel. He struck again and again and presently I went to help him by holding the chisel so he could strike a harder blow. But first I cautioned him to make sure he hit the chisel and not my hand. Slowly we cut a hole into the side of *Flyaway* and, oddly, I thought it an act of desecration.

The hole was about a foot by six inches and at last Byrne was able to bend back the flap of aluminium so that he could look inside. As he did so some brown powder dropped out to lie on the sand. 'Yeah,' he said. 'An integral fuel tank.'

'What's the powder?'

'You always get gunk in the bottom of a tank no matter what you do. The gasoline is filtered going in and filtered coming out but no gas is pure anyway, and you have chemical instabilities and changes.' He put his hand inside and withdrew it holding a handful of the powder. 'More in here than I would have thought, though. If I was Billson and entering a race I'd have the tanks scoured and steam-cleaned before starting.'

I looked at the handful of dried sludge as he put it to his nose. 'More than you would have thought,' I repeated.

'Don't put too much into that,' he advised. 'This is the

first time I've looked inside a fuel tank. It ain't a job that's come my way before. There were over three hundred gallons in this tank and God knows what was happening to it while it was evaporating. Constant changes of temperature like you get here could have started all kinds of reaction.'

'All the same,' I said, 'I'd like to have a sample of that stuff.'

'Then find something to put it in.'

I'm old-fashioned enough to use a soap shaving-stick and mine came in a plastic case. It hadn't seen much use in the desert and I'd grown a respectable beard which, Byrne told me, was flecked with grey. 'Pretty soon you'll look as distinguished as me,' he had said. I broke off the column of soap and we filled the case with the brown powder and I screwed the cap back on and, for safety, secured it with an adhesive dressing from Byrne's first aid kit.

By that time it was past midday so we prepared a meal. As we ate Paul said, 'When are we leaving?'

Byrne glanced at me and I knew the same thought was in both our minds – we had a burial detail to attend to. He said, 'Early tomorrow.'

I said nothing to Paul until we had finished eating and had drunk our tea. Then I put a new film in my camera because I wanted a full record. I said, 'Paul, brace yourself; there's something I must tell you.'

His head jerked and he stared at me wide-eyed, and I knew he'd guessed. 'You've found him. You've found my father.'

'Yes.'

He got to his feet. 'Where?'

'Not far from here. Are you sure you want to see him? Luke and I can do what's necessary.'

He shook his head slowly. 'No – I must see him.'

'All right. I'll take you.'

The three of us went to the cave and the tears streamed down Paul's face as he looked down at what was left of his father. There were still scraps of flesh and skin left attached to the bones but it was brown and mummified, and a few tendrils of hair clung to the skull which otherwise was picked clean.

I took some photographs and then we began to brush the sand from the skeleton. Underneath the thin layer of sand was rock so we could not bury Peter Billson. Instead we piled a cairn of stones over the remains, Paul sobbing all the time. Then we went back to *Flyaway*, Byrne carrying under his arm the tin box which had been next to the body. There were a couple of other things we had buried with Billson; two packets bearing the name of Brock, the pyrotechnic company. One contained flares, the other smoke signals. Neither had been used because a rescue plane had neither been seen nor heard.

Standing next to *Flyaway* Byrne held out the box to Paul. 'Yours,' he said simply.

He took it and then sat down on the sand and laid the box in front of him. He looked at it for a long time in silence before he stretched out with trembling fingers to open it. This was nothing like opening a Christmas present. There were a lot of papers inside.

In his last days Peter Billson had kept a diary, written in his log-book. I don't propose to go into this in detail because it is most harrowing. A proposal has been made that it be published in a future edition of the *Journal of the Royal Aeronautical Society*. I'm against the idea. A man's mental agonies when facing death ought to be private.

There was Billson's flying licence, a sealed envelope addressed 'To my darling, Helen', a worn leather wallet, a pipe and an empty tobacco pouch, a Shell petrol carnet, a sheaf of bank notes – British, French and Nigerian, and it was strange to see the old big British five-pound note – and a few other small odds and ends.

Paul picked up the letter addressed to his mother. His lower lip trembled. 'I ought to have treated her better,' he whispered, then handed it to me. 'Will you burn that, please? Don't open it.'

I nodded. Byrne stooped and picked up a card. 'The compass deviation card,' he said. 'Not more than a degree and a half out on any course.' He handed it to me. 'It don't matter if a compass has deviation as long as you know what it is.'

Printed on the card was a compass rose around which were written figures in ink. It was signed by the compass adjuster and dated the 4th of January, 1936. I turned it over and saw something scrawled on the back. *I wonder how bloody true this damn thing is?* I nudged Byrne and showed it to him, and said in a low voice, 'He was beginning to guess in the end.'

The diary told Byrne what he wanted to know about the landing. 'He *was* a good flier, Paul,' he said. 'This is how he got down. His engine had quit and he was coming down in a glide with an airspeed of fifty-five knots. There was a low moon and suddenly he saw rocks between him and the moon, so he stalled her. He pulled her nose right up and that lost his speed and his lift at the same time, so he fell out of the sky damn near vertically. What he called a pancake landing. Never heard it called that before. He says, "The old girl pancaked beautifully but I'm afraid both oleo legs are broken – one badly. Never mind, she wouldn't take off from here anyway." '

I read the diary. He had lasted twelve days on two and a half gallons of water. At first the handwriting was firm and decisive but towards the end it degenerated into a scrawl. During the last few days he was apparently feverish and had hallucinations, communing with the painted men on the wall of the cave. The last entry was in a surprisingly firm hand and was a plea that his wife and young son be well looked after. The thought of the £100,000 insurance on his life seemed to comfort him a lot.

Byrne grunted and stood up. 'A guy like that deserves better than a heap of stones. He needs a marker.' He strode to *Flyaway* and jumped up on to the wing, then made his way up the fuselage until he was astride the cowling of the big radial engine. There was a banging and I saw he was unshipping the propeller.

That gave me an idea. I found the piece of aluminium we had cut from the side of the fuselage and, using the chisel and a small hammer began to incise letters. Paul came over to see what I was doing and stayed to help. When I thought we had finished I said, 'That's it, Paul.'

'No – there's something I want to add.'

So he guided the blade of the chisel while I thumped with the hammer and we added the fourth line so that our rough plaque read:

PETER BILLSON
AIRMAN
1903–1936
Fly away, Peter

Twenty-Nine

That seemingly small task took longer than I thought and by the time we had finished the sun was setting. We had our evening meal and went to sleep early. At dawn the following morning Paul and I helped Byrne take out the last two bolts that held the propeller to the shaft and we lowered it to the ground using a rope made up of bits and pieces of the donkey harness. Byrne and I carried to it the grave in the cave while Paul brought the plaque. We set the propeller upright near the grave and Byrne fastened the plaque to the boss using some wire he had found in *Flyaway*.

Then we stood there for a while, doing nothing, but just standing there. Byrne said, 'I guess Billson was the first guy to see those pictures in here in a few thousand years. Maybe this propeller and the inscription will still be there in a thousand years from now. Aluminum don't rust and things change slow in the desert. It's a good marker.'

After a while we went away, leaving Paul to his own thoughts.

In spite of the hobbles the donkeys had moved a fair way in search of grazing and it took us a while to find them and it was an hour before we got them back to the camp. Paul had come back looking sombre and helped us load them. It was time to go.

We took one last long look at *Flyaway* and then began the awkward business of coaxing the donkeys through the narrow cleft in the rock. When we got them out Byrne said, 'Okay – back to Tamrit. Maybe three days.'

Paul said, 'Do you mind waiting a minute? I won't be long. I just want . . .' He swallowed convulsively and looked at me. 'You didn't take a picture of the plaque. I'd like that.'

I glanced at Byrne who said, 'All right, Paul, but not more than fifteen minutes. Tether those donkeys firmly. We'll stroll ahead.' He pointed. 'That's the line we take.'

I unfastened my bag and took out my camera. 'Shall I come with you, or can you take the pictures?'

'I can do it,' he said, so I gave him the camera and he went back through the cleft.

Byrne said, 'Funny thing, this flesh and blood. You wouldn't think he'd feel like that about a man he hardly knew.' He tugged at the donkey rein. 'Let's go; he can catch up.'

We went at an easy pace, threading our way among the rocks for about half a mile. I looked back and said, 'Perhaps we'd better wait for Paul.'

'Huh?' said Byrne abstractedly. He was staring at the ground. 'Been camels here.'

I looked down at the enormous pad marks in the sand. 'You said there were wild camels.'

Byrne dropped on one knee. 'Yeah, I know I did – but wild camels don't repair their own pads.' He traced a line on one of the footprints. 'This one cut its foot and someone put a leather patch on.'

I frowned. 'Can that be done?'

'Sure. I just said so, didn't I?' He stood up and looked around. 'And there it is.'

I turned and, coming up from behind us was a man riding a camel – the Arab who had been with Kissack. He whistled shrilly and from our front came an answering whistle. There were five of them altogether; Kissack and the Arab, and Lash and his two musclemen, all mounted on camels and with no less than six baggage animals. There were no weapons in sight but that didn't mean a thing.

Lash looked down at us from the enormous height a camel confers. 'Mr Byrne,' he said pleasantly. 'And Mr Stafford. Well met. I didn't expect to find you here. Looking for frescoes, I take it?'

Kissack said, 'You're a long way from Kano, Stafford. You've come the wrong way.'

'And there's someone missing.' Lash snapped his fingers. 'What was his name? Ah, yes – Billson. Where is Mr Billson?' One of the men behind him muttered something, and he added, 'And the Tuareg who were with you?'

Byrne dropped the leading rein of his donkey and put his foot on it. 'Paul went sick so they took him back to Djanet.' It was a good improvised lie.

'Strange that we didn't meet him,' observed Lash. He beckoned to the Arab, who came close to him. Lash tossed him the camel reins and the Arab coaxed the camel to its knees and Lash dismounted awkwardly. He had not been riding in the Tuareg manner with his feet on the neck of the camel, but had stirrups. He grimaced. 'Damned uncomfortable beasts.'

'No call to ride them if you don't want,' said Byrne. 'You'd do better with a Tuareg saddle instead of that Chaamba rig.' He jerked his head at the Arab. 'His, I suppose.'

'You suppose correctly.' Lash waved his hand and all the men dismounted, the camels grunting discontentedly. 'Cat got your tongue, Mr Stafford?'

'I've found nothing interesting to say, so far.'

'Oh, you will,' he assured me. 'I'm certain you will. You've both already met Kissack so there's no need to introduce him. As for my other friends, they have no English.'

'Friends!' I said. 'Not guides?'

Lash smiled thinly. 'Propinquity breeds friendship. From the direction you're taking it seems you are returning to Tamrit. Do I gather that you've found what you were looking for?'

'Yeah, we found some paintings,' said Byrne. 'And I guess these are new ones – not seen before.'

'You weren't looking for frescoes,' said Lash flatly. 'Let's cut the cat and mouse act, shall we? You were looking for an aeroplane. Did you find it?'

'I don't know what business it is of yours,' I said.

Lash looked at me unsmilingly. 'Or yours, either. You wouldn't take a warning back in London. You had to play the thick-headed hero and meddle in things that don't concern you.'

So there it was said outright – Lash had been responsible for having me beaten up. 'Who's paying you?' I asked.

'Still meddling? That's dangerous. Now, where's Billson?'

'You've just been told,' I said. 'He went back to Djanet three days ago. He had an injury which was inflamed.' I touched my own shoulder. 'Here.' I was careful not to look at Kissack.

The play of expression on Lash's face was interesting because what I had just said could be circumstantially true. He dismissed Billson for the moment. 'And the aeroplane – where is it?'

'What airplane?' asked Byrne.

Lash sighed. 'Look, Byrne; don't play with me. That's just being stupid.' He turned away and began to talk to the Arab in low tones. The Arab remounted his camel, urged it to its feet, and began to backtrack along the way we had come. If he went far enough he'd find the donkeys Paul had left tethered outside the cleft in the rock. He might even find Paul.

Lash turned back to face us. 'Where's that aeroplane? And don't ask which aeroplane. It's a Northrop "Gamma" 2–D, built in 1934 and called *Flyaway*. It was crashed around here in 1936 by Peter Billson.' As Byrne opened his mouth Lash held up his hand. 'Don't tell me you don't know what I'm talking about. That would be a big mistake.'

Before Byrne could reply Kissack said, 'You're wasting time, Mr Lash. Let me try.'

'Shut up!' said Lash coldly.

Byrne said, 'I don't know what you're talking about.'

'All right,' said Lash wearily. 'We'll try it your way, Kissack.'

There was suddenly a gun in Kissack's hand. He stepped

forward and looked at us speculatively. 'The old geezer knows more about the desert than Stafford, I reckon; so he'd be a better guide.' I looked at the pistol he lifted; the muzzle was pointing directly between my eyes and I knew I was close to death. 'If you don't tell us, Stafford will be dead meat.'

It seemed an eternity before Byrne said, 'Okay – it's about ten kilometres back.'

A grunt of satisfaction came from Lash, and Kissack said, 'Do I kill him anyway, Mr Lash?'

'No,' said Lash. 'We might need him again – and for the same reason. Search them.'

They found our pistols, of course. Kissack checked the loads on the three donkeys. 'You had a rifle – where is it?'

I realized it had been packed on one of Paul's donkeys. Byrne said, 'Left it behind in the Ténéré. Too much sand and the action jammed. That's the only reason you're still alive, Kissack.'

Kissack's face whitened and he lifted the pistol again and pointed it at Byrne. 'What, for Christ's sake, did you do to Bailly?'

'That's enough,' commanded Lash. 'We're wasting time. Help me get up on this bloody camel.' They all remounted and now they all had guns showing except Lash, who seemed to be unarmed. 'About face,' he ordered. 'Now, take us to that aeroplane. No tricks, Byrne, or you'll be shot in the back where you stand.'

And so we retraced our steps. I glanced sideways at Byrne whose nose was beakier than ever. He didn't look at me but gazed ahead with a bleak expression. All he had bought was time – ten kilometres' worth of it – say, four or five hours. Then it would all start again.

I wondered about Paul – Byrne had given him fifteen minutes and he ought to have shown up by now. I prayed to God that he would live up to his reputation. Be a *nebbish*, Paul, I thought. Be the invisible man.

I tramped along, conscious of the guns at my back, and a

rhyme chittered insanely through my mind over and over again:

> As I was going up the stair,
> I met a man who wasn't there;
> He wasn't there again today,
> I wish to hell he'd go away!

We hadn't been moving long when the Arab appeared and reined his camel alongside Lash. There was a muttered conversation, and Lash called 'Stop!' I stopped and looked back. Lash said silkily, 'More tricks, Byrne? I warned you about that. Follow Zayid.'

The Arab moved in front of us and veered to the left on a course which would take us directly to where we had left Paul. Byrne grunted and shrugged imperceptibly. It seemed that Zayid was a good tracker – good enough to call Byrne's bluff.

We came to the cleft in the rock and there were no donkeys and no sign of Paul. If he was a *nebbish* he had also the characteristics of a boojum because, wraithlike, he had 'softly and suddenly vanished away'. Byrne looked at me and raised his eyebrows, and I shook my head to indicate that I didn't know, either. The little man who wasn't there had indeed gone away.

There was a bit of discussion in French with Zayid pointing out the imprint of donkey hooves in the sand and a clear indication they had gone through the cleft. Lash said, 'Kissack, get down and go through there, and tell me what you see.'

Kissack dismounted and, with drawn gun, went through the cleft. He disappeared from sight because there was a bend half way through and then all was silence except for the snuffling of a camel behind me. Suddenly there was a shout, incoherent and without words, which echoed among the rock pillars, and Kissack came back, yelling excitedly, 'It's there, Mr Lash; the bloody plane is there!'

'Is it?' Lash seemed unmoved. 'Zayid!' The Arab helped him dismount. 'Now let's all go and look at this aeroplane which is unaccountably ten kilometres out of position according to Mr Byrne's reckoning.'

There was no choice for it so we went. The camels were too big to go through the cleft so Zayid hobbled them and left them outside, but they took the donkeys through. And there stood *Flyaway* just as we had left her. Zayid and Lash's hired thugs from Algiers weren't very much interested, but Lash and Kissack were. They went towards her, Lash at a steady pace and Kissack practically dancing a jig. 'Is it the one, Mr Lash?' he asked excitedly. 'Is it the one?'

Lash took a paper from his pocket and unfolded it, then studied it and compared it with what was before him. He peered at the side of the fuselage and said, 'Yes, Kissack, my boy; this is indeed the one.'

'Christ!' said Kissack, and jumped up and down. 'Five thousand quid! Five grand!'

'Keep your damned mouth shut,' said Lash. 'You talk too much.' He swung on his heel and stared back at us. 'You – come here!' Byrne and I were hustled forward, and Lash pointed to the hole we had cut. 'Did you do that?'

'Yeah,' said Byrne.

'Why?'

'We found Billson's body. We wanted to mark the grave.' He nodded up towards the engine. 'That's also why we took the propeller.'

'You buried the body?'

'What there was of it. The ground is pretty hard. We built a cairn over it.'

Lash showed his teeth in a grim smile. 'So that's what you did. Then all is not lost.' I didn't know what he meant by that. 'Where is the body?'

Byrne told him. 'Get that propeller, Kissack,' said Lash. 'Take Zayid with you. But first tie these two – arms behind them and ankles secured.'

So we were tied up and left to lie under the rock wall of

the gully. Kissack and Zayid went off to find the grave and Lash and the other two ducked into the cleft. Where they were going I didn't know. I said, 'Sorry to have got you into this, Luke.'

He merely grunted and wriggled, and in his struggles with his bonds he fell against me and knocked me over. I fell heavily and a stone dug into my breastbone. When I got back into a sitting position I was panting. 'It's no good,' he said. 'They know how to tie a guy. Struggle and the knots tighten.'

'Yes. What do you think he's going to do?'

'About the airplane – I don't know. But if you're right about what you heard in Bilma he's sure as hell going to kill us. Why he hasn't done it yet I don't know.'

I looked down at the sand on which I had fallen. The imprint of my body was there, but there was no stone. And yet I had felt it. 'Luke! Remember that stone axe-head you found at the Col des Chandeliers? It's in the pocket of my *gandoura*. Think you can get it out?'

I fell on my side and he wriggled around with his back to me, his bound arms groping for my chest. It was a grotesque business, but he got his hands into the pocket and explored around. 'It's right at the bottom.'

'Got it!' Slowly his hands came out under my nose and I saw he grasped the small object between his fingers. It wasn't very big – not more than an inch long – and was probably more of a stone scraper than an axe-head. But the edge was keen enough.

'Trying to bite free?' said an amused voice behind us. Byrne dropped the scraper and it fell to the sand and I rolled on to it. 'You'll need strong teeth to bite through leather thongs,' said Lash.

I turned my head and looked at him. 'Do you blame me for trying?'

'Of course not, Colonel Stafford. It's the duty of every officer to try to escape, isn't it?' He squatted on his heels. 'But you won't, you know.'

'Get lost,' I said sourly.

'No – it will be you who are lost. If your bodies are ever found they'll look something like Billson's, I imagine. But they won't be found near here – oh, dear me, no! We couldn't have a coincidence like that.'

He turned his head at the clanging of metal on rock, and I followed his gaze to see his men coming through the cleft, each carrying two jerricans. They carried them over to *Flyaway* and set them down, then went away again. Lash's attention returned to us. He said to Byrne, 'I've been going over what you've told me since we met this morning and I've come to a conclusion, Byrne. You're a damned liar!'

Byrne grinned tightly. 'You wouldn't say that if I had my hands free.'

'Yes, you lied about practically everything – about the position of this aeroplane, about looking for frescoes – so why shouldn't you have lied about Billson? It would fit your pattern. Where is he?'

'He left us three days ago!' said Byrne. 'His shoulder was bad and getting worse. That was where Kissack shot him. He'd had a hard time in the Ténéré and it had opened up again and, like the goddamned fool he is, he said nothing about it because he wanted to find his Pappy's airplane.'

'So you know about that.' Lash glanced at me. 'Both of you.'

'When I found out how bad his shoulder was I was feared of gangrene,' said Byrne. 'So I sent him back with Atitel and Hami. I guess he's travelling slow, so he should be going down from Tamrit about now.'

'I wish I could believe you.'

'I don't give a hoot in hell whether you believe me or not.'

The men came back carrying four more jerricans which they put with the others. I watched them go back through the cleft. Lash clapped his hands together lightly. 'So, according to you, Billson never came here.'

'Not if he went back three days ago.'

'It doesn't matter,' said Lash, and stood up. 'I won't take

the chance. Billson won't leave North Africa. He's a dead man, as dead as you are.'

He went away and Byrne said, 'A real cheerful feller.'

'I wonder where Paul is?' I said in an undertone.

'Don't know, but I ain't putting my trust in a guy like him. Any help from him is as likely as a snowstorm on the Tassili. Where's that goddamn cutter?'

I groped around for a full five minutes, sifting the sand. 'Got it!'

'Then hold on to it, and don't let go. We may have a chance yet.'

Kissack and Zayid came back carrying the propeller. Kissack showed the plaque to Lash who laughed. He didn't toss it aside but walked over to where the donkeys were patiently waiting and carefully stowed it. Then he climbed up on to the wing of *Flyaway* and looked into the cockpit. 'He'll see that the compass is missing,' I muttered.

'Maybe not,' said Byrne.

Lash made only a superficial investigation of the cockpit but then climbed up on to the fuselage and opened the cargo hatch. He peered inside, then said something to Kissack who was standing below. He seemed highly satisfied. He next made his way up the fuselage towards the engine where he sat astride the cowling just as Byrne had done. He picked up something and examined it, laughed again and tossed it down to Kissack, and pointed to us.

Kissack walked in our direction. He stood over us and held something in his fingers. 'Where's the spanner that fits this?' It was one of the nuts that secured the propeller to the engine shaft.

'Find it yourself,' said Byrne.

Kissack kicked him in the ribs. I said quickly, 'It's packed in a tool kit aboard that donkey – the one in the middle.'

Kissack grinned at me and went away. Byrne said, 'No need to help them, Max.'

'I'm not. I don't want them searching all the loads. The compass is packed among my kit.' I looked across at Lash.

'Did you leave all the nuts there?'

'Yeah – in a neat row on top of the engine cowling. I'm a real tidy guy.' His voice was bitter.

Lash's men came through the cleft carrying four more jerricans; that made twelve and they apparently went back for more. A jerrican holds a nominal four gallons – actually a little more – so there was fifty gallons standing there on the sand. I said, 'What the hell do they want with all that water?'

'What makes you think it's water?'

I blinked in astonishment. 'You think it's petrol!'

'They're putting the propeller back, ain't they?'

'They're crazy,' I said. 'They can't fly it out of here.'

'They don't intend to,' said Byrne. 'Remember Paul's Land-Rover? I figure they're going to burn it.'

Destroying evidence of what? I watched them replace the propeller. It was a much more laborious task for them to put it back than it was for us to take it off. At one time all five of them were engaged on the job and it was then that I took a chance and had a go at cutting the thongs around Byrne's wrists. Holding the polished and sharpened stone blade I sawed at the leather without being able to see what I was doing because Byrne and I were back to back.

Suddenly he said, 'Enough! They've finished.' I palmed the blade and twisted around again to look at *Flyaway*. Kissack and Zayid were handing up jerricans to Lash, who stood on the wing and was pouring petrol into the auxiliary tank. The other two were still engaged in ferrying more jerricans. Lash put fifty gallons into the tank and there was still another fifty available because I counted twenty-four jerricans in all.

'Three camel loads,' said Byrne. 'I did wonder about all those pack animals.'

Lash and Kissack came over to us. Byrne looked up at them. 'I said it to Wilbur and I said it to Orville – "It'll never get off the ground."'

'Very funny,' said Lash. 'Kissack's come up with a suggestion. He thinks we ought to put one of you into the cock-pit.' He studied us, then turned to Kissack and said objectively, 'It can't be Byrne – he's too old and it might show. If it's anybody at all it'll be Stafford.'

Kissack shrugged. 'Suits me.'

Lash looked at me. 'I don't know,' he said reflectively. 'The clothes are wrong.'

'They'd be burnt.'

'Mmm. Then there are the teeth. This plane's going to be found sometime, Kissack, and someone might decide to do a thorough investigative job. If they discover the wrong man in the cockpit, then a hell of a lot of questions are going to be asked.'

'After more than forty years!'

'Stranger things have happened. No, on balance I think we'll leave things as they are. We have Billson's body so let's leave it at that. It'll look as though he got out before the plane went up.' Lash looked down at me and smiled. 'Don't let your hopes soar, Stafford. It's merely a reprieve.'

I said, 'You're a cold-blooded bastard!'

Kissack kicked me in the ribs and Lash caught his arm. 'Don't do that. I detest gratuitous violence.'

Kissack said, 'Gratty-what violence?'

'I mean I don't get my kicks out of it as you do.' Lash turned and looked at *Flyaway*. 'It doesn't *look* crashed,' he complained. 'Not so it would burn out. We'll have to raise the tail and tip the whole plane forward on to the engine.'

'Hell, that thing's heavy!'

'Not as heavy as all that, and there are five of us. All we have to do is to lift up the tail and put stones under it. When we get the pile of stones high enough it'll tip forward like a see-saw. But first, some petrol, I think.'

They walked away towards *Flyaway* and Lash climbed up on to the wing again. Kissack handed him a full jerrican and Lash poured it into the cockpit, and then poured another into the cargo compartment. Then he did the same thing again with two more jerricans and I saw the shimmering haze of evaporating petrol above the aircraft. It was like a bomb and only needed a spark to explode.

All five of them assembled at the tail. While four of them lifted the other piled stones underneath and gradually the tail rose higher and higher. While all eyes were off me I got busy with the stone blade at Byrne's wrists. I didn't see *Flyaway* tip over but when I looked her fuselage was at forty-five degrees and her tail was pointing to the sky. The rending noise had been the propeller bending under the sudden weight of the engine as it hit the ground.

They poured more petrol into her and Kissack used the last can to lay a trail across the sand. He didn't want to be too close when he tossed in a naked flame. He was quite a competent arsonist. Lash, standing close by us, took a paper from his pocket; I think it was the same one he had used to identify *Flyaway*. 'I won't need this any more,' he said conversationally, and lit one corner with a cigarette lighter. He held it up to make sure it was aflame, then tossed it into the petrol-soaked sand.

At first nothing happened. In the bright glare of the sun it was impossible to see the flames as they ran towards *Flyaway*. But then she exploded in fire; flames gouted out of the cockpit with a roar as though under forced draught, and ran up the fuselage right up to the tail and rudder until she was totally enveloped.

The donkeys brayed and plunged in fright. Lash shouted, 'Get those bloody donkeys out of here!' I don't think he had realized until then how much heat so much petrol would generate. They rounded up the donkeys and pushed them through the cleft, then went through themselves, leaving us lying there.

I took the opportunity of trying to cut the thongs at Byrne's wrists again, but he snatched himself away. 'For Christ's sake!' he said. 'Roll over against the rock and keep your head down. That goddamn auxiliary tank will be going up any second.'

We rolled over and huddled against the rock, keeping our

faces away from the burning aeroplane. Behind us, seventy yards away, the auxiliary fuel tank exploded like a bomb and I felt a wave of searing heat. There was a pattering noise all about and something hit me in the small of the back. When I looked at *Flyaway* again she had blown in two, and her tailplane and rudder were lying some distance from the forward section. One wing was also detached.

And I had lost my stone blade.

After that the flames died down very quickly and Lash came back. He looked down at us quizzically. 'Feeling a trifle singed? Never mind, it will make your hair grow.'

'Go to hell!' said Byrne.

Lash ignored him and looked at the wreck of *Flyaway*. 'A really nice job,' he said with satisfaction. 'I had considered using gelignite but it might not have looked right. This looks perfectly natural. Anyone who goes to the movies knows that crashed aircraft burn well.' He beckoned to Kissack. 'Get these two on their feet and walking. We'll visit the grave.'

Kissack bent down and cut the thongs at my ankles and he wasn't particularly considerate about it because he cut me, too. I got to my feet laboriously because my hands were still tied behind my back and I lost my balance. Lash and Zayid led the way, with Byrne and me following, Kissack behind us with a pistol in his hand. The other two tagged on behind.

The cairn of stones had been disarranged and Billson's skull was showing. Lash looked down at it unemotionally. 'Well, we've got the body but we can't leave it like this, can we? I mean, the man wouldn't have died and conveniently buried himself.'

He gave orders in French and his men began to dismantle the cairn. I said, 'How did you know the plane would need burning?'

Lash shrugged. 'I didn't. If it had burned forty years ago it would have saved me a considerable amount of trouble. But I didn't take the chance. I never take chances. I came prepared for anything.'

He looked down as the desiccated corpse was revealed. 'Kissack wanted to put this in the cockpit before we burned the plane – but Kissack is a fool, as I'm sure you've learned. As soon as he told me there was an arm missing I vetoed that suggestion. Everything must not only look right – it must *be* right. I never take chances.'

The body was soon wholly uncovered. Lash looked down at it. 'Is this as you found it?'

'Yes.'

'I don't believe you. He would have left a message of some kind – left his papers.' His head came up and he stared at us. 'Where are they?'

'Maybe you just burned them,' said Byrne. 'You didn't search that airplane too well.'

'But you did,' said Lash. He turned to Kissack and said abruptly, 'When we get back down there I want those donkeys unloaded and everything searched.'

'All right,' said Kissack. He held the pistol negligently in his hand, muzzle down.

I wasn't worried about Billson's papers because Paul had them, wherever Paul was, which was probably a long way over the horizon by now. But if our stuff was searched they'd find the compass. Why in hell I was worried about that I don't know; it should have been the least of my worries.

I said, 'Kissack!'

'What?'

'When you burned Paul Billson's Land-Rover did you search it first?'

'What the hell? No, I didn't. What's it to you?'

'Nothing. You're getting paid five thousand pounds for this job, aren't you? I bet Lash is getting ten times as much.'

Lash's eyes flickered. 'Mr Stafford exaggerates.'

I stared at Kissack. 'Didn't Lash tell you?'

'Tell me what, for God's sake? What's Billson's Land-Rover got to do with my five thousand quid?'

I shrugged. 'Just that Billson was carrying quite a lot of cash. More than five thousand – much more. I can't believe

286

Lash didn't tell you.'

'How much more?' Kissack said hoarsely.

'Fifty-six thousand in British currency. It was in his suitcases in the back of the Land-Rover.'

Kissack's eyes widened, and he whirled on Lash. 'Is that true?'

'How would I know?' said Lash in a bored voice. 'Keep your cool, man. Stafford's just trying to needle you.'

'Is he, now? I wonder?'

Lash lost his boredom. 'Damn it, if I'd known do you think I wouldn't have told you? Do you think I'd have stood by and let you burn money? I'm not such a – '

He had no time to say more because there was a shockingly loud bang from quite close and the top of Kissack's head blew off, spattering grey fragments of brain all about. His knees buckled and he collapsed to the ground, letting the pistol fall as he did so.

Paul Billson always did over-react.

Thirty

An army rifle, even one of First World War vintage, is intended to kill men at ranges of up to a thousand yards or more, and an averagely good marksman finds it a comfortably good tool at four hundred yards. Paul Billson was not an averagely good marksman; in fact, he was not a marksman at all and later confessed that it was the first shot he had ever fired, whether in anger or otherwise. But even Paul Billson could not miss killing Kissack at a range of fifteen feet.

By his account he had gone to the grave and taken his photographs, then spent some minutes in contemplation. He had then gone back, picked up his two donkeys and followed the line Byrne had given him. He had spotted us surrounded by Lash's men on camels and tactfully drew aside. Luckily for him – and us – he had gone over rock, otherwise Zayid might have seen his tracks. He watched us led into captivity and wondered what to do about it.

He didn't say so but I think his first instinct was to make a run for it, yet I might be maligning him. Anyway, where was he to run? It was three days on foot back to Tamrit and he must have known that he could never find his way there by himself. But whatever his thoughts were he decided to stick around. And he discovered that Byrne's Lee-Enfield was packed on one of his donkeys.

He went away and found a hole among the rocks and tethered the donkeys. One of them was inclined to bray, which frightened him because he thought it might be heard and they'd come looking for him. But he did the right thing. He unloaded the donkeys, hobbled them as he had seen

Byrne do, and turned them loose. Then he looked at the rifle.

He had seen guns at a distance but had never handled one, nothing unusual in an Englishman of his age who had missed war service because of physical unfitness. There are not that many guns floating loose about Luton. He fiddled about with it, being careful not to touch the trigger, and worked the bolt action, trying to find the principle by which it worked. Eventually, more or less by accident, he pressed a catch and the magazine fell into the palm of his hand. It was empty, which was why no bullets were being inserted into the breech.

He thought about that for a moment and soon came to the conclusion that the ammunition would not be kept far from the weapon. He knew that Byrne was in the habit of keeping a full magazine in the pouch slung around his neck but surely there must be more bullets somewhere. He began to search through the loads he had taken from the donkeys and eventually found an opened packet containing eleven rounds.

When he tried to put bullets into the magazine they wouldn't fit so he tried them the other way around and they went in sweetly, compressing the leaf spring in the magazine. He found that it held five bullets. He pushed the magazine into the rifle and worked the action slowly and was rewarded by the sight of a cartridge being pushed firmly and smoothly into the breech. He now had the rifle loaded.

He knew there was such a thing as a safety-catch and soon found the small switch-like lever on the side of the rifle which would cover or uncover a red spot. His problem was that he didn't know when it was on and when it was off. It never occurred to him to take out the magazine, eject the round from the breech and then test the trigger with an empty gun. At last he reasoned that red would mean danger, so that when the red spot showed the safety-catch was off. He covered the red spot and stood up, holding the rifle.

Paul was not a man of action, rather a man of reaction. He

could be pushed – by men, by circumstances, or as English, the journalist, had pushed – but it was not his habit to initiate action. So he stood there, irresolute, wondering what was the best thing to do. He then decided that it would not be a good idea to walk in on Lash and company by way of the cleft in the rocks which was now the common highway to *Flyaway*; instead, he would try to approach from the other direction. That was a good idea.

He found a canteen and filled it with water, put the remaining six bullets into his pocket, and then set off to explore, carrying the rifle somewhat gingerly as though it might explode of its own volition. He knew his direction to the cleft so he set off at right-angles to that, skirting the base of a rock pillar. To anyone knowing Paul Billson it must have been an unlikely sight.

He kept track of his progress by counting his paces, and when he had counted two hundred double strides he veered to the left and carried on. After five minutes he stopped in his tracks because he heard voices. Cautiously he peered round a rock and saw Kissack and Zayid passing by within spitting distance. They were carrying a propeller.

That gave him his location; he was somewhere near his father's grave. He waited a while and then stepped out to where they had walked and immediately knew where he was, so he walked a little way until he came to the cave where his father was buried. The rocks of the cairn had been rudely tumbled aside and he saw the white bone of his father's skull. That angered him very much and he trembled with rage.

His impulse was to walk down to *Flyaway* and shoot Kissack, but he reined himself in. He had no illusions about his prowess with a rifle and seriously doubted if, when it came to the push, he *could* kill Kissack – not in a straight shooting match. And then there were the others. I rather doubt if the plight of Byrne and myself crossed his mind at that time.

He stopped over the grave and picked up a rock, intending to rebuild the cairn. Then he paused with the rock still held in his hand and thought about it. Logical thought did not come naturally to Paul Billson; as I have said, he was a man who reacted to stimuli. But he thought now and carefully replaced the rock where he had found it, then went away and sat behind a rock out of sight of the cave to work things out.

Presently he saw smoke drifting overhead, and then came the dull, echoing thud as the auxiliary fuel tank of *Flyaway* exploded. He assumed, correctly, that *Flyaway* was being destroyed. He didn't know why, but then, very few people did. He stood up and looked towards the source of the smoke, again irresolute.

Then he turned and looked through a gap in the rocks towards the grave. Paul didn't know it but he was standing by what a rifleman would consider a perfect loophole. Two rocks standing on a third, the gap between them about six inches. The depth of the gap was nearly three feet, and from where he was standing he could see the grave, about twenty feet away. There were even two flat ledges on which he could plant his elbows to give aiming support.

Chance, circumstance, and the odd workings of Paul's mind had put him in exactly the right place at the right time. Soon he heard voices.

A little later he fired the rifle.

The muzzle blast of an army rifle fired at close range can be quite frightening. I suspect that, given the standard army firing squad of eight men, even if they all missed the victim would probably die of shock. That single shot, coming unexpectedly, froze everybody into a tableau as Kissack fell bonelessly to the ground.

The bullet that smashed into the back of Kissack's head passed through him as though he wasn't there. It entered the cave, ricocheted around the walls and came out *spaaang*, giving Zayid a fright. But it wasn't that which broke the tableau; it was the dry metallic clatter, coming from nowhere in particular, as Paul worked the action to put another round up the spout.

291

Lash pulled a pistol from nowhere at exactly the same time as Byrne dived for the gun Kissack had dropped. It's difficult to do a rugby tackle when your hands are tied behind your back but I did my best and went for Lash's legs. His pistol exploded and I felt a smashing blow in my left arm and tumbled to one side. But I had brought him down.

Then bullets were buzzing over me like bees as Byrne shot over and past me, and out of the corner of my eye I saw Zayid go down in a tumbled heap. Paul added to the row with another blast just as Lash recovered enough to raise his gun intending to shoot at Byrne. I swung my legs around and booted at his wrist just before Byrne got him. Byrne was shooting police-fashion; square on to the target and in a crouch, with arms extended and both hands on the butt of the pistol. He pumped three shots into Lash who jerked convulsively, then flopped about on the ground and began to scream.

Paul fired again and the bullet ricocheted from rock to rock. Byrne yelled above Lash's screams, 'Paul, stop shooting, for Christ's sake! You'll kill us all.'

I tried to lever myself up, but I used the wrong arm and got a jolt of pain. When I finally sat up and looked around I saw the bodies of Zayid and Kissack and Lash, who was screaming just as Bailly had screamed in the Ténéré. The other two had vanished. It had all happened within, perhaps, twenty seconds.

Byrne yelled again. 'Come out, Paul. Show yourself.'

Paul came from behind a rock. His face was white as paper and his hands shook uncontrollably. Byrne stepped forward and caught the rifle as it fell. 'Did you fill the magazine?'

Paul nodded wordlessly.

'Any more ammunition?'

Paul dug his hand into his pockets and passed the cartridges over. He stared at Lash and then clapped his hands over his ears to shut out the endless screaming. I wanted to do the same but I couldn't lift my left arm. When a man is killed in the films he folds up decorously and has the decency to die quietly; in real life it's different.

Byrne pulled back the bolt of the rifle and an empty brass case flew out. He slammed the bolt forward and locked it and then, without warning, stepped over to Lash, put the muzzle of the rifle to his temple, and pulled the trigger.

The shot crashed out and after the echoes had died away the silence was shocking. Byrne looked at me and his face was drawn and haggard. 'My responsibility,' he said harshly. 'Three bullets – one in the belly. He wouldn't have lived. Best this way.'

'Okay, Luke,' I said quietly. So died a man who said he detested gratuitous violence but who would kill coldly to a plan. In my book Lash had been worse than Kissack.

Byrne was reloading the rifle. 'You hurt?'

'I caught one in the arm – I'm flying on one wing.'

He grunted. 'You two wait here,' he said, and went off without another word.

Paul walked over and looked down at Lash. 'So quick,' he whispered. Whether he was referring to what Byrne had done or to the entire action I didn't know. He turned his head. 'You all right?'

'Help me up.' My left arm was beginning to really hurt; it felt as though an electric shock was being applied at irregular intervals. As he hoisted me to my feet I said, 'You did well, Paul; very well.'

'Did I?' he said colourlessly.

'These bastards were seriously considering burning me in the plane,' I said. 'And if I know Kissack he'd have liked to burn me alive – and so would Lash if he thought it would contribute to realism.' I paused; I was waiting for the sound of shots but all was silent.

Paul turned a puzzled face towards me. 'What was it all about, Max?'

'I don't know,' I said. 'But I'm going to find out. And now, for God's sake, will you cut me loose? But be careful with my arm.'

*

Byrne came back half an hour later. The rifle was slung over his shoulder and he was leading two pack camels. He leaned the rifle against a rock and said, 'No problem,' then held out his wrists. 'I don't remember breaking free,' he said. 'I just did it. You did well with that stone chopper.'

'The other two men?'

He indicated Lash. 'The paymaster is dead, so no pay – no fight. Trash from the Maghreb. I gave them three camels and water and told them to get to hell out of it. They won't bother us none.' He tossed the leading rein to Paul and unslung a box from the pack saddle. 'Let's see your arm.'

He pronounced it to be broken, which I already knew, set it in a rough and ready way and put it in an improvised sling. 'We'd better get you back to civilization,' he said.

But there was much to do before that. Paul helped him load the three bodies on to the camels and they went away. Where they went I don't know but they came back two hours later without the bodies. In that time I had finished rebuilding the cairn over Billson's body. Byrne laid the aluminium plaque on top. 'No propeller,' he said wryly. 'Can't shift it again.'

We cleaned up around the cave, picking up spent cartridge cases and other evidence, then went back to *Flyaway*, and Paul looked at the blackened wreckage and shook his head. 'Why?' he asked again.

No one answered him.

'We leave tomorrow at dawn,' said Byrne. 'But this time we ride.'

And so we did, with Byrne grumbling incessantly about the damnfool way the Chaambas rigged their camels for riding.

Thirty-One

As Edward FitzGerald might have put it, 'Djanet was Paradise enow'. Four days later Byrne saw me settled comfortably in a hotel room, then went away, probably to see Atitel and to tell him that his broken leg was worth ten camels, after all – delivered to Bilma at the beginning of next season. I wondered how much a broken arm was worth.

When he came back he had done that, and more. He had also gone to the telegraph office and cabled Hesther Raulier. I don't know exactly what he'd put in the cable but it was enough for Hesther to promise to send a chartered aircraft to Djanet to return Paul and me to Algiers. 'I'd like for you to get that arm fixed,' he said. 'But not here. Hesther knows the right people in Algiers – it can be arranged quietly.'

I nodded. 'Then we've got things to do,' I said. 'Is there such a thing as a Commissioner for Oaths in Djanet?'

'Huh?'

'An American would call him a Notary Public.'

His brow cleared. 'Sure there is. Why?'

'I want to put down in writing everything we found wrong with *Flyaway* – all about the compass and the stuff in the bottom of the main fuel tank. And I want you to sign it before an official witness. I'll sign it too, but we'll keep Paul out of it. Do you think you can find a typewriter anywhere?'

'There's one in the hotel office,' he said. 'I'll borrow that.'

So I spent half a day typing the statement, with many references to Byrne to elucidate the more technical bits. I did it one-handedly but that was no hardship because my typing is of the hunt-and-peck order, anyway. Next morning we went to the notary public and both of us signed every

295

page which also had the embossed seal of the notary public. It didn't matter that he couldn't understand the content; it was our signatures he was witnessing.

Then I brought out my plastic shaving-soap container and that was put into an envelope and sealed and Byrne and I signed our names across the flap. I watched Byrne laboriously writing his name in an unformed handwriting, his tongue sticking out of the side of his mouth like that of a small schoolboy. But it came out clear enough – Lucas Byrne.

As we left the official's office Byrne said, 'You got ideas?'

'Some – but they're pretty weird.'

'Could be nothing but. It figures. If you find any answers let me know.'

'I'll do that,' I said.

The three of us lunched at a restaurant and inhaled a few beers and then Byrne drove us back to the hotel to pick up our bags and then the few miles to In Debiren where the airstrip was and where a Piper Comanche awaited us. Paul, who once didn't have the grace to thank anyone for anything, positively embarrassed Byrne, who adopted a 'Shucks, 't'warn't nuthin' ' attitude.

I said, 'Paul, get in the plane – I want a couple of last words with Luke.' Once he was out of earshot I said, 'He's right, you know; thanks aren't enough.'

Byrne smiled. 'I hope to God you're right.' He produced an envelope, sealed and with my name on it. 'This is for you. I told you I'd bill you. You can settle it with Hesther.'

I grinned and tucked it in the pocket of my *gandoura* unopened. 'What will you do now?'

'Get back to the Aïr and my own business – go back to leading the quiet life. Give my regards to Hesther.'

'I'll give her your love,' I said.

He looked at me quizzically. 'You do that and she'll laugh like a hyaena.' He took my hand. 'Look after yourself, now. From what I hear, the big cities can be more dangerous than the desert.'

'I'll bear that in mind,' I promised and got into the Comanche.

So we took off and, as the plane circled the airstrip I saw that Byrne hadn't waited. The Toyota was trailing a cloud of dust and heading south to Bilma and, from there, to the Aïr.

At first, during the flight north, I was preoccupied with my own thoughts and gazed sightlessly at the vast dun expanse which flowed below. There were too many damn loose ends to tie up and I couldn't begin to see where to start.

Presently I took out Byrne's envelope and handed it to Paul. 'Can you open that for me?'

'Of course.' He ripped off the end, shook out the contents and gave it back to me.

As Byrne had promised he'd billed me, and it was all set out clearly, payable in pounds sterling. His own services he had put down as a guide at £30 a day; at thirty-three days that came to £990. Then there was the purchase of gasoline – so many litres at such-and-such; oil and new tyres; camel hire – and the purchase of five camels at £100 each. He also added in half the cost of a new Toyota Land Cruiser which seemed quite steep until I remembered how Kissack had shot Byrne's truck full of holes in the Ténéré. Altogether the bill came to a little over £5000.

There was no charge for saving life. Byrne was one hell of a fellow.

As I put it away Paul said happily, 'I'm looking forward to seeing that editor's face again.'

'Um – Paul; do me a favour. Don't go off pop as soon as we get to London. I don't want you to tell anyone a damn thing until I give you the word. Please!'

'Why not?'

I sighed. 'I can't tell you now, but will you believe me when I say it's for your own good? In any case, you can't tell anyone about Lash and Kissack.'

Again he said, 'Why not?'

297

'Jesus!' I said. 'Paul, you *killed* a man! Shot the top of his head right off. You don't want to open that can of worms. Look, you can tell the newspapers about finding *Flyaway* and your father's body, but just give me time to find out something, will you? I want to discover what the hell it was all about.'

'All right,' he said. 'I won't say anything until you say I can.'

'And you won't *do* anything, either. Promise?'

'I promise.' He was silent for a while, then he said, 'I don't remember much about my father. I was only two when he died, you know.'

'I know.'

'About the only thing I can remember was him bouncing me on his knee and singing that nursery rhyme; you know, the one that goes, "Fly away, Peter! Fly away, Paul!" I thought that was a great joke.' So would Billson. Paul rubbed his chin. 'But I didn't like my stepfather much.'

I cocked my eye at him. 'Aarvik? What was wrong with him?'

'Oh, not Aarvik; he came later. I mean the other one.'

I said, 'Are you telling me your mother married *three* times?'

'That's right. Didn't you know?'

'No, I didn't,' I said thoughtfully. 'What was his name?'

'Can't remember. He wasn't around much, and I was only a kid. After I was about four years old he wasn't around at all. It's all a long time ago.'

Indeed it is, Paul; indeed it is!

He didn't say much after that revelation and neither did I. We lapsed into silence and I was still mulling it over when we landed at Algiers.

The big Mercedes with the Arab chauffeur was waiting by the hangar as the Comanche taxied up and we were soon wafted luxuriously to the heights of Bouzarea overlooking Algiers. If the chauffeur was surprised at carrying a Targui he didn't show it.

We stopped at the small door in the wall which opened as silently and mysteriously as before, and Paul and I walked towards the house. Hesther Raulier was still lying on the chaise-longue and might never have moved but that she was wearing a different dress. As we approached she put down her cigar and stood up.

Suddenly her monkey face cracked into a big grin and she laughed raucously. 'Jesus, Stafford! What in hell do you think you're doing? Auditioning for *The Desert Song*?'

She put me to bed fast and summoned the doctor who, apparently, was on tap immediately. She said, 'Luke put a couple of words into his cable that meant something bad – stuff I hadn't heard since the Revolution – so I got in Fahkri. He's used to gunshot wounds and knows how to keep his mouth shut.'

Dr Fahkri examined my arm, asked how long ago it had happened, and then told me the bullet was still in there. He deadened the arm, sliced it open and took out the bullet, stitched it up again and put on a proper splint. I said to Hesther, 'Better have him look at Paul. He took a bullet in the shoulder about a month ago.'

She spoke to Fahkri in Arabic and he nodded and went away, then she turned to me. 'What happened out there?'

'Kissack happened,' I said. 'He and a man called Lash – and four others.' I gave her an edited version of what had happened, and ended up by saying, 'I don't know what we'd have done without Luke Byrne.'

'Luke's a good man,' she said simply. 'But what was it all about?'

'Whatever set it off was in England. I suppose Paul really started the ball rolling but he triggered something, a sort of time bomb that was lying around for forty-two years. I've got a few questions to ask. If I find any answers I'll let you know.'

'You do that.' She stood up. 'You can't go back to England dressed as a Targui.'

I shrugged. 'Why not? London is full of Arabs these days, and nobody there could tell the difference.'

'Nonsense. I'll get a tailor in tomorrow and you'll have a suit the day after. You and Paul both.'

We stayed in Algiers for four days, more so I could recuperate from Fahkri's surgery than anything else. I lazed about and read the English newspapers that Hesther bought me so that I could catch up on the news. Everything was going to hell in a handcart, as usual.

Once, referring to Paul, she said, 'That guy's changed – changed a lot. He's quieter and not as nervy.'

I grinned. 'God knows why. What happened to him is enough to make anyone go screaming up the wall.'

On the fourth day we left on an Air Algérie flight to Orly. The interior of the plane was decorated in a tasteful shade of emerald green. Green may be the Arab colour but this plane had pictures of jaunting cars and scenes from Killarney because it had been bought second-hand from Aer Lingus. However, it got us to Orly all right and we transferred to the London flight.

An hour later we were at Heathrow. It was raining and it looked as though it had never stopped since I had left.

Thirty-Two

I had telephoned Heathrow from Orly and so there was a car waiting with a driver, since I could not drive a car with a broken arm. He drove us the short distance to the Post House Hotel and I told him to stick around while I booked in. There were reservations for Paul and me in adjoining rooms, so we went up and I got him settled.

Paul, of course, was dead broke – he hadn't a penny – and that suited me fine because I wanted him immobilized. I didn't give him any money, but said, 'Paul, stay here until I get back. If you want anything, order it – it's on the house. But don't leave the hotel.'

'Where are you going?'

'I have things to do,' I said uninformatively.

I went down to the lobby, cashed a sheaf of travellers' cheques, picked up the driver, and gave him an address in Marlow. As we left the hotel-studded environs of Heathrow I reflected that the Post House was the ideal sort of anonymous caravanserai to hide Paul; I didn't want his presence in England known yet, nor mine, either.

The car pulled up outside Jack Ellis's house and I walked up and rang the doorbell. Judy Ellis opened it, looked at me uncertainly, and said, 'Yes?' interrogatively.

I had met Jack's wife only three or four times. Stafford Security Consultants Ltd was not the kind of firm that drew wives into the business orbit; we had other ways of ensuring company loyalty, such as good pay. I said, 'Is Jack in? I'm Max Stafford.'

'Oh, I didn't recognize you. Yes, he's just got back. Come in.' She held the door wide and let me into the hall while making all the usual excuses wives make when the boss drops in on an unexpected visit. The place didn't look all that untidy to me. 'Jack,' she called. 'Mr Stafford's here.'

As I stood in the doorway of the living-room Ellis rose from an armchair, laying aside a newspaper. He looked at me questioningly. 'Max?'

I was suddenly aware of the beard – now neatly trimmed by a barber Hesther had brought in, the light-coloured suit of a decidedly foreign cut, and the black silk sling which cradled my left arm. I suppose that to Jack it was a disguise. 'Hello, Jack.'

'Well, for God's sake! Come in.' He seemed glad to see me.

I was aware of Judy hovering in the background. 'Er . . . this isn't a social call, Jack. I want to talk to you.'

'I hope to God it isn't,' he said. 'And I want to talk to you. Where have you been? Come into my study.'

He hustled me away and I smiled pleasantly at Judy in passing. In the study he offered me a chair. 'What's wrong with the arm?'

'Just broken.' I smiled. 'It only hurts when I laugh.'

'God, I'm glad to see you. You just disappeared, and I didn't know where to look. All hell's been breaking loose.'

'I've not been away long – just over a month,' I said mildly. 'You haven't lost your grip in so short a time?'

'If you want to put it that way, I suppose I have.' His voice was grim. 'But I never had much grip to begin with, did I?'

It was evident that something was griping him so I said, 'Give me a drink, sit down and tell me all about it.'

He took a deep breath, then said, 'Sorry.' He left the room and returned with a tray on which were bottles and glasses. 'Scotch okay?' I nodded, and as he poured the drinks he said, 'As soon as you left the whole character of the company changed.'

'In what way?'

'Well, as a minor example, we're now letting dogs out

without handlers.' He handed me a glass.

'Starting with Electronomics,' I suggested.

He looked at me in surprise. 'How did you know that?'

'Never mind. Go on.'

He sat down and looked broodingly into the glass which he held cradled in his hands. 'The big thing is that we're now up to our necks in industrial espionage. You've been away six weeks and I'm already running three penetration exercises.'

'Are you, by God? On whose authority?'

'Charlie Malleson twisted my arm.'

I stared at him. 'Jack, you're not there to take instructions from Charlie. He's just the bloody accountant – a number juggler. You're supposed to be standing in for me – running the operational side – and that doesn't mean penetration operations. We're in security; that's what the name of the firm means. Now, how did Charlie twist your arm?'

Ellis shrugged. 'He just told me to do it.'

'Didn't you squawk?'

'Of course I bloody well squawked.' His ire was rising. 'But what the hell could I do? I'm not a shareholder, and he brought Brinton in to back him up, and when the bosses say "Do!", you do. Max, this last week I've been on the verge of quitting, but I held on in the hope that you'd come back.' He stuck his finger out at me. 'Any moment from now I'm going to get instructions to penetrate one of our own clients. That would be a laugh, wouldn't it? Playing both ends against the middle. But it's not what I joined the firm for.'

'Not very ethical,' I agreed. 'Take it easy, Jack; we'll sort this out. You say Charlie brought in Lord Brinton?'

'The old bastard is in and out all the time now.' Jack caught himself. 'Sorry. I forgot he's a friend of yours.'

'Not particularly. You say he comes to the office frequently?'

'Two or three times a week. He has himself driven two whole blocks in his Rolls-Royce.'

'Does he have access to files?'

Jack shrugged. 'Not through me. I don't know about Charlie.'

'Oh, we can't have that.' I thought about it for a moment, then said, 'I talked about you to Charlie before I left. It was agreed that if you could handle my job then you'd be made managing director. That would entitle you to a parcel of shares because that's the way we work. I was going to start operations in Europe – go for the multinationals. Didn't Charlie say anything about this?'

'Not a word.'

'I see.' I sipped my scotch. 'This is a surprising development but it's not what I came to see you about. Remember what we were doing just before I left?'

He nodded. 'Looking for a half-wit called Billson.'

'Well, I found him, and that led to other things. I want you to re-open the account of Michelmore, Veasey and Templeton, but do it quietly. Don't open a formal file, and keep all details locked away from prying eyes.'

'Same as before?'

'Exactly the same as before. No one sees it – especially not Charlie or Brinton. Now, this is what I want you to do.' As I reeled off my requirements Jack's eyes got bigger. I ended up by saying, 'Oh yes; and that analytical chemist must be a forensic type, able to go on to the stand in court as an expert witness.'

He looked up from the notebook in which he was scribbling. 'Quite a packet.'

'Yes. Now, don't worry about what's happening to the firm. Leave that in my hands and I'll sort it out. Carry on as usual. One more thing, Jack; I'm not in England. You haven't seen me tonight. I'll arrive at the office unexpectedly one day. Okay?'

He grinned. 'Catching them in the act?'

'Something like that.'

I went away leaving Jack a great deal less troubled in the mind than when I'd arrived. I gave the driver Alix Aarvik's address in Kensington and sat back wondering how that pair of cheapjack bastards thought they could get away with it. It was very puzzling because I was the majority shareholder.

Alix Aarvik was in and pleased to see me. As she ushered me in to the living-room she said, 'Oh, you've hurt yourself.'

'Not irrevocably. Have you been keeping well?'

'I'm all right. Would you like coffee?'

'Thank you.'

She was busily domestic for a few minutes, then she said, 'I like your beard – it suits you.' She suddenly blushed because she'd said something personal to a comparative stranger.

'Thank you. I might keep it on that recommendation.' I paused. 'Miss Aarvik, I've found your brother.' I raised my hand. 'He's quite well and undamaged and he's back in England.'

She sat down with a bump. 'Oh, thank God!'

'Rather thank a man called Byrne; he got Paul out of most of the holes he got himself into. Paul will tell you about it.'

'Where was he?'

I thought of Koudia and Atakor and the Tassili. 'In North Africa. He found his father, Miss Aarvik.' Her hand flew to her mouth. 'I suppose the story will be breaking in the newspapers quite soon. A complete vindication, making nonsense of all the malicious speculation.'

'Oh, I'm so glad!' she said. 'But where is Paul now?'

I wondered whether or not to take her into my confidence. She was much more level-headed than Paul, but in the end I decided against it. The truth, if and when it came out, would be so explosive that the fewer in the know the better, and there must be no possible way of Paul getting to know it.

I said carefully, 'Newspapermen in a hurry can be highly inaccurate. We'll be holding a press conference in a few days' time and Paul and I are honing our statements — making sure they're just right. I'd rather he wasn't disturbed until then.'

She nodded understandingly. 'Yes,' she said. 'I know Paul. That would be better.'

'You may find that Paul has changed,' I said. 'He's different.'

'How?'

I shrugged. 'I think you'll find that he's a better man than he was.'

She thought about that for a moment but couldn't make anything of it. 'Were you with Paul when you found . . . the body?'

'Yes, and so was Byrne. We helped Paul bury it.' I neglected to say that we'd helped him twice.

'Who is Byrne?'

I smiled. 'A difficult man to describe. You could call him a white Targui, except that a lot of Tuareg are as white as we are. He says he used to be an American. A very fine man. Your brother owes him a lot.'

'And you, too.'

I changed the subject. 'Are you still with Andrew McGovern as his secretary?'

'Yes.'

'I'd like you to do me a favour. I'd like to meet him.'

'That can be arranged,' she said.

'But not very easily the way I want to do it. I want to meet him *not* at his office, and without him knowing who I am. This is a matter of some discretion, an assignment on behalf of a client.'

'That *will* be difficult,' she said, and fell into thought. 'His lunches are usually business affairs. Can't you see him at his home?'

'I'd rather not. I prefer not to take business into people's homes.' Considering that I'd just busted in on Jack Ellis and here I was in Alix Aarvik's flat that was a non-starter, but she didn't notice.

'He has no lunch appointment for the day after tomorrow,' she said. 'On those occasions he hardly eats at all and, if it's fine, he nearly always takes a walk in the gardens of Lincoln's Inn. If it's not raining he'll probably be there. Would you know him if you saw him?'

'Oh yes.'

She spread her hands. 'Then, there you are.'

I made leave-taking motions, and she said, 'When will I be seeing Paul?'

'Oh, not long. A week, perhaps; not more than ten days.' I thought that if I didn't get what I wanted within ten days I probably wouldn't get it at all.

I didn't leave all the work to Ellis. For instance, I spent an interesting morning in the Public Records Office, and on my way to see McGovern I called in at Hatchard's and browsed through the current edition of *Whitaker's Almanac*. Although it told me what I wanted to know I bought it anyway as part of the dossier.

Eight days later I had all I needed. I primed Ellis to let me know the next time Lord Brinton visited the office, then sat waiting by the telephone.

Thirty-Three

I pressed the button in the lift and ascended to the floor which held the offices of Stafford Security Consultants Ltd. The girl travelling up with me was one of our junior typists; probably somebody had sent her out to buy a packet of cigarettes or a bar of chocolate or something illicit like that. She looked at me and turned away, then looked at me again as though I were someone she ought to recognize. It was the beard that did it.

I stepped into the familiar hallway, walked into Reception and straight on through towards my own office. Barbara the receptionist said, hastily, 'Here, you can't . . .'

I turned and grinned at her. 'Don't you recognize your own boss?'

I carried on, hearing, 'Oh, Mr Stafford!' I went into my office and found Joyce hammering a typewriter. 'Hi, Joyce; is Mr Ellis in?'

'You've hurt your arm.'

'And gone all hairy. I know. Is he in?'

'Yes.'

I walked in on Ellis. 'Morning, Jack. Got the rest of the bits and pieces?'

'Yes.' He unlocked the drawer of his desk. 'The chemist's report and the marriage certificate. It was 1937, not '36.'

I nodded. 'There'd be a mourning period, of course.'

'What's this all about, Max?'

I unlocked my briefcase, using one hand, and he dropped the papers into it. 'Better you don't know. Is Brinton here?'

'His Nibs is with Charlie.'

'Right – stand by for fireworks.'

I walked in on Charlie cold, without announcement,

ignoring the flapping of his secretary. He was sitting behind his desk and Brinton was in an armchair by his side. The armchair was new, but Brinton was noted for attending to his own creature comforts. If Charlie had seen fit to get an armchair then it meant Brinton was a frequent visitor.

Charlie looked up at me blankly, and then the penny dropped. 'Max!'

'Hello, Charlie.' I nodded at Brinton. 'Morning, my lord.'

'Well, I'm damned!' said Brinton. 'Where did you spring from? I see you've hurt your arm. How did you do that?'

'Skiing can be dangerous.' A perfectly truthful statement, if not responsive to the question. I drew up a chair, sat down, and put the briefcase on the floor.

'Where were you? Gstaad?' Brinton was his old genial self but Charlie Malleson seemed tongue-tied and wore a hunted look.

I said, 'I've been hearing some bloody funny stories about the company so I came back.'

Charlie's eyes slid to Brinton who didn't seem to notice. He still retained his smile as he said, 'From Ellis, I suppose. Well, it's true enough. We've made some changes to improve the profitability.'

'Without my knowledge,' I said coldly. 'Or my consent.'

'What's the matter, Max?' said Brinton. 'Don't you like money?'

'As much as the next man – but I'm particular how I earn it.' I turned to Charlie. 'You didn't take that clause from the Electronomics contract. So this was being cooked up as long ago as that. What the hell's got into you?' He didn't answer, so I said, 'All right; from now on we go back to square one.'

Brinton's voice was almost regretful as he said, ' 'Fraid not, Max. You don't have all that much of a say any more.'

I looked at him. He still wore the big smile but it didn't reach his eyes which were cold as ice. 'What the devil are you talking about? I own fifty-one per cent of the shares – a controlling interest.'

He shook his head. 'You did. You don't now. You made a mistake, the elementary mistake of a man in love. You trusted someone.'

I knew it then. 'Gloria!'

'Yes, Gloria. You went off in a hurry and forgot about the seven per cent interest in the firm you'd given her. I bought her shares.' He wagged his head. 'You should pay more attention to proverbial sayings; there's a lot of truth in them. Hell hath no fury like a woman scorned. See what I mean?'

I said, 'Seven plus twenty-five makes thirty-two. That's still not control.'

His grin had turned reptilian. 'It is if Charlie votes with me – and he will. It seems he's been a trifle worried lately – his financial affairs have become somewhat disordered and it's definitely in his interest to increase the profitability of the company. It fell to me to point out that simple fact.'

'I don't suppose you had anything to do with his financial disorder,' I said acidly. Brinton's grin widened as I turned to Charlie and asked quietly, 'Will you vote with him?'

He swallowed. 'I must!'

'Well, by God! What a bloody pair you are. I was prepared for his lordship to pull a fast one, but I didn't think it of you, Charlie.' He reddened. 'You came to see me at my club just before I left. I thought then that you wanted something but I couldn't figure what it was. Now I know. You wanted to find out if I was still going on holiday even though I'd left Gloria.' I jerked my thumb at Brinton. 'He sent you to find out. No wonder both of you were urging me to go. You were giving me the fast shuffle so that Brinton could grab Gloria's shares.'

Brinton chuckled. 'It was her idea, really. She came and offered them to me. Max, you're a simpleton. You don't think I'd let all the valuable information in your files go to waste. A man could make millions with what you've got here.'

'You let me build up the reputation of the company, and

now you're going to rape it. Is that it?'

'Something along those lines,' he said carelessly. 'But legally – always legally.'

I said, 'Brinton, I have something for your ears only – something I don't think you'd like Charlie to know about.'

'There's nothing you can say to me that anyone can't hear. If you have something in your gullet, spit it out.'

'All right,' I said. 'Kissack won't be coming back.'

'What the devil are you talking about?' he demanded. 'Kissack? Who the hell is he?'

I hadn't scored with that one. Of course, he might not know of Kissack who was pretty low on the totem pole – a hired hand. I tried again. 'Lash won't be coming back, either.'

That got to him! I knew by the fractional change in the planes of his face. But he kept his end up well. 'And who is Lash?'

'Lash is the man who hired the men who beat me up,' I said deliberately. 'Lash is the man who hired Kissack to k—'

Brinton held up his hand abruptly. 'I can't stay here all day. I have things to do at my place. You can come with me and get rid of this nonsense there.' He got to his feet creakily.

I cheered internally. I had the old bastard by the short hairs, and he knew it. He went ahead of me and I paused at the door and looked back at Charlie. 'You louse!' I said. 'I'll deal with you later.'

I went with Brinton to the basement and we solemnly drove two blocks to the basement of another building and ascended to his penthouse where the coal fire still blazed cheerfully. All the time he didn't say a thing, but once on his own ground, he said, 'Stafford, you'd better be careful with your statements or I'll have your balls!'

I grinned, walked past him and sat in an armchair by the fire, and put down my briefcase. He didn't like that; he didn't like not being in control, and that meant he'd have to follow me. He sank into an opposing chair. 'Well, what is it?'

'I'd like to tell you a story about a bright, ambitious young engineer who married a woman who had just come into money. She hadn't won the pools or anything like that, but the life of her previous husband had been insured for a hundred thousand pounds. This was in 1937, so that's a lot more money that it sounds like now – maybe half a million in our terms.'

I stopped but Brinton made no comment. He merely stared at me with cold eyes. 'But what this woman didn't know was that this bright young engineer who, incidentally, was Canadian like yourself, had murdered her husband. His name was John Grenville Anderson, but he was commonly known as Jock. He was born in 1898 which, by another coincidence, would make him exactly as old as you.'

Brinton whispered, 'If you repeat those words in public I'll take you to court and strip you naked.'

'It was the name that foxed me,' I said. 'We've had quite a few Canadian peers but none of them have tried to hide behind a name. Beaverbrook was obviously Canadian; Thomson of Fleet not only retained his own name but advertised his newspaper connection. But Brinton doesn't mean a damned thing, either here or in Canada. There's a little place called Brinton in Norfolk but you've never been near it to my knowledge.'

I leaned down and opened the briefcase. 'Exhibit One – a photocopy of a page from *Whitaker's Almanac*.' I read the relevant line. ' "Created 1947, Brinton (1st.) John Grenville Anderson, born 1898." A most anonymous title, don't you think?'

'Get on with this preposterous nonsense.'

'Exhibit Two – a copy of your marriage lines to Helen Billson early in 1937. You didn't stick with her long, did you, Jock? Just long enough to part her from her money. A hundred thousand quid was just what a man like you needed to start a good little engineering company. Then the war came, and Lord, how the money rolled in! You were in aircraft manufacture, of course, on cost plus a percentage until your compatriot, Beaverbrook, put a stop to that. But by the end of the war you'd built up your nest-egg to a couple of millions, plus the grateful thanks of your sovereign who ennobled you for contributing funds to the right political party. And not just a tatty old life peerage like we have now. Not that that made any difference – you had no legitimate children.'

His lips compressed. 'I'm being very patient.'

'So you are. You ought to have me thrown out neck and crop. Why don't you?'

His eyes flickered. 'You amuse me. I'd like to hear the end of this fairy story.'

'No one can say I'm not obliging,' I said. 'All right; by 1946 you'd just got started. You discovered you had a flair for finance; in the property boom of the 'fifties you made millions – you're still making millions because money makes money. And it all came out of the murder of Peter Billson whose widow you married.'

'And how am I supposed to have murdered Billson?'

'You were his mechanic in the London to Cape Town Air Race of 1936. In Algiers you delayed him so he'd have to fly to Kano at night. Then you gimmicked his compass so that he flew off course.'

'You can never prove that. You're getting into dangerous waters, Stafford.'

'Exhibit Three – an eight-by-ten colour photograph of *Flyaway*, Billson's aircraft, taken by myself less than two weeks ago. Note how intact it is. Exhibit Four – an affidavit witnessed by a notary public and signed by myself and the man who took out the compass and tested it.'

Brinton studied the photograph, then read the document. I said, 'By the way, that's also a photocopy – all these papers are. Those that are a matter of public record are in the appropriate place, and the others are in the vaults of my bank. My solicitor knows what to do with them should anything happen to me.'

He grunted. 'Who is Lucas Byrne?'.

'An aeronautical engineer,' I said, stretching a point. 'You'll note he mentions a substance found in the main fuel tank. Here's a report by a chemist who analysed the stuff. He says he found mostly hydrocarbons of petroleum derivation.'

'Naturally,' sneered Brinton.

'He said mostly,' I pointed out. 'He also found other hydrocarbons – disaccharides, D-glucopyranose, D-fructopyranose and others. Translated into English it means that you'd put sugar into the fuel tank, and when Billson switched over from the auxiliary his engine froze solid.' I sat back. 'But let's come to modern times.'

Brinton stretched out his hand and dropped Byrne's statement on to the fire. I laughed. 'Plenty more where that came from.'

'What about modern times?'

'You became really worried about Paul Billson, didn't you, when you found he was practically insane about his father? He was the one man who had the incentive and the obsessiveness to go out to find *Flyaway* in order to clear his father's name. You weren't as worried about Alix Aarvik but you really anchored Paul. I had a long chat with Andrew McGovern about that the other day.'

Brinton's head came up with a jerk. 'You've seen McGovern?'

'Yes – didn't he tell you? I suppose I must have thrown a bit of a scare into him. He had no objection to employing Paul because you were paying all of Paul's inflated salary. He jumped to the natural conclusion: that Paul was one of your byblows, a souvenir of your misspent youth whom you were tactfully looking after. And so you tethered Paul for fifteen years by giving him a salary that he knew he wasn't worth. It's ironic that it was you who financed his trip to the Sahara when he blew up. I dare say the payments you made through the Whensley Group can be traced.'

His lips twisted. 'I doubt it.'

314

'McGovern told me something else. He didn't want Stafford Security pulled out of the Whensley Group – it was your idea. You twisted his arm. I don't know what hold you have on McGovern, but whatever it is you used it. That was to stop me carrying on the investigation into Paul Billson. You also got McGovern to send Alix Aarvik to Canada but that didn't work out, did it? Because I got to her first. So you had Lash have me beaten up. I don't think McGovern likes you any more. I suppose that's why he didn't report back to you that he'd seen me – that and the fact that I told him he'd better keep his nose clean.'

Brinton dismissed McGovern with a twitch of a finger. 'You said Lash isn't coming back. What happened to him?'

'Two bullets through his lungs, one through the belly, and another through the head at close range – that's what happened to Lash. There are three dead men out there, and another with an amputated foot, and all because of you, Jock. All because you were so scared of what Paul Billson might find that you put out a contract on him.' I tapped my arm in its sling. 'Not Gstaad, Jock; the Tassili. You owe me something for this.'

'I owe you nothing,' he said contemptuously.

'Then we come to a man called Torstein Aarvik who married Helen Billson.' I drew a photocopy of the marriage certificate from my briefcase. 'This really shook me when I saw it because legally she was Anderson, wasn't she? Helen had lost sight of you so she took a chance. She married Aarvik as the widow Billson without divorcing you. It was wartime and things were pretty free and easy and, besides, she wasn't too bright – I have Alix Aarvik's word for that. But you knew where she was because you'd been keeping tabs on her. I don't know how you separated her from her money in the first place but you used her bigamous marriage to keep her quiet for the rest of her life. She couldn't fight you, could she? And maybe she wasn't bright but perhaps she was decent enough to prevent Alix knowing that she's a bastard. Now who's the bastard here, you son of a bitch?'

'You'll never make this stick,' he said. 'Not after forty-two years.'

'I believe I will, and so do you, or you wouldn't have been so bloody worried about Paul Billson. There's no statute of limitations on murder, Jock.'

'Stop calling me Jock,' he said irritably.

'You're an old man,' I said. 'Eighty years old. You're going to die soon. Tomorrow, next year, five years, ten – you'll be as dead as Lash. But they don't have capital punishment now, so you'll probably die in a prison hospital. Unless . . .'

He was suddenly alert, scenting a bargain, a deal. 'Unless what?'

'What's the use of putting you in jail? You wouldn't live as luxuriously as you do now but you'd get by. They're tender-minded about murderous old men these days, and that wouldn't satisfy me, nor would it help the people you've cheated all these years.'

I put my hand into my pocket, drew out a calculator, punched a few keys, then wrote the figure on a piece of paper. It made a nice sum if not a round one – £1,714,425.68. I tossed it across to him. 'That's a hundred thousand compounded at a nominal seven per cent for forty-two years.'

I said, 'Even if Scotland Yard or the Director of Public Prosecutions take no action the newspapers would love it. The Insight team of the *Sunday Times* would make a meal of it. Think of all the juicy bits – Lady Brinton dying of cancer in virtual poverty while her husband lived high on the hog. Your name would stink, even in the City where they have strong stomachs. Do you think any decent or even any moderately indecent man would have anything to do with you after that?'

I stuck my finger under his nose. 'And another thing – Paul Billson knows nothing about this. But I can prime him with it and point him at you like a gun. He'd kill you – you wouldn't stand a flaming chance. You'd better get out your cheque book.'

He flinched but made a last try. 'This figure is impossible. You don't suppose I'm as fluid as all that?'

'Don't try to con me, you old bastard,' I said. 'Any bank in the City will lend you that amount if you just pick up the telephone and ask. Do it!'

He stood up. 'You're a hard man.'

'I've had a good teacher. You make out two cheques; one to the Peter Billson Memorial Trust for a million and a half. The rest to me – that's my twelve-and-a-half per cent commission. Expenses have been high. And I get Gloria's shares, and you sell out of Stafford Security. I don't care who you sell your shares to but it mustn't be Charlie Malleson.'

'How do I know you won't renege? I want all the papers you have.'

'Not a chance in hell! Those are my insurance policies. I wouldn't want another Lash turning up in my life.'

He sat down and wrote the cheques.

I walked the streets of London for a long time that afternoon with cheques in my pocket for more money than I had ever carried. Alix Aarvik and Paul Billson would now be all right for the rest of their lives. I had put the money into a trust because I didn't want Paul getting his hands on it – he didn't deserve that. But the not-too-bright son of a not-too-bright mother would be looked after.

As for me, I thought 12½% was a reasonable fee. It would enable me to buy out Charlie Malleson, a regrettable necessity because I could no longer work with him. Jack Ellis would continue to be a high flier and he'd get his stake in the firm, and we'd hire an accountant and pay him well. And Byrne would get something unexpectedly higher than the ridiculous fee he'd asked for saving lives and being shot at.

At the thought of Byrne I stopped suddenly and looked about me. I was in Piccadilly, at the Circus, and the lights and crowds were all about me in the evening dusk. And it all seemed unreal. This, the heart of the city at the heart of the world, wasn't reality. Reality lay in Atakor, in Koudia, in the Aïr, in the Ténéré, on the Tassili.

I felt an awful sense of loss. I wanted to be with Byrne and Mokhtar and Hamiada, with the cheerful man who, because his name used to be Konti, was a murderer. I wanted to say hello again to the giraffe in Agadez, to sit beside a small fire at an evening camp and look at the stars, to feel again the freedom of a Targui.

I stopped and pondered, there among the hurrying crowds of Londoners, and decided to give Byrne his fee in person. Besides, it would also give me the opportunity of swapping dirty limericks with Hesther Raulier.